THE WINNERS OF NINE BOOK AWARDS transcending the genres of science fiction, environmental fiction, and action-adventure, ***The Girl Who Rode Dolphins*** and ***Dolphin Riders*** have proven themselves thrillers with a labyrinth of spellbinding twists, turns, and thunderous action that takes readers on a roller coaster ride of nail-biting suspense and explosive adventure.

Upon its original debut, ***The Girl Who Rode Dolphins*** received the following multiple awards:

- ***Winner of Best Epic Adventure of 2008***
  BooksandAuthors.net
- ***Winner of Best Science Fiction Epic Adventure of 2008***
  BooksandAuthors.net
- ***Winner of Science Fiction Genre***
  2009 Green Book Festival
- ***Finalist in Action Adventure Category***
  2009 National Indie Book Excellence Awards
- ***Winner of Environmental/Green Fiction Category***
  2010 International Book Awards Competition
- ***Winner of the Talking Category***
  2015 Animals, Animals, Animals Book Festival
- ***Honorable Mention Awardee in Science Fiction Category***
  2015 London Book Festival

Dolphin Riders, the sequel to ***The Girl Who Rode Dolphins***, is an ensuing adventure combined with political intrigue that promises to captivate readers with enthralling action and mysticism on a scale every bit as intense if not greater than the first book.

- ***Official Selection Winner of Action/Adventure Category***
  2016 New Apple Summer eBook Awards
- ***Finalist In Action/Adventure Category***
  2016 Beverly Hills Book Awards

Following their original debuts, both books were re-released in 2026 by Seaworthy Publications, Inc. as a five-part cliff-hanger series as follows:

The Girl Who Rode Dolphins, 3rd Edition

- Part 1 - Gaia's Intervention
- Part 2 - Gaia's Heartbeat
- Part 3 - Retribution

Dolphin Riders, 3rd Edition

- Part 4 - Creation
- Part 5 - Survival

Survival

Part 5
of
The Dolphin Riders Series

Dolphin Riders
3rd Edition

Survival

Part 5
of
The Dolphin Riders Series

Dolphin Riders
3rd Edition

by

Michael J. Ganas

SEAWORTHY PUBLICATIONS, INC. • MELBOURNE, FLORIDA

Survival
Part 5 of the Dolphin Riders Series
Dolphin Riders Series, 3rd Edition

ISBN 978-1-9966191-12-4
eBook ISBN 978-1-966191-13-1

Published in the USA by:
Seaworthy Publications, Inc
6300 N Wickham Rd.
Unit #130-416
Melbourne, FL 32940
E-mail orders@seaworthy.com
www.seaworthy.com

Library of Congress Cataloging-in-Publication Data

Names: Ganas, Michael J., 1946- author | Ganas, Michael J., 1946- Girl who rode dolphins
Title: Gaia's intervention / by Michael J Ganas.
Description: Third edition. | Melbourne, Florida : Seaworthy Publications, Inc, 2026. | Series: The dolphin riders series ; part 1 | "The girl who rode dolphins 3rd edition" | Summary: "Former Navy SEAL Jake Javolyn, a part-time smuggler by necessity and dive boat operator by profession, has come to Haiti in search of something. Hiring his boat out to Dr. Franklin Grahm, a renowned marine zoologist, Javolyn sets course for Navassa Island, only to stumble across a beautiful girl in the open sea. Encircled by a pod of six white bottlenose dolphins, the girl is found riding a seventh, much larger but similar creature. Upon rescuing the girl from the nets of a tuna trawler crewed by vicious members of a drug cartel, Javolyn soon discovers the girl has strange and unusual powers. Even more amazing are her companions, for they are unlike any sea mammals he has ever encountered. They possess forelimbs with hands, super-intelligence, and can speak in human languages. From then on, he is plunged into a world of the supernatural and confrontation with iniquitous forces bent on vengeance and the capture of nature's most recent miracles. A stunning rollercoaster ride of epic adventure, Gaia's Intervention is the first book in this blockbuster series, an ecological saga that will leave readers spellbound and enthralled with its superb mix of intense action, environmental issues, and mysticism"-- Provided by publisher.
Identifiers: LCCN 2026000755 (print) | LCCN 2026000756 (ebook) | ISBN 9781966191049 v. 1 paperback | ISBN 9781966191056 v. 1 epub
Subjects: LCSH: Dolphins--Fiction | LCGFT: Ecofiction | Action and adventure fiction | Fantasy fiction | Novels | Fiction
Classification: LCC PS3607.A4385 G35 2026 (print) | LCC PS3607.A4385 (ebook)
LC record available at https://lccn.loc.gov/2026000755
LC ebook record available at https://lccn.loc.gov/2026000756

Dedication

To my gemstone, Harriet.

Table of Contents

Facts x
Introduction xiv
Chapter One: Inducing Fear 1
Chapter Two: Kicking Ass 8
Chapter Three: A Star Gone Nova 25
Chapter Four: Getting Away 29
Chapter Five: Extreme Nausea 32
Chapter Six: Not Intimidated 38
Chapter Seven: Foiling The Pursuers 53
Chapter Eight: Unexpected Calmness 62
Chapter Nine: Walls of Pure Gold 73
Chapter Ten: Reunion of Twins 81
Chapter Eleven: Superyacht Disabled 91
Chapter Twelve: Robo-fish Problem 101
Chapter Thirteen: Moonpool Surprise 113
Chapter Fourteen: A Wild Guess 124
Chapter Fifteen: Bomb Found 137
Chapter Sixteen: Ez Hacks in 145
Chapter Seventeen: Chopper Destroyed 159
Chapter Eighteen: World's Largest Ship 165
Chapter Nineteen: The Order Revealed 175
Chapter Twenty: Scaling The Kraken 187
Chapter Twenty-one: Rebooting the System 208
Chapter Twenty-two: Sliding Into the Abyss 225
Chapter Twenty-three: Jamming In Progress 237
Chapter Twenty-four: Unseen Foe 248

Chapter Twenty-five: Madman On The Loose 258
Chapter Twenty-six: Watch and Learn 272
Chapter Twenty-seven: Right on the Edge................. 282
Chapter Twenty-eight: Disaster Approaching 294
Chapter Twenty-nine: Holographic Projections 312
Chapter Thirty: All is Possible.................................. 325
Chapter Thirty-one: Shark Bait................................ 344
Acknowledgments... 362
About the Author.. 364

Facts

Haiti is currently the poorest country in the Western Hemisphere, a Caribbean nation beleaguered by economic strife, dismal squalor, and political instability, a land of defoliation and ecological ruin. It is a place with a violent past, punctuated by a succession of bloody rebellions and previously governed by a long line of statesmen and dictators whose policies were either inept, ineffectual, unpopular, corrupt, or oppressive. The Duvalier dictatorships of father and son, however, proved to be the most corrupt, oppressive and violent, and under their brutal regimes Haiti suffered deeply.

Francois "Papa Doc" Duvalier ruled Haiti from 1963 until his death in 1971 when his son Jean-Claude "Baby Doc" Duvalier took over the reins of power. Under the Duvalier governments, the population was kept in a state of fear, terrorized by the regime's secret police force, the Tonton Makout. They were also known as the VNS, Volunteers of National Security, and Papa Doc referred to them as his "civilian" military, while the citizens called them "the bogeymen." They were recruited mostly from Haiti's slums and were used to crush all opposition, often imprisoning without trial, torturing, and even killing individuals considered enemies of the state.

An estimated 60,000 Haitians were murdered at the hands of the Tonton Makout, which had a standing force of roughly 10,000 loyalists. Papa Doc made sure his secret police outnumbered the Haitian army by a factor of two in order to assure that he did not get overthrown in a coup. Both Francois Duvalier and his son also took advantage of the people's strong belief in voodoo to control the population. Consequently, much of the citizenry believed them to be voodoo spirits. To this day, voodoo, merged with Catholicism, is the religion of choice embraced by most Haitians.

Misappropriation of government funds amounting to hundreds of millions was common practice under Baby Doc's tyrannical rule, and in the wake of intense political unrest and pressure from the United States to step down, he was finally forced from power in February of 1986, whereupon he fled to France. A wealth of evidence shows various drug cartels to be firmly entrenched in present-day Haiti, where the political climate, endemic poverty, and a breakdown in civil rule makes it an ideal staging area for the transshipment of illegal contraband, where public officials are often threatened or corrupted by bribery to keep a blind eye to drug trafficking.

Navassa Island is a small, uninhabited island, which lies in the Caribbean Sea between Haiti and Jamaica. The island originally belonged to Haiti before being claimed in 1801 as an unorganized, unincorporated territory of the United States, which currently administers it through the U.S. Fish and Wildlife Service.

Malique is a fictitious fishing village that lies roughly midway between the real cities of Saint-Marc and Gonaives along Haiti's western coastline. It has been created solely for the purpose of this novel.

Al Qaeda is an actual present-day organization of Islamic extremists bent on the destruction of the United States and its allies. To this day this terrorist group continues to flourish despite the loss of its originator and leader, Osama Bin Laden, who was killed by a team of U.S. Navy Seals when they stormed his hideout in Pakistan during a bold raid that occurred in 2011.

All mention of Haiti's former leadership and historical events, both past and modern day, are based on documented history and are used as a backdrop for the writing of this novel. In this way, history has been merged with fiction.

All characters, creatures and unusual settings that play a key role within the novel's plot are entirely fictitious and have been created solely for the reader's intrigue and entertainment.

Michael J. Ganas

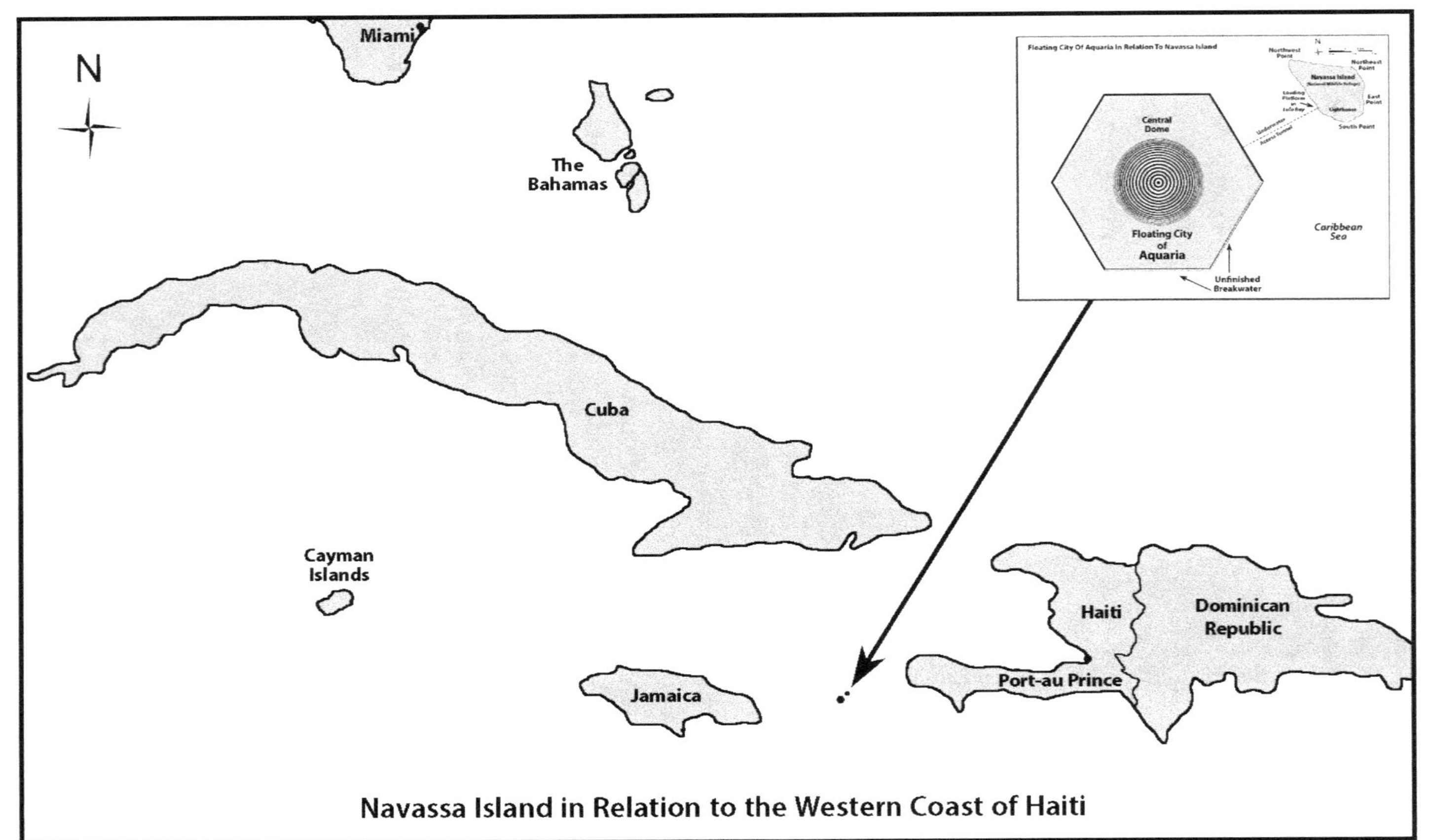

Navassa Island in Relation to the Western Coast of Haiti

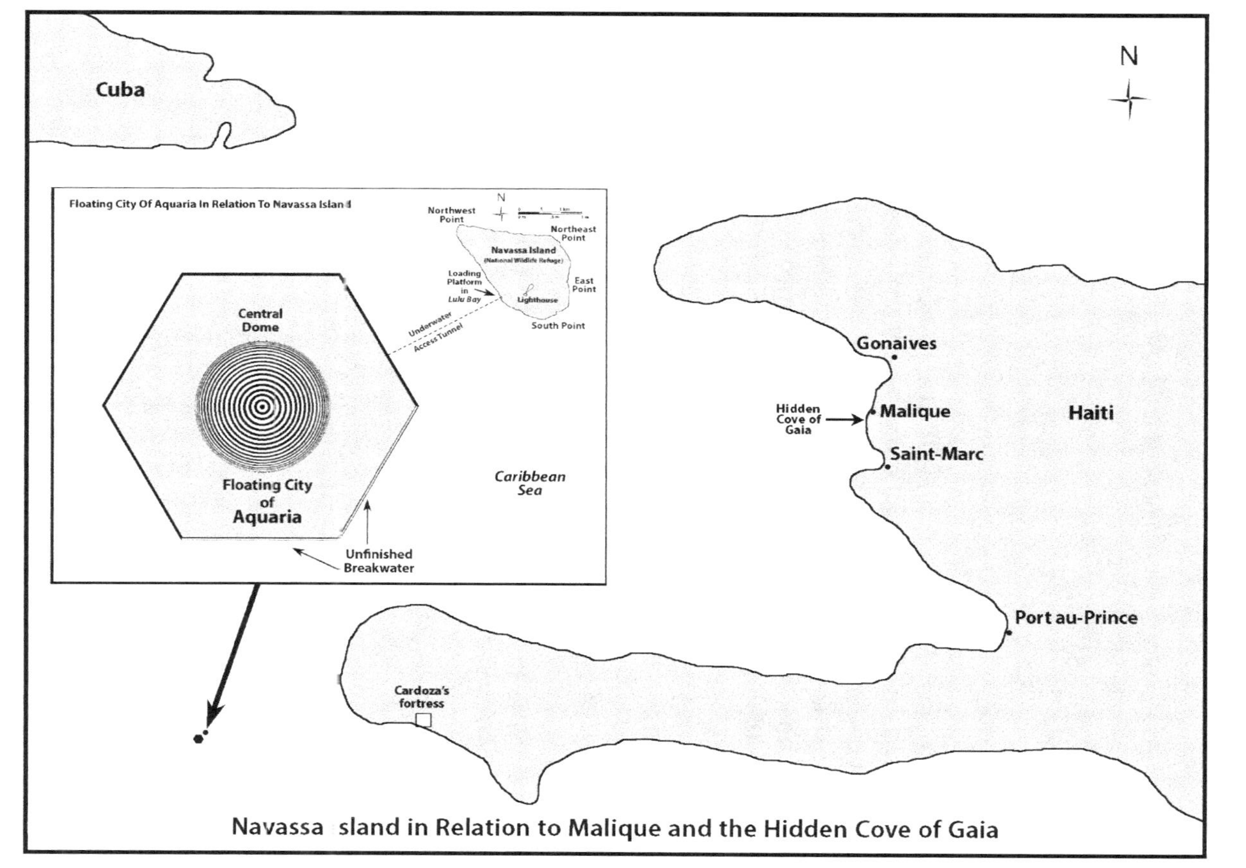

Navassa sland in Relation to Malique and the Hidden Cove of Gaia

Introduction

In Dolphin Riders, Third Edition: Part Four – Creation, Rafael Cardoza, a powerful drug lord and the pod's longtime nemesis, is killed and his fleet of aerial drones and ships destroyed as Jake, Destiny, and the dolphins strike back. But now Jake must rescue Mort, a man who was held prisoner by the drug lord. Trapped in Cardoza's fortress, Jake and Mort must fight their way out against superior odds.

Chapter One: Inducing Fear

Malikai Allotey stared open-mouthed, finding it difficult to accept what he was seeing. Where Cardoza's huge aircraft hangar had stood, flames were licking high into the night sky. Straining his eyes against the glowing inferno, he looked in vain for the Chinook troop transport, but the tandem rotor helicopter was also gone. A few moments earlier, he had overheard alarmed shouts coming from some of Cardoza's men scurrying about in confusion, and he had climbed up into the turret of the stronghold's east tower to confirm the cause of their panic. Turning, he addressed the lanky individual standing next to him.

"How did this happen?" he asked, his tone shrill.

Lamont shrugged laconically. "I don't know."

"Give me your radio!" Allotey screeched, his mind churning over the implications of this unanticipated loss. With his mode of transportation now destroyed, he was temporarily stranded. Even worse, the intricate plan so meticulously crafted had fallen apart, and with it, payment for his services. Like the hangar, the money he was to receive had also gone up in flames.

Lamont extended a reluctant arm to offer the radio, and as he did, Allotey snatched it rudely from his hand. Hitting the transmit button, Allotey screamed into it like a woman. "This is Malikai. Do you hear me, Rafael?"

"I have already told him what happened," Lamont said in a manner that suggested both annoyance and contrition.

Allotey ignored him, screaming more fervently this time. "All the drones have been destroyed. Do you hear what I am telling you, Rafael? Where was your security? Maximus is going to be furious."

As Allotey said this, another man climbed into the tower to join him. Captain Alvarez stared pensively in the direction of the blaze. The storm had now passed, and with no downpour to impede the flames, the fire continued to burn fiercely.

"We have come under attack by saboteurs," Alvarez announced gruffly.

Allotey's hysteria suddenly evaporated, and he turned to study the Chilean captain with startled eyes. "Are you certain of this?"

Alvarez leaned out of the turret and pointed down. "Look below you! The moat is only half full."

Allotey looked down. With the storm's cloud cover now gone, the moon had re-emerged directly overhead to reflect a soft glow off the water girthing the fortress. But now the level had dropped by a good fifteen feet.

"Where did the water go?"

"There is only one place for it to go," Alvarez snapped. "The lower level is no doubt flooded. They must have used explosives to breach the moat wall. Did you not feel the blast? It shook the foundation."

Allotey's flummoxed expression abruptly turned. "Are they in the building?"

"I don't know," Alvarez snapped again. "But the destruction of the hangar may not have been their primary objective. It may have been a diversion."

Allotey tensed. "Deploy the men! Station them at all the potential entry points, including the stairs leading to the lower levels."

"I have already done that," Alvarez growled irritably.

At hearing the approach of footsteps echoing dully, Alvarez drew his *corvo* and shouted out a command. "Identify yourself!"

"It is Dr. Ermstine. Don't shoot!"

A few seconds elapsed before Ermstine crowded his paunchy bulk into the turret, his manner grave. "Is what I am hearing true? Have all the drones been destroyed?"

"I am afraid so," Alvarez grumbled.

Ermstine shot a quick glance at all three men. "Where is Rafael?"

"We do not know," Allotey offered dismally. "He does not answer my calls." He was about to say more, but a distinct slapping sound suddenly caught his ears. *Whap, whap, whap!* Poking his head out of the turret in an effort to locate the source, he immediately jerked back as a large object abruptly shot by, the tip of its main rotor blades seemingly inches away from the tower as it passed. A powerful floodlight on the aircraft was aimed down, illuminating the water in the moat. Slung beneath it, he saw a large rectangular box suspended a few feet above the water.

Puzzled by the sight, Allotey leaned out to risk another look. The box had to be at least thirty feet long and six feet wide in his estimation.

Lamont raised his weapon, prepared to unleash a salvo at the receding whirlybird, but Alvarez pushed the muzzle down before it could be leveled. "You fool!" the Chilean captain admonished sharply. "Do you not recognize an ally?"

Allotey looked at Alvarez. "Are you able to contact him?"

Alvarez pulled a handheld radio from his belt, adjusting the frequency before he spoke. "This is Captain Alvarez, do you read me Reaper?"

A strained moment of expectation elapsed as all four men listened hopefully for a response. When one did not come back, Alvarez tried another hailing frequency before repeating himself. The enervating din of chopper blades ebbed quickly as the Hind followed the moat around the side of the fortress, continuing to keep its floodlight trained on the water. The Russian's deep voice erupted from the radio just as Alvarez was about to switch channels again. "This is the Reaper."

"We have come under attack," Alvarez blurted savagely. "You are advised to fire upon any movement you detect beyond the walls of this citadel. As must be obvious to you, Cardoza's hangar to the east has been completely destroyed by infiltrators."

A moment of silence ensued before Zinova responded gruffly. "Let me speak to Cardoza."

"He is currently unreachable," Alvarez replied hotly. "The moat wall has been breached by explosives, and it is possible he may have been caught in the flood when it filled the lower level."

"My contract is with Cardoza, not his underlings, and it does not involve keeping this facility secure."

"Then why are you flying reconnaissance around our perimeter?" Alvarez asked in bewilderment.

"Cardoza requisitioned me to move a shark from his trawler to the moat, which I have now done. Since the task is complete, my services here are now finished."

At hearing this, Allotey's face turned puce. He was beside himself with rage. "I will speak to him," he hissed. "Give me your radio."

Pompously he yelled into the speaker, attempting to take charge of the situation. "This is Malikai Allotey, Special Envoy of the United Nations. As a ranking official within this world conclave, I am empowered to commission the services of military contractors whenever circumstances dictate such a need." Although he knew this was not true, he was desperate enough to advance this absurd prevarication. Adjusting his tone to one of benevolence, he threw in a bonus. "Name your fee and I will consider it."

When the Reaper did not immediately answer, Allotey's patience exploded. "Just name your fee," he shouted shrilly, "and I will see that you get paid."

"Twenty million in Euros, and all of it up front," Zinova's disembodied voice came back.

Allotey's jaw dropped. "That is preposterous," he wailed.

"No more preposterous than the claim you just made about your empowerment," Zinova grunted. "Do you think I am an imbecile? I have dealt with UN emissaries before and know they hold no such power."

The sound of the Hind suddenly grew louder, and Allotey saw that it had returned to hover eerily before him, presenting a broadside view with its floodlight now turned off. He glanced below, noticing that the large box it had previously carried was now absent. The Hind's starboard cabin door was open and he could see several men looking back at him, their weapons aimed in his direction. With slowly widening eyes he stared apprehensively as the chopper pivoted around to face him head on. In the moonlight he could vaguely distinguish someone in the chin bubble idly working the controls. Sitting further back behind a canopy was the pilot, who he presumed to be Zinova. It was then he realized he was looking into a twin set of gun barrels protruding from a pod situated under the chin bubble.

Fearing for his life, Allotey thought quickly. "Alright, alright, I have something better to offer you."

"And what might that be," Zinova said, his tone chaffing and sardonic.

"Gold!" Allotey let the word hang for one extended moment to wet the Reaper's appetite. "I can get you tons of it, far more than twenty million in Euros," he rambled on hurriedly.

"You have it with you?"

"Unfortunately no, but I can tell you where you can find it."

"Where?" As Zinova asked the question, the aircraft's floodlight came back on, its powerful beam blinding him.

Allotey threw a hand up to shield his eyes. "It is stored in the floating city of Aquaria," he squealed.

The Reaper let out a harsh laugh. "What good does that do me?" He laughed again. "You make it sound as though I will be able to just walk in there and help myself."

"That is exactly what I am saying," Allotey pleaded quickly. "At this moment the UN is mobilizing a task force to take over the city. As its ranking representative in the Caribbean, all authority concerning Aquaria's temporary governance will revert to me once the facility is secured. I will have full command in taking inventory of its assets, including the stockpiles of precious metals."

The Hind continued to hover ominously as though the chopper itself were mulling the proposal. Zinova looked on, studying the faces in the castle turret and considering the sincerity of the offer. Allotey and the other men averted their eyes from the floodlight's intense glare to avoid burning their retinas. Aquaria, he knew, was a thriving enterprise, and based on that alone there was no reason not to believe Allotey's claim. If tons of gold actually existed there, then he wanted a share of it. Though he hadn't been able to substantiate it as yet, all his instincts told him he had lost both Hinds on the operation Cardoza had hired him to perform, causing him to severely chastise himself endlessly. He had stupidly let his own airship get hijacked simply because he had drastically underestimated Javolyn, but he wouldn't let that happen again. And though he had tried, he had been unable to contact Badger, making him conclude that the other Hind was also gone.

As the Reaper thought about these things, he pondered these lost assets, knowing he had to replace them as quickly as possible. If word ever got out that he had suffered a failed mission, his reputation was certain to crash and burn. The demand for his services would diminish rapidly, not to mention the fees clients were willing to pay. Men of Spetsnaz caliber were hard to replace, and Hinds even harder. Hinds were incredibly expensive on the black market and he would need a ton of money to pay for them.

"What do you want of me?" Zinova found himself asking.

"I want you to get us out of here," Allotey shrieked.

"I only have room for three more people aboard this bird, and I see four of you."

Allotey shot a glance at Lamont. "Then one of us will stay," he blurted. "Can you pick us up from the topmost battlements?"

Zinova opened his mouth to speak, but a flash of light out of the corner of his eye drew his attention to what lay beyond his port window. With the storm now gone, moonlight shed sufficient light on the ocean to give him an unobstructed view of the bay, and he clearly saw the entire stern of the *Southern Star* rise up a few feet before falling back into a foaming sea. A rapid succession of several more flashes ensued at scattered locations on the water, and Zinova glimpsed the rear section of Cardoza's super yacht, *Usurpar*, getting consumed in a flaring fireball. Another explosion enveloped the stern of the *Northern Comet* a split second before another flash erupted amidships of the *San Pedro*. The tugboat that had carried supplies ashore was the last to elicit this dazzling display, with the entire vessel spewing flaming parts in all directions. Within seconds, all the vessels began to flounder and sink, and even at his present distance from the disasters he could see men leaping into the sea to escape the drowning ships.

Zinova's radio suddenly resounded with Allotey's panicky voice again. The tone was pleading. "Do you hear me? We will wait for you on the battlements. I will make you a rich man."

The Reaper brought his eyes back to the men in the turret. Judging from the swath of destruction, he knew the attacking force had to be sizable. This could not possibly be the work of a small force of men. In that moment he made a decision.

"Three of you is all I will take," Zinova grunted. "But if you are lying to me about the gold, my men will drop each of you into the ocean from ten thousand feet." Pulling lightly on the Hind's collective lever, he put a slight amount of additional pitch in the main rotor blades. As the aircraft began to rise, he spoke quickly into the intercom. "We are going to evacuate a party of three on the battlements above," he instructed the crew in the language of his homeland. "Stay alert! This facility has come under attack, so be prepared to fend off infiltrators."

Chapter Two: Kicking Ass

Jake treaded his way lightly on the stone steps, his senses on full alert. With only a half-spiral to go, he stopped and whispered to the man behind him. "Stick to me like glue!" he ordered gently.

Rising up the remaining distance, he poked his head above the landing. Three men, two of them wearing United Nations blue helmets, were just taking up positions to monitor the immediate area, their heads swiveling back and forth nervously. He surmised the man lacking UN garb to be one of Cardoza's goons. Ducking down quickly, he activated his Portable Holographic Projector, sliding it over the lip of the top landing and off to one side so that it would not be directly between him and his adversaries. He was unsure of what to expect, but he nevertheless had to give it a try. Based on what Phillipe had told him just before leaving the *Southern Star*, the UN troops may have found a way to counter the effects of the dolphin art using drugs. Phillipe had seen the blue helmeted captain lift a small convex cap strapped to his thigh and slap down hard on a tiny nodule the cap had protected. The captain had done this just prior to activating Option 2 on the Masker he had taken from Kalid and had remained unaffected by the hologram while his men had fallen violently ill. The captain had made reference to a drug, berating his men for not taking it. Upon learning of this, Jake had immediately asked Achilles for a visual accounting of the event. Achilles had then conjured images of what Perseus had witnessed through Phillipe's eyes, projecting them into Jake's mind as though Jake were viewing a movie, and he was not surprised to see the pockmarked face of Captain Francisco Alvarez leering back at him. The tiny nodule Phillipe had described was in full view, making him conclude that it was a tiny syringe, and he knew that Alvarez had injected himself with something.

Mat had also alerted Jake to the hologram's possible ineffectiveness against UN troops during his last conversation with him. Mat had related Kalid's description of what had taken place prior to his wounding. Kalid had said that the hologram had at first worked and then it didn't.

With these things weighing heavily on his mind, Jake stood fast, waiting for something to happen. His concerns were partially allayed by a loud howl of pain, and he poked his head up a second time to glimpse a man writhing on the floor, his body jerking like a jackhammer. The man was not one of the UN mercenaries, and he could plainly see that the blue helmets were alternating confused gazes between the stricken man and the hologram, their faces harboring scowls. Strapped to the right thigh of each commando was a small convex cap similar to the one Alvarez had worn. One other conspicuous item Jake had not noticed before was the sheathed corvo the mercenaries carried, and he immediately knew these men were members of Alvarez's team.

Taking full advantage of the situation, Jake sprang up and let loose with the Sledgehammer, squeezing off two quick shots. The frag-12 rounds caught their intended targets, exploding on impact and blowing gaping holes through the Kevlar body armor protecting the chest of each commando. Both men went down, killed instantly.

Jake scooped up the PHP and turned it off, avoiding eye contact with the light show as he did so. Pocketing the device, he glanced back at Mort to see how he had reacted to the display. The fear Mort had manifested a moment earlier was now gone, replaced by a faraway look of serenity and contentment.

Turning, Jake noticed the Cardoza goon had stopped twitching and was trying to stand. Taking a few quick steps, Jake unleashed a vicious kick that caught him on the side of the head. The man went down again and lay quiet.

Moving back to Mort, Jake took him by the shoulders and shook him hard. "Stay alert!" he ordered. "Better that you're scared than languid."

With UN troops supposedly immune to the dolphin hologram, he wondered if the PHP was worth using any longer. He had no time to consider culling out possible good guys, for to do so would surely get him killed. In light of the present situation, his only option was to assume every man he came upon deserved what he was going to dish out.

Pulling Mort along with him, Jake rounded a bend and nearly ran into three more blue helmeted commandos, catching them by surprise. At close to point-blank range he fired from the hip. Two of the commandos were thrown back violently as the rounds tore through their body armor and slammed them brutally against a wall. The third man dropped to a knee and nearly got off a shot, but Jake was quicker and fired again. The frag-12 caught him full in the face, disintegrating his head. In a weird knee-jerk reaction, the Uzi he had been holding flew backwards to go clattering across the stone floor.

Jake turned to study Mort again, happy to see the serenity supplanted by fright once again. He knew fear could sometimes be a good thing when a person's life was on the line. Fear got the adrenaline flowing. Fear made an individual fight harder.

Continuing on at a trot, Jake was careful to avoid the smear of brain tissue, blood and shards of bone that littered the floor before him. Mort was not as careful, and his feet nearly slipped out from under him as he followed in Jake's wake. In an effort to keep from falling, he managed to get a hand on Jake's shoulder, holding on for support.

"Watch your step!" Jake chided, holding his voice to a whisper. Clearing the mess, he stopped and removed Mort's hand. If they were going to survive, it was critical his body and limbs remained unimpeded. "You know how to use a firearm, Mort?"

Mort shook his head nervously.

"Well, you're about to learn," Jake said, continuing to monitor the passageway before him. Reaching down, he snatched up the Uzi dropped by the commando he had beheaded. Removing the clip, he checked to see if it was topped off with bullets. Satisfied, he replaced the clip and chambered a round, making sure the weapon's safety switch was on before he handed it over to Mort.

Mort looked terrified, holding the Uzi as though the metal comprising it was toxic to the touch. "How do I operate it?" he asked timidly.

"It's really simple. Just point it at your target and pull the trigger," Jake instructed soothingly, doing his best to quell Mort's unease. "Just be mindful where you aim it, and above all, don't point it in my direction. Can I count on you, Mort?"

When Mort nodded numbly, Jake put the weapon's safety in firing mode. Though Mort's inexperience with a firearm was a potential liability to both of them, some deep inexplicable instinct told him it was the right thing to do under the present circumstances.

"Just remember to keep your finger off the trigger until you have a target to shoot at," Jake said. "You ready, Mort?"

Mort took a deep breath, letting it out slowly before nodding vigorously. "I'm ready," he finally acknowledged.

Jake turned and resumed moving down the corridor again. Up ahead he saw another ninety-degree bend. "You know where this passageway leads, Mort?" he whispered over his shoulder.

"There's an open courtyard just beyond the turn," Mort answered back, his tone seemingly calmer now.

Jake nodded, reaching for something in his utility belt. He only carried one baseball grenade and hoped it would be enough. Pulling the pin, he held down the spoon, advancing cautiously toward the bend. Hugging the wall, he risked a peek around the inside corner. He was immediately met by a hail of bullets. Withdrawing his head and ducking down low, he released the spoon on the grenade, counting off two seconds before tossing it into the courtyard beyond. Contained by stone walls on each side, the detonation was loud and piercing as it sent out shrapnel in all directions.

Feeling wildly indestructible and lightheaded, Jake sprang out into the open. A few low-watt incandescent lights spaced at intervals along the courtyard's outer perimeter provided just enough illumination for Jake to see, and with reckless abandon he let loose with the Sledgehammer, whipping the muzzle around to take out the first two men he came upon. Both were blue helmeted commandos, already bloodied and staggering from the grenade. The frag-12 rounds exploded against their Kevlar chest protectors and hurled their bodies backwards as if tugged by some mighty hand from behind. Three other blue helmets were already down, two of them unmoving and seemingly mortally wounded. One of them, however, was trying to rise to his feet, dazed and bleeding profusely from the shrapnel that had peppered his neck. Taking no chances, Jake pumped off another round, catching the commando in the side and nearly cutting him in half.

Totally consumed by the warrior's lust for battle, Jake took in the courtyard at a glance, looking for other adversaries. From discussions with Belachek, he knew it wasn't so much a courtyard but an area between the inner and outer defensive walls. Based on Belachek's description, he knew the inner wall was actually the façade of the keep, the main living quarters situated in the center of the stronghold.

Jake tensed at the sound of drumming, a low pitched cadence that grew quickly and echoed out into the open area where he now stood. Looking for the source, his eyes were drawn to an arched entrance on the inner wall side, and he recognized the beat of running footsteps in a tunnel. Bolting headlong from the entrance like horses leaving a starting gate, three of Cardoza's thugs were suddenly before him. Startled by Jake's presence, the lead thug skidded to a halt and attempted to raise his weapon, but before he could do so his accomplices flew into him from behind, knocking him off balance. In rapid succession, all three were flung back as the Sledgehammer's explosive rounds found their mark.

Another sight grabbed Jake's attention, one Belachek had briefed him on. It was the Bengal tiger within a large cage situated within a recessed section of inner wall off to his left. He had once seen a rendering of Cardoza's pet carnivore on the ceiling of the mystical chamber behind the cove's majestic waterfall, but now he was actually seeing it with his own eyes. The beast was pacing back and forth, barring its fangs and roaring ferociously, maddened by the scent of blood and carnage filling the courtyard. Years earlier Destiny had claimed the rendering had originally portrayed Jake being mauled by the tiger, but by the time Jake had viewed it, the rendering had changed to show Walter McPherson as the mauling victim.

The clatter of an Uzi abruptly pulled Jake from this momentary reflection, and he spun around in reaction to the sound. Mort had fired his weapon, and to Jake's amazement he saw another blue helmeted commando stagger back as several rounds collided against his body armor. Jake followed up with a round of his own, and the commando was knocked off his feet as though tackled by an NFL linebacker.

Jake looked at Mort with newfound respect, surprised that the man had held up under such stressful duress. If not for Mort's alertness, the Chilean mercenary would have surely got the drop on him. "Nice job,

Mort!" Jake praised as he scanned the courtyard again. "Any suggestions which way we go from here?"

Mort pointed toward the courtyard's far end. "That way!"

A familiar sound suddenly impinged on Jake's awareness, escalating quickly from a soft susurration to a discordant din. Glancing up, he glimpsed a spotlight playing back and forth on the ramparts above. The spotlight's beam abruptly steadied, and Jake suddenly found himself caught in its blinding glare.

"Get back!" he shouted, grabbing Mort forcefully by the arm and hauling him roughly out of the light. No sooner had he done that, sparks flew up from the stone pavement as a shower of 7.62 millimeter rounds suddenly rained down. Bullets seemed to be ricocheting everywhere as Jake raced for the entrance on the inner wall side, and in less than two seconds he reached the safety of the nearest passageway. Dragging Mort with him, he moved well back from the entrance.

A storm of rounds continued to carom and hammer the opening, sending splinters of stone and fragmented bullets zinging and humming down the passageway but miraculously missing both men. With them no longer visible to the gunner, the sound of heavy machine guns immediately cut out, upon which Jake ran back to the entrance to risk a peak. For one brief moment the spotlight moved searchingly about the courtyard before infringing on the battlements higher up. Jake watched as the silhouette of the Hind shifted beyond his line of sight, the cacophonous din of its powerful engines and rotor blades fading to a dull whine as the stone battlements reflected the sound away.

Prepared to venture back out into the courtyard again, Jake pulled up short as movement caught his eye. The tiger had gotten free of its cage and was now roaming the courtyard. Jake watched as it moved silently among the dead men, sniffing the sprawled bodies before singling one out. Hunkering down on all fours, it began to feast.

Mort moved up behind Jake to crane his head over Jake's shoulder. "This is not good," he said dismally. "That animal's a killer. How do you suppose it got loose?"

"Some of those rounds must have hit the locking bolt on the cage," Jake offered, "but we can't stay here. Stay behind me and don't make any sudden moves." Mort did not protest or cower in fear as Jake ventured beyond the entrance and crept noiselessly along the inner wall.

Sensing the men, the tiger stopped its gnawing and went rigid. Lifting its head, it locked fierce yellow orbs on Jake, a low throaty growl rumbling forth from behind barred, bloodied teeth.

One of the things Jake had heard about big predatory cats was that you didn't look them directly in the eyes, otherwise you immediately invited attack since the cat would take it as a challenge. But something deep down made Jake do just that, something he could not explain. Keeping his Sledgehammer trained on the beast, Jake moved slowly along the wall with Mort sticking to him like glue. Unless it attacked, he had no reason to kill the beast.

The Bengal remained tense, its head swiveling slowly as it fixated on both men sidling past, the low growl continuing to rumble unabated from its throat, and for one fleeting moment Jake expected it to spring. But the tiger suddenly relaxed, dropping its fierce gaze from Jake and resuming its feeding.

Jake blew out a sigh of relief and picked up the pace, turning only once to look back at the cat, which was now ignoring him and feasting contentedly. Based on Belachek's rough sketch of the place, Jake assumed they were heading toward the portcullis. If they were going to escape this place, the drawbridge needed to be in the down position.

Jake opened up a mental link to his bond mate. *What's your status, Achilles?*

We're still avoiding detection, JJ, the dolphin shot back, *but it's doubtful Franklin can continue holding his breath each time I submerge. His condition is fragile. On the bright side, all of Cardoza's vessels have been sunk.*

Jake projected another thought. *Is the drawbridge still up?*

Unfortunately, yes, JJ. Stuck in this moat, Destiny and I have no way of helping you.

Jake continued following the inner wall, reaching where it turned ninety degrees. Taking a quick peak around the corner, he saw that the area beyond was deserted.

Mort grabbed his shoulder, speaking softly. As though he had heard Jake's interchange with Achilles, he said, "We don't need the drawbridge to get out of here."

Jake's expression turned hopeful. "Another way?"

"Yes, about fifty paces ahead there's a doorway a short distance from the gatehouse. It gives access to a portal that opens to the moat."

You hear that, Achilles?

Yes, JJ. I noticed a wooden hatch cover to the south side of the drawbridge just before Fernando dropped me in the moat.

Hold tight, Achilles, I'm going to make a try for it.

Jake turned to Mort. "I hope you're good at sprinting, Mort, because I need you to run like the wind." Having said that, Jake leapt past the corner and raced diagonally for the opposite wall, running in the direction of the gatehouse. Scanning the corridor before him, he prepared to dodge more bullets. In moments he reached the door Mort had described without taking any fire. Finding this odd, he did a quick mental count. So far he had taken out eleven commandos and four of Cardoza's thugs, with one enormous shark dispatching Cardoza and three more of his goons. Altogether, that added up to nineteen men. Perhaps that accounted for most, if not all, the combatants he would face.

The actual number is twenty-one, Achilles corrected, reading his thoughts again.

You mean there were two others? Jake shot back.

Yes, Destiny says she zapped two more of Cardoza's boys just before we reached her, but they either drowned or became shark chow.

Good to know, Jake replied. *So I take it Destiny's getting back to her old self.*

Seems that way.

We better cut the chatter, Achilles. More bad guys might be lurking about. Even though the exchange had occurred in less time than it took to blink, Jake knew a distraction of this sort was potentially dangerous.

With Mort right behind him, Jake examined the door, judging it to open inwardly. Reaching for the door handle, he pushed. The door appeared to be made of solid oak planks and would not budge. "Move back!" he yelled at Mort, aligning the barrel of the Sledgehammer with the door's locking mechanism and stepping away. Just before squeezing the trigger, he caught movement out of the corner of his eye. An assailant poked his head around the side of the gatehouse wall, bringing a weapon to bear on him. Jake spun and fired before the man could get off a shot. The round went high, barely missing the assailant and sending a shower of stone fragments to explode from the wall above his jutting head. For emphasis, Jake let loose another shot as the man ducked back out of sight, sending more stone shards flying.

Turning, Jake pumped off another shot, this time disintegrating the door handle and blowing a jagged hole through the heavy oaken plank supporting the lock. The impact swung the door inward and Jake hastened the movement by throwing a shoulder against the wood. "Go!" he yelled, looking back at Mort and stepping aside.

As Mort sprang through the opening, Jake pivoted to squeeze off another shot. The frag-12 detonated with a muffled sound, this time meeting flesh and bone as it caught the same assailant full in the face as he foolishly leaned out again from his place of cover. Leaping through the doorway, Jake grabbed the edge of the door and slammed it closed. Someone had forgotten to turn off a single low-watt light bulb that lit the room beyond, and he grabbed the first object he saw. It was a large table with piles of paper littering its top. Sweeping the paper off it, he discovered it was quite heavy. The table was topped with a slab of granite and had a cast iron frame.

"Give me a hand!" Jake yelled, glancing briefly at Mort. Grunting laboriously, both men managed to slide the table up against the door. Lying nearby was a stack of small crates, and without hesitation Jake lifted the topmost one, placing it on the table to block off the hole in the door. In rapid succession he stacked a few more crates on the table, noticing the strain they put on his back in moving them.

"Why was Cardoza holding you prisoner?" Jake grunted, hefting another box.

Mort was breathing hard from the exertion, but managed to speak in gasping, halting sentences. "I was a hostage. He was using me as leverage so as to keep my twin brother working for an associate of his, a man of incredible wealth and affluence. We're scientists. We used to work for the U.S. Department of Energy at Los Alamos. We-"

Mort suddenly stopped moving boxes, laboring for breath.

"Take a rest, Mort," Jake said, moving one last box into place. "You were about to say?"

"We retired from government service five years ago to go into business for ourselves. We lent assistance to Uncle Sam as private contractors. My brother specialized in electronics and computers, I in laser science. After Cardoza kidnapped me he somehow learned about our breakthrough."

"What kind of breakthrough?" Jake prodded encouragingly.

"Percy and I were on the threshold of a new idea that would revolutionize laser weaponry. Up to now the most powerful laser developed only puts out thirty kilowatts of energy. Our design, however, could unleash ten times that amount. At least in theory. Without me, Percy could not possibly construct such a weapon. It was not his area of expertise. But together we could. Cardoza wanted the design. When I refused to give it to him he threatened to kill me."

"An interesting story," Jake said.

"There's more to the story than just that," Mort huffed. "My brother and I managed to compile a mountain of incriminating evidence against Cardoza's associate, a man who heads a cabal conspiring to control the world. The reach of this man is enormous. He has tentacles embedded covertly in all the major governments across the globe. Cardoza is subservient to this man, who they call the *Sublimis*."

Jake frowned with puzzlement. "*Sublimis?*"

"The *Sublimis* is the head of the snake that controls the organization. He is at the top of the pyramid of power. The cabal has existed for generations, with the title being passed down from father to son through the ages, and now they have become more powerful than ever. The *Sublimis* knows we have acquired evidence against him and all his associates, and Cardoza has been assigned the task of retrieving it."

"So did you give it to him?"

"No. My brother has it stored in a place they'll never think to look, one you might say is right under their noses."

"That is quite an extraordinary story," Jake muttered, his attention preoccupied with the objects now bracing the door.

Satisfied for the moment, he eyed the room. It was a moderately-sized chamber, obviously used for storage. While stacks of boxes, crates and various other items cluttered the walls, one object grabbed his immediate attention. A long wooden shaft the size of a telephone pole dominated the room's center, and attached to its tip was a pulley. The pole was aligned with the hatch that was supposed to be their way out. The pole sat on rollers in a long guide embedded solidly in the floor. A sturdy T-bar situated at its aft end rose up to the height of a man's waist, and he immediately ascertained its purpose. With a man on each side of the pole pushing against the T-bar, the pole could be slid forward or moved back. From what Jake could see, the pole could be extended through the hatch and out over the moat, making him wonder what it was used for, though it reminded him of a buccaneer's cannon waiting to be fired once its muzzle portal was opened.

"You're looking at Cardoza's latest form of amusement," Mort said, correctly reading Jake's curious expression. "He lowers men from it to feed the sharks. I was to be their next meal."

"Well, you don't have to worry about Cardoza anymore. One of his sharks had him for dinner," Jake murmured absently, continuing to study the contraption. Moving to the hatch cover, he saw it was hinged at the top and had a heavy sliding bolt that locked it down. It could be raised by using a ratchet pulley that connected to a chain attached to its lower edge.

Jake slid back the locking bolt and grabbed the chain, but stopped short to survey the room again, curious to know what was stored here. His eyes fell upon a large cluster of wooden boxes stacked up against a side wall, all labelled with the word *AZUCAR*.

Achilles immediately translated, sensing Jake's puzzlement. *The word means sugar in Spanish.*

Jake sent back an assessment. *An army couldn't eat that much sugar in a year.* Reaching for a crowbar that lay on the floor next to one of the stacks, he pried off the cover of the topmost box. Probing around momentarily, a smile overtook his features. "Now look what we've got here," he announced blithely.

Mort moved closer to peer inside the box. "What?"

Jake pulled out a small brick-like object. "TNT!" he mumbled softly. He counted thirty-three similar boxes. "There's probably enough here to blow half this place to dust."

Jake swept the room searchingly again, spotting a crimper sitting atop an adjacent stack several feet away. Knowing what such a tool was used for, he scrutinized the small cardboard box that sat next to it. His smile grew larger when he looked inside the box. "Just what the doctor ordered," he remarked jubilantly, "blasting caps and fuse." Removing a three-foot length of coiled fuse, he inserted one end into a blasting cap and secured it with the crimper. Pushing the cap into the small brick of TNT, he placed the brick back in the box he had taken it from. The box held a total of forty bricks, each brick weighing one pound.

"You never told me your name," Mort said, watching the procedure intently.

Jake removed his K-bar from its sheath and sliced through the cord, shortening its length by a foot. "My friends call me Jay Jay."

"Thanks for saving my hide," Mort said.

Jake glanced up with a sober expression. "I'd hold off on the thanks for the time being if I were you. We're not out of the woods yet." Pulling a tiny butane lighter from a pouch on his utility belt, he flicked it several times to test the flame. On the third flick, the flame caught and held steady. "Do us a favor, Mort, and open the hatch."

Mort placed the Uzi down on the floor next to the hatch and grabbed the vertical section of chain attached to the ratchet pulley. Pulling it down, he forced the hatch cover to swing into the room and pivot toward the ceiling.

Jake moved to the opening and poked his head out, seeing that the drawbridge was still up. Withdrawing his head, he stepped back to light the fuse. "I suggest you make the plunge, Mort," he said calmly.

The fear Mort had previously shown was back with a vengeance, and he stood fast on the lip of the hatch opening, uneager to jump. "What about the sharks?"

"They're going to be the least of your worries if you don't get moving."

"I should tell you I have a problem with heights," Mort stammered nervously as he looked down at the water. With the surface of the moat considerably lower, the drop would be close to thirty feet.

A heavy pounding suddenly reverberated against the door to the chamber. Jake glanced behind him to see the table bracing it move back several inches. Abruptly, he snuffed out the lighter and picked up the Sledgehammer. Firing back to back rounds into the door below the level of the table, he was careful to miss the heavy crates he had placed on top of it. God only knew what was in them, and the last thing he needed was to set off an explosion. The pounding abruptly stopped as the rounds blew open the door's lower portion, and a muffled scream followed.

"Give me your weapon, Mort!" Jake commanded sternly as he strapped the Sledgehammer over his shoulder.

Mort turned, reaching down to retrieve the Uzi where he had left it, glad to step back from the precipice. Jake spoke quickly as Mort rose back up and handed him the weapon. "Sorry, Mort, but out you go." Mort let out a startled cry as Jake gave him a powerful shove, and he fell backwards through the opening, dropping from sight.

Jake spun around as more pounding resumed, and he saw the table begin to inch back again. Based on what was stored in the room, he had to assume they wouldn't dare fire their weapons through the door. Taking full advantage of this, he took careful aim with the Uzi and fired. The clip emptied in seconds, sending a barrage of rounds streaming through the jagged holes in the door's lowest section and invoking additional screams.

A sudden vision flashed before Jake's eyes, and he saw two of Cardoza's goons go down on the opposite side of the door, their shins bloodied. Another goon lay off to one side, his left leg blown off at the knee where a frag-12 had caught him a moment earlier. Four more thugs scurried in quickly to drag the first two men out of the way as four blue helmets moved in to place a heavy steel plate against what remained of the lowest section of door. With the shield in position, they picked up a heavy length of pipe that was being used as a battering ram.

The vision blinked out just as the pounding resumed, and Jake saw the door begin to lurch inward inch by inch with each powerful strike. Tossing the Uzi aside, he grabbed the lighter, flicking it savagely to ignite a flame. Though it sparked, it would not light this time. Stubbornly he kept at it, cursing as he ran his thumb over the roller again and again. Almost ready to give up, a flame suddenly caught on the wick and held, and without hesitation he applied it to the fuse. Satisfied that the fuse was silently burning, he placed two more boxes in front of it. Seeing that it was now effectively hidden, he turned and dove through the hatch. From his stint in the Seals, he was quite knowledgeable on the use of explosives, and based on the length of fuse he had cut, he knew he had roughly two minutes to get away from the devastating blast that would be forthcoming.

Spinning in midair like a cat, Jake adjusted his body posture to meet the water feet first. On the way down he caught a fleeting image of the drawbridge, suddenly aware that it was coming down. Driven deep by the force of his plunge, he felt Achilles' powerful forelimbs latch onto him. A heavy glare beamed down into the water, giving him a shadowy glimpse of the surrounding murk.

Where are the others? Jake asked Achilles, surprised at not seeing any forms clinging to his back.

Franklin and Mort are a safe distance away where I left them standing in waist-deep water. I discovered a narrow ledge below the surface that juts out from the fortress.

What about Destiny? Jake projected the query like a shotgun blast.

Achilles was suddenly unresponsive, and before Jake could press him again, the surrounding water was abruptly alive with a cascade of small projectiles zipping by like wind-driven hailstones. A muted though familiar buzz reached Jake's ears an instant later, and he immediately knew the cause of the sound. He didn't bother to look up. The image was sharp and distinct in his mind's eye, and he saw the Hind hovering ominously above the moat as though he were viewing it from high up.

Without hesitation, Achilles dove deeper to escape the fusillade, bolting along the canal's rocky bottom at full speed. *Where's Destiny*? Jake demanded as he was pulled along. Already he sensed they were well beyond the glaring light and the firestorm of rounds.

She's with Esmerelda, Achilles finally answered.

You're not making sense, Jake fired back.

You'll understand soon enough, was all Achilles would offer.

Bringing the Hind to a hover, Zinova played the spotlight over the water looking for the man he had seen leap from the fortress. His gunner had riddled the water in the exact spot where the man had landed, yet he could not detect any sign of blood on the surface. Pivoting the chopper around, he cast the light in the opposite direction. A voice suddenly came over the intercom. "One of our passengers is becoming troublesome," his second in command grumbled in annoyance.

"Which one?" Zinova asked, continuing to scan the water.

"The UN emissary. He demands we leave at once."

Zinova looked down the length of the canal, hungering for at least one kill to appease his rage. His involvement with Cardoza had cost him far too much.

"Perhaps we should toss him into the moat," Drakov appealed.

"Let him be!" Zinova muttered. He would need Allotey to recoup his losses. Continuing to hover, he adjusted the spotlight to illuminate the drawbridge. It was now fully lowered, and under the light he noted seven blue helmeted commandos taking positions along each side of the bridge, their weapons pointed down at the water. As far as he could tell, they also sought the man who had leapt from the fortress.

With a deft touch of the cyclic and a little pressure on the left foot pedal, Zinova faced the Hind away from the drawbridge and moved slowly along the moat, keeping the spotlight aimed down at the water. "Everyone is to stay alert!" he commanded his crew brusquely. "I want these infiltrators dead."

Under the searchlight's intense glare, nothing escaped his scrutiny as he brought the aircraft down the length of the moat along the west side of the castle. Something suddenly caught his attention along the fringe of the beam, and he immediately refocused the light as he brought the aircraft to a hover again. He could have sworn he saw the head of a man duck under the water immediately adjacent to the castle wall.

"Boris, fire your guns in the center of the beam!" he ordered his gunner.

The water was chopped into a frothing maelstrom as Boris opened up with the twin machine guns, some of the rounds catching the stone above the waterline and emitting a shower of sparks.

Boris kept the barrage going for several seconds before letting up on the trigger. "If anyone was down there, I'm sure I got him," Boris replied smugly.

"If you got him, the water should be red with his blood," Zinova growled dubiously.

"Then the sharks will get him," Boris riposted evenly, noting the large fin suddenly coming to the surface along the water's edge.

Zinova continued to hover, deciding which way to go as he eyed the fin. It occurred to him the shark below him might very well be agitated by something in the water. Perhaps it was on the scent of human prey as Boris contended. The fin jutting above the surface suddenly charged ahead, moving in the direction of the drawbridge. Opting to follow it, he began to swing the chopper around. Halfway through the turn, the Hind's windshield rattled as though pelted by a storm of pebbles.

"We're taking fire!" Boris yelled.

From the impacts, Zinova knew they were being assailed by small arms fire. Looking for the source, he spotted dual muzzle flashes at three o'clock. Leaning the aircraft over, he adjusted the spotlight to illuminate a cluster of small trees fronting a jumble of large boulders fifteen meters beyond the moat's edge, but before he could angle the chopper into firing position, the flashes were gone. Boris, however, was not to be denied. Through his seat, Zinova felt the vibration of the Hind's twin 30s opening up.

Bringing the chopper closer to the target, Zinova eyed the area as Boris let up on the guns. The possibility of taking additional hits did not concern him. He knew the Hind was invulnerable to small arms fire. "I don't see anything," he grumbled in a soft hiss, his eyes playing back and forth over the boulders. Slowly, he brought the Hind around to circumvent the trees and rocks, meticulously searching the ground for signs of assailants.

"There has to be at least two of them down there," Boris stated bluntly. "I distinctly saw two muzzle flashes."

"These infiltrators are like phantoms," Zinova grunted in a tone caustic and guttural. "No sooner do we catch sight of them, they disappear." Frustrated, he brought the Hind to the outer rim of the moat, slowly working the light over the ground.

Feeling it safe to do so, Destiny rose to the surface on the north side of the drawbridge and glanced behind her. Seconds earlier the Hind had passed overhead, sweeping the water with its powerful spotlight before flaring into a hover. Treading water, she saw the drawbridge begin to come down just as Jake leapt clear of the fortress. Turning, she looked in the opposite direction. Under the moon's pervading glow, she discerned the huge fin knifing the surface and bearing straight at her. Try as she might, she found she was not able to control or influence the creature's behavior in any way. This one was different, certainly not like the animal that had killed Cardoza. Nevertheless, she was not afraid as the great fish bore down on her. The white shark just recently dropped in the moat was enormous, a killing machine nearly thirty feet in length. Yet she sensed a familiar presence wafting from it that seemed to reach into her very thoughts. The presence had substance, and it suddenly resonated with astounding clarity.

This is the same creature that took me long ago, Esmerelda said, *but now my spirit controls it rather than Erzulie.*

You know what we must do, Destiny chimed.

Yes, my child, though it will not be easy. The water may not be deep enough.

All is possible if we believe strongly enough, Destiny reminded her, grabbing hold of the fin and straddling the shark's broad back.

Yes, all is possible, Esmerelda maintained, forcing the creature as deep as the water would allow.

Chapter Three:
A Star Gone Nova

Jake realized just how close he had come to losing Franklin and Mort, and strangely enough it was the shark that had killed Cardoza that saved them. Using his bio-sonar, Achilles had sensed the approach of the creature as it homed in on the ledge supporting the two men.

You sure it's the same shark? Jake queried as he rode his bond mate's back.

Without a doubt, and apparently she's still hungry, Achilles replied, grasping each man firmly under an armpit as he bolted through the murk. He had snatched them away before the shark reached them, but now the strain of carrying three men while eluding the pursuing beast was taxing even his incredible endurance.

Unfortunately, she's forcing us back where we don't want to be, Achilles added, *and if I don't surface immediately, both Franklin and Mort will drown.*

The fact that the shark was in attack mode perplexed Jake. *Can't Destiny control it like before?*

She says the creature will not respond. Controlling marine creatures does not always work, especially with unpredictable predators like sharks.

How much time do we have? Jake asked, knowing Achilles was like a keen biological clock with an extraordinary sense of time.

Not much, maybe thirty seconds at most. But to make matters worse, Destiny tells me there's commandos on the drawbridge with their weapons aimed at the water. It seems we're effectively hemmed in, I'm afraid, and at this moment I'm out of options. I have no choice but to surface to save Franklin and Mort.

Jake held on tight as Achilles broke the surface and lifted his charges so that their heads were above the water. Both men gasped audibly before inhaling sharply, sucking air into oxygen-deprived lungs. Glancing behind him, Jake espied the Hind further back, its spotlight tenaciously roving the ground along the moat's outer perimeter and moving slowly in his direction. Looking ahead, he saw the commandos spread out along the drawbridge. To make matters worse, he discerned the head of another blue helmet poke out from the portal he and Mort had jumped from.

Grabbing the Sledgehammer strapped to his shoulder, Jake brought the barrel around to bear on the opening above him in one smooth lightning-like motion. The thought that they had run out of luck sprang to the forefront of his mind, and he wondered if things could get any worse than this.

Whatever you do, don't shoot at the commandos on the drawbridge, otherwise you'll risk hitting Destiny, Achilles cautioned.

Unsure what Achilles meant, Jake squeezed the trigger before the man looking down at him could align his own weapon. The possibility of a misfire was allayed as the Sledgehammer abruptly discharged. Built for low recoil, it barely bucked as a frag-12 rocketed from its muzzle to explode against the portal's upper lip. Though the shot missed its intended target, the blue helmet screamed out in pain as shrapnel found its way into unprotected parts of his torso, arms, and neck.

Water began kicking up all around Jake as men on the drawbridge began shooting. Jake's next thought was projected like thunder as he sought to escape the enfilade. *Take us under, Achilles*!

Achilles seemed to hesitate, and just as quickly as it started, the enfilade ceased. Jake saw commandos being flung from the drawbridge as a monstrous form barreled into them like a runaway semi. It had leapt up from the water on the opposite side of the bridge with enough momentum to completely traverse the structure. With no guard rails on the bridge to impede it, it plummeted to splash down with crushing force on several of the blue helmets it had sent flying into the water.

Jake stared transfixed for one brief moment, aware that Destiny was astride the huge creature. Glancing behind him, he saw the orientation of the Hind change, the chopper's pilot seemingly cognizant of what had just happened. *Get us out of here, Achilles!* Jake ordered, the thought issuing from his mind like a thunderbolt.

With powerful flicks of his tail, Achilles shot ahead, quickly gathering speed but keeping to the surface this time. He was making for the north side of the drawbridge, attempting to put distance between them and the impending explosion. Riding her strange mount, Destiny was suddenly abreast of Jake. "I'm going to keep the other shark away from you," she yelled. Abruptly she fell back, prepared to protect Achilles' rear as Jake's bond mate sounded, pulling Franklin and Mort along with him.

Though he was more than a hundred meters away, Zinova had caught sight of the disturbance, seeing additional muzzle flashes coming from the vicinity of the drawbridge. Barely illuminated under the pale glow of a gibbous moon, he had discerned a dark form rise up to snuff out those flashes before falling back into the water. Puzzled, he lowered the Hind's nose, throwing power into the churning rotor blades. Picking up speed rapidly, he followed the moat's outside bank to investigate. Already he could see a few blue-helmeted men floundering feebly in the water.

Hungering for a kill, he scanned the area below, hoping to spot infiltrators. Another flash erupted off his starboard side, this one intense and huge like a star going nova, and had he been looking directly at it he would have been temporarily blinded. Stunned by its sheer magnitude and ferocity, he was jarred violently in his seat as something slammed heavily against the fuselage. This was followed by a fleeting onslaught of lesser impacts against the airframe, and with startling swiftness, the Hind leaned precariously to port, the tip of its main rotor coming dangerously close to the ground. A highly experienced pilot, Zinova reacted quickly, fighting madly to regain control of the aircraft, which was now spinning wildly, blown away from the fortress like a leaf caught in a force-5 hurricane.

Drakov's alarmed voice suddenly blared over the intercom with deafening volume. "We've been hit!"

Furiously working the controls to keep from crashing, Zinova barely managed to arrest the Hind's dizzying spin, slowing the counterclockwise rotation before bringing it to a halt. Still, the chopper continued to lean heavily to port, and he had to compensate by tilting the main rotor to starboard. It was touch and go for several more seconds before he was able to level the sturdy aircraft, and bringing it to a hover, he noticed something didn't feel right.

"Bring us down!" Drakov yelled, his tone uncharacteristically fearful.

Zinova pivoted his head to glance out his port window. A long cylindrical object protruded at an awkward angle from the side of the cabin. Looking to his right, he saw the same thing, though the object didn't extend as far. Without hesitation, he spotted a small patch of ground devoid of vegetation and set the Hind down, facing it toward the fortress. Staring straight ahead, he was astonished to find that he was now several hundred meters from the impregnable stone walls, but even more astonishing were the flames and smoke billowing from the structure. As far as he could tell, a good portion of the structure had been obliterated.

Chapter Four: Getting Away

Having managed to escape the blast, Achilles swam around the undamaged portion of the fortress, eventually reaching the south side. Discerning a suitable place in the rock levee that defined the moat's outer periphery, he released his charges. Assisted by Jake, Franklin was first to climb up using seams and crevices in the abutted stones as handholds. Mort quickly followed, eager to get beyond the reach of predators.

Ascending to the bank, Jake joined up with both men, cautiously taking in his surroundings. Visibility was obscured. A slight breeze had sprung up carrying tendrils of dense smoke from the explosion. A fire continued to rage in the western sector of the fortress, which now lay in total ruins. Sensing movement off to his right, he pulled the Sledgehammer from his shoulder, prepared to use it.

"Don't shoot!" a voice petitioned breathlessly. Two dark forms abruptly materialized out of the haze as they de-activated their cloakers, and Jake recognized Belachek and Jimenez.

Jake addressed the former Spetsnaz operative. "Any idea where that Hind is?" he asked, taking inventory of the sky above through the pall of smoke.

"We saw it go down somewhere to the west," Belachek said. Both he and Jimenez were breathing heavily, and Jake could tell they had rushed here as fast as their legs would carry them. "We were able to fire upon it to keep my old boss distracted and away from you," Belachek rambled on, "but his Hind may have been damaged by the explosion."

Jake stared back in mild surprise. "How do you know it was Zinova?"

"I saw him come into the hangar before we blew it up. He had seven of his men with him. They left with the third Hind he always keeps in reserve."

"You saw his bird go down?"

"Not actually, but it appeared to be spinning out of control when it disappeared from sight."

Jake let out an imperceptible sigh of relief, suddenly willing to gamble that Belachek's assessment was correct. He had felt the brutal shock wave issuing from the blast, and with the Hind not far behind, he was certain it had to be damaged if not destroyed altogether.

Pulling a small handheld radio from one of the waterproof pouches on his utility belt, he brought it to his lips and spoke softly. "Rogue Dog to Fly Boy, come in!"

Jake had to repeat himself before a reply came back garbled with static. "Fly Boy is at your disposal." An easing of anxiety was apparent in Fernando's voice.

"Achilles awaits you for extraction on the moat's south side," Jake instructed. "I don't know if you noticed it, but be on the alert for another Hind in the immediate vicinity. We think it was damaged and went down, but we can't be sure."

"I'm on my way," Fernando shot back eagerly.

Jake put away the radio, looking down into the moat as a curtain of smoke parted. Moon beams twinkled off a turbulent set of expanding ripples, indicating movement just below the surface. His face remained impassive as he projected a concern to his bond mate. *How's our girl doing, Achilles?*

She's fending that brute off me at the moment. It's a good thing Destiny's shark is bigger than the one chasing me, otherwise I'd be expending far more energy than I am now.

Jake turned to Belachek. "I'd be obliged if you and Jimenez would escort these two gentlemen down to the end of the pier where the submersible is standing by," he said, setting his gaze on Franklin and Mort hovering at his side. "Destiny and I will meet up with you as soon as Achilles is extracted."

Belachek nodded stoically. He seemed to have no problem with Jake calling the shots, but Franklin interceded quickly, laying petitioning eyes on Jake. "I prefer to stay with you, son. I have to know that my daughter is safe."

"No need for that," Jake said. "Once Achilles is pulled from the water, she'll be coming."

Franklin was adamant. "I want to see for myself that she's safe."

Jake was on the verge of objecting, but abruptly caved at seeing the look of resolution on his father-in-law's face. "All right, Dad," he acquiesced.

Belachek stared at Mort quizzically. "Who is this man?" he asked, as if noticing him for the first time.

"His name is Mort, a guy Cardoza had locked away in his underground dungeon before I broke him out," Jake said.

Mort cut in before Jake could say more. "Once we're away from this awful place, I'll explain why I was being held prisoner."

Belachek shrugged nonchalantly, but spoke gregariously. "And I will look forward to hearing about it." Setting his mismatched eyes on Jake again, he posed a question of his own. "Did you get Cardoza?"

Jake smiled soberly, turning to indicate the moat. "Let me just say one of his pets got all choked up over his demise."

Belachek grinned, glad to see the mission had succeeded. Placing a guiding arm over Mort's shoulder, he started to lead Mort away but stopped short. Turning, he looked back at Jake. "Stay safe, my friend," he uttered in an amiable tone. "Let us hope my former boss was killed. A man like that will not accept defeat, and as far as I know, you are the first to defeat him. If he is still alive, he will come after you like a maddened animal after all the problems you have caused him." That said, he disappeared into the night with Mort and Jimenez following.

Chapter Five: Extreme Nausea

Walking around the Hind, Karloff Zinova assessed the damage with a critical eye. Though dents marred the armored sides in various places, both the main and tail rotors had miraculously escaped the rain of stone and debris catapulted by the blast. But these were not the things that concerned him. It was the long cylindrical timber exceeding thirty feet in length that extended from both open doors of the aircraft's main cabin. Lodged at an odd angle, most of it jutted cantilever from the port side door. It was this that had been the cause of the Hind's instability following the explosion, for it had created a significant moment that had made the chopper list heavily to port. By some strange quirk of luck, however, it had not wrought any structural damage to the airframe, though it had killed two of his men and the black man called Ermstine as it swept through the cabin.

"Push harder!" Zinova snarled, ordering three of the five remaining men under his command to rid the timber from the cabin. He had already posted two others as sentries, positioning them fifty meters forward on opposite sides of the Hind to interdict the possibility of a sneak attack by infiltrators. But now he was considering bringing them back.

"It will not move," Drakov groaned in exasperation, straining with all his might against the steel T-bar protruding perpendicular from the bottom of the pole. While it provided a place of leverage for multiple hands to push against, its very existence required that the timber be retracted from the Hind's starboard side since the jutting bar would catch obstacles if they tried moving the short end through the cabin.

Zinova went around to the opposite side of the Hind and positioned himself against the end of the pole's long side farthest from Drakov, prepared to pit his bearlike strength against the unyielding timber, but heaving to no avail he cast wrathful eyes on Allotey and Alvarez standing idly apart from the task. "Both of you pitch in and help," he barked furiously. "Unless we remove this timber, we're not going anywhere."

Alvarez lowered his pack, moving quickly to lend a hand, but Allotey hesitated momentarily, appearing resentful of being ordered about like a lackey. The prospect of hard physical exertion was foreign to him. Mumbling under his breath, he joined in to push against the obstinate object keeping them grounded.

With all eight men grunting hard, the timber lurched forward, moving several inches before stopping, and Zinova could see it was lodged more firmly between supporting stanchions within the cabin.

"We need to use the winch," Drakov gasped. Relaxing his hold on the T-bar, he retrieved a heavy-duty come-along winch and two lengths of ¾ inch nylon rope from one of the Hind's storage compartments. Tying one of the ropes off to the base of the T-bar where it met the timber, he knotted the rope to one of the winch's two hooks. Securing the second rope to the remaining hook, he pulled the rope taut before looping it snugly around the trunk of a nearby tree and tying it off. Designed to handle up to five tons, he began ratcheting the winch. "Let's hope this works," he said hoarsely, dubiously eyeing the rope, which would yield long before the winch reached its maximum capacity. He knew that if the rope snapped, someone would likely get hurt pretty badly. "I'll winch as we push," he stated, leaning his weight up against the T-bar.

Once again the timber lurched as everyone pushed hard, but this time it crept forward as the winch added to the effort. Seconds, then minutes ticked by as the pole continued to inch forward. "Just a little more," Drakov grunted, speaking more to the winch than the men assisting him. In another moment the timber sprang free, the end of it falling from the cabin floor and landing with a heavy thud as it met the ground.

Another sound suddenly caught Zinova's attention, and he motioned everyone to keep quiet. Listening, he realized it was the drone of another chopper. "Everyone in the aircraft!" he bellowed in a deep, guttural growl.

"You'll fly us to the colony?" Allotey asked tensely, wondering if Zinova had changed his mind about taking him to Aquaria.

Zinova stared at the UN emissary, seeing a man filled with fright. "You better be right about the gold," he threatened. "If you are wrong I will kill you."

Allotey paled noticeably, his usual arrogance completely absent. He had no doubt the Reaper meant to carry out the threat should the colony fail to show any gold.

Jake watched apprehensively as Fernando brought the helicopter to a low hover, submerging the sling into the water. Visibility opened up quickly as a potent blast of rotor wash dispersed smoke from the fire, allowing the moon to reassert its soft pervasive glow over the surrounding landscape. Another moment passed before Achilles' familiar essence reverberated in Jake's head. *I'm ready to go, JJ.*

Not bothering to use the radio, Jake looked up at the chopper's cockpit and twirled a finger in a circular motion. Fernando nodded in understanding before putting pitch into the main rotor, and seconds later the sling went taut, lifting Achilles' twelve-hundred-pound mass slowly from the water. As the whirlybird headed for the ocean carrying its heavy burden, Jake moved to the edge of the canal, reaching down to haul Destiny up the last few feet from the rocky embankment. The surface of the moat rippled heavily below her as the gargantuan shark she had been riding sounded, its huge dorsal fin disappearing from sight.

Embracing his wife in his powerful arms, Jake gave her a passionate kiss. "We better get moving," he finally murmured, begrudgingly releasing her. "Once Fernando dumps Achilles back in the ocean, I want you and your father to fly back to the cove with him. I think it's best you stay with the children and your mother."

"You're going back to Aquaria, aren't you!?" Destiny said.

"I have no choice. I can't leave Mat and Jacob alone to fend off a UN task force."

"There's nothing you can do," Destiny protested wearily.

"Perhaps," Jake concurred, "but I have to try." He turned to glimpse the chopper as it moved farther away, the whir of its blades rapidly diminishing.

Grabbing her hand, he led her and Franklin down the slope leading to the shoreline. Two-thirds of the way down, Destiny stopped short, looking back the way they had come. "This is not over, Jay Jay."

Jake went rigid. A vision of the Hind suddenly emerged in his mind's eye, and a moment later he heard the distinctive drone of its engines escalating swiftly in pitch. "Run!" he urged, the word automatically ensuing from his lips in a throaty wail. Now familiar with the instrumentation these Russian-made whirlybirds were equipped with, he knew Zinova would readily see Fernando's chopper on his radar screen.

Jake immediately sent out a rapid-fire warning to his bond mate, the thought leaping from his mind like a gazelle escaping a lion. *Jump as soon as you clear the beach, Achilles!*

As he ran, Jake glanced over his shoulder to spot the Hind coming on quickly. In a few more seconds it would be in firing range of Fernando, who had not yet reached the ocean. In that fleeting moment he knew he had one option to fall back on, and one option only. Pulling the PHP he had retained from his utility belt, he stopped running and depressed the activation button, holding the device above his head. A momentary delay ensued before a holographic projection of the dolphin art sprang into the night sky, its enigmatic pulsing streaks of multi-colored light twisting and interlacing directly in front of the approaching attack helicopter.

Please let this work, Jake pleaded inwardly as the Hind bore down on them.

As soon as he lifted off, Zinova activated the aircraft's radar system. Throwing maximum pitch into the main rotor, he forced the Hind straight up like a runaway elevator. Checking the system gauges on the instrument console, he saw that all the readings were in the normal range. Confirming this, he could feel no odd vibrations shuddering through the airframe. By some strange quirk of luck, he knew that the Hind's power train had miraculously escaped damage.

Fully airborne, he had a bird's eye view of what remained of Cardoza's lair. The westernmost portion had collapsed, leaving a mound of stone and timber rubble that sloped down into the moat and disappeared below the waterline. Flames burned heavily, evoking a billowing curtain of dense smoke that drifted off to the south. And while a section of the drawbridge was still intact, what remained of it lay upside down, deposited more than fifty meters west of the canal alongside the road leading to the fortress. Lying on its side next to it was the large cargo container he had used in moving the shark to the moat. Transporting the shark had been Cardoza's last request of him, a task which he now knew had been all for naught, for he was certain Cardoza had perished, and with the drug lord gone, no payment would be forthcoming.

Gaining a height of 300 meters, he slowed the aircraft's vertical ascent and studied the radar screen. Just as he suspected, a blip showed up. It was flying at low altitude and moving directly away from him on a southern heading.

The voice of his gunner came over the intercom. "Look at your screen!" Boris exclaimed briskly. "He's south of us."

"I see him," Zinova grumbled. Lowering the aircraft nose, he brought the Hind into a steep dive, descending through a pall of smoke to come up behind the unknown intruder. Certainly it had to be part of the force that had attacked the fortress, he surmised. And if he was wrong, what difference did it make?

"Take him out with a missile!" Zinova ordered, catching sight of the whirlybird. It looked to be a relatively small helicopter with something slung beneath it.

"With pleasure," Boris replied, eager for a kill. "I will scatter pieces of him all over the beach." As he armed a missile, a swirl of bright lights suddenly danced before his eyes. Confused, he stared transfixed for less than half a second before being assailed by extreme vertigo. With his brain feeling as though it was going to explode, he ripped off his flight helmet and clutched his skull. The scream that left his lips was abruptly cut off as a sudden rush of vomit rose up from his stomach to spew from his mouth.

Reeling from the onslaught of holographic light, Zinova felt his stomach begin to churn in reaction to the invisible vise crushing his head. Too late to stop it, a gush of bile spurted from his lips to splatter across the control panel. As though from far away, the voice of Alvarez rang out to rise above the other screams echoing in the cabin behind him. "Don't look at it!"

Using all his will, Zinova instinctively closed his eyes, fighting back the illness sweeping over him. He was one of those rare individuals who was able to function in the midst of debilitating dizziness and pain, having once been considered for cosmonaut training by the Soviets. Testing him in a high speed centrifuge, they had discovered he could withstand a g-force of twenty for better than two minutes without losing consciousness. But that was when he was much younger. This, however, was unlike anything he had ever before experienced, and it took every ounce of his remaining willpower to keep from blacking out. In the midst of his torment, he vaguely perceived the Hind yaw stiffly to starboard, and in that instant he knew he was losing control of the chopper. Having enough presence of mind to keep from crashing, he pushed down hard on one of the foot pedals to counter the dangerous yaw. Sensing the airframe pivot back beneath its main rotor, he knew he had overcompensated when the Hind spun violently in the opposite direction. Risking a peek, he opened his eyes. The display of swirling lights was now gone, the Hind having moved past the source of emission. Nevertheless, the severe nausea still festered, and he let go with another involuntary burst of vomit that drenched the console.

Too sick to continue flying, he knew he had no choice but to set the Hind down. Somehow he was able to change course, just barely managing to avoid plunging the chopper into the ocean looming before him. In his present condition he dared not try landing on the beach, which was strewn haphazardly with large boulders and outcroppings of rock. But he needed to land without having to consider hazardous obstacles. His only option was Cardoza's airstrip a little ways upland. Fighting off the debilitation draining him, he used his iron will to combat it. Again, he upchucked, unable to stop the surge of bile and vomit leaping from his throat. Just a little further, he urged himself on, guiding the Hind clumsily past the smoldering ruins of Cardoza's hangar. Desperate to reach the runway that lay before him, he wondered if he would be able to land the Hind before unconsciousness overtook him.

Chapter Six: Not Intimidated

Amphitrite was not intimidated by Swensen's hulking form as he looked down at her with a cold expressionless stare, knowing the man amounted to nothing more than a physically powerful machine ready to carry out the wishes of its master. The real threat resided in the smaller man, and within his eyes she saw the fiery blaze of a psychotic killer many times more potent than anything she had ever before encountered. Unlike the rabidly malicious but now deceased Colonel Ternier whose ambitions had never been achieved, here was a persona that had reached the absolute apex of power yet still hungered for more. Power from any source, she knew, created an appetite for additional power, but before her sat a megalomaniac who aspired to control the wealth of the entire world. If the devil existed in physical form, this was surely him, she concluded, but she also knew that by no means was he acting alone.

Comfortably ensconced in a cushioned chair in the uppermost cabin of the yacht's superstructure, Maximus put down a cup of tea from which he had been sipping. Tinted acrylic windows bordering the oval room along its perimeter provided a three hundred and sixty-degree unobstructed view of the sea in all directions. Casually, he turned his head to take in the small village nestled along the shoreline three miles distant. A soft halo of pink silvery light crowned the steep hills behind it, imparting a fairytale-like setting to the scene. Studying it briefly, he brought his gaze back to Amphitrite. "What is your relationship to the children?" he asked.

Amphitrite kept her gaze fixed and unwavering as she looked into Maximus' soulless, ruthless eyes, sensing a burning cauldron of impatience lurking just below the surface. Thankfully, Zimbola had trusted her insights enough by not putting up any resistance against the boarding party sent from the *Numquam Satis* that had stormed aboard the *Angel* nine hours earlier. And though he and the rest of them were now prisoners, she sensed none of them had as yet been harmed. For the moment, she would appease the man sitting before her by answering his questions truthfully. Something deep inside her told her this was the appropriate action to take. "I am their grandmother," she willingly admitted.

Maximus stared, finding this hard to believe. The woman looked far too youthful and attractive to be a grandmother, appearing to be in her mid-thirties at most. Either she was one of those rare individuals able to resist the ravages of time, or she had assumed the role of grandmother in name only without having any genetic relationship to the children.

"Their biological grandmother?" Maximus questioned, testing the full context of her assertion.

"Yes."

Deciding to accept her claim, he lifted the cup to his lips again, seeming to smile subtly before putting it back down. "Their grandmother," he uttered with satisfaction. "That is most convenient!"

Leaning forward, he placed his elbows on the table and tented his fingers. "Then I'll have to assume you are also the biological mother of the Dolphin Girl."

"Yes."

He turned his head again to scrutinize the village once more. "You and your people have made great strides over the last several years, obviously accomplishing the impossible. But tell me, how is it that a small contingent of seemingly simple and impoverished Haitians was able to get the funding for such a grand undertaking?"

"I sense fear within you," Amphitrite murmured softly. "The thought of more sea colonies coming on line scares the daylights out of you. You see them as an impediment to your own insidious interests."

Maximus smirked wolfishly. "Not at all. I actually applaud your efforts in succeeding to build such a thriving enterprise. It was a monumental undertaking. Unfortunately, you will soon discover those efforts were all in vain once a UN task force seizes your operation. Control of it, including all its assets, will then fall to me, at least indirectly."

Maximus paused for effect, enjoying the moment before going on. "Building an operation of that scale had to have cost Tursiops at least one hundred billion in U.S. currency, yet I know for a fact not one bank, corporation or other entity on the face of the earth provided the funding to build it, nor would they have risked financing it had you applied for loans. This led me to conclude that your people used something to barter with, and that something had to be gold. Through various sources I have learned this to be true. The question is, where did you get such a huge quantity of it?"

Amphitrite smiled sardonically. "The earth is a marvelous super-organism. You're correct about no one on the face of the earth willing to finance our vision, so *Gaia* herself provided for us what no one else would have been willing to do."

Maximus frowned, puzzled by the word. "*Gaia*? Who is this person?"

"I'm surprised you never heard of her. She is the embodiment of our Mother Earth."

For several seconds Maximus stared at her as though she were insane, then abruptly sneered. "You're telling me the planet provided you with the gold to fund your operation."

"Yes."

A mocking laugh erupted from Maximus' lips. "Did she just hand over tons of it, no questions asked?" His laughter suddenly ceased, changing over to a rabid snarl as he shot another look toward the village. "No doubt you found a gold mine, and it's probable it's located somewhere near Malique."

Amphitrite remained calm, not offering anything.

Maximus suddenly relaxed, seemingly bringing his anger under control for the moment. "How much gold do you currently have and where is it stored?" he asked. Though his tone was raspy, he posed the question casually, as though requesting current weather conditions.

"Enough to build at least five more colonies of equal size," Amphitrite stated without hesitation.

The statement invoked surprise in Maximus' countenance, and he responded with another flare of annoyance. "Do not toy with me, woman. That much gold could not possibly exist outside known reserves currently held in vaults around the world."

Amphitrite kept her gaze direct. "*Gaia* holds far more gold than even you can imagine."

"You'd be surprised at what I can imagine," Maximus grumbled irritably. "But it's a known fact that only one ounce of gold actually exists for every 400 ounces traded on world markets."

"Believe what you want. Nevertheless, *Gaia* has all the resources she needs to heal the wounds men like you inflict upon her."

Maximus studied her closely, looking for signs of insanity. "Let's assume I accept what you're telling me," he finally said. "What I don't get is how your people were able to bring forth such a colossal engineering feat. Where did the know-how and technical skills come from to build machinery capable of harvesting energy directly from the ocean?"

Amphitrite responded quickly, her comportment remaining steady and enigmatic. "What *Gaia* lacks, she simply creates."

Once again, Maximus frowned. "What does that mean?"

"She spawns the intelligence necessary to build such machinery."

Understanding slowly replaced the clouded look dominating Maximus' features. "Those creatures," he blurted. "Those strange white beasts with hands. They are the ones that created Aquaria, aren't they?"

"The only way you could possibly know about them is through those robotic fish you sent into the colony to spy upon us. Using them to plant explosives, your objective was to discredit us in the eyes of the world."

Maximus grinned fiendishly. "Yes, and it worked beautifully." Pausing, he took another sip of tea before resuming the conversation. "I've studied the concept behind ocean thermal energy conversion, trying to make sense how Aquaria makes it work, and based on the information I've obtained, the colony's seven OTEC power plants should not be able to work."

"Maybe I can enlighten you," Amphitrite offered.

Maximus seemed pleased that the woman was willing to cooperate. "For one, the seafloor directly beneath Aquaria maxes out at nine hundred and fifty feet," he pointed out. "At that depth, the ambient water temperature and nitrate concentration are insufficient for harvesting the vast amounts of energy and food the colony is obviously producing. For another, your surface water intakes don't conform to a standard OTEC model. You use seven identical pipes that extend horizontally out to the offshore berthing facility near the island. Why go to the expense of constructing lengthy intakes when it is so much simpler to draw in surface water immediately contiguous with the OTEC plants?"

Amphitrite remained stoic as she shed light on the riddle. "For any OTEC process to work effectively, a minimum temperature differential of forty degrees Fahrenheit must exist between the surface and deeper waters. But by increasing this differential further, greater amounts of energy can be produced. We solved this problem by preheating the surface water at the island's offshore berthing facility. That is why the surface intakes extend so far from the power plants."

"To preheat that much water would require enormous amounts of energy," Maximus said, "maybe even more than what your OTEC generators are capable of producing. Where is that energy coming from?"

"Hydrogen gas."

"If what you're telling me is true, it sounds as though the process would be close to a break-even wash in energy production." Maximus shook his head doubtfully. "Doesn't seem practical to have the hydrogen Aquaria produces channeled back to the berthing facility to be used for producing more energy."

"The hydrogen does not come from Aquaria," Amphitrite said. "It comes from another source."

"From where, then?"

"From deep under Navassa Island."

Maximus stared as though impressed. "A subterranean vent," he concluded. "How convenient! Obviously, your people found a way to put it to good use, just as you have done with the *guano* mined on the island. I hear you supply it to Haitian farmers free of charge to double and triple their crop yields. But it seems something has been added to this miracle fertilizer. Not only is it exceptionally potent, it also has an unknown ingredient that makes indigenous crops resistant to chemicals that would normally kill them. Isn't that so?"

Maximus smiled smugly when Amphitrite didn't answer. There would be ample time to learn the fertilizer's secret. At the moment, however, he wanted to stay focused on the mysteries Aquaria harbored. "How is so much algae produced? The water beneath Aquaria lacks the nitrates in sufficient quantity needed to grow algae," he contended. "The water is not deep enough."

"We are able to harvest water from deep down in the Cayman Trench, well beyond 3,300 feet where nitrate concentrations begin to level out."

"But your vertical intakes go straight down," Maximus objected with a dark scowl. "They can only end at the seafloor beneath them."

Amphitrite knew he would never have been able to detect what actually lay down there. Navassa Island was the truncated apex of an enormous undersea mountain that sat on the edge of the Cayman Trench. Cold deep water currents flowing along the edge of the trench coming in contact with warmer water from above continually produced odd thermal effects that would distort sonar rays. Add to that the strange and unpredictable electrical fields and anomalies produced by those marvelous creatures dwelling at that depth and the T-crystals they produced and the end result was 'noisy water' that wreaked havoc on sonar and video equipment.

"An assumption on your part, but a valid one even though the ambient acoustical and electrical interference directly below Aquaria would have prevented you from seeing what lay down there."

"And what would that be?"

"*Thurentras!*"

"What the hell are *thurentras*?"

"*Gaia* has the ability to create life forms necessary to carry out objectives. In this case she created creatures to draw cold, nitrate-laden water up from the depths. The vertical intakes collect the water the *thurentras* harvest from the Cayman Trench and bring it to the colony above."

For several seconds, Maximus remained mute, his face contorting with a flood of mixed emotions before settling on a look of intense avarice. "These creatures you speak of, I assume they sit stationary on the seafloor?"

"Yes."

Maximus took another sip from his cup. "That art your colony produces is…" He paused, seeming to grope for the right words. "I suppose arcane and debilitating would be suitable words to describe it since it induces extreme vertigo in people when they look upon it, yet all your colonists seem immune."

Amphitrite allowed herself a small smile. "For reasons we don't fully understand, only those who are truly evil will become ill when viewing it," she stated, seeing the man's eyes flash briefly.

Maximus quickly regained control of himself. "Your people don't use drugs to keep from getting sick?"

"No."

A fleeting, skeptical look crossed Maximus' face like a dark cloud scudding over a roiling sea. "Which brings us back to my first question," he grumbled. "Where do you mine the gold?"

"There is no need for us to mine it," Amphitrite replied, deciding it was time to be evasive. "As I told you, *Gaia* provided it." Amphitrite gauged his reaction, seeing the dam holding back his growing impatience ready to burst.

"Where is it stored?" Maximus demanded, the question coming out in a sharp hiss. "If you want to see your grandchildren alive again, I suggest you tell me." His cheeks and forehead seemed to swell, darkening further with a network of gray veins that pulsed and ticked erratically, making him appear like a cobra on the verge of striking.

"Not far from here," Amphitrite baited calmly. "If you wish, I can take you there."

Maximus settled back into his chair, once again in charge of his emotions. The woman's capture was appearing far more fruitful than he had anticipated, collaborating what Senator Van Heflin had told him about there being a cache of the precious metals somewhere near Malique. The young man taken from the woman's boat, though weak and apparently convalescing from a serious injury, had further substantiated this upon intense interrogation. Maximus had learned his name was Alex Trekov and that he had been part of a team sent by the Reaper to take control of a cove in the vicinity of Malique. Under questioning, Alex had told him about the gold bars littering the ground in the forest that bordered a deep gorge gouged by a plunging waterfall.

So, Maximus surmised, a humorless grin coming to his face in piecing together the whole picture. *Rafael wanted the gold for himself, so he used Zinova to get it. I thought I noticed ire in his eyes when Van Heflin brought up the subject during the fortress meeting. I shall deal with him at the appropriate time.*

Mulling this, he set a probing gaze on the nearby coastline. Though he had known for some time now about the gold, he had mistakenly assumed it was all stored in Aquaria or the adjacent island.

Curious to see for himself, Troy Jacob kept his face plastered to the lone circular window within the small but lavishly furnished ship's quarters, though the effort wasn't necessary. Through the eyes of his bond mate, he would have seen the small coastal village anyway. Moving toward the village on a slow but steady course off the ship's starboard side was the *Avenging Angel*. From *Alpha*, he had learned that the *Angel* had been towed behind the huge vessel on which he was currently being held. Upon capture, he and his twin sister, accompanied by their grandmother, had been locked in the room. But an hour earlier, his grandmother had been taken away by two burly crewmen, and according to *Alpha*, she, Zimby and Hector had been led back aboard the *Angel* under the watchful eyes of twelve armed men, one of them a large blonde haired individual the size of Zimby.

Redirecting his gaze, Teejay spotted the dorsal fins of two other pod members. Turning, he looked at his sister, placing his lips to her ear. "Athena and Natalie are here," he whispered.

Melody nodded. "We've got to find a way off this ship," she whispered back, scrutinizing the locked door to the plush sleeping quarters.

"I wonder what they did with Alex," Teejay mumbled in a hushed tone. "He wasn't with grandma and Zimby when they took them aboard the *Angel*."

"He's probably locked away in another room," Melody guessed. "He was still a little weak when they took him from the *Angel*." She started to add more, but the lock to the door suddenly clicked audibly, and a bald headed, middle aged man poked his head into the room. Scrutinizing the children with kind eyes, he gestured with a finger to his lips. Glancing furtively behind him, he entered the room, pulling a pushcart used for serving meals in with him. A jumble of hardware and electronic parts littered the top of the cart. Shutting the door behind him, he quickly pocketed a key into a white lab coat.

"Who are you?" Melody queried warily.

"Keep your voice down," the man cautioned. "I'm here to help you."

Teejay pointed to an object set on a pivot attached to one of the walls. "We're being watched," he warned. This was something his grandmother had pointed out to him and his sister before she was led away.

The man smiled. "Don't worry, I've disabled the camera. I'm going to get you out of here."

Teejay appeared dubious. "What about the cameras set along the corridor outside?"

"All the cameras along this sector of the ship are inoperable at the moment. In another minute they'll notice the problem," the man said, checking his wristwatch. "But I have a little diversion set to go off five seconds from now. Grab hold of something to brace yourselves."

A sudden dawning alighted in the expression of both children, and they automatically grabbed hold of a nearby bedpost. A heavy tremor suddenly shot through the ship, immediately followed by a cacophony of blaring alarms.

"Hop aboard!" the man urged, lifting up one side of the cloth that draped over all four sides of the pushcart. "We don't have much time."

Sensing the man could be trusted, the twins climbed on the cart, barely able to squeeze into the tight space. "Where are you taking us?" Melody asked as the cloth dropped back down to hide them.

"I know that both of you swim like fish," their liberator explained hurriedly, opening the door and looking both ways to make sure the coast was clear before pushing the cart out into the corridor. "I also know that your dolphins are here," he elucidated further. "There's a small platform near the stern about thirty feet above the water. Do you kids have any fears about jumping?"

Teejay and Melody eyed one another with solemn looks. "We're not afraid," Teejay answered for both of them.

"What about you?" Melody asked. "Will you be coming with us?"

"I'm not a very good swimmer, I'm afraid to say, and I have a problem with heights." The man gasped breathlessly, nearly breaking into a trot as he pushed the cart along.

"But what if they find out you helped us escape?" Melody pressed.

"It's a risk I'm willing to take."

"Why are you doing this?" Teejay asked.

"I'm doing this for myself as much as I'm doing it for you. These are bad people and I'm tired of being afraid of them."

"Then why do you work for them?" Teejay needed to know.

"Because I'm a coward. They extorted my skills, and I was too afraid to refuse."

"You're not a coward!" Melody consoled soothingly, liking their savior even more. "How can you be if you're helping us? Can you tell us your name?"

"You can call me Percy."

"Kinda like Phillipe's bond mate, Perseus, without the eus," Teejay said. "In Greek mythology, Perseus was a hero. He saved *Andromeda* from *Cetus*, a gigantic sea monster."

"Quiet down, children!" Percy said brusquely. "We have visitors."

The twins' ears immediately perked at the sound of pounding footsteps resounding through the corridor. "What just happened?" they heard Percy say. "I felt something jar the ship."

"There was an explosion and our surveillance cameras stopped working," a disembodied voice grunted irritably. "Where are you going with that cart?"

"I'm on my way to the moon pool. Thought this serving cart would be useful for carrying spare parts," Percy replied smoothly. "One of the robofish isn't working right. Maximus will have my head if I don't get it fixed right away."

The twins noted three pairs of booted feet just below the cloth concealing them. The muzzle of a rifle barrel suddenly poked under the cloth to lift it higher. "Whatcha got under there?" Just as the cloth began to come up, another heavy jolt rocked the ship, this one more severe than the first. Abruptly, the cloth dropped, followed by a rumble of running feet.

"Be on the lookout for saboteurs," the same voice shouted back as the men bolted down the corridor. "We might be under attack."

Teejay let out a tense sigh. "That was close."

"I anticipated this would happen," Percy said, "so I rigged a second charge to go off."

"You timed it that way?" Melody asked incredulously.

"It was a good approximation," Percy said, moving the cart around a corner and opening a door. "A good scientist strives to be as precise as possible, trying to factor in all the possibilities. Anyway, climb on out, we're here."

Just as Percy had described, the twins found themselves on a small platform that overlooked the sea. Actually a sundeck that jutted out from the hull, it had two reclining lounge chairs set back from a low transom railing. Casting their eyes to the east, the children saw that the *Angel* had almost reached Malique's small harbor.

Melody glanced down, espying Alpha and Omega in the water below before turning to Percy. "Why don't you come with us? We'll make sure you don't drown."

Percy produced an avuncular smile. "I'm better off here where I can be a thorn to these people. The owner of this vessel is the cause of Aquaria's troubles. He wants to take control of the colony and will go to any lengths to get it." A grimace came to his face as he said this. "He's the evillest man I've ever known and the source of most of the world's problems. He is incredibly rich and powerful, with a vast organization serving him that is capable of orchestrating and manipulating world events to get what he wants. He and his cabal must be stopped."

Though they were children, both twins were far smarter than their years would suggest, and they took in the words with a profound understanding. "What's his name?" Teejay asked.

Percy spit out the answer as though disgorging something foul tasting. "Malcolm Maximus. Now I suggest the two of you get going before they discover you're missing."

Both children gave Percy a fervent hug, then climbed over the railing. "We'll always remember what you did for us," they chorused, giving him a farewell smile. Showing no fear, they launched themselves into perfect swan dives, cleaving the water with fluid grace.

Zimbola eased off the throttle, bringing the engine to a gentle idle as the *Angel* glided smoothly against the pier. He watched as Hector jumped off the vessel to tie off the stern. With a weapon trained on him by one of the armed men who had followed him onto the pier, Hector's expression was sullen. Another of the henchmen leapt onto the dock to grab a bow line flung by one of his teammates stationed on the bow. With two captors guarding her, Amphitrite was escorted off the *Angel*.

Several villagers had come out onto the pier in greeting, but at seeing the ominous band of hard looking men clad in black and the wicked-looking weapons brandished by them, they made a hasty retreat back to the village.

A basso voice rumbled behind Zimbola, a voice almost as deep as his own. "Get off the boat!"

Zimbola turned with an impudent scowl, wondering if he could take a slug from the Glock 42 aimed at his gut and still take on the man holding it. Presenting a dour gaze behind dark sunglasses, the Nordic giant waved the pistol casually as though reading his thoughts.

"A time will come when you don't have that gun to keep me from crushing your throat," Zimbola threatened brazenly.

The threat seemed to hit a nerve, and Zimbola sensed a flash of anger behind the coal-black lenses that hid Swensen's eyes. The man's momentary pique quickly dissolved, however, falling back into the same icy stare Zimbola had been forced to absorb during the short boat ride.

"Move!" Swensen rumbled again.

Continuing to glare belligerently, Zimbola exited the pilothouse and climbed down the steps, mulling what it would take to rile this man. The Nordic displayed little emotion, acting more like an automaton than a human. The dark, round lenses cloaking the man's eyes seemed to accentuate this perception all the more, and with his crew cut of ash blonde hair and prominently jutting lantern-shaped jaw, he gave Zimbola the impression of a huge insect with mandibles stoically sizing up prey. And though he stood an inch shorter than the Jamaican's imposing height, the width and thickness of his shoulders appeared to match Zimbola's powerful physique.

But it was those infernal glasses that caused Zimbola to scrutinize the man a little more closely. All these captors wore them. They did not look like normal sunglasses. And then he realized it was the small node attached to the bridge connecting the lenses that gave the glasses an odd appearance. Studying the frame further, he noticed something else. It resided on one of the temple extenders that allowed the glasses to hug the man's face. Another small node sat on the left extender directly above the ear. All at once it became apparent to him that the central node was a camera and the ear node a radio transmitter. Someone was monitoring this excursion from a remote location. He could only surmise that person was the owner of the super yacht they had previously been taken aboard, though he had not as yet seen the man.

Just before he disembarked the *Angel*, Zimbola was handed a large backpack by one of the other men. "Put this on!" the man ordered curtly. The backpack was light and felt empty, and as he strapped it on, Zimby saw that Hector was already wearing a similar one.

Forced to trek along behind Amphitrite and her two escorts, Zimbola purposely slowed his pace, openly displaying an unwillingness to cooperate with these men. Whenever he did this, he was prodded harshly in the buttocks with the muzzle of a short-barreled machine pistol the man directly behind him wielded. Except for Swensen, all the men carried identical weapons. Having been tutored by Jake on various types of firearms, Zimbola recognized the weapons to be F-2000 assault rifles, currently one of the most sophisticated and deadly lightweight combat weapons on the planet.

Reaching the end of the newly renovated pier, Zimbola was marched along the red brick pathway that wound its way through the picturesque village. Malique was unlike the typical ramshackle hamlet found along the Haitian coast, exhibiting well-kept structures in brightly painted colors that dotted a landscape rich in vegetation. Everywhere he looked, a sense of pride permeated the sedate, idyllic atmosphere the village conveyed.

Knowing what lay along one side of the path a little further on, Zimbola stared hopefully ahead, anticipating a certain reaction from the two men walking alongside Amphitrite. But the reaction he expected did not come. Conspicuously positioned next to the path was a moderately sized billboard with a glass surface, and behind the glass was an eye-catching exhibit of the enigmatic albino art.

Zimbola was truly dumbstruck when Amphitrite's escort trudged past without a falter in their step. *How can this be?* he wondered. *These men are evil, and evil people always succumb to the art.* When Amphitrite walked past the exhibit with not a hint of hesitation, he could only conclude that she knew this would happen. *Perhaps some of the others will become ill*, he consoled himself. Forcing himself to remain calm, he prepared to take advantage of such a possibility should it arise.

This spark of hope quickly faded as the rest of the group moved on without any signs of sickness. *I have to trust her instincts, Zimbola reminded himself. She was the only one able to defeat Erzulie, the evil witch of the voudun, when no one else could.*

Continuing to move along the path, the group encountered several more exhibits of the dolphin art, each one different while still harboring the same underlying theme of arcane surrealism. When no one fell ill, Zimbola's disappointment changed over to acceptance. With regret, Zimbola eyed the PHP affixed to the top of the exhibit residing at the center of the village as they passed it. *If only it were night,* he thought wistfully, knowing holographic displays of the art were so much more effective than the simple two-dimensional creations at inducing illness in those with iniquitous tendencies. At night the PHP would have been activated to shed a soothing aura over the village, but daylight tended to attenuate the three-dimensional projections, making them barely visible under a bright sky.

As he looked around, Zimbola saw no residents roaming the village, aware that they had fled to their homes. What little that remained of Zimbola's faith crumbled further as Amphitrite led the group beyond the brick path's terminus. She was now taking them along the trail that wound its way into the hills. The thought that she was actually leading them to the cove was disconcerting. Plodding onward, he berated himself harshly for his weakening resolve. *I must have faith in her,* he vowed. *I must believe.*

Chapter Seven:
Foiling The Pursuers

Maximus sat at the multi-screened console, closely monitoring what the remote cameras were showing. At the moment, the woman was leading his men into the forested hills that rose up beyond the village. As always, he made it a habit to let others carry out his objectives, especially where the possibility of danger existed. And in this case, he had to assume the potential for it was quite high. The excruciating pain and vertigo he had suffered when he tried to take down the Hind was something he never wanted to experience again. Having failed to use the drug specifically developed to combat it, he had been defenseless against the swirling lights that had coalesced before his eyes, a three-dimensional manifestation of the mysterious art produced by the colony. The memory of it made him twinge. He was certain his brain had been on the verge of exploding during the ordeal, and it had taken him hours to fully recuperate after the event. If something similar to that existed in Malique, he would rather avoid it, uncertain just how effective the drug would be if he came into visual contact with those lights. And while he had made sure his men were injected with it prior to going ashore, he knew such a drug might not work for everyone, particularly since it had only been tested against two-dimensional representations of the strange art. During testing, holographic representations had not been considered. For these reasons he had decided to stay behind, directing the operation from the safety of his vessel. But now he wondered just how safe he was in view of recent events.

Scowling with pent up fury, he continued to mull over the likely suspects among those still aboard the *Numquam Satis* who might have perpetrated those events. It infuriated him to know that portions of the video surveillance system had failed just prior to the blasts that had jarred the ship, particularly the camera that provided real-time viewing of the room where the children were being held. Ruling out the possibility of infiltrators, he was now convinced that one of the crew had tampered with the system. Certain that the culprit had to have a good working knowledge of electronics to pull off such a stunt, he systematically narrowed the field. Although the two explosions set off in the port side storage holds did not cause excessive damage, he deduced these were merely diversions designed to cloak a higher aim. And that aim had succeeded all too well, for now the children were missing. As soon as the disabled cameras had come back on line, Maximus had immediately seen that the children were no longer in the room. A frenzied search of the entire vessel by the ship's crew quickly ensued, only to come up empty so far.

The ship's intercom suddenly buzzed sharply, and Maximus snatched up the phone expecting to hear good news. "We've searched everywhere, sir," a disgruntled voice uttered. "They're nowhere to be found."

"You're absolutely certain of this?" Maximus screamed, now thoroughly enraged. Without the children, his trump card was lost.

A brief moment of silence followed before a nervous reply came back. "I'd stake my life on it, sir."

"You had better be right, otherwise you're going to lose it," Maximus snarled in frustration. "Launch two skiffs and search the sea between us and the shore. Those children are good swimmers, so they might be heading for the village."

Maximus slammed down the phone, continuing to reduce the list of suspects one by one through a process of elimination, finally arriving at one name only, and that name was Percy Osgood. He found this rather strange. Though Osgood was a mechanical genius, he was also a withdrawn and timid sort, certainly not the type of person to put his life on the line. Furthermore, Maximus held something that ensured Osgood's continued cooperation. He had Percy's twin brother, Mortimer, locked away in Rafael's fortress, ransoming him in exchange for Percy's skills. But Mortimer had certain information that could potentially have damaging consequences to Plagiarius if that information ever became public, and Maximus had ordered Rafael to use whatever means necessary to find out where that information was kept and to destroy those files.

Overall, though, Maximus sensed he had the upper hand, and while it didn't make sense that Percy would risk his brother's life by committing sabotage, all the evidence seemed to point his way.

Picking the phone back up, Maximus called another member of his staff. "Bring Percy Osgood to me," he ordered shrilly.

Riding their bond mates, Teejay and Melody traversed the three miles of open water quickly, only periodically coming to the surface when they needed to breathe. Reaching Malique's main pier in just under twelve minutes, they approached the *Avenging Angel* with utmost caution, coasting alongside and looking up at her stern.

"I don't think anyone's aboard," Melody whispered to her brother, noting the unusual stillness hanging all about them. It was a calm morning, with a glassy, flat sea abutting the shoreline. Only a few boats were currently tied up alongside the long pier, including the 70-foot *Exoco*, a high-speed hydrofoil used for quickly transporting supplies to and from Aquaria. Both twins knew the vessel had been named after a family of flying fish called *Exocoetidae*. Flying fish had exceptionally large pectoral fins that acted as wings, allowing them to glide above the sea for short distances whenever they leapt from the water to escape predators. With dual hydrofoils jutting out on each side of it, the boat clearly resembled its namesake.

At seeing no one among the few vessels, Melody realized that most of the local fishermen would have already taken advantage of the superb conditions, putting out to sea at sunup. Strangely though, she could see no villagers anywhere in the quaint little hamlet, and the quietude was overpowering.

Straddling Alpha, Teejay risked craning his head to scan the area beyond the village. Almost instantly, he caught sight of several black-clad troopers climbing the steep trail that led up into the hills. Following their progress a moment longer, he saw them disappear into the forest. Hunkering back down, he spoke quietly. "I see them. They're taking the trail that leads to Gaia. Looks like Grandma's leading them there just like she said she would."

The escalating drone of an outboard engine made both children turn. A small boat carrying three men was heading in their direction. Further back, another motorboat was running a zigzag course over the sea, the men aboard it swiveling their heads back and forth in search of something. "I think they know we escaped and are looking for us," Melody said calmly. "Got any ideas?"

Teejay scrutinized one of the nearest piles supporting the pier. He could see that the tide was close to full ebb, judging how low the ocean surface had receded from the high-water mark. Swinging his gaze seaward, he eyed the closest boat for several seconds before his face broke out in a mischievous grin. "As a matter of fact, I do."

Amphitrite continued to lead the way, taking the path that wound through the hills until it ran abreast of the bowl-shaped chasm. "The thing you seek is down there," she said to her escorts.

The men on each side of her stopped to gawk, with the one on her right pulling off his sunglasses to make sure the apparatus was not deceiving his eyes. Falling away below them was a place of wonder, a breathtaking vista of tinted flora hugging the tiered walls that surrounded a limpid blue-green pool with a mirror-like surface. At the far end of the basin, a gush of whitewater tumbled lazily down, sending up a prismatic mist that separated the sunlight into a rainbow of primary hues. Even at this distance, the multitude of fauna darting among the lush vegetation was evident. Birds and butterflies in a myriad of colors seemed to be everywhere.

In moments, the rest of the men caught up, nudging Zimbola and Hector before them. Swensen looked down, seemingly taking in the magnificent scenery with cold indifference. "She says it is down there," the man who had removed his glasses muttered gruffly, addressing the Nordic leader.

Swensen turned to Amphitrite. "Is there a way down there?"

Amphitrite nodded. "But I advise you to watch your step. The way down can be treacherous in places." Without another word, she led them further on, finding the crude ladder that descended to the uppermost tier.

One of the men suddenly shouted, removing some underbrush a short distance away. "There's a bunker over here, but it appears to be empty."

"Make sure it is," Swensen barked sternly.

Without hesitation, six of the band fanned out to form a skirmish line around the enclosure. A minute of cautious investigation ensued before the same man yelled back from inside the bunker. "It's definitely empty, nothing in here."

Amphitrite held back a smile. Unbeknownst to Jay Jay, she had left instructions with members of the cove's security force just prior to departing the cove on the *Angel*. Because they deemed her to be a mambo, a high voodoo priestess, they had carried out her wishes without question. The men were to stop manning the bunkers, at least temporarily, and they were to hide the dual fifties and ammunition in the forest, including the headphones that allowed communication between the bunkers.

Satisfied that there was no apparent danger, Swensen turned his gaze back on Amphitrite, the dark glasses giving a chilling edge to his unwavering stare. "Lead us on, woman, but do not forget who holds your grandchildren."

"If anything happens to those children, I swear by Agwe that I will send you to hell," Zimbola growled, gritting his teeth and fixating Swensen with a fierce, penetrating stare of his own that promised mayhem. Like the villagers, his belief in Caribbean folk religion derived from African mysticism was unshakable, and Agwe was a spirit that ruled over the sea.

A scowl transcended Swensen's face, with the veins on his bull neck bulging to the surface and ticking like a metronome. This was the first show of anger Amphitrite had seen in the man. "When the time comes, I will give you the chance to back up your meaningless threats," he spat in agitation, his deep voice rumbling like an earthquake.

Once again, Amphitrite refrained from smiling. A while earlier, Athena had communicated with her telepathically, and she knew about the children's escape. Unfortunately, she could not convey that to Zimbola.

Having filled their lungs with deep inhalations, Melody and Teejay held on tight as their bond mates submerged and darted for the open sea. Covering a distance of a thousand meters, they rose back to the surface south of the village and well away from the nearest boat.

"Over here!" Melody and Teejay taunted, laughing and waving their arms wildly over their heads. Though they knew their pursuers were too far away to hear them, they continued these antics until they were sure they were spotted.

With both boats coming on rapidly, the children submerged again, this time angling back toward the coast. Coming up for air, they saw both boats circling their last position, the men aboard them peering down into the water expectantly.

"Over here!" the twins yelled in unison, resuming their previous antics.

As soon as the boats turned in their direction, Alpha and Omega shot into the depths, the children clinging fast and exhilarated by the pursuit. They were enjoying the game, unconcerned about the danger hanging in the balance. Randomly changing course, they came to the surface again and again, gradually drawing their pursuers farther and farther south. Gauging that they were now close to the cove's entrance, they separated, veering off in different directions, with Omega cruising along the bottom and taking Melody through the narrow channel that provided a way through the barrier reef. With the tide at full ebb, jagged corals lay inches beneath the surface on both sides.

Getting through the reef, Omega turned north, following the intertwined mass of pulsating tentacles that lay atop the sandy bottom like bundled cables. These were the tentacles that extended thousands of feet deep down into the Cayman Trench, endlessly harvesting the tiny gold grains that rose up from hot fissures in the earth's crust. Had Melody and her mount followed the tentacles to their ultimate source, they would have come upon the two huge pumpkin-shaped *thurentra* residing in the cove.

Forty meters from the channel, Melody was brought to the surface, whereupon she waved her arms wildly again. "Over here!" she shouted at the top of her lungs.

The driver of the nearest boat immediately caught sight of her, and maddened by the elusiveness of his prey, swung the runabout around and gunned the outboard to maximum power, coming straight at her with an enraged look on his face. This time she would not get away.

Caught up in the heat of the moment, the driver failed to notice the barrier reef lurking just below the surface. Plowing on at full speed, his rage abruptly turned to befuddlement as a grating crunch resounded. With razor-sharp coral ripping through the hull, the small watercraft jerked sideways and flipped, hurling all three passengers into the water. Screams filled the air as the boat landed atop two of the men, the bottom of its hull facing the sky. Partially pinned between the port gunwale and jagged calcareous growth, both men wailed pitifully as an expanding ring of crimson bespoke of their injuries. Flung further away, the driver lay wedged amid a dense cluster of staghorn coral, his head and torso above the water. Bleeding profusely from a multitude of lacerations, he stared vacantly in Melody's direction, too confused as yet to comprehend what had just happened.

A measure of sorrow caught up with Melody as she looked upon the stricken men. She hated to see suffering of any kind, even if it was caused by the reckless doings of these men. Sitting calmly astride Omega, she watched as the second boat slowed, the ruffians aboard it taking in the scene before them. Bespectacled with dark sunglasses, the trio showed little concern for their injured companions, focusing ominous gazes on Melody like predators deciding how they would go about capturing her.

The boat was identical to the first, a twenty-foot open fishermen with a center console. As it slowed further, the driver shifted his scrutiny to what lay below the surface. Coasting to a crawl, he turned the boat to the south and paralleled the outer edge of the reef, searching for a way through it. As Melody watched, she saw the driver's lips moving as though he were speaking to himself and not to his partners. One of the other men was assisting him, leaning over the port side and peering intently down into the water while the third man kept his gaze locked on Melody.

"There!" yelled the man leaning over the side, gesturing wildly to the steersman. "I see a way in."

The steersman nodded, immediately spotting the opening. Abruptly, he turned the boat, angling it away from the entrance and swinging it around to face the channel head on. He hung there momentarily, glancing back in Melody's direction. "If she tries to escape again, shoot her!" she heard him say, her heart skipping a beat as she noticed the third man lift up a rifle with a scope, aiming it directly at her.

In spite of the sudden fear gripping her, Melody held her position, knowing what was about to happen. Two objects broke from the water with blurring momentum, rising up on opposite sides of the boat and leaping over it. Yelps of surprise knifed the air as all three men were swept from the vessel.

With no one to steer it, the boat moved sluggishly beyond the reach of the men, and Melody caught sight of her brother rising to the surface next to it. With Alpha lending support, he managed to clamber up over the side and get behind the controls. Turning the steering wheel, he let the boat coast forward a few seconds longer before pointing the bow back toward the reef.

"Hey!" one of the floundering men screamed upon spitting out a mouthful of water. "Bring back our boat!"

Throwing the throttle all the way forward, Teejay leapt over the side just as the boat took off with a burst of speed. Rejoining Alpha, he watched in fascination as the hull hit the shelf of coral and jerked upward. A split second later, the outdrive snagged against the leading edge of the stationary obstacle, nearly tearing off the outboard motor. Careening wildly, the boat finally came to a stop, its hull ripped apart.

"We'll get you for this," another of the men shrieked, treading water and shaking his fist at Teejay.

Teejay ignored the threat, submerging with his mount to join his sister moments later. As he rose up next to Melody, Athena and Natalie came to the surface beside him.

"Nice job!" Melody marveled at her brother. Turning her head, she brought a loving gaze to Athena and Natalie. "Congratulations! Those jumps were perfectly timed."

"Shall we?" Teejay remarked, a broad grin clinging to his face as he looked at the others.

"Yes!" effused Melody.

"Then off we go," said Natalie.

Without another word, all six slipped below the surface.

Chapter Eight: Unexpected Calmness

Maximus was beside himself with rage at seeing what had happened to his men. Riding adolescent albino dolphins, those little brats had made fools of them, purposely luring them further and further south until the first boat slammed into a reef. He had watched the whole thing unfold through the remote cameras attached to the sunglasses his men wore. Deciding he could not let this game go on, he had ordered the men in the second boat to kill the girl if she tried to escape again. That was just before he caught a fleeting image of something leaping up to sweep the men into the water. Freeze-framing the blurred image on the video recording, he saw that it was another albino dolphin, this one much larger than the ones the children were riding. Also captured within the frame was the gray tail fluke of another dolphin streaking in the opposite direction. With only one of the men managing to keep from losing his glasses, he had observed the boy climb aboard their boat and send it crashing into the reef. After that, he saw two large dolphins, one albino and one gray, join both siblings and their mounts, only to disappear below the water.

A distressed voice crackled over the radio. "We need assistance, sir. Will help be coming soon to evacuate us?"

Maximus ignored the plea. *Screw them,* he thought bitterly. *Let them suffer for their stupidity.* Should he decide to rescue them, it wouldn't be until later, and the loss of the two boats would be coming out of their pay. Switching channels, he brought his attention back to Swensen. "Status?" he rasped.

"The woman says it's in a cave behind the waterfall, but we already found ten gold bars." Swensen shifted his gaze to show the small stack of gleaming bars sitting on the sandy beach. In the background, Maximus could see the nearness of whitewater tumbling into the gorge.

"Where did you find them?"

"Right where you see them. I don't advise touching them, they could be rigged with a bomb. Perhaps I should use the woman to test them."

"No, use the short captive to move them, but first have the men fall back to a safe position."

Maximus studied the one called Hector closely as Swensen ordered him to move the bars. Hector shrugged, glowering up at the Nordic before advancing on the stack and tossing them aside one by one until all ten formed a disorderly pile.

"Test one of the bars to see if they're real," Maximus instructed as Swensen rejoined the shorter man.

On the screen, a knife suddenly came into view, and with the point of the blade thrusting down sharply into one of the bars, Swensen used his considerable brawn to gouge a small cavity into the metal. Holding the bar up, he gave Maximus a close up perspective of his handiwork. "Seems real enough," Swensen said.

"Good, now have the woman take you and your men into the cave, including the captives, but leave two of the men behind as a rear guard."

Within moments, Maximus saw Amphitrite begin to scale the steep crag to the left of the falls, her two escorts struggling to keep pace with her. Shifting screens, he saw the arms of the lead escort reaching out for handholds among the numerous crevices and fractures, and as they climbed higher he realized the ascent was precarious. With the water so close and spray coming off it, moss clung to the rock in many places, making the going slippery.

Changing back to Swensen's perspective, he watched as the lead man followed the woman still higher. She was climbing with the nimbleness of a gibbon and he was having difficulty keeping up with her. An instant later, he bellowed out in horror as he lost his grip, and Maximus saw the man's head smash into a rock outcropping as he plunged into the tumultuous water below.

"Forget about him!" Maximus ordered impatiently. "Just keep the men moving. Finding the gold is all that matters."

Uncharacteristically, an eerie sense of superstition suddenly gripped Maximus, and he had trouble sweeping it aside. The thought that the rainbow might have been a precursor of calamitous events grew irrationally large in his mind, and he wondered if more were yet to come. Through Swensen's glasses, he had seen it arching over the falls when the woman had led his band to the rim of the gorge. *Was it merely coincidence,* he asked himself? Already he had lost the children, with six of his men currently stranded on the reef, three of them no doubt seriously injured. And now one of his men had died. A vision of the double rainbow he had seen arching over Aquaria and the island behind it abruptly assailed him to increase his growing unease, and it took considerable effort to quell the feeling. Angrily, he reminded himself how much he hated the sight of rainbows.

"Leave him!" Swensen yelled down, stopping the two men left behind on the beach from wading into the water to search for their fallen comrade. "No sense trying to retrieve a dead man."

Both men looked up, nodding in acquiescence.

Following behind Amphitrite's guard, Hector groped his way cautiously along the slippery rock with Zimbola right behind him. Reaching out for another handhold, Hector lost his grip, and had not Zimbola reacted instantly, Hector would have been another casualty. As though he had anticipated what was about to happen, Zimbola leaned forward to snare his longtime friend by the wrist to keep him from falling. Holding on with one hand to the rock, the tips of his banana-size fingers held fast to a crevice as he hauled Hector back up with the other. In moments, both men were again working their way higher along the path Amphitrite had chosen.

Several anxious minutes passed, but no other mishaps occurred. With the remainder of the party finally reaching the gloom behind the falls, the armed men began turning on small flashlights they carried. When Amphitrite casually reached for something along a side wall, her lone remaining escort stopped her, blocking her arm with his weapon.

"It's only a lantern," she said, raising her voice to be heard above the thunder of the falls.

Swensen intervened quickly. "Let her use it!" he commanded gruffly. Several men began to remove their sunglasses to see better in the dim light, but Swensen's curt admonishment stopped them from doing so. "Keep your glasses on!" he growled.

When Amphitrite flicked on the battery-powered lantern, the nearby shadows disappeared to reveal a succession of murals painted along the cave walls. The murals receded into the darkness that lay beyond the glow of the lantern. Playing their lights back and forth, Maximus' henchmen eyed the paintings curiously. Enthralled by the grim scenes the murals depicted, they followed Amphitrite deeper into the subterranean cavern. Visual representations of Hispaniola's early history were laid bare, showing the arrival of the Spanish conquistadors and the subsequent atrocities they inflicted on the native people.

Holding to the rear of the procession, Swensen's voice boomed out again, echoing like a bass drum in the confined quarters. "Stay alert!" he warned. He could tell the murals were distracting the men.

Several moments later, Amphitrite stopped, seemingly reaching the back of the cave where jumbles of fallen rock blocked further progress. Where she currently stood, the pervading roar of the falls had diminished considerably, now reduced to a gentle susurration.

"I see no gold in here, woman," Swensen accused suspiciously.

"There's a passage behind the rock, but getting through is a tight squeeze," she said. "I doubt it will accommodate a man of your size." She turned her gaze to Zimbola, adding, "The *Avenging Angel's* captain has never been able to go beyond this point, and you are just as big."

"Show me!" Swensen said.

Continuing to hold the lantern, Amphitrite sidled her petite body around the largest boulder, leaving only a thin glow of light streaming back as she disappeared from sight. "Most of your men should be able to squeeze through," her disembodied voice echoed back.

"Keep thinking about your grandchildren," Swensen reminded her. "You hold their lives in the balance. Any trickery on your part will be the end of them." He shot a berating look to her immediate escort. The man stood fast, staring at the narrow opening with distrust. "Follow her!" he ordered. "Test the opening to see if she is lying."

Holding his weapon out in front of him with one hand, the escort overcame his reluctance and squeezed around the bend. A moment later, his voice came back, strained with exertion. "I think she's telling the truth, sir. I can barely squeeze through."

Turning his gaze on two of the nearest men, Swensen barked out another order. "Both of you will stay behind with me to guard the big one." His jaw clenched as he threw a hard stare at Zimbola. "The rest of you will follow the woman and communicate back what you find. I'm placing you in charge, Ratillo."

"What about him?" Ratillo asked, indicating Hector.

"Take him with you, but two of you go in ahead of him."

"I cannot get through wearing this pack," Hector protested haughtily.

"Take it off then and hand it through to the man in front of you," Swensen spat irritably. "You'll need it to carry gold."

Removing the backpack, Hector pushed it through the opening to the trooper that preceded him. He had never been in this cave, and a feeling bordering on claustrophobia gripped him as he squeezed his fireplug frame into the rocky entrance. Once through, the pack was shoved roughly back into his hands, and he was prodded forward to make room for the others coming through. Looking past the men in front of him, he saw Amphitrite. In spite of their situation, she appeared unusually calm as she stood before a flight of steps carved into the stone. The light from her lantern illuminated a shaft that rose up steeply.

Amphitrite made subtle eye contact with Hector as several more grim-faced troopers crowded in behind him to scrutinize their tight quarters. Though her expression was guarded, he knew her well enough to know that something was going to happen, and very soon.

Maximus cast livid eyes on the monitoring screens. They had all gone blank, filled with the dull gray graininess of static. Once Swensen and his men had entered the cave, he had lost all contact with them. Obviously, something was interfering with the transmission, most likely the cave's rocky interior.

Switching channels, he reverted to the sunglass cameras worn by the two lone sentries left behind on the beach adjacent to the base of the falls. It was as though he were looking through their eyes as images sprang onto two of the screens to replace the gray static. One showed the cascading waterfall while the other revealed a serene scene of the cove waters stretching away to the far end of the gorge.

The ship's intercom came alive, buzzing harshly to intrude into his thoughts. "We have located Percy Osgood, sir. Are you ready to receive him?"

A dark frown immediately consumed his face. "Yes, bring him in here now."

Moments later, Osgood was escorted into the control room accompanied by two members of the ship's security.

"Leave us!" Maximus rasped sternly, throwing a contemptuous gaze at both guards. They were well acquainted with the look. They had failed miserably in their duties by letting the children get away.

Both men turned, withdrawing from the room quickly to escape the withering stare.

Maximus remained seated, tilting his head in a sideways glance to study Osgood. Expecting to see the same fidgety expression Osgood always wore in his presence, he was surprised when he saw something different. The man appeared quite relaxed, with no sign of the usual edginess showing on his face. As a matter of fact, he could swear he detected a smirk residing just below the surface.

Indicating the screens behind him, Maximus frowned darkly and said, "As you can see from the monitors, I have lost contact with all but two of the men I sent ashore. Nine cameras are not working. Why is that?"

Percy stared at the two screens, his eyes coming to rest on the one showing a chasm-like setting. The image was stunning. The place seemed to flourish with life in a spectrum of pulsing colors.

"I'm not sure," Percy muttered distractedly, his mind racing along and trying to formulate another plan of action. He was thinking on his feet, and this latest development was something he might be able to use.

"You said those glasses would be exceptionally reliable when you designed them," Maximus grumbled in annoyance.

Boldly, Percy stepped past Maximus and leaned over the computer keyboard set off to one side. "Give me a sec to troubleshoot the system. Is the rest of the shore party at the same location?"

"No," Maximus said, rapidly losing patience with the scientist. "They're in a cave behind the waterfall you're looking at. Is that causing interference?"

Percy manipulated keys swiftly. "Possibly," he said. A map of the nearby Haitian coast replaced the screen showing the falls, with two flashing dots depicting the relative distance between the *Numquam Satis* and the shore party. Pulling up the GPS coordinates of the shore-based dot, he memorized the location, less than five miles from his current location. Without Maximus knowing what he was doing, he made a few more adjustments to the system settings before the real-time view of the waterfall once again settled on the screen.

"There you go," Percy said, smiling with satisfaction as three other screens suddenly came alive. "I increased the signal."

Maximus gazed critically at the darkened images fading in and out and overlaid with static. "What about the others?"

"Unfortunately, that's the best I can do. Wherever those other men are, the rock surrounding them must be far too dense to allow video transmission. As it is, the three signals we're currently receiving from the cave are very weak."

Shifting his eyes between the three monitors, Maximus could just barely make out an image of the largest captive, who seemed to have an incessant scowl plastered on his face. He was being closely watched by the three men guarding him. Based on the primary screen, one of those men was Swensen.

Maximus pointed to the screen representing his bodyguard. "Will he be able to hear me?"

"He should," Percy replied.

Hitting the transmit button, Maximus said. "Can you hear me, Swensen?"

The image from Swensen's camera abruptly moved, facing away from the captive's scowling face. The response that came back was barely audible. "You're coming in very weak, but I can hear you."

"What happened to the others?"

"They moved deeper into the cave where the gold is located. The passage was too narrow for me to follow, so I sent six of the men ahead with the woman and the short one."

"Are you able to communicate with them?"

"No, but I will keep you informed as soon as they get back."

"Good," Maximus said. "I will expect to hear only good news."

Ending the transmission, he eyed Osgood. Necessity had dictated he avoid breaching the subject of the missing children until the scientist got the remote camera system up and running again.

"Two children in my custody managed to get off this ship with someone's help," Maximus said, keeping his rage at a simmer for the moment to gauge Osgood's reaction.

Osgood remained calm, far more relaxed than he should have been even if he was innocent of abetting the children. This uncharacteristic change in behavior made Maximus feel uncomfortable. Tranquil demeanors rattled him.

"And you think I am the party responsible," Percy said, his tone serene.

"Well, are you?" Maximus growled, his wrath abruptly surfacing like a burst of hot gas rising rapidly from the ocean depths.

"Yes, I helped them. I also disabled your video system and planted those explosives."

Maximus gaped, suddenly speechless at the man's forthright audacity. That he would openly admit he had done these things was the last thing he had anticipated.

Overcoming his astonishment, Maximus found his tongue. "Then you have signed your brother's death sentence," he stated, nearly stammering out the words.

Percy chuckled. "No, I haven't. Mortimer escaped Cardoza's clutches." With his eyes abruptly coming alive with defiance, he let the statement sink in to further unsettle Maximus' composure before going on. "You probably don't even know that Cardoza is dead. Your plan to unleash *Sterilis* on Haitian farmland has gone up in smoke. All the drones have been destroyed along with much of Cardoza's compound."

Maximus stared dumbly, barely able to speak. "That's impossible!" he croaked. "You're bluffing."

"No, I'm not." Osgood threw a confident look at the bank of monitoring screens. "See for yourself. You have access to satellite imagery. Would you like me to pull it up for you?"

Without waiting for an answer, Osgood leaned over the computer keyboard again. With the deftness of a concert pianist, his fingers played swiftly over the keys to bring up an image of the Caribbean on the center screen, which was larger than the others. The display changed quickly, enlarging through a rapid sequence of magnified images that homed in on Haiti's southwestern peninsula.

Maximus was numb as he looked upon the final picture. A good third of Cardoza's fortress lay in ruins. Shifting his eyes, he saw what was left of the hangar one mile to the east. Only rubble and charred portions of aircraft littered the landscape. Out in the bay and along the shore, he discerned masses of floating debris, some of it having already washed up on the beach. But there were no vessels sitting at anchor. Both the *Southern Star* and *Northern Comet* were gone, along with Cardoza's luxury yacht, *Usurpar.*

"How did you know about this?" Maximus uttered feebly, still in shock. "You had no access to this room."

Osgood studied the screen, his eyes roving over the detailed imagery as if seeing it for the first time. "Mortimer got word to me."

"But how?" Maximus demanded gruffly, suddenly coming out of his stupor.

"Have you forgotten that I am an electronic whiz? Even your seemingly airtight computer security lock could not prevent communication between me and my brother."

Maximus' voice gained volume, now rasping with outrage. "Someone must have helped your brother escape."

"Yes, someone did, and that man is on his way here. If he was able succeed against Cardoza, I can only imagine what he is capable of doing to you."

Maximus shot a hand to the intercom, slamming his fist down on the button. "Guards!" he shrieked.

Osgood looked upon Maximus with repugnance, slipping a hand into a pocket on his lab coat. "You're finished, Malcolm. I'm going to make sure your insidious schemes never come to fruition. My brother and I have all the evidence we need to expose you and your organization to the world."

"I am the world," Maximus crowed mordantly, rising to his feet. "I control it."

Osgood smiled. "But for how much longer once this information gets out. Mortimer and I know about *The Order* and what it is trying to achieve."

The door behind Maximus suddenly burst open, the same two guards entering the room with their weapons drawn.

"You'll tell me where you keep this information," Maximus hissed.

"Or what? You'll torture me." Osgood laughed, lifting something from the pocket and holding it up.

Maximus stared at the small device, his eyes shifting back to the unbearable smile on Osgood's face. "What is that?"

"Should my thumb come off this button, this ship will be destroyed along with everyone on it. There are enough explosives aboard to do that."

"You would sacrifice yourself to kill me?"

"As the old saying goes, 'the ball is in your court,'" Osgood chortled, noticing that the hard expressions the guards wore had changed over to terror.

A troubled look fell across Maximus' face, and he swallowed noisily as though gulping down a disagreeable morsel of food. Nervously, he eyed the device held in Osgood's hand, wondering if it was truly a detonator. Gambling on a hunch was something foreign to his nature, and in making decisions he had always made it a habit to stack the deck in his favor before betting on the outcome. To gamble on the possibility of a bluff had the potential of getting him killed. He realized he had no choice but to negotiate a deal. "What do you want?"

"Have your pilot fly me to shore." Osgood was referring to the helicopter sitting aboard the ship's landing pad. A second chopper sat in an enclosed hangar abutting the pad.

"How do I know you won't destroy the ship once you're off it?"

"You don't. But I know you still have another hostage aboard, and I prefer to avoid soiling my soul with the blood of an innocent unless you force me to. All I want is a ride to shore. Beyond a mile, the signal from this device won't reach the ship, and the coast is farther away than that."

Maximus studied Osgood closely, failing to understand this sudden change that had come over him. The man carried a casual, carefree air, completely devoid of the one thing he valued most for carrying out his goals, and that was fear.

"Very well," he rasped in feigned resignation, his mind quickly racing ahead with a plan of reprisal. He would accommodate Osgood's wishes for the time being, but once the helicopter was away, he would move the ship further out to sea to ensure it was beyond the range of a potential detonation signal, assuming that the scientist was not bluffing and that he would keep his word about not using it. After Osgood disembarked the aircraft, he'd have the pilot fly into the gorge to pick up two of the mercenaries under Swensen's command and fly them to where Osgood was dropped off. Then they would track him down and bring him back after the device was destroyed.

"I should give you fair warning that any move or perceived trickery on the part of your men to disarm me will be met with the destruction of this ship. Then I shall see you all in hell."

Percy was surprised at the calmness of his own voice. Strangely, he felt not the slightest bit of fear as he faced Maximus and his cohorts. His mind was clear, unhampered by dread or anxiety as it once was in the presence of this man. But he knew the cause. It was the mysterious display of interlacing lights he had been exposed to just before Maximus had lost control of the drone. The feeling it had evoked in him had been euphoric. And even now he could sense its effect lingering within him.

Maximus turned, focusing a stern gaze on the two guards. "Escort him to the landing pad and see that he gets off the ship without any interference. Is that understood?"

After both men nodded apprehensively, Maximus looked back at Osgood, his eyes ablaze with pent up anger. "I'll notify the pilot to take you ashore. Now go! Get off my ship."

Chapter Nine: Walls of Pure Gold

Ratillo glanced around the square chamber wearing a scowl. Under the weakening glow of the lantern held by Amphitrite, his features quite distinctly resembled what his namesake suggested. Strangely, he was fond of the moniker bestowed on him by his fellow comrades in arms.

"I see no gold in here," the "*Rat*" grumbled.

"Look upon the walls," Amphitrite said.

Flashing his small flashlight directly on one of the walls, Rat was nearly blinded by the light reflected back at him. Even the dark glasses he wore failed to suppress the intense yellow radiance. Stepping closer, he ran a hand over the mirror-like surface. It was smooth and polished, and as he explored it further, he saw a caricature of his rodent-like image staring back at him, grotesquely distorted as though he were observing himself in a fun house mirror. All around him, other members of the six-man squad were doing the same.

Rat brought a bewildered gaze back to Amphitrite. "What is this?"

"The walls of this chamber are made of pure gold," Amphitrite said.

As if to confirm her claim, Rat ran his fingers along the surface again, then looked around the room as though he might have missed something. "What good does this do us?" he complained heatedly, bringing his eyes back to Amphitrite. "There's nothing to carry out with us."

"Maximus asked that I show you where the gold was kept, and I've done that," Amphitrite stated calmly.

With a snarl on his face, Rat moved toward her, drawing an arm across his chest to give her a vicious backhand slap, but stopped short as a cascade of light suddenly poured down from the ceiling above. Startled, he looked up.

A whirlpool of glimmering bands spun counterclockwise, the eddy of luminosity quickly gathering speed and growing brighter, and Rat imagined he was glimpsing a far-off galaxy in deep space. Intrigued, he could not tear his eyes away as the whirlpool expanded to reveal individual glowing points, the space between them opening up swiftly to show vast gulfs of nothingness. The illusion was mesmerizing, and he had the sensation he was traveling at many times the velocity of light as he flew into the heart of the swirling mass.

"The pursuit of physical gold is merely an imitation of the true gold," Amphitrite said, remembering the words she had spoken long ago when she had cleansed Chester Hennington of all the rot that had built up inside of him. She sensed these men were diametrically different and beyond help, however, truly nefarious by nature, and it stood to reason their wickedness would at least approximate the man they worked for. But if she couldn't help them, she would do what she could to rid the planet of them.

"There is a great deal of difference between true and false gold," she continued. "It is the longing for real gold that causes man to collect the imitation gold."

"Are you implying the walls of this room are made of fake gold?" Rat grunted, keeping his eyes fixated on the overhead display.

Amphitrite ignored the question, sermonizing further. "Because gold represents the color of light and spiritual inspiration, man has unconsciously pursued this divine light by seeking an imitation of it much the way a small child satisfies itself by playing with toys. In this way man attempts to gratify this craving of the soul by seeking the false gold, ignorant that the true gold lies like a hidden spark deep within his heart, his innermost being."

Rat frowned, continuing to look up. "What are you talking about, woman?"

Amphitrite kept her voice neutral, without emotion. "But I see no hidden spark within your heart, only darkness. Men like you will never know the true gold."

Rat grimaced in annoyance, and for one fleeting moment she thought he would look away from the ongoing light show.

"Do you know where physical gold comes from?" Amphitrite asked him.

Rat stared hypnotically, wondering why this woman would ask such a stupid question. "Gold mines!" he muttered absently.

Amphitrite glanced around, aware that all six of her captors were fully entranced by the sight as a lone star loomed up, its surface sending out a deep violet radiance that only the hottest stars could emit.

"Gold comes from heavy element stars that are far more massive than our sun," she said. "After several million years of generating energy by fusing light elements into heavier ones, these stars eventually run out of fuel. But in the process, so much iron builds up in their core that the star can no longer support its own weight. When this happens, immense gravitational forces collapse the ball of iron in upon itself, causing it to erupt in a cataclysmic explosion called a supernova. This eruption provides the necessary heat to fuse iron into gold, scattering it to other parts of the galaxy where it combines with other elements and space dust to form new solar systems."

The men stood transfixed as the star erupted in a blinding flash to send out a rush of matter and lethal radiation in all directions.

As Amphitrite spoke, she moved next to Hector, who also appeared entranced. "Following a *supernova* explosion, a small dense star composed primarily of neutrons is all that remains. These neutron-rich stars are called *pulsars*. They become highly magnetized and rotate at a dizzying rate, releasing incredible amounts of energy."

Amphitrite grabbed hold of Hector, pulling him close and placing a hand over his eyes. Making sure to look away, she said. "But at the center of these pulsars is a black hole, capable of sucking in anything that comes near it, including dark matter."

Amphitrite closed her eyes as a gale of swirling wind suddenly cropped up, nearly lifting her and Hector off their feet. Men screamed out in panic, their cries of alarm fading away rapidly as though they were falling into a deep well.

The rush of air died quickly, and sensing that the danger had passed, Amphitrite opened her eyes and glanced around.

Except for herself and Hector, the chamber was empty.

The wails of the advance party carried in the confined quarters before fading altogether, and by the time they reached Swensen's ears, the sound was reduced to an indecipherable whisper. Moving close to the narrow fissure in the rock that prevented him from accompanying the men, he poked his head in. "Did you find anything?" he shouted into the opening.

When no reply came back, he repeated the query, only to be met with an unsettling silence that was overlaid by the pervasive rustle of the falls.

Zimbola sneered. Strange things seemed to happen whenever Amphitrite was involved. "Do not expect your men to return," he badgered mockingly.

Swensen spun, aiming his pistol at Zimbola's face. "I have had enough of you," he spat ominously, the dark glasses giving him the look of the android in *The Terminator* movie. "Maybe I should kill you now."

Zimbola gazed at the firearm with disdain. "That is the only way a man like you will be able to kill me…with a gun."

Maddened with rage, Swensen's finger tightened on the trigger, and if not for the voice of Maximus suddenly coming alive in his ear, he would have fired the weapon. "What is happening?" Maximus demanded.

Turning his back on Zimbola, Swensen spoke quickly as the two mercenaries assisting him kept their assault rifles trained on their captive. "I am not sure. I heard something further back in the cave, but the men do not answer when I call to them."

"Perhaps they're too far back to be heard," Maximus said.

"Maybe," Swensen replied, turning a sour gaze back on the hulking Jamaican, who faced the two men guarding him a ferocious, challenging demeanor. "Do you have any problem with me terminating the big one? He is becoming a nuisance."

Maximus hesitated only momentarily. "Then get rid of him."

A menacing smile crossed Swensen's face. That was all he needed to hear. With sadistic intent, he pointed the Glock at Zimbola's knee. He would make the big man suffer before he killed him.

At that moment, Amphitrite emerged from the fissure in the rock. "Your weapons will not work in here," she said calmly.

Swensen turned at the sudden intrusion, looking behind her in expectation. When no one else appeared, he bared teeth like a maddened dog. "Where are the others?" he rumbled.

"Your men are gone."

"What do you mean gone?"

"They are no longer with us; they are gone from this earth."

Swensen stared, stunned and confused by the implication. "Do not joke with me, woman. What happened to my men?"

"The darkness took them."

The voice of Maximus blurted in Swensen's ear to further fan the flames of his growing rage. "Kill her! Then have your men find out what happened to the others. If there's gold in there, you'll find it without the woman's assistance."

Though he was still bewildered, Swensen's lips curled up into a malicious grin, anxious to carry out the order. But first he would kill the big one, nice and slow as he had planned.

As he raised the Glock, he heard something hum, the sound quickly gathering strength as though heralding the approach of a swarm of bees from the mouth of the cave. The buzz escalated sharply into a piercing whine, causing Swensen to grimace with pain. Lifting a hand to his ear to block the sound, an intense light many times the brightness of the sun suddenly flared before his eyes. Blinded, he gripped the glasses and tore them from his face, instinctively knowing them to be the cause of his discomfort. Blinking and trying to regain his vision, he vaguely perceived two dull thumps resound in the confined quarters. Something clattered harshly on the cave floor, and an instant later he felt a powerful hand grip the wrist of his gun-toting hand.

Squeezing the trigger several times in reaction, Swensen was surprised when the Glock failed to discharge. But if it would not fire, he would use it as a bludgeon. Bracing himself, he used his massive legs and arms to break away from the man grappling with him, but as he did so the gun was yanked from his hand and sent caroming off a wall.

"I told you I would kill you," Zimbola grunted.

Still blinded, Swensen managed to grab an arm, twisting and turning to counter the impossible steel-like grip imposed on him. He knew the Jamaican would be strong, but he found it inconceivable that a human could exert this much strength. At an early age, he had learned to use his superior size and brawn to bully people, establishing himself as a troublemaker on the streets of Oslo where he had developed a fondness for intimidation. Rarely had he ever come across anyone that could match him in brute strength. Pounding someone into a comatose state was something he greatly enjoyed, and it was this propensity for violence that had led him to the wrong side of the law. Only a merciful judge had kept him from going to prison, giving him the option of serving in the Norwegian army to avoid incarceration, and it was in the military where he had taken up wrestling, eventually winning a spot on Norway's Greco-Roman wrestling team. The darkness within him proved to be an asset, and he had learned how to channel it into an unparalleled string of wins for the team. This ultimately took him to the Olympics where he might have medaled if not for being disqualified in a semi-final match in the super heavyweight division eleven years earlier. Frustrated by an exceptionally skilled opponent and unable to restrain the darkness welling up inside him, he had bitten off a finger of his foe. Deeply embittered by the loss, he had competed in a strong man competition a year later, easily winning the event against fifteen of the world's most powerful men. But since then, he had become even stronger with the help of weekly injections of human growth hormone and anabolic steroids, all provided to him by Maximus, who had recruited him to be his personal bodyguard. Yet the man now opposing him seemed to be every bit as strong, and this shocked him.

Pivoting and using his hips, Swensen maneuvered for advantage using his wrestling skills to throw his opponent off balance. Still very much blinded, only spots danced before his eyes in the limited light. Vision, however, would not be necessary for him to execute a throw. Being slightly shorter than Zimbola, he worked his long gorilla-like arms under Zimbola's to clamp them around his torso in a powerful bear hug. Unfortunately, attempting his favorite move, a belly-to-belly vertical *suplex*, would be foolhardy since it would require lifting his opponent in a high overhead arch and falling back on his own neck on the rocky floor.

Both men struggled like two massive bull elephants locking tusks, turning and driving each other against the cave walls, each vying to knock the other off his feet. With small boulders and rubble littering the floor at this juncture in the cave, it was only inevitable that one of the men would stumble.

A harsh grunt left Zimbola's lips as his left ankle met one of these obstacles, and with Swensen forcing him back, the huge Jamaican lost his balance, the side of his head colliding harshly against a rocky surface. Swensen was on him in an instant, straddling him in a full mount and raining down a hail of thunderous punches. Dazedly, Zimbola reached up through the storm, managing to force a thumb the size of a cucumber into Swensen's throat. The Nordic immediately gagged, clutching his injured windpipe with both hands and wheezing hoarsely. Lifting a leg, Zimbola hooked it around Swensen's head and swept him away. Rising to his feet, he crouched low and drove a shoulder into Swensen's gut. Swensen expelled a low grunt as the wind was driven from him, but he recovered quickly, reaching out blindly to hook an arm around Zimbola's neck.

Ponderously, both giants grappled, breathing heavily as they pivoted and danced, striving for superior leverage. Swensen tried for a hip throw but nearly tripped over the two guards Zimbola had taken out. Both of them lay unconscious, one atop the other in a fallen heap. Regaining his balance, he caught Zimbola with a stiff forearm that opened up a gash under his left eye. Shaking off the blow, Zimbola countered with an overhand right that landed solidly on Swensen's jaw. With a fist the size of a cannonball, he followed up with a vicious left. The Nordic's face distorted in a grimace of pain as blood splattered from his broken nose. Staggering back, he latched onto Zimbola's wrist to keep from falling down. Again, they danced and whirled, tenaciously locked up in battle and alternately slamming each other into walls of rock but still managing to hold their feet. Both men were now gasping for air and drenched in sweat, bleeding profusely from a multitude of contusions and cuts about their face and arms.

Sensing that his opponent's endurance was beginning to flag, Zimbola bulled Swensen around, aligning him with the fallen guards. Timing his move, he shoved him violently away. A stunned look of horror swept over Swensen's face as he was sent flying backwards over the men, the back of his head thudding heavily into a boulder as he landed flat on his back.

Swensen stared up with glazed eyes as Zimbola fell on top of him. "The evil fire that burns within you must be extinguished," Zimbola gasped, his left hand grasping Swensen by the throat. Bunching a fist, he came down hard with his right hand, hammering it into Swensen's face like a piston a half dozen times. With his features turned to a bloody pulp, Swensen somehow found the strength to turn onto his stomach to avoid the pulverizing blows. Straddling his adversary's back, Zimbola gripped Swensen's head in his powerful hands and heaved up, cranking it to one side with all of his remaining strength. A sickening crunch echoed sharply as vertebrae snapped, and Swensen's body jerked spasmodically before going slack.

Zimbola rolled off Swensen's inert body and lay on his back, closing his eyes and fighting for breath. Something touched his face, and he realized Amphitrite was kneeling over him with a hand on his cheek. He knew she was healing his injuries with her miraculous touch.

"Is he dead?" Zimbola asked, continuing to gasp. Never had he encountered a man so strong.

"Yes, and so are the other two."

"I didn't think I hit them that hard," Zimbola said, mildly surprised by her statement.

Hector was suddenly hovering over both of them. "What now?" he asked. "There are two more of them outside the cave."

Amphitrite looked up and smiled. "Something tells me they won't be a problem."

Chapter Ten: Reunion of Twins

Percy Osgood sat in the spacious cabin of the EC 135, one of two helicopters stationed aboard the massive super-yacht. The high-end luxury chopper manufactured by Eurocopter was typical of Maximus, who indulged himself in the most expensive and extravagant state-of-the-art equipment found on the market. With its plush interior, the rotary-wing aircraft seemed to focus entirely on the needs of high-net worth individuals.

Percy glanced down as the chopper lifted off the landing pad and sped away. As he had anticipated, the *Numquam Satis* was already moving further out to sea to increase its distance from the detonator held in his hand. Allowing himself a small smile, he took his thumb off the device and let out a sigh of relief. To his own amazement his bluff had succeeded beyond his wildest expectations. The device was not a detonator but a sending unit he had quickly assembled to interface with the sunglass communication system he had designed, and having gained access to the ship's main control room, he had been able to reprogram the system right under Maximus' nose.

Slumping back into the comfortable handcrafted leather seat, he wondered where this cunning boldness had come from that had allowed him to rescue the children and escape from Maximus' clutches. He had always thought himself to be a coward, but this newfound courage confounded him. Putting aside this self-appraisal, he checked out the reading on the unit's tiny display screen.

Keying the intercom, he said, "Take us on a heading of 120 degrees."

A moment later, the aircraft banked moderately to starboard to take on the new heading. "You made a big mistake in going against Maximus," the pilot grumbled. "You have signed your own death warrant."

Percy ignored the comment, continuing to monitor the screen. According to the reading, Swensen's team was less than four miles away to the southeast where the land along the coastline rose up steeply. Oddly enough, the location closely matched the coordinates Mortimer had given him. Long ago, both brothers had developed a modified version of the *Khoisan* click language indigenous to some tribes of southern Africa, using their tongues to articulate 'click' consonants of varied inflections through which they could communicate in a coded conversation of their own, and it was while Percy was hastily putting together the device he held in his hand that he received a message from his brother on a short wave instrument he had turned on. To anyone listening in, it would have sounded like inconsequential noise emitted by one of the many electronic gadgets filling his lab, but to Percy it was like the sound of a concerto symphony. Mortimer was safe with the man who had rescued him, and soon they would arrive at the prearranged location he had sent him, which was a short distance away. His brother had also given him an ETA.

Using a specially prepared program, Percy had replied back to his brother to apprise him of his plans. Checking his watch, he saw that the estimated time of arrival was less than five minutes away.

As the chopper reached the land, Percy scanned the rugged terrain below him, and it was only moments later that he spotted a cascading waterfall spilling into a gorge. The sight took his breath away. With the sun now directly overhead, the sunlight accentuated a kaleidoscope of vibrant colors carpeting tiered slopes that fell away into a mirror-like lagoon of blue-green water. Near the base of the falls, he spotted two lone figures lingering on a narrow strip of white sand.

"Bring us lower and fly doughnuts over the gorge below us," Percy instructed the pilot.

"Maximus said I was only to drop you off," the pilot protested.

Percy leaned forward and held up the device. "See this! It's a microwave detonator. All I have to do is take my thumb off the button and the *Numquam Satis* is deep-sixed. If you want a ship to fly back to, you'll do as I say."

"The ship's too far away for the signal to reach it," the pilot insisted, remembering what Maximus had told him.

"No, it's not," Percy lied. "This device has a range of twenty miles."

The pilot let out an incomprehensible curse before doing as directed, and Percy felt the change in inertia as the chopper dipped lower to swing around in a tight counterclockwise bank. Looking out the port side window, he was staring almost straight down as he studied the layout of the elongated amphitheatre of dazzling hues. He immediately discerned a narrow doglegged channel that connected the basin of water with the ocean, and as the aircraft swung beyond the escarpment that hid the chasm from the sea, he glimpsed the two skiffs caught up on the reef along with several of the men that had ridden in them. Two other men had managed to make their way ashore, appearing stranded on a slender ledge that sat below a sheer wall of rock. Hearing the chopper, they looked up hopefully, no doubt believing Maximus had sent the aircraft to rescue them.

Movement under the water drew Percy's eyes, and he perceived a torpedo-like object better than thirty feet in length slide past the men sitting atop the ledge. At first he thought it was a huge sea creature, but as the chopper looped for another pass, he saw that it had entered the channel that gave way to the lagoon.

"How long am I to keep flying circles?" the pilot suddenly peeved.

"Bring us to the beach near the falls and maintain a hover!" Percy ordered.

The two guards on the beach kept their weapons lowered as the EC 135 descended and came closer to hang stationary at a height of thirty meters above the water. Still wearing the sunglasses, they stared stoically up at the chopper as though expecting its arrival.

Percy aimed the device in his hand, depressing the button and sending out a signal. Both men abruptly reeled, dropping their weapons and raising their hands as though to shield their eyes. Tearing off the sunglasses, they appeared to stagger around blindly.

A satisfied smile came to Percy's face as he took in the scene. The device had worked perfectly, its signal causing an overload in the audio receptors and the tiny light emitting diodes embedded in the sunglass lenses. Wherever the rest of the shore party was, the overload would cause a chain reaction throughout the system, deafening and blinding anyone wearing the glasses.

Something rippled the water close to shore, drawing Percy's attention to the disturbance, and an instant later he espied a man rise to the surface and wade onto the beach. Held within the man's hands was an odd looking firearm, its muzzle trained on the two blinded guards.

One of the guards seemed to regain his vision, and scrambling for his dropped weapon, he plucked it from the sand to fire upon this unanticipated interloper. Too late on the trigger, the guard's body was hurled violently back as the interloper fired first. By this time the second guard reacted, pulling a handgun from a holster, only to be thrown back as a powerful round plowed into his body.

"Drop me off on the beach!" Percy commanded the pilot.

"Are you crazy?" the pilot shot back.

"Do it or so help me I'll destroy the ship," Percy said.

"Okay, okay!"

Percy opened the side door as the chopper dropped low to hover a few feet off the sand. Jumping clear, he looked back to watch the helicopter climb above a towering ridgeline to disappear.

Jake Javolyn came over to him cradling the Sledgehammer in his arms. "You must be Percy, Mort's twin brother," he said. "You look just like him."

Percy gripped Jake's hand, shaking it vigorously. "Thank you for rescuing my brother. I am indebted to you, sir." Looking past Jake, he scanned the water. "Where is he?"

Just as he asked the question, *Johnnie* broke the surface twenty meters from shore, its top hatch popping open. A moment later, Mort climbed out onto the hull and waved to him, a broad smile clinging to his face. Several more objects were suddenly alongside the sub, and Percy heard the laughter of two children. In a flash, Melody and Troy Jacob were whisked to shore by their bond mates.

"Do me a favor and hold this," Jake said to Percy, handing him the Sledgehammer and kneeling down to embrace his children as they rushed into his arms.

"Dadoo!" they screamed, hugging him fiercely.

Jake stood, holding a child in each of his brawny arms. "He saved us, Dadoo," they both chorused in unison, looking at Percy in admiration. "He snuck us off that bad man's ship."

Jake kissed each child tenderly on the forehead before setting them back down in the sand. "I think I am much more indebted to you, sir," he said to Percy, who watched eagerly as Mort was towed to shore by Achilles. Percy handed him back the Sledgehammer and waded out into the water to embrace his twin brother.

The sound of another whirlybird caught Jake's ear, and looking up, he spotted Fernando's chopper coming over the cove's southern rise. A minute later, the Bell Ranger set down on the beach, and Destiny and Franklin climbed from the fuselage. Almost immediately, both children dashed over with gushing exuberance to greet their mother and grandfather, cries of unrestrained joy issuing from their lips.

While on his way back from the Bay du Milieu, Jake had learned of the *Avenging Angel's* hijacking and the subsequent kidnapping of everyone aboard, including his children, but by the time he had been informed of this through Achilles, the children had already escaped. For reasons he was still trying to fathom, his mother-in-law had purposely instructed the dolphins accompanying her to withhold this information from the remainder of the albino telepathic network until the time was right to do so. Not even Destiny had known about the situation. But upon hearing of it, Jake had immediately gotten word to Fernando not to land in the cove. Rather he was to standby at the Devil's Horn until Jake felt it safe for him to enter the hidden sanctuary.

As the moment wore on, Phillipe, Victor Belachek, and Jimenez climbed from *Johnnie*'s hatch to join the party ashore. Jake became aware of movement by the falls, and glancing up, he saw Amphitrite, Zimbola and Hector making their way down from the hidden cave.

Upon reaching the beach, Belachek had a brief word with Percy before approaching Jake with a sober expression. "My son is still aboard that ship."

"Yes, I know," Jake said, expelling a deep sigh. He had learned this from Achilles, who had been apprised of the situation by Alpha and Omega.

Belachek held his gaze with those strange, mismatched orbs of his. "Are you going to help me get him back?"

Jake knew he could not refuse him. If not for Belachek, much of Haiti's farmland would have been contaminated and rendered useless for growing crops, at least for several years to come. But with time growing short and a need to get back to Aquaria, he was suddenly confronted by a storm of indecision.

"Yes, I'll help you," Jake said, placing a hand on Belachek's shoulder. "Come with me."

Intruding upon Mort's reunion with his twin brother, Jake looked to Percy. "One other person is still being held prisoner aboard that ship. Do you know where he's being held?"

Maximus stared at one of the screens showing the receding Haitian coast, his head reeling from what had befallen him. First it had been the children escaping, followed by the death of Cardoza and the destruction of the drones. To make matters worse, the Osgood brothers had also slipped away beyond his grasp, at least temporarily. Even the prized robo-fish Percy had designed were gone, further adding to his woes. He had thought to use the speedy units to chase down the children in the open sea, but Estrada had informed him they were missing from the yacht's moon pool. A highly loyal employee that Maximus had assigned to be Percy's assistant, Estrada was the only person other than Percy capable of programming and operating the robo-fish. He had planned on using the autonomous units to further discredit the colony by setting off explosions on Navassa's pristine reefs just prior to the UN invasion of Aquaria.

And as if to add insult to injury, another rainbow suddenly materialized above the distant shoreline, arching high over the village of Malique and framing it perfectly. The very sight of it rankled him, and he couldn't help but wonder if it was yet another omen of more bad things to come.

Ever since he had witnessed the double rainbow hanging above Aquaria and Navassa Island, his troubles had begun to mount.

A meticulous schemer, Maximus was not used to his carefully laid plans going awry, and lately it seemed as though he had been thwarted and outmaneuvered every step of the way. Mulling this, he remembered his last conversation with Percy Osgood.

"*'Someone must have helped your brother escape.'*

'Yes, someone did, and that man is on his way here. If he was able succeed with Cardoza, I can only imagine what he is capable of doing to you.'"

A mental image of Jake Javolyn suddenly loomed large in his mind, and with it, his utter hatred of the man. It had to be Javolyn, he told himself. The former Navy Seal was the only one he could think of with the training and military knowhow to take on a man like Cardoza and come out on top. Here was the man at the heart of his problems, he and all those who worked for Tursiops.

But then there was the matter of the Osgood brothers. "*Mortimer and I know about The Order and what it is trying to achieve.*" Percy had said. The very thought of it disturbed him to no end, and he knew under no circumstances could he ever let that information get out, for if it did, it could potentially bring down *The Order*, exposing from the shadows all those associated with it. But if it somehow managed to leak out, he would use the full clout of the mainstream media in concert with *fifth column* government officials to dismiss it as just another conspiracy theory concocted by lunatics. With public apathy currently at an all-time high, even hard facts could be turned into nothing more than malicious gossip and scuttlebutt, deflected and quashed by the net of deception purposely emplaced to mold the perceptions and opinions of citizenry. Conspiracy theories were in abundance these days, he well knew that many of them were actually true. Nevertheless, he preferred that information never get out.

Over the centuries, the clandestine organization had continued to become ever more prosperous and omnipotent at the expense of the masses, manipulating world affairs to gratify its insatiable hunger for more and more power and riches. If left to flourish, *The Order* would soon control the entire planet, achieving complete dominance over humanity and establishing the global feudal system it had always sought. It would be a system in which there would only be three classes of people, the super-elite, the elite and the peons, with the peons forced to perform all the work.

The thought of the plan being disrupted evoked a deep sense of outrage in Maximus. Only the highest-ranking members within the organization had knowledge of the plan's full context, but bringing them all together for face-to-face clandestine discussions without arousing the suspicions of government officials not connected with the cabal was not always easy, nor advisable. But closed door sessions of the *Bilderbergs* usually presented an opportunity for this to happen, and he made it a habit to take full advantage of these annual summit meetings of the world's elite. Though the press openly acknowledged such forums, as was typical of these gatherings, the agendas and list of attendees was kept strictly confidential. Security was always airtight, sponsored by a strong military presence within the hosting country, and no one other than attendees would be privy to what was discussed. During these meetings it was generally agreed that only the most affluent deserved to govern, for if left to control its own destiny through moral convictions and unworkable dead-end ideals, the mainstream factions of the human race were just too stupid to do an adequate job of governing themselves. In the end, they would undoubtedly destroy the planet through runaway breeding that would ultimately deplete all of its precious resources. Only men like himself, plutocratic elites who shared pragmatic beliefs, would be able to save it, though as a rule the planning of sinister agendas at such meetings were generally avoided unless circumstances dictated it.

Each year when these forums took place, Maximus would take aside those members of *The Order's* royalty he had marshalled to attend and conduct a separate closed-door session to chart out new or revised goals or report on objectives already underway, though on the surface these discussions would undoubtedly be perceived to be quite unsavory and repugnant to even the most radical *Bilderberg* factions not connected with *The Order*. Lurking at the heart of these discussions, however, was their primary mission, which ultimately entailed establishing a feudalistic world government in combination with a form of slavery in which the peons would produce all the wealth for the other two classes to enjoy at their leisure. The only socialism that would exist would involve providing just enough of the basic necessities needed to sustain the slaves. But first the world population had to be greatly reduced to a more manageable level, and the ways and means by which they would accomplish it were laid out in detail.

Scowling, Maximus brought his eyes to the other screens, all of which remained blank. Seconds earlier, his link to the shore party had suddenly ended, with the network of screens connected to them flaring brightly in unison with an unbearable audio screech that had temporarily deafened him. And then the system had gone inexplicably dead. But just before it happened, he had seen his helicopter fly into the gorge and come to a hover, observed through the glasses of the two rear guards left outside the cave.

Keying the radio, he hailed his pilot. "Report!?"

The pilot's tone was grave. "A man rose up out of the water and killed the two guards outside the cave. I had no choice but to drop Osgood off and get out of there. I'm now inbound for the ship."

Maximus stiffened as though pierced by a lance stabbing deep into his gut, but he quickly gathered himself. "Do not land!" he ordered. "I need you to pick someone up in Port-au-Prince."

"Who?"

"Shut up and stand by!" Maximus snapped irritably. He needed to think this out a bit more carefully. As he mulled the situation, a revised plan formed rapidly in his mind.

Snatching up his cell phone, he activated a programmed number and placed the device to his ear. Though it rang only three times, to Maximus it seemed to take forever before a familiar voice answered. Talking curtly in coded Latin, Maximus spoke quickly, barking out several instructions before ending the call. Hastily, he called another number, not really expecting anyone to answer since it was possible that person was dead. Even so, he had to make sure. From what he had seen of Cardoza's stronghold, he doubted anyone could have survived the destruction.

He was just about to hang up when someone answered after the sixth ring, but he had trouble hearing the person on the other end due to a pervading drone in the background. Again, he gave instructions in coded Latin, receiving some information in return.

Another idea came swiftly to him, and Maximus placed one more coded call, this one to someone that was currently in the floating city of Aquaria. The phone only rang twice before that person answered and a quick exchange ensued. Finally satisfied, Maximus hung up and glimpsed the EC 135 circling his ship.

Knowing that his radio link with the pilot was encrypted, Maximus hailed the pilot again. "You're to pick up Senator Brent Van Heflin. He and another man will be waiting for you. Get them back to this ship without delay."

He knew it was quite fortunate that the senator was currently meeting with the Haitian Minister of Agriculture. It made him easily accessible. It meant he could be delivered to the ship in less than an hour to discuss what he had in mind.

Chapter Eleven: Superyacht Disabled

Mat Daniels stood at a window high up in Aquaria's central tower with Amelia Amhurst at his side. They were in the same room where Jacob had shown Amelia the doctored newscasts. As they looked out to sea, they could see a fleet of ships gathering on the horizon, one of them an aircraft carrier.

Amelia turned, setting a questioning gaze on Jacob, who sat glumly at his desk. "What are you going to do?"

"Nothing at the moment," Jacob said.

"Do you think they're going to send in troops?"

Jacob nodded. "Undoubtedly."

Amelia thought about the strange art scattered all around the colony. Out of curiosity she had asked Mat about it, and he had explained what it did to viewers, though if this were true, she wondered why a bad egg like Bolder had not gotten ill from it.

"Then your art should neutralize them," she said hopefully.

Jacob shook his head dejectedly. Jay Jay had gotten word to him about the antidote UN troops had been using to combat the art. "I don't think so," he muttered dolefully. "They seem to have found a way around our passive line of defense."

"How?"

"I've since learned they inject themselves with a drug that allows them to bear up to the art's debilitating effects. I'm sure that any UN forces breaching this facility will have already taken the necessary precautions to avoid possible sickness."

Amelia's eyes widened with horror. The memory of seeing Bolder inject himself with something came rushing back with frightening clarity. "My god!" she cried. "I saw my cameraman inject himself with a drug he claimed was for controlling Hepatitis C. He had been vomiting just before injecting himself."

Mat wheeled away from the window to look at her. "Are you certain of this?"

"Yes."

"Then I better go see what he's up to," Mat said tersely. Pulling a cell phone from his pocket, he spoke quickly as he strode briskly to the door. "Ez, I need a fix on Eric Bolder."

Amelia watched him go before bringing her gaze back to Jacob. "Are you sure you don't want to evacuate the residents?"

"As a precaution, they have already been sent ashore to the nearby island," replied Jacob.

Amelia stared back in surprise. Earlier on, she hadn't noticed any mass exodus leaving the floating city, and now that she had thought about it, she hadn't seen any residents on Aquaria's lower levels when Mat had given her a quick tour only an hour ago. Nevertheless, she wondered how nearly ten thousand people managed to reach the island without a convoy of boats to transport them. "How were you able to move them so quickly?" she uttered in amazement.

"We have a tunnel that connects with an underground facility on Navassa," Jacob said softly.

"Can it accommodate all those people?"

"Yes."

"But will they be safe."

"Safe enough for the time being," Jacob acknowledged. Seeing her concern, he added, "I've already given the people the option to leave Aquaria completely, but no one wants to go back to their old lives. As we already know, the American administration is willing to abide by the UN ruling to cede Navassa back to Haiti, and since the majority of residents are Haitian nationals, I see no reason why they won't be able to stay. Unfortunately, strings will be pulled to install others to administrate the running of this complex, though I can't eliminate the possibility they'll close this place down."

"Do you honestly believe the Haitian government will allow that?"

Jacob did not immediately answer, rising up from his desk to look out a window behind him. He stared briefly in the direction of Navassa Island before turning back to her with an expression of deep reflection on his face.

"During the last several years, Tursiops has put considerable effort into rooting out the corruption that exists within the Haitian government. In doing this, we even used bribery in order to urge some officials to enact policies favorable to its citizenry and the welfare of the nation as a whole. And while some progress was made, it still wasn't enough."

Jacob expelled a tired sigh. "In the end, greed will be the determining factor whether or not this enterprise survives. If greed prevails, then Aquaria is finished."

Amelia opened her mouth to say more, but a disembodied voice she had previously heard broke into the conversation to cut her off.

"Jacob, three submarines have just joined up with the UN armada," Ez interjected smoothly. "One of them fits a kilo class profile while the other two appear to be the latest Varshavyanka class variety."

Jacob shook his head in frustration. He hadn't expected submarines, particularly the kind Ez had identified. These were Russian built vessels. Such submersibles usually exceeded 4,000 tons and were powered by diesel-electric engines. And while all three were designed for stealth, it did not necessarily mean they carried Russian crews, for he knew the Russians routinely sold military hardware to other countries. The fact that submarines had joined up with the UN task force confronting them now added an ominous edge to what was about to take place.

Mat Daniels found Bolder in Level H, one hundred twenty feet below sea level. He was standing with his back to Mat, aiming his camera through a large window of acrylic Plexiglas that provided a magnificent view of the immediate marine environment. At the moment, a huge school of skipjack could be seen drifting by lazily beyond the glass, seemingly herded by a school of gray dolphins.

Mat moved up behind the shorter man, aware that they were currently the only two people at this location. Sensing someone at his back, Bolder spun.

"I take it the footage you're recording will be photo-shopped just like your other work," Mat said snidely. Looking down, he noticed a medium size duffel bag at Bolder's feet. "What's in the bag?"

"None of your business," Bolder said, regarding Mat with hateful eyes.

Mat stepped closer. "As head of security for this facility, it's my business to know."

Bolder bent to set the camera on the floor next to the duffel bag, rising back up and riveting Mat with a pugnacious gaze and bunching his fists. "You were lucky last time, but this time you're gonna find out what the real *Boulder* is made of."

Mat shrugged, more than happy to accommodate the man's wishes. "Let's get it on then." With his guard lowered, he stuck out his chin, presenting it as an easy target. "Swing for the fences."

"You bet I will."

Bolder lunged, rearing back with his right arm and throwing everything he had into an overhand haymaker.

Mat barely leaned back in time to avoid the attack, feeling the wind from Bolder's knuckles miss his jaw by less than a millimeter. The speed of the move surprised him. He had underestimated this squat, powerfully built man, realizing he had to take him more seriously.

Bolder saw the look on Mat's face and sneered. "That was your first mistake."

"And what might that be?" Mat said, circling to Bolder's left with newfound respect.

"You stupidly assume a man with a build like mine will be slow. I've cleaned out bars filled with guys like you."

"Congratulations!"

Mat studied Bolder's footwork, aware that his opponent moved like a seasoned fighter. Unless he could connect with another groin kick, he doubted he would be able to take the man out with only one well-placed strike like before. Nevertheless, he snapped out his left foot to test the water as Bolder bore in on him again. Though the maneuver was lightning quick, Bolder blocked Mat's foot, slapping it away with the edge of his hand before it reached the area between his legs.

Mat winced. Bolder's hand felt as though it were made of stone.

"Forget about using the same move," Bolder grunted, leering admonishingly. "It'll only work once on a guy like me. I'm a quick learner and faster than you think."

Mat danced swiftly to his right before Bolder could trap him up against the Plexiglas window. "Amelia tells me she saw you inject yourself with a syringe," he said.

"So what of it?"

"That's why you haven't taken ill. The people you work for know about our unique art and found a way around it."

Bolder frowned maliciously, stalking Mat like an angered bull looking to gore a matador.

"That's right. And once UN troops storm this place, your operation will be finished. They'll all be inoculated to withstand whatever it is that ridiculous art does to people."

"Did it ever occur to you why Amelia never got sick from it and you did?" Mat asked.

"Don't care."

"Only the wicked become sick."

"Is that so! Sounds like a crock."

Bolder suddenly rushed forward again, unleashing a savage right cross, but Mat correctly anticipated the punch, shifting his body weight left to avoid the strike.

"We've never been able to fully understand why the art works," Mat went on, "but it seems to be a visual stimulus that triggers some kind of neurological mechanism in a person's brain. With wicked people, it brings on a severe case of motion sickness."

Bolder attacked again, throwing a flurry of punches, but Mat moved quickly to avoid the barrage.

"We can do this all day," Mat needled. He noticed that Bolder was beginning to wheeze. "I doubt a paunchy bastard like you can keep this up for another minute without falling down."

"Go to hell!"

"Either you're in poor physical shape or that drug is sapping you," Mat continued to badger. "And once it wears off, you'll be sick as a dog."

In desperation, Bolder came at him again, swinging wildly, but Mat could see he was now moving slower, with his punches lacking the same authority as before.

"Stop jumping around and face me like a man," Bolder gasped.

"I'll make a deal with you. You tell me who you work for and I'll stop moving."

Bolder was fatiguing fast, his mouth open wide to suck in air. "You know…very well who I work for…it's the IBC."

Mat smiled, shaking his head. "Wrong answer! Give me the person's name!"

Bolder ceased his stalking, bending at the waist to brace his hands against his knees. He was gasping hard.

"Pooped already?" Mat taunted. "Maybe I should call down a gurney to have you wheeled back to your chopper so you can fly the hell out of here."

Unexpectedly, Bolder reeled. He sank to one knee and clutched his chest with his left hand.

Mat took a step closer, no longer regarding the man as dangerous. "Looks like you're having a heart attack," Mat said unsympathetically.

Bolder's gasping suddenly stopped. He was holding something in his right hand.

Too late, Mat realized what it was as two tiny objects lodged in his chest. Grimacing in severe pain, he found himself jerking crazily on the floor. The involuntary muscle contractions seemed endless as Bolder rose up to stand over him.

"Suckered you in good," the shorter man said smugly. "That was your second mistake, falling for a ruse like that. Hope you enjoyed being electroshocked." Abruptly, he pulled up on the wire to retract the two dart-like electrodes embedded in Mat's chest.

The pain immediately subsided, but before Mat could get back on his feet, Bolder gave him a vicious kick that landed square on his chin. That was when darkness flooded his consciousness.

Percy withdrew another small device from a pocket on his lab coat. Looking to Jake, he said, "I don't know if anyone noticed them missing, but right after I helped your kids escape, I launched two robo-fish Maximus carries aboard his yacht."

Jake stared at the device. The memory of the mechanical fish probing the colony came to mind all at once. "Maximus used those fish to recon Aquaria and set off explosions, didn't he?"

Percy nodded abashedly. "I'm afraid so. I'm the one who designed them."

Jake studied the unit. It had a small screen embedded in it. "You can control them with that thing?"

"Yes. The fish are normally preprogrammed to autonomously carry out assigned tasks, but this little baby can override those functions."

"What do you suggest?" Jake asked, failing to see how the robo-fish could be used to rescue Alex.

Percy grinned. "Diversion! Fish One is carrying explosives. If we take out the vessel's props, the ship will be dead in the water. The crew's attention will be focused on the disturbance. While they're busy checking out the damage, you can get aboard through the moon pool located amidships."

Jake pondered the plan. In sinking all of Cardoza's vessels back in the *Bay of Anse du Milieu*, Hercules and Phillipe had used up the remainder of the highly potent explosives brought along for the mission. And he had to forget about frying the circuitry that operated the engine system of the *Numquam Satis*. The sub operated by Abdel was currently too far away to put the T-BEMP it carried to good use.

"What about the hull doors?" Jake pointed out, seeing an obvious impediment to the plan. "If they're closed, we won't have access to the moon pool."

Percy's grin broadened. "Fish Two is outfitted with a remote control that can open the doors. Once the ship stops moving under power, it will activate the doors to swing open. The fish has to be in the immediate vicinity of the doors to do that."

"What about an alarm? Won't the bridge detect the doors opening?"

"Normally, yes, but I deactivated the warning system just before I released the fish. There's only one man aboard the ship who has the know-how to bring the system back online."

"How do you know he hasn't already done that?"

"I changed the password. Without the new one, reactivating it is impossible."

"What are the chances of anyone being in the moon pool once the hull doors open?"

Percy's grin slid away. "The odds of that happening should be quite low. My guess is all the technicians will be down in the engine room where there's a small hull door for sending out a ROV on an umbilical to assess the damage."

To Jake, the plan still seemed highly risky, but then again, taking risks was in his blood. "Where are those fish?"

"One mile offshore and standing by. But we'll need to get within a half mile of them to use this device. Beyond that, they'll be out of range to receive the override."

Jake wheeled, studying the faces all around him before singling out his wife. He could tell she already knew what he was thinking.

"This is going to be a five-man mission. Fernando, I'll need you to drive *Johnnie*." He caught Franklin's look of disappointment as he said this. "Sorry, dad, but you've done more than your share already." Turning his head, he looked up at his over-sized friend. "Zimby, I'm going to need you to back me and Victor up once we board the vessel. Percy, you'll stand by with Fernando."

"What about me?" Phillipe interjected.

"And me?" said Jimenez.

"I need both of you to stay here to safeguard the women and children."

Phillipe opened his mouth to say more, but Jake cut him off. "I'll be counting on you to keep them safe," Jake said firmly. "Do you have a problem with that?"

Phillipe would not meet Jake's eyes. He could tell Jake was still peeved at him for having remained aboard the *Southern Star*. "No," he uttered dejectedly.

Jake placed a hand on Jimenez's shoulder. "Round up the men and get them back in the bunkers pronto. There's no telling what might be headed this way again."

Jimenez nodded, happy to oblige.

Looking to Victor, Jake said, "We better get moving if we're going to get your son back."

Jake glanced at his watch. A feeling of growing impatience was seeping rapidly into his bones. "How you making out, Percy? Are the fish picking up a signal?" He looked back expectantly as Mort's twin brother continued to manipulate the tiny keyboard on the handheld device.

Percy's face was consumed in deep concentration. "I didn't have a chance to test out this little gizmo," Percy explained absently. "I slapped it together in the heat of the moment, so it's understandable that a few bugs have yet to be worked out."

"We've got to get moving," Jake uttered in exasperation.

Percy's expression suddenly changed as he monitored the small screen, his eyes coming alive like those of a man stumbling upon a new discovery. "I see the problem." He turned to Jake. "But I'll need to work on the fish in a dry environment. I need to open them up."

"How do you propose to do that?" Jake asked, his patience almost at an end.

"Open the chamber and let the dolphins out. If you swallow the fish and dewater the chamber, I can correct the problem."

"How long's that going to take?"

"Two minutes, give me two minutes."

Jake turned to Fernando as Victor and Zimbola looked on, their expressions filled with apprehension. "Do as he says, but make it quick."

Jake queried his bond mate. *You following this, Achilles?*

Yes, JJ, I'll let Hercules know you're going to spit us out.

Fernando opened *Johnnie*'s maw to evacuate the dolphins and pull in the robo-fish, both of which were floating stationary side by side ten feet below the ocean surface. A hiss ensued as water was being expelled under pressure from the interdiction chamber.

Satisfied that the chamber was fully dewatered, Jake opened the access hatch to let Percy crawl through.

"Take a look at this," Fernando said.

Jake brought his eyes to bear on the monitor Fernando indicated. *Johnnie*'s periscope had been raised, and on the viewing screen he saw where it was aimed.

"Magnify the view!" Jake ordered.

"Looks like the same chopper that dropped off Percy," Fernando said.

Jake watched the helicopter land on the *Numquam Satis*. The vessel was still moving under power. From his angle of approach, he saw that the yacht was enormous, easily surpassing eight hundred feet in length.

"Are you at full magnification?" asked Jake.

"Afraid so," Fernando replied. He studied the aircraft as the main rotor began to slow. "Aside from the pilot, looks like two others getting off. Too far away to tell who they are, though."

Jake nodded. "Keep pace with them," he said. "Don't want them to get too far ahead of us."

Chapter Twelve: Robo-fish Problem

Maximus eyed the Haitian Minister of Agriculture shrewdly, wondering how much it would cost him to get what he wanted. Bronte Pharah was tall and lean, a relative newcomer to the position he held. Maximus had instructed Van Heflin to bring Pharah with him.

Pressed for time, Maximus got right to the point. "Play ball with me, Mr. Pharah, and you'll be a very rich man."

Pharah shot an indignant look at the senator seated across from him. In clipped, carefully enunciated English, he said, "I thought I was invited here to discuss Haiti's future prospects for agricultural development." He turned a displeased gaze back on Maximus. "If you thought you could bribe me, you are mistaken."

Maximus smiled. So he wants to up the ante by playing hard to get, he thought amusedly. He had dealt with Pharah's kind before. "You confuse bribery with career advancement," Maximus said. "What I am offering you is the administration of Aquaria once Navassa is ceded back to Haiti. You would be placed in charge of its day-to-day operations."

Pharah's irritated expression softened a bit. "My expertise lies in the field of agronomy. I know nothing about marine aquaculture."

"An in-depth knowledge of marine farming will not be required. I don't know if you are aware of it, but Aquaria is a highly profitable enterprise. As head of its day-to-day operations, you would share in its profits. You would become a multi-millionaire almost overnight."

A mask of skepticism quickly gathered on Pharah's features. "How do you propose to get me installed as its head? That decision can only be made by Haiti's president. First, he would have to appoint me to the post, then the appointment would have to be approved by the prime minister and ratified by the national assembly."

Maximus glanced over at Van Heflin. "Leave that to us. I'm sure the senator here can use his considerable congressional influence to have a clause inserted in the ceding agreement to have you placed in charge. What say you, Mr. Pharah? Does my proposition interest you, or are you set on spending the remainder of your career in a position with little financial reward?"

Pharah appeared uncomfortable. He had a wife and five children to support, not to mention two elderly parents that required constant care. The temptation to take the offer was quite strong, though he had no misconceptions about what he would be giving up if he accepted it. His integrity would be lost. He would be nothing more than a puppet dangling on strings controlled by this man. He was proud of his integrity. It had set him apart from his bureaucratic peers, many of whom were steadily enriching themselves through the usual corruption that was so prevalent among government officials. The majority of that corruption, he knew, involved bribes associated with the drug trade. Haiti offered the perfect environment for transshipping vast amounts of illegal narcotics and cocaine.

"What say you, Mr. Pharah?" Maximus repeated, his raspy voice taking on an overtone of vexation.

"I'm not a person prone to making snap decisions," Pharah said. "I will need time to think this over."

Maximus held back the cloud ready to descend on his face, presenting a feigned grin instead. In speaking with Allotey, he had learned that Dr. Herbert Ermstine had been killed. But even if he were still alive, the planned rebellion he had hoped to incite had been snuffed out with the destruction of the drones. The only way he was going to control Aquaria, at least for the short term, was to install a Haitian national to run it, a man who would be directly under his control. And the first thing he needed from that man was to halt the export of the enriched *guano* fertilizer to Haitian farmers. Once that was accomplished, he'd have the mined *guano* contaminated with the *Sterilis* compound before resuming exports. At that point, drones would no longer be needed to spread the deadly mixture over Haitian farmland.

"What if I sweeten the offer by throwing in a bonus?" Maximus said.

Pharah hesitated. "I don't know…I-"

"Does $200,000 in U.S. currency seem reasonable enough, cash up front?"

Maximus lifted a lid on a box that had been sitting on the table and slid it across so that Pharah could view the contents. He had kept it in reserve for a moment like this. He knew such a sum would be a tempting windfall to any bureaucrat within a third world country like Haiti.

Pharah stared at the money for several seconds, appearing like a starving man hungering for food. With an unexpected abruptness that surprised both Maximus and Van Heflin, he pulled his eyes away and stood up, eyeing both men contemptuously. "I cannot accept this," he said angrily. "I am not for sale."

"What if I told you your family is in great danger," Maximus snarled, no longer able to keep up the pretense of civility. "Would you be willing to take the money if it would keep them safe?"

Pharah's composure unraveled further, turning to shock. As though hit with a sedation dart, he slumped down heavily into his chair, a beaten man.

The two minutes Percy had said it would take to correct the robo-fish problem turned into twenty, then thirty. Jake knew he had to do something and do it quickly. But with Maximus' vessel cruising along at close to full power, gaining access to the ship was going to be made extremely difficult if not altogether impossible.

In spite of this, Fernando continued to shadow the vessel, hanging back 1.000 meters off its stern. Every so often he would raise the periscope, looking for anything unusual to happen. Finally, something did happen.

"There's another whirlybird approaching the ship," he announced.

Jake stared at the monitor, knowing that Fernando had left it on full magnification. "That's a Hind." He turned to Belachek. "Tell me if I'm wrong, Victor, but that chopper looks like the one Zinova was flying."

Victor studied the screen as the Hind set down on the ship. "I think you are right."

Jake crowded close to the screen. From *Johnnie*'s present position relative to the ship, they had a perfect angle for an unobstructed view of the highest portion of the vessel's superstructure. He saw two men ascending the stairs leading up to the landing pad. The Hind's main rotor continued to spin as four figures emerged from it to meet the two men. It was evident a discussion was taking place as the ship plowed on. The discussion appeared heated at times, but even at full magnification the gathering of men was still too far away for Jake to be certain of this. Several minutes passed before the meeting ended, upon which five of the men climbed aboard the Hind, leaving one man behind. Another moment passed before the Hind lifted from the landing pad to dip low over the water before gaining height and speed as it drew away.

Percy suddenly poked his head from the hatch leading to the interdiction chamber. "Problem solved," he said enthusiastically. Pulling himself from the hatch, he dogged it off. "You can flood the chamber."

Jake kept his eyes glued to the screen as Fernando opened the valves to re-flood the chamber.

"Looks like the ship's starting to pick up speed," he said, surprised at how fast it was accelerating. Reaching across the control console, he turned on *Johnnie*'s side scan sonar and checked a digital readout. "She's past forty knots and pulling away fast."

Percy stepped up next to him to observe the gauge. "She can go a lot faster than that, I'm afraid to say."

"How fast?"

"Better than sixty knots."

Jake frowned. "A ship that size," he retorted dubiously. "How is that possible?"

"She's outfitted with a Wartsila-Sulzer turbocharged diesel engine usually fabricated for pushing supertankers. But it was specifically designed to also burn nitro fuel."

The answer stunned Jake. With a degree in mechanical engineering, he knew that nitro fuel was actually a highly combustible combination of methanol and nitromethane, with the nitromethane typically comprising anywhere from ten to forty percent of the mixture. He was well aware that nitro engines could turn better than 50,000 rpm as opposed to ducted-fan aircraft engines, which could only go as high as 25,000.

"What percent nitromethane does it use?" Jake asked, continuing to watch in dismay as the ship pulled farther and farther away.

Percy read the look in Jake's eyes. "Fifty percent. The vessel usually cruises on diesel, but if Maximus decides to switch over to nitro, even the robo-fish are going to have a tough time gaining on her."

"Where on the ship are the nitro tanks located?"

"There's only one tank. It holds one hundred thousand gallons, and it's just forward of the diesel tanks."

Jake glanced over at Victor, seeing the deep concern etched on his countenance. Abruptly he turned to face Percy with a stern gaze. "Did it occur to you we run the risk of setting off the nitro if we blow the screws?"

"I don't think there's any chance of that happening."

"Why not?"

"The entire ship's outer hull consists of six-inch titanium plates. Inward of them, the plates are reinforced with ply-layered composites of titanium, carbon, and ceramic mesh capable of stopping a small torpedo. The stern is even more heavily shielded."

Jake's mind raced along in analytical mode. "Even so, maybe it would be safer to try boarding her via helicopter."

Percy's response was emphatic. "Forget it! Maximus has two hidden twenty millimeter cannons aboard her, one near the bow and the other near the stern. Anything coming near the ship that is perceived as a threat will be immediately blown out of the sky."

Jake sighed in frustration. "Then I guess we better proceed with the original plan. How we doing Fernando?"

"The fish are out and the dolphins back in."

Percy pressed a button on his handheld remote, and through the forward viewing portal Jake saw the duo of robo-fish dart rapidly away.

"The ship's speed just passed sixty knots," Fernando announced.

"Then we have to assume Maximus has switched to the nitro fuel," Percy stated.

"Take us to full throttle," Jake ordered, now wondering if the mechanical fish had the speed to catch up with the ship. A vigilant glance at the instrumentation on *Johnnie*'s control panel told him that his quarry was on a bearing headed directly toward Aquaria. Already the *Numquam Satis* was within ten miles of the floating city.

From the bridge of the *USS Carl Sagan*, Captain Alfred Delila kept the spyglasses trained on Aquaria's outer perimeter five miles distant. In his early fifties, he was a tall man with an easy smile, but as he studied the complex, a frown came to his face.

Lowering the glasses, he handed them to Lieutenant Myron Johnson. "Tell me what you see, lieutenant."

Johnson, a youthful black man with the build of a football running back, brought the glasses to his eyes, shifting them several degrees right, then left for a good twenty seconds before turning back to the captain. Appearing puzzled, he said, "No oil slicks or billowing clouds of soot, if that's what you're implying, sir. All I see is a pristine environment."

Captain Delila's face clouded further. "Precisely. We were told these people are despoilers of the marine habitat, but I don't see anything that would suggest that. Unfortunately, we have our orders."

Johnson nodded sagely. "But it doesn't mean we have to like them, captain."

The captain turned his gaze to the carrier's deck. The *Carl Sagan* was the latest addition to the U.S. Navy's fleet, an ultra-modern vessel of electronic wizardry. Directly below him were two AW101 helicopters, each prepared to airlift a squad consisting of sixteen Navy Seals onto the landing pads of Aquaria's central structure. The multi-purpose rotary-wing aircraft were massive, powered by three turbo-shaft engines. They were the result of a joint venture by British and Italian engineers, sold to the UN and recently assigned to the carrier for the impending invasion.

Delila swiveled his head to look further down the ship's runway where four heavily armed F/A Super Hornets were currently standing by. Looking at his watch, he turned back to Johnson. "Your men have been briefed and are ready to go?"

"Yes, sir."

Out of curiosity, Delila asked, "Any of them need the drug?"

"No, sir. We were all tested, and it seems none of us experienced the vertigo the art is supposed to bring on."

This did not come as a surprise to the captain. He had seen examples of the strange art and had experienced a sublime sense of euphoria each time he looked upon one of the enigmatic creations.

Without making it obvious, Delila studied the lieutenant with a critical eye. He had seen the man's file, but seeing him in person proved far more interesting. At twenty-four, Johnson seemed far wiser than his years would suggest. A standout during Seal training, he had all the tools necessary to qualify him as a leader of elite warriors. Johnson was undeniably smart and crisply efficient. And now he would lead the Seal teams into the heart of Aquaria to take control of the floating city. But first he must await the arrival of the UN envoy assigned to the task force, the overall figurehead of the operation. The envoy would be accompanied by a U.S. senator, both of whom were to immediately follow on the heels of Johnson's team once they secured the city. Once the city was secured, the envoy would then assume command of the facility. But even before the mission commenced, a briefing was to take place in which explicit instructions were to be issued by the envoy.

Scanning the sky, Delila looked for the Hind that was supposed to deliver Malikai Allotey, Special Envoy of the United Nations' Council on World Ecological Affairs. He found it odd that Senator Brent Van Heflin, Chairman of the senate's Science and Technology Committee, would be with him. The communique had come in a half hour earlier from command headquarters. Delila was not to proceed with the operation until Allotey and the senator arrived.

Delila hated this assignment. Having his ship turned over to the whims of a non-military bureaucrat representing a conglomeration of foreign nations did not sit well with him. He was aware of the corruption that existed within the UN, and all his instincts told him there was something wrong with the whole affair. He had seen strange things occur during his twenty-eight years in the military, with orders coming down from higher-up that didn't make sense, and this operation reeked of it.

Swiveling his head, Delila looked across the water at several other nearby ships comprising the UN's multinational task force, his gaze searching out the profile of a large low-squat vessel floating stationary less than a thousand meters away. Disdainfully he eyed the 4,000-ton Kilo class submarine. Built by the Russians, it was yet the latest addition to Iran's growing naval fleet. Renowned for being able to resist heavy radio and electronic interference, the diesel-electric submersible was equipped with four 533mm torpedo launchers and ten missile launchers. Purchased at a price of $800 million, it had been named the *Iron Fist* and was currently commanded by Captain Sayyari Habibollah, an officer within the Islamic Revolutionary Guards branch of the Iranian navy and a devout member of Hezbollah, a radical Islamic militant group firmly entrenched within the government of Iran. Habibollah, he well knew , had a long-standing history of being a loose cannon and was notorious for trying to provoke international incidents. Delila had had run-ins with the man while captaining aircraft carriers on two separate occasions in the past, once in the Straits of Hormuz and once in the Gulf of Oman, and each time Habibollah had made threatening runs at his ship in Ghadir class submarines, which were far smaller in size than the one he was now commanding. Among other things, rumor had it that Habibollah was one of the instigators during the takeover of the American Embassy in Tehran in 1979. Unfortunately, and much to his dislike, they were now on the same team, forced to work together at the whims of unknown, and most likely unsavory parties with holds on the strings of power.

Delila scanned the sea farther to the south, spotting two more vessels with low profiles that appeared identical. He had been thoroughly briefed on their capabilities. These were Varshavyanka class diesel-electric submarines recently purchased from the Russians by Venezuela. Ostentatiously named *El Martillo* and *El Yunque*, which translated to *The Hammer* and *The Anvil*, they were essentially upgraded versions of the Kilo class model Iran had purchased, designed for conducting anti-shipping and anti-submarine missions in relatively shallow water. Each Varshavyanka class vessel could accommodate a crew of fifty-two and was equipped with eighteen torpedoes and eight surface-to-air missiles. They featured stealth technology with extended combat range for striking land, surface, and underwater targets. Intelligence reports showed them to have advanced hull architecture, optimal level of control process automation, and low noise emission while cruising underwater. Above all, they required low maintenance and were highly reliable.

With this in mind, Delila mulled a follow-up report he had received about these vessels. A third Varshavyanka class sub was due to be transferred to Venezuela, bringing the entire cost of all three subs to over $1 billion. Though the Russians had given the Venezuelan government a line of credit totaling $800 million, Delila wondered how the South American country could afford such extravagant and expensive military hardware. In spite of the fact that Venezuela was oil-rich, it currently had an ailing economy primarily due to widespread corruption within its government. A recent report he had read by Transparency International, a non-governmental international organization that monitors and publicizes corporate and political corruption globally, ranked the country among the top twenty most corrupt nations on the planet, alleging that $22.5 billion in Venezuela's public funds had been transferred to foreign accounts, with half that money being unaccounted for by any of its government officials. And now rumor had it that its government was allied closely with Iran, providing indispensable support to Hezbollah in its quest to destabilize American influence in the Western Hemisphere.

Delila pondered this knowledge. Even if the submarine purchases were based entirely on credit, a most unlikely scenario, Venezuela could ill afford that scale of defense spending. A combination of prolonged drought and alleged government inefficiencies had plunged the country into crippling cuts in domestic spending, particularly on hydroelectric power generation, which its citizens desperately needed.

"Captain, we have contact," a radioman behind Delila suddenly blurted. "The UN envoy is inbound and will land in the next three minutes."

Delila scanned the sky, spotting a small speck approaching from the east and growing larger by the second. "Give him clearance to land," ordered Delila, watching the aircraft draw closer.

Lieutenant Johnson spoke up as the distinct lines of the helicopter became apparent. "Sir, don't you find it strange that the envoy would be showing up in a Hind."

Delila gave a subtle nod. "Yes, lieutenant, I find it very strange."

Maximus studied the two photographs held in his hands, his eyes periodically shifting from one to the other in near metronome cadence. "I'll get you sooner or later," he muttered to himself. Sitting in the vessel's observation room that gave a 360-degree view of the sea, he placed the photos on the table before him to look back at Haiti's rapidly receding coastline.

A soft rap on the door resounded just before it opened, and Alex Trekov was led into the room by two guards. Extending a hand, Maximus motioned him to a chair, taking quick inventory of the youth's condition. From all outward appearances, the young man seemed to have recovered significantly since being brought aboard his vessel.

"Tell me what you know about Karloff Zinova," Maximus said, asking the question in Russian, one of the five languages he was fluent in. From the earlier interrogation with the youth, he had learned that Alex only spoke Russian.

Alex shrugged. "I cannot offer much, only that he used to be a Spetsnaz operative who turned mercenary. I worked for him only a few short months and rarely had direct contact with him. That was left to his two lieutenants."

Maximus thought about the burly bear of a man he had met on the landing pad a short time earlier, the infamous Reaper Cardoza had told him about, and if not for Javolyn, the Reaper would have sustained an unblemished track record in carrying out clandestine missions. But with Javolyn having bested him, he knew Zinova was now thirsting for revenge. He had seen it in the man's eyes. Retribution, he well knew , was a great motivating force. It drove people relentlessly on, turning them into ravenous beasts who would stop at nothing to get what they wanted. Maximus used people the way a farmer used a blade to shear sheep, and he would make full use of that motivation to capture Javolyn and his wife once and for all. With Cardoza presumed dead, he had struck a deal with Zinova during that short meeting, and at Allotey's urging, promised him a share of any gold found on Aquaria or Navassa. Once the gold was secured, he would then use Zinova to launch a foray into the cove to take possession of the remaining precious metal cache.

"You are obviously a very rich man," Alex said, interrupting Maximus' thoughts. He looked enviously about the room with its exquisitely expensive furnishings. "Perhaps if I worked for you, I might be able to someday enjoy such riches."

Maximus sat back in his chair, eyeing the youth appraisingly before replying.

"So you fancy yourself working for me, do you? What skills do you offer?"

The question seemed to throw Alex off balance. "I am a soldier, a mercenary for hire."

A sneer crossed Maximus' features. "And not a very good one," he scoffed. "Was that your first mission?"

Alex looked away, unwilling to admit it was.

"What happened to you back there?" Maximus pressed. "You weren't wounded, yet you seemed to be recovering from an illness."

Alex stood, opening his shirt to reveal pink scar tissue where a .50 caliber round had pierced his abdomen. "I was shot in the stomach."

Maximus stared, scrutinizing the remnant of the wound dubiously. "No one heals that quickly."

"Believe what you want, but I did. I would have died, but they did something to me, something I cannot explain."

"Who?"

"Two women. They were helped by strange looking creatures."

"Was one of those women aboard the vessel we took you from?"

"Yes."

"What about the other? Describe her!"

"She was young and very pretty."

Maximus reached for one of the photos sitting on the table, pushing it forward for Alex to see. "Is this her?"

Alex scrutinized the photo taken by the robo-fish during its surveillance of Aquaria. It showed a girl wearing a face mask as she rode a huge albino dolphin, her ebony hair streaming back. "I think so."

"What about the creatures? Did they look anything like the one she's riding?"

"Yes, they were white. One of them was bigger than the rest, maybe the same one in the picture."

"What about this one? Did they have any unusual anatomical features?"

Maximus pushed another photo across the table. It displayed two white dolphins with prehensile appendages extended from beneath their pectoral fins. Each one held a socket wrench and appeared to be tightening bolts on a submerged structure.

"Yes, they all had hands."

Maximus held the youth's gaze for several seconds. "Either you're lying about being shot or these people have the ability to heal life threatening injuries rather quickly."

"I am telling you the truth," Alex said.

Maximus rose up from his chair to contemplate what Alex was telling him, suddenly feeling a need to pace the room. But as he did so, he was nearly knocked off his feet by a powerful shock wave that coursed through the ship. Klaxons immediately blared as he caught himself from being thrown to the deck. The normal though barely detectable vibration that told him the ship was underway was now gone, and he felt the vessel rapidly losing its forward momentum.

Maximus got on the intercom to the engine room. "What happened?" he screamed.

"Our drive shafts are gone!" someone from engineering answered in a strident voice.

Chapter Thirteen: Moonpool Surprise

Holding onto Percy as he clutched Achilles' dorsal fin, Jake broke the surface of the moon pool amidships of the *Numquam Satis*. Letting go, he climbed from the water to take rapid inventory of his surroundings. The chamber above the pool was cavernous, and at the moment was bathed in only limited lighting. Perhaps this was normal for this sector of the ship when no activity was taking place, he surmised, for the immediate area appeared to be devoid of any crew members. Blending in with shadows provided by an overhead gantry, Jake hung still for several more seconds to ensure this was the case. Satisfied that no one was around, he slipped off the Sledgehammer strapped to his shoulder. Calling to his bond mate in that silent mode of communication they used, he had Achilles lift Percy from the water to deposit him on the steel grating walkway bordering the pool. Motioning Percy to his side, he summoned his bond mate again.

Achilles, pass the word to Hercules to bring in Victor and Zimby.

Jake looked down at the moon pool, knowing it was too small to accommodate *Johnnie*'s elongated dimensions. Minutes earlier, Achilles had scanned the opening to confirm this, after which he had poked his head above the moon pool's water to recon the area surrounding it. With Fernando holding *Johnnie* steady below the ship's hull, Jake and Percy were the first to climb into the craft's interdiction chamber before being purged into the open sea, upon which it had only taken seconds for Achilles to whisk them up into the bowels of the ship. And with Hercules now being called upon, the giant albino had rapped twice on *Johnnie's* forward viewing port to let Fernando know it was time to flood the chamber again and spit out the two men awaiting to be let out. Since the turnaround time to accomplish this was relatively quick, there was no need to have any of the boarding party outfitted with self-contained breathing apparatus. But with Percy not being a seasoned diver like the others, it had taken considerable coaxing on Jake's part to keep him from panicking.

"Remain calm and remember to expel some air from your lungs as Achilles takes us up, otherwise you'll risk suffering an embolism," Jake had instructed him. "You'll only be submerged for a few seconds."

Jake kept his vigilance on full alert, his eyes constantly roaming the chamber. Even though Percy had ensured him he had permanently disabled the surveillance cameras in the immediate area prior to launching the robo-fish, he had the sensation he was being watched.

The sound of burbling water echoed softly as Hercules breached the moon pool's limpid surface, with Zimby astride the dolphin's back directly behind Victor. With the sea being relatively calm, the rise and fall of water in the pool was minimal.

Gesturing silently, Jake motioned them toward him as they hauled themselves from the water. Both men were heavily armed, with Victor wielding the AK-104 he had used back at the cove, and Zimby clutching a firearm that was once a favorite of Jake's, and that was his trusty MK-23 Stoner, a rapid-fire assault weapon that had been popular among Navy Seals during the Vietnam War. With a drum magazine that held 150 rounds of 5.56mm ammo, the Stoner could unleash overwhelming suppressive firepower at a rate of 850 rounds per minute.

Once the men had regrouped, Jake looked to Percy, holding his voice to a whisper. "Where to now?"

Percy pointed aft where a flight of stairs rose up from the lowest part of the chamber. "This way," he said softly.

Stealthily, the four-man team moved rapidly up the stairs with Jake leading the way. At the top was a grated catwalk that formed a ring above the moon pool. Suspended another ten feet above it was another grated catwalk surrounding the gantry used for lowering equipment into the water below. Jake scrutinized the upper catwalk, which was concentric with the one he stood on. Seeing that part of it along the far side was shrouded in darkness made him feel uneasy. Percy stepped past Jake, making for a nearby computer terminal attached to the railing on brackets.

Jake grabbed him by the arm, speaking quietly. "What are you doing?"

Percy looked past him to Belachek. "I'm going to hack into the ship's surveillance system to confirm if Victor's son is still where they put him."

Jake nodded. "Okay, but be quick about it."

Hovering over the keyboard, Percy's fingers danced over the keys. On the screen above the keyboard, a real-time scene of the room where Alex was being held was suddenly displayed.

"He's not in there!" Percy muttered in disappointment.

"Well see if you can find him," Jake said.

Percy manipulated more keys, bringing up images showing other sectors of the vessel. Most of the scenes were devoid of crew, but a few showed handfuls of black-clothed men carrying automatic weapons, whom Jake surmised to be members of ship's security.

"Bingo!" Percy suddenly uttered, a satisfied smile coming to his face.

The screen showed Alex being led down a hallway, a guard on each side of him.

Victor stared over Percy's shoulder, relief falling across his face. "He seems to be fully recovered."

"You know the best way to get to that part of the ship?" Jake asked Percy.

"Yes. My guess is they're taking him back to the room where he was being held."

"Then show us the way," Jake ordered.

All four men froze as the unmistakable sound of firearm bolts being drawn snicked loudly overhead. "Drop your weapons!" a gruff voice said.

Jake looked up to see a balding, bespectacled man in a white lab coat staring down at him from the upper catwalk's railing. On each side of him were three black-clad, Kevlar-vested troopers with machine pistols aimed down. Rapidly assessing this unexpected predicament, Jake analyzed their chances of survival. Had he been alone, he would not have hesitated to put up a fight, blasting away in spite of the odds and the drop these men had on him. But in that instant of decision, discretion won out, though the urge to swing his weapon upward in a lightning-like fashion and squeeze the trigger was almost overpowering.

The bespectacled individual seemed to read his thoughts. "Don't even think about it," he warned brusquely.

"Do what the man says," Jake said, giving Zimby a covert wink before placing his weapon on the steel grating. For reasons he could not rationalize, he did not feel his team was vulnerable. Not so willing to follow Jake's lead, Victor hesitated.

Jake spoke softly out the side of his mouth. "Easy there, Victor. You'll have to trust me on this."

With great reluctance, Victor put his weapon on the grating.

"A wise decision," the spokesman from above said. Swinging his gaze to Percy, he leered gloatingly. "I'm rather surprised you would attempt something like this, Percy. I figured you had something to do with the ship losing power. Right after the explosion, I scanned the surrounding sea using the hull cameras. That's when I spotted one of the robo-fish you stole. No doubt you sacrificed the other one, using its payload of high-grade explosive to take out the ship's screws. Maximus is going to enjoy getting his hands on you for what you did to his yacht."

Percy stared back, a defiant look on his face. "I should have known you would be lurking about, Estrada. I thought I recognized your sickening odor when I climbed aboard."

Estrada's smirk fell away like lead shot, turning immediately to a scowl. "I'm going to enjoy hearing you scream."

"And I'm going to savor the thought of you being locked behind bars for the remainder of your days," Percy riposted evenly.

"What do you mean by that?"

Now it was Percy's turn to smirk. "Everything Maximus has been planning is going to be revealed to the world. *The Order* is finished."

"That's impossible!"

"No, it's not. I was able to hack into the encrypted agenda and long term goals of your nefarious cabal, making files and storing them away in a place where Maximus would never find them. Recorded in those files are hundreds of names along with transactions, dates, and objectives to be achieved, all aimed at enslavement of the masses."

"You won't be around to release those files," Estrada contended.

Percy snickered tauntingly. "No matter what happens to me, the information those files contain are destined to fall into the right hands. You won't be able to stop that from happening. The world is going to find out very shortly about the true nature of Plagiarius and Unus Universitas, including *Omicron-7,* the planned *Morior* blights and the dispersal of *Sterilis.*"

Estrada let out a constrained laugh, the same gloating leer returning to his face. "It won't matter if anyone else has access to that information. How are they going to disseminate it? I don't think you realize *The Order* controls most major media outlets around the world. The information would be immediately suppressed."

Percy's retort was swift. "Do you really think you can stop it from leaking into the social media on the worldwide web? One way or the other, the truth will eventually find its way into the public domain. Trying to contain it will be futile."

Estrada's leer evaporated again. "The mainstream media will dismiss it as nothing more than fabrications made by lunatic conspiracy theorists. The media will counter the leaks with a barrage of deceptions designed to keep the public distracted. They are like sheep. Their apathy makes it easy to lead them down the path of ignorance."

"What about governments?" Percy said. "Do you think they'll be able to ignore these claims?"

"*The Order* controls all the major powers like puppets on a string. It will not be in the interests of governments and world leaders to acknowledge the claims. They'll insist they have no credibility and are unsubstantiated. They'll distance themselves from the rumors, continuing to cultivate the contrived philanthropic and humanitarian goals portrayed by Plagiarius and Unus Universitas. They'll avoid impugning the integrity of government officials and bureaucrats already on the payrolls of these industrial giants. No matter which way you go, you're going to be outmaneuvered and outplayed at every turn in the road. You're-"

Estrada was abruptly distracted as the water in the moon pool suddenly erupted. Jake saw a fountain of spray shoot upward, and in the midst of that fountain were two white objects streaking side-by-side, one much bigger than its companion. Estrada and the six troopers barely had time to turn and glimpse what Jake was seeing, and by then it was too late.

A cacophony of startled screams rang out as two sets of twin prehensile appendages sprang out from beneath pectoral fins. With the objects reaching the apex of their leap, the smaller set of arms enfolded Estrada and the closest trooper on his left, pulling them from the catwalk. Achilles fell backwards, clutching them firmly to his body. Reflexively, the trooper fired his weapon, but his arm was pinned and a dozen rounds caromed harmlessly off steel fixtures off to one side. In the same instant, Hercules was able to embrace all three men on Estrada's right with his wider span, pulling them down with him as gravity took over. A huge splash flew upward as both albinos met the water and disappeared, bringing the men with them.

Jake reacted quickly, snatching up his Sledgehammer and firing off two shots that toppled the last two troopers from their perch. An instant later, they too, disappeared below the moon pool's surface, the water turned red from their mortal wounds.

"So much for the element of surprise," Jake grumbled.

"It's obvious Maximus knows we're here," Percy said, leaning back over the computer terminal and hitting more keys. "And to make matters worse, Alex is not in the original room where they were keeping him." A succession of images showing various sectors of the ship played rapidly across the monitor. "They're taking him to the helipad!" he suddenly exclaimed, stopping on one that showed Victor's son being escorted up a steep flight of stairs by the same two guards as before.

"Are you sure of that?" Jake blurted.

"Why else would they be taking him up the only way to the chopper?" Percy pulled up another image. Four pairs of eyes scrutinized the screen to observe a helicopter sitting on the helipad. Someone was just climbing into the pilot's seat. "That's the pilot," Percy said. "If you hurry, you might be able to stop him before he takes off." Switching screen images, he saw one of Maximus sitting in the ship's control room, a dark scowl consuming his face.

"If I were a gambling man, I'd wager Maximus is getting ready to jump ship."

"Which way to get there?" Jake demanded.

Percy pointed at a closed door at the end of the catwalk. "Follow the corridor on the other side of the door. There's a second door thirty feet away that gives access to a stairwell. Go up ten flights. The helipad is at the top." Pulling up more images on the monitor, he added, "As of this moment the entire way is clear. Now go!"

Jake hesitated, seeing that Percy continued to manipulate the keyboard. "Aren't you coming?"

"No, I can do a lot more good here."

"Okay," Jake shot back, "but stay put. We'll be getting off the ship the same way we came in, so be ready for a quick departure once we return." Abruptly, Jake turned and sped down the catwalk with Victor and Zimby on his heels.

Indecision gripped Maximus. Estrada had alerted him that the ship was about to be boarded, and he had instructed Estrada to bring the invaders to him as soon as they were captured. But now, Estrada was not answering his pages, and try as he might, he could not pull up any images on the computer screens. For reasons unknown, he was effectively locked out of the ship's surveillance system, and without it he felt like a blind man groping about in darkness. A feeling of fear swept over him, intensified all the more by the ship's current situation. Without its screws, the *Numquam Satis* was not going anywhere.

Maximus made a decision and contacted his pilot, who was standing by atop the landing pad. "Is everyone aboard yet?"

"The Russian is," the pilot said, "but Pharah is still not here. You want me to crank 'er up?"

Maximus detected impatience in the reply. It was obvious his pilot was eager to get going. "Yes, we're getting off the ship."

"What's our destination?" the pilot asked.

"The *Kraken*."

Maximus got on the ship's radio, hailing Restoff, the leader of his remaining security. "What's the holdup with Pharah?" he rasped heatedly.

"He got sick and had to use the toilet. I didn't think you'd want him soiling the chopper, but they're bringing him up now. Where are you, sir? All the cameras stopped working."

"I'm in the control room." As an afterthought, Maximus said. "How many men with you?"

"Sixteen, not counting myself. Six others are with Estrada. Another two are with Pharah and two more with the Russian."

"Then you should have no trouble neutralizing the intruders. There are only four of them. I'll expect you to either kill or capture them, but bringing them to me alive is preferred. Is that understood?"

"Yes, sir."

It wasn't until the third flight of stairs that Jake, Victor and Zimby encountered opposition. The stairwell was positioned amidships of the yacht, providing access to each deck through a set of doors, one located to port and the other to starboard. With Jake leading the way, he was almost to the fourth landing when the port side door burst open. Firing from the hip, he caught the trooper coming through with a frag-12 round to the throat that hurled the man backwards into another Kevlar-vested companion following on his heels. Jake fired again before the second trooper could recover, the shot blowing a gaping hole through his body armor and killing him instantly.

Scrambling as fast as his legs would carry him, Jake was halfway up the sixth flight when he heard the starboard door below him open. Trailing up the rear, Zimby let loose with the Stoner, sending a hail of bullets into three more troopers that cut them down quickly. In the confined space of the stairwell, the sound was deafening, reverberating off the walls like a chainsaw on the verge of exploding.

On the eighth landing, the doors on both sides opened at the same time, and Jake took out another two troopers as Victor unleashed a withering enfilade that caught three more armed adversaries before they could raise their weapons.

Jake stopped momentarily to pluck two *flashbangs* from the web belt of one of the men he had killed. He recognized them as M84 stun grenades, non-lethal explosive devices used to temporarily disorient an enemy's senses. Designed to produce a blinding flash of light and disabling noise without causing permanent injury, they could induce a short bout of blindness and loss of hearing in an adversary. *Flashbangs* were often carried by Navy Seals on covert missions, and Jake had utilized them on more than one occasion in the past.

Jake tossed one of the grenades to Victor. "Might come in handy," he remarked. Noticing a small walkie-talkie also attached to the dead trooper's web belt, he grabbed that too.

Leaping for the ninth flight, Jake's legs began to burn with the rapid ascent, Victor now right beside him. An alarm suddenly went off in his head, the same sense of presentiment he had recently experienced ever since being revived from his near-death state back in the cove.

"Get down!" Jake yelled, shoving Victor harshly to one side and stopping his headlong rush.

Taking the last four steps in a single bound, Jake reached the next landing and pulled the pin on the *flashbang*. Opening the port side door, he tossed it through. In his mind's eye he had clearly seen them coming even before they showed themselves. One of the two troopers approaching the door fired his weapon, but Jake sprang to one side of the doorframe to avoid the lethal volley of rounds that swarmed past.

Jake covered his ears and averted his eyes to avoid the blinding flash and jarring concussion as the grenade detonated. Stepping calmly back into the doorway, he turned the Sledgehammer loose on the troopers as they staggered about, unleashing two shots in quick succession. A third man lay on the floor, still stunned. Scrutinizing the fallen man, Jake saw that he was unarmed and wore a dark business suit.

"Don't shoot!" the man screamed, suddenly regaining his senses, his eyes fluttering open like those of a person waking up from a deep sleep and trying to orient himself to his surroundings. "Don't shoot!" he pleaded again, shielding his face with both hands as though to ward off a bullet.

Jake took in the hallway to make sure it was clear of other troopers before stepping over the man, his weapon at the ready. "Who are you?" he demanded.

"Bronte Pharah," the man cried, "Minister of Agriculture in Haiti. "They were holding me against my will."

Jake pulled Pharah to his feet, somehow certain the man was telling the truth. "Come with me!" he said. "Stay close and don't lag behind."

"But-"

Jake cut him off sharply, his reply curt. "There's no time for explanations. Just keep close if you want to get off this ship alive."

Victor was nowhere to be seen as Jake came back onto the landing with Pharah following. Jake shot a quick glance to Zimby, who was keeping a close watch on the stairs below. "Where's Victor?" he demanded.

Zimby indicated the final flight with jerk of his head. "Up there."

The whine of a turbine suddenly intruded its way into Jake's awareness, its growing pitch telling him there was no more time to lose. Bounding up the final flight of stairs, he headed for the lone door that supposedly gave way to where the sound was coming from. As he flung the door open, he saw that he had emerged out into the open below the helipad. Prudently, he looked to both sides to make sure he wasn't walking into an ambush as the roar of the whirlybird's turbine assaulted his ears. From the sound he knew the aircraft was on the verge of liftoff. Another set of stairs with a railing on each side rose up steeply to the lip of the platform supporting the chopper. Quickly, he ran up the steps, shouldering his way against the downdraft of heavy rotor wash pummeling him. Victor was at the top with his AK-104 aimed at the aircraft.

Taking a rapid assessment of the situation, Jake saw that the side door to the chopper was open. Alex stared back with a guard on each side of him, his expression unreadable. One of the guards held an Uzi submachine pistol to the lad's head as another guard wearing a headset pointed his weapon back at Victor. Sitting in the co-pilot's seat was a man Jake assumed to be Maximus, a set of headphones clamped to his head. An incongruous mix of both rage and smugness filled the man's countenance as he glimpsed Jake arriving on the scene.

Helplessly, Victor watched as the main rotor bit the air to lift the chopper sluggishly off the platform. He didn't dare fire his weapon. Even with well-placed shots that disabled the engine or took out the pilot, he risked ricocheting or fragmenting bullets that could kill his son or rupture the fuel tank, which could turn the aircraft into a raging inferno. He was effectively stalemated.

As the chopper rose higher and began to swing away, Jake saw Maximus' face change as he spoke into his lip mike. It was the look of a man on the brink of delivering a deadly blow to a hated enemy, and once again an inexplicable bout of presentiment took hold of him.

Even before the second guard could discharge his weapon, Jake launched himself sideways to tackle Victor and send both of them rolling along the edge of the helipad. A barrage of rounds caromed fiercely off the steel deck, narrowly missing both men.

The helicopter turned as its pilot moved it out over the water, its side door now facing away and nullifying the guards opportunity to fire in their direction again. Jake rose to his feet, watching the chopper race away. Turning, he took in Victor's anguish. The man appeared lost and forlorn as he stared fixedly at the object taking his son into the distance.

Jake sympathized with him. Being a father himself, he could well understand what the man was going through at that moment.

Chapter Fourteen: A Wild Guess

Mat came awake with a start. Recognizing the person shaking him, he realized it was Samuel. "What happened?" he asked groggily.

"You were unconscious," Samuel said.

Aware of a dull pain, Mat raised a hand to his chin and flinched. Gingerly he groped his jaw, wiggling it back and forth to test it for a possible fracture. Though it was swollen and his fingertips came away with a slight smear of blood, he could tell it was not broken.

A remembrance of the fight with Bolder and how he had been suckered came oozing back. Mat stiffened, shooting a quick glance around the immediate area. Bolder was gone. "Where'd the news guy go?"

"Ez says he's in the access tunnel leading to Navassa."

Mat rose to his feet. "Whatever he's up to cannot be good," he said. An ominous feeling welled up in him as he thought about the duffel bag Bolder had carried.

"What's the latest with the UN task force?" Mat asked.

"A helicopter landed on the aircraft carrier. Ez says it's similar to the one Jake and Fernando commandeered. Three large submarines are also out there with the other ships."

"Damn!" Mat said, feeling more helpless than ever. "Any word from Jake?"

"No."

Mat looked beyond the acrylic window that gave a view of the hydrosphere that lay beyond. A swarm of bluefin crowded close to the glass, blocking what he was trying to see. Abruptly, the mass of tuna scattered, driven away by two albinos streaking past. It was as though the dolphins had read his mind and had purposely interceded to disperse the obstruction.

Mat's cell phone rang. "I instructed the dolphins to clear the fish out of the way," Ez said without preamble as soon as he answered. "Gauging his current pace, Bolder will reach the shipping platform in ten minutes."

Mat shot a glance at the window again. From this angle he could see the transparent access tunnel as it disappeared into the watery void beneath the algae lagoons. Though his jaw still throbbed, the cobwebs clinging to his thoughts were beginning to clear. Checking his wristwatch, he was shocked to see he had been comatose for almost forty minutes. "What took you so long in sending help?" Mat accused, speaking bitterly into his cell phone.

"With the exception of Jacob and Amelia," Ez shot back, "everyone has been evacuated to Navassa. I decided to avoid compounding Jacob's responsibilities by alerting him to your predicament, so I contacted Abdel and had him send Samuel."

"Where are you going?" Samuel said as Mat stepped past him.

"I'm going after Bolder."

"I'll help you."

Mat shook his head, still feeling a little woozy. "No. Stand by with Abdel in the sub. It's possible we may need to use the T-BEMP to stop those vessels." The fact that not one but three submarines had joined up with the UN task force was a bad omen. Deep down, Mat knew the T-BEMP option stood little chance. The UN vessels would detect the sub and most likely destroy it long before it got within range of their engines. But at least it was an excuse to keep Samuel out of harm's way for the time being.

Samuel looked grim. "You're the boss."

Mat started to leave, but Samuel reached down and lifted two items off the floor near his feet, handing one of them over. "Ez thought you might need these," he said.

Immediately recognizing his utility belt with spare ammo clips and holstered Heckler and Koch USP-9 submachine pistol similar to Jake's,

Mat nodded appreciatively as he strapped it about his waist. That accomplished, he hefted the other item. "What's in the knapsack?" he asked.

"A cloaker and a Masker."

Harnessing the knapsack to his shoulders, Mat broke into a trot, chastising himself as he did so. He had severely underestimated Bolder, and there was no telling what the IBC cameraman had hidden in that duffel bag he carried. But one thing was for sure that he could not refute. Bolder was a dangerous man.

Plagued by a feeling of failure, Jake had no other choice but to vacate the ship. Victor had become pensive, appearing like a lost soul and showing signs of intense remorse. It was apparent a huge chunk had been torn from his heart, and Jake had to keep reminding him to stay alert.

Retracing the way they had come, the walkie-talkie Jake had taken from the dead trooper suddenly buzzed noisily with static. "Raven calling Unit Three, report!"

Jake raised his arm for Victor, Zimby and Pharah to stop. Quickly, he adjusted the volume control to reduce the sound issuing from it.

"Raven calling Unit Three, report!" the voice repeated with a touch more urgency behind it.

Jake listened, wondering if Unit Three was one of the teams he and his accomplices had taken out. The latest batch of troopers he had come across had been in groups of two and three.

The disembodied voice grew angry. "Answer me, Unit Three!" When no response occurred, the same voice issued another command. "Calling all units, has anyone seen Unit Three?"

"This is Unit One. Negative on the query," a different voice replied.

"Unit Five here!" another voice barked out in alarm. "We found Unit Three terminated on Level Four of the mid-ship stairwell."

The radio went silent for several seconds before Raven came back. "Units Two and Four, why aren't you answering?" When no reply ensued,

Raven issued another order. "Unit Five, proceed with caution up the stairwell."

"This is Unit Five, we're on our way."

Raven came back again. "What's your location, Unit One?"

"Ninth level, starboard corridor. I just found Unit Four, both shot dead."

"What about the Haitian Minister?"

"He's not here."

"Well find him!" Raven growled. "But first I want you to assist Unit Five. If these raiders are still in the stairwell, you'll be able to trap them between you."

Jake turned. "Hand me your *flashbang*," he whispered to Victor.

With the grenade in his hand, Jake proceeded down the stairs slowly, working his way toward the fifth level. He was about to peek over the railing to see if he could catch a glimpse of the men comprising Unit Five, but suddenly realized this wasn't necessary as another vision flashed in his mind's eye. Painted on one of the walls on each landing were big black letters that indicated the level of the ship. Three men had just passed Level Five and were padding silently up the stairs.

Jake turned again. "Keep your hands on your ears and close your eyes," he whispered to the others, mimicking these actions with his hands and eyes. Pulling the pin, he dropped the grenade over the railing.

Even with his hands clamped firmly over his ears, the concussion jarred him. Rushing down the stairs, Jake found the troopers reeling about in stunned confusion, and it was fairly easy for him to finish them off quickly.

"Get back to the moon pool!" Jake said to the others. "I'll follow you."

Zimbola hung back, not willing to leave Jake behind. "I'm staying with you," the big Jamaican said.

From the adamant look on Zimby's face, Jake knew it would be futile to convince his friend otherwise. Instead, he looked to Victor, who still appeared numb. "We'll get your son back, Victor, but right now I need you to get Minister Pharah to the moon pool. The dolphins will be waiting."

The words seemed to snap Victor out of his fugue. "Come with me," Victor said to Pharah, grabbing him by the arm. Pharah looked frightened as he eyed the stairs above Jake, but he turned and let Victor lead him away.

Jake's radio buzzed again. "Raven, this is Unit One. I believe Unit Five has engaged the raiders, judging from the sound. My ears are still ringing."

"Acknowledged," Raven replied brusquely. "Bring any captives to the engine room. I'll be waiting for you there."

Jake made sure Victor and Pharah had a significant lead before eyeing the three troopers he had cut down, looking hopefully for more flashbangs clipped to their utility belts. At seeing none, he turned to Zimby. "I have an idea," he said. "Let's take up a position behind the port side door."

Zimby nodded and both men made a hasty exit through the door. Quickly, Jake explained what he had in mind.

Having retained the PHP after his encounter with Zinova near Cardoza's stronghold, he pulled it from a pouch on his web belt and held it at the ready. Leaning against the backside of the door, Jake peeked through the narrow panel of glass that provided a view of the Level Five landing. Sending out a mental query, he called to his bond mate. *How you doing, Achilles?*

Standing by below the moon pool, Achilles answered. *For the record, there's a keel hatch near the ship's stern where they sent out a ROV on an umbilical to assess the damage to the propulsion system.*

Thanks for the update, Jake said, keeping a wary eye on the stairs above the landing. At that moment, a booted foot appeared, treading cautiously on the next step down.

Motioning for Zimby to get ready, Jake waited for the opposition to show itself, discovering that Unit One consisted of three men. Withdrawing his face from the glass before the lead trooper glanced in his direction, he knelt low and nodded. Standing to one side of the doorway, Zimby flung the door open. With a flick of the activation button, Jake tossed the PHP onto the landing and ducked back behind the wall. He had no idea whether or not these men had immunized themselves to the effects of the dolphin art, but he had to at least give it a try.

All three troopers reacted at the same time, sending a torrent of Uzi rounds through the open doorway. And just as quickly as the barrage had started, it stopped, and wails of intense agony broke the air. Risking a peek around the doorframe, Jake saw that all three troopers had dropped their weapons and sunk to their knees, each clutching his head as though struck by an invisible demon.

Jake looked over at Zimby and rose to his feet. "Let's go!" he said.

Stepping back out onto the landing, Jake was overcome by that same feeling of ecstasy that always accosted him whenever he looked upon the holographic display. With the stress of mortal combat keeping him hair-trigger tense, he found comfort in the three-dimensional geometry as it pulsated before him, and he had trouble looking away from its soothing glow. Though he could have aimed his Sledgehammer and put all three foes out of their misery, he could not bring himself to do so. He was well aware of the potential danger he brought upon himself by staring at these displays too long. Simply put, they weakened the survival instinct. Suddenly calmed by the kinetic art form dancing before his eyes, he willed himself on past the portable holographic projector, leaving it behind and taking the next flight of stairs down. He would let the PHP remain where it lay and serve out its intended function, and that was to hold the downed troopers at bay.

Only when Jake reached the next landing down did the grip of euphoria and well-being begin to subside, and a quick glance behind him showed Zimby following with a subdued, mesmeric expression clinging to his face. It was as though the Jamaican had just undergone a profound religious experience.

Sitting at the controls of the utility cart, Mat moved swiftly along the tubular access tunnel that would take him to the offshore platform. He had traversed its full length only once before to reach the subterranean complex on Navassa Island, and that had been immediately following its construction when he had traversed it on foot. And though it ran directly under the offshore platform to connect with the island, a smaller diameter manhole rose vertically from it to interface with the platform's lowest level. Each end of the tunnel was blocked by a circular hatch door with a dogging wheel that had to be turned by hand. Another overhead hatch at the top of the manhole allowed access onto the platform. As a rule of safety, users were required to batten down the doors upon entry or exit, but he had discovered that Bolder had left the tunnel's entrance hatch ajar. Unfortunately, the wiring systems and mechanisms for automatically opening and closing the hatches remotely had not yet been completed, which made it impossible for Ez to lock down the hatches at the other end to keep Bolder from getting through. And to make matters worse, no Aquarians were currently on the platform to secure the hatch from the other side. Because of the imminent invasion of the facility by UN troops, the majority of Aquarians had been evacuated to the nearby island via the tunnel hours earlier.

Made of clear acrylic polymer, the tube had an inner diameter of eight feet. Schools of various fish species swarmed just beyond the glass as he stared intently ahead looking to catch up with the man who had knocked him senseless. Two recessed grooves located forty-five degrees below the mid-height of the tunnel on each side and running parallel with it provided slotted guides for the cart's runners.

Just before giving chase, Ez had reminded Mat about the utility cart, which lay stored in a nearby locker next to the tunnel entrance. Because he had never used the cart, he had to rely on Ez for instructions on its operation, which was simple enough. Designed for easy storage, the cart was portable and compact, but could be unfolded for transporting equipment through the tunnel. Weighing slightly less than sixty pounds, Mat had found it easy to insert its runners into the recessed guides of the tunnel and get underway. He saw that there was a problem, however, as he stared at the simple gauges attached to the cart's handlebars. The lone battery providing power to the cart was low on juice. Someone had forgotten to recharge it.

Staring intently ahead, he looked for movement, but all he saw was the circular interior of the tube reduced to a pinpoint in the distance. As he moved on, he saw that the seafloor had risen considerably, with vast clusters of thriving coral reef and fish life coming into view beneath him. Though he had moved along the tunnel at a rate much faster than most world class athletes could run in an all-out sprint, he could see that the cart was beginning to move slower, much slower as the battery expended the remainder of its power. Mat estimated he had traversed almost two miles of the three-mile-long access tunnel as the cart suddenly slowed to a crawl, and realizing it was no longer doing him any good, he hopped off and began running. Taking deep breaths, he felt a continuous rush of air at his back. This told him that the blowers located within the floating city were still active. Movement of fresh, breathable air within the access tunnel had been crucial in allowing nearly ten thousand people to reach the island.

Upon reaching the moon pool, Jake found it to be vacant. Sending a mental query to Achilles, he asked if Victor, Pharah, and Percy were aboard *Johnnie*.

Victor and Pharah have returned, Achilles informed him, *but Percy was not with them. I have to assume he's still aboard the ship.*

A bad feeling suddenly took hold of Jake, and he let his bond mate know it. *This is not good. I can't leave without him.*

That's understandable, JJ. Fernando is still standing by.

Jake looked over at Zimbola. "I need you to get aboard the sub."

The Jamaican shook his head adamantly. "You're stuck with me whether you like it or not."

Jake was about to argue this, but the radio he had taken from the downed trooper suddenly squawked. "Raven to Units One and Five, give me an update?"

The reply that immediately followed surprised Jake.

"This is Unit Five." Though muffled in static, the voice sounded strained. "We have neutralized the intruders. We were forced to kill all four of them and have no captives. Unit One is with me but their radio took a bullet and is not working."

A moment of dead silence followed before Raven came back. "You sound funny, Unit Five. Everything okay?" A hint of suspicion was obvious in his tone.

"Took a round in the leg but I'm still able to walk. I also lost a man," Five said.

Jake had trouble believing what he was hearing. He was certain he had killed the three men comprising Unit Five. *How could this be?*

Another short pause ensued before Raven came back, his tone now sounding petulant. "Do you have the Haitian in custody?"

"No."

"Head to the moon pool!" Raven ordered impatiently. "He might be trying to board a sub directly under it. We spotted it with our ROV camera."

"If he's there, Estrada will get him," Five answered.

"Estrada's dead," Raven rebuked testily. "His body floated past the ROV. That's when we sent it amidships and saw the sub."

"What about using one of our torpedoes to destroy it?" Five recommended.

"The torpedo hatches refuse to engage," Raven railed in frustration. "They won't open. The ROV hatch is the only one that works, and the techs were forced to open it manually. Now go!"

"We're on our way," Five said.

Jake turned to Zimby and shrugged. "I don't get it. I could have sworn we took out both units."

"You did."

Jake spun, startled by the voice at his back. Percy emerged from the shadows.

"You almost got yourself killed," Jake admonished sharply, easing up his finger on the Sledgehammer trigger. "I assume that was you on the radio."

"Always had this talent for mimicking voices," Percy offered.

"But for what purpose?" Jake needed to know.

"I had to be sure I disabled the hull torpedoes before we left the ship."

Jake frowned. "You never mentioned this ship had torpedoes."

Percy smiled disarmingly. "I doubt it would have made a difference had I told you. As it is, I was able to shut down most of the systems that would have caused us problems, including their internal communications." His gaze fell on the small radio clipped to Jake's utility belt. "It forced them to use those crude walkie-talkies."

"Any idea where Maximus is headed?" Jake asked.

Percy nodded. "He's on his way to the *Kraken*. He owns it."

"The mega-tanker? How can you be sure?"

"I was able to intercept his last transmission." Moving past Jake, Percy made his way over to the computer terminal he had used before. "If you'll indulge me for one moment, I'd like to show you something."

"Whatever it is, be quick about it," Jake grumbled impatiently. "We've got to get going."

"You might find this important," Percy said airily, his fingers playing rapidly over the keyboard again. "Maximus made sure to have a link installed within the onboard surveillance system. It provides real-time viewing of the *Kraken* whenever she's within thirty miles of this ship." The rear deck of an enormous oil tanker as seen from a camera perched high up abruptly sprang into view on the computer screen. "You're looking at her as I speak, so she must be within range."

Jake stared, his eyes falling on a large helicopter that had just settled on one of the tankers landing pads, its main rotor slowing. The chopper was much too big to be the one Maximus had escaped on. Placing a hand on Percy's shoulder, Jake said, "Does that bird hold some meaning to you?"

Percy's features hardened. "Bounty hunters. Maximus hired them to kidnap my brother."

Jake continued to stare as several armed men raced up onto the pad and into the chopper's main cabin. Several seconds elapsed before two figures were ushered out, their hands shackled firmly behind their backs. Two others emerged from the cabin door, following behind the two being led away.

"Are you able to zoom in?" Jake asked, suddenly growing edgy. There was something oddly familiar in the way one of the captives walked.

Percy went to work on the keys once more, and a second later Jake's fear was confirmed.

Turning his head, Percy read the anger blazing across Jake's face. "Do you know them?"

Jake did not answer. He could feel his bond mate's fury growing in concert with his own. The sensation gathered strength before suddenly fading.

Achilles reined in his mushrooming ire, though it was analogous to holding back a volcanic eruption. The dolphin knew a show of anger would do nothing to help the situation, aware that too much of Jake resonated within him. With considerable effort he got control of his emotions, easing his way into Jake's thoughts again with a profound delicacy.

JJ, I just received word the Hind touched down on an aircraft carrier positioned near Aquaria. Ez saw it land forty minutes ago.

The delay in news evoked a tad of petulance in Jake's reply. *And she thought to inform you of this now?*

No, JJ, we were in range of her underwater broadcasts just before you climbed into the moon pool, but I thought it wise not to lay more bad news on you.

Jake was still annoyed. *Anything else you forgot to tell me?*

You had enough on your plate to deal with, JJ, so I thought it best not to tell you before. Three submarines are also on station with the UN task force. Ez has a bad feeling about their intentions and strongly suggests you get back to Aquaria on the double. She'll fill you in on everything once you arrive.

Jake was suddenly aware of Percy appraising him with a penetrating stare. "I hate to intrude on your thoughts," he apologized, "but what's our next move?"

Jake let out a troubled sigh. "I need time to think this out, but right now I suggest we get back on the sub and get away just in case Raven is able to re-engage those torpedoes."

The huge head of Hercules broke the surface of the moon pool as Jake uttered this.

A sudden idea struck Jake, and he explored it further by conferring with his bond mate, taking only milliseconds to get Achilles' opinion.

Aquaria's outer breakwater is less than five miles away, his bond mate informed him.

Do you think we can get their cooperation? Jake asked.

They have never refused us, Achilles reminded him.

Jake looked at Percy. "I have an idea," he said, quickly laying out the rudiments of a plan. "Think you can do it?"

Percy's eyes narrowed. "I'll give it my best shot," he said. Abruptly he went back to working keys on the computer terminal.

Jake set his eyes on Zimby. "I want you to get Mr. Pharah back aboard *Johnnie* and have Fernando hightail it to Malique to drop the two of you off."

Seeing the scowl coming to Zimby's face, Jake cut him off quickly before he could object. "It's important you get him away from all this. You can get back to the cove using one of the company jeeps. I need you there to protect everyone, especially the children."

"What about you?" the black goliath grumbled.

"As soon as Fernando drops you off, he is to get back here pronto. Have him bring back a grappling hook with at least a hundred and fifty feet of rope. I know Kobe has both aboard the *Exoco*, which should still be docked there."

Jake glanced at his watch. "Tell Fernando to squeeze every ounce of speed he can get out of *Johnnie*. This vessel will likely be at Aquaria's southern perimeter by the time he gets back. Round trip shouldn't take more than an hour."

Zimbola was reluctant to leave, though he knew it would be unwise to question his friend's instincts and judgement in situations like this, knowing his partner was usually right most of the time, and following some minor bickering, finally jumped down into the moon pool to climb aboard Hercules' back. Pharah, however, was not so eager to join him, bearing the expression of a frightened child being led to the dentist's chair, and Jake had to literally shove him into the water to get him to go.

Thankful that both men finally disappeared below the waterline, Jake watched as Percy continued to jab away at the keyboard. Out of the clear blue an image of the remaining robo-fish suddenly flashed like a beacon in the back of his mind, and with it a bolt of raw, inexplicable intuition. Looking over Percy's shoulder, he voiced another question. "All your incriminating files on Maximus are stored in the remaining mechanical fish, aren't they?"

Percy stopped punching keys and turned his head, his expression filled with amazement. "How did you know?"

"Call it a wild guess," Jake muttered distantly as another idea came together within his thoughts. "I have one more request of you. That is, if you're willing to trust me."

Percy's reply came quickly. "Fire away!"

Chapter Fifteen: Bomb Found

Bolder reached the vertical manhole that rose up to connect with the offshore platform. Like the tunnel he had just traversed, it also appeared to be made of the same clear acrylic polymer material, giving him a three hundred and sixty-degree view of the undersea environment beneath the platform. Breathing hard and slinging the duffel bag he carried over one shoulder, he climbed the twenty rungs embedded on one side of the manhole. Ascending to the top, he turned the dogging wheel in the middle of the hatch that barred his way. It required little effort to swing it down, and he quickly hauled his bulk upward through the opening. On the other side was a maze of pipes, cables and electrical conduits that branched out in various directions before rising up through a ceiling that appeared to be constructed of the same sea cement Jacob had described during his interview with Amelia.

Taking a moment to study this elaborate but confusing network of interlacing components, he made his way forward. Even before he entered this area, the access tunnel's transparency had given him an excellent view of the seven huge pipes running parallel with it, and he could clearly see that they all connected with the massive substructure in which he now found himself. According to information Maximus had given him during their last phone call, the platform received vast amounts of hydrogen gas ducted into it. Housed within the substructure were chambers that burned the gas in order to raise the temperature of surface waters in Lulu Bay. Maximus had emphasized how this process was key to increasing the temperature differential between surface and deep waters that drove the OTEC turbines within Aquaria's central structure, making them even more efficient at producing electrical power.

But Maximus suspected another process that also took place on the offshore platform, informing Bolder that the natural fertilizer harvested on the nearby island was likely being supplemented by unknown ingredients prior to being shipped off to Haitian farmers, and it was these ingredients that made their food crops immune to the effects of the Omicron-7 compound.

Setting down the duffel bag and unzipping it, Bolder removed a small object contained within and clicked a tiny switch to the 'on' position before placing it behind a large grouping of ductwork. Satisfied that it was well concealed, he reached for the bag and made his way over to a grated stairway off to one side. Pleased with himself, he climbed the stairs, eventually reaching the top four flights up.

Finding himself in the small warehouse he had seen situated on the platform when he had flown over the complex, he glanced around. Bags of what he assumed to be fertilizer were stacked up on pallets along three walls. Within their midst sat a forklift with its forks lowered and nearly touching another pallet loaded with a low stack of small wooden boxes. He judged them to be about twelve inches on a side and slightly more than four inches high. Curious as to what the boxes contained, he stepped closer and leaned over to inspect one of the topmost boxes, which had a hinged lid secured by a small hasp-like fastener.

Unsnapping the hasp and lifting the lid, his eyes bulged in astonishment at what lay inside. Within the box lay three gold bricks. Assuming the recessed lettering spelling 24 karats stamped on the highly polished surface of each brick was for real, he was looking at gold in its purest form.

Awestruck, Bolder stared for a few more seconds before trying to heft the box, gripping the wooden handles that jutted from each side and finding that it hardly moved. Gold, he knew, was heavier than lead, far heavier. Shifting his stance, he placed his feet on top of the stacked boxes and re-gripped the handles, throwing his back into to the lift and using all his bull-like strength to raise the container from the pallet. His eyes widened, certain the weight was close to four hundred pounds. No wonder there were so few boxes on the pallet, he thought. Too many would have exceeded the lifting capacity of the forklift.

Setting the box back down, his mind abruptly surged into high gear. If his calculations were correct, he might be able to come away with seven boxes of the precious metal, and that would be cutting it close. Aside from what he was to be paid for his part in the mission, this was to be a windfall bonus he had least expected.

Whirling around, Bolder eyed the three large articulated roll-up bay doors that provided access to the platform deck. All were in the closed position. Striding quickly to the nearest one, he activated the switch that raised it. A low hum ensued as the jointed panels began to slide upward on their rollers. Bolting back to the gold-bearing pallet, he placed the duffel bag atop the boxes before hopping onto the forklift and turning the starter key. He was familiar with operating forklifts, having operated one during a summer job in his youth when he had loaded trucks at a plant in Michigan that manufactured car batteries. As it rumbled to life, he eased the forks under the pallet, raising it no more than six inches above the floor, intent on keeping the center of gravity low as he moved the load. Looking behind him, he backed the forklift through the bay door and out onto the deck.

Mat climbed up through the manhole to find the hatch open. Cautiously he poked his head up through the opening, glancing around sharply looking for an ambush. At seeing no-one, he pulled himself the rest of the way through, taking a moment to reseal the hatch and dog it off.

Puzzled as to what Bolder was up to, his mind continued to rove over several possibilities when his cell phone suddenly vibrated. Pulling it from his pocket, he saw that the incoming call was from Ez.

"Bolder is out in the open on top of the platform," Ez informed him. "I can see him clearly. He used the forklift to move a pallet of the gold we use for bartering out onto the deck."

Mat knew Ez was accessing Aquaria's camera system, which would give her views of the platform from various angles. Some of the cameras were located on the platform while others were mounted high up on Aquaria's central structure. "What's he doing now?"

"He has some kind of gadget in his hands. A close up view suggests it to be some kind of remote control."

This puzzled Mat even more, but Ez interrupted his thoughts before he could voice another question.

"The IBC chopper is lifting from the pad. It has no pilot, so it's probable Bolder is controlling it with the remote."

"Where's the chopper headed?" Mat blurted.

"Directly for the platform!" Ez said.

"It's obvious he's looking to get away from here-" Mat's words trailed off as he realized there could be only one reason why Bolder had come this way. "Because he planted a bomb," he added flatly to complete the sentence.

A helpless feeling accosted him as he considered the consequences that would befall the colony if his speculation was true. Even a small detonation would trigger a chain reaction in the hydrogen gas being ducted to the platform. The explosion would be disastrous. Not only would it completely obliterate the platform, but it would also likely destroy the intake pipes leading to the OTEC generators, at least a portion of them. Without power, the colony's operations would come to a complete halt, and it would take months to repair the damage and get the facility up and running again.

Mat looked around in desperation, his eyes roaming searchingly over the forest of conduits and cables that lay all about him. If there was a bomb hidden among this hodgepodge of components, he had to find and disarm it immediately.

From the bridge of the *Carl Sagan*, Captain Delila watched the two massive AW101 choppers lift from the carrier to ferry their contingent of Navy Seals in the direction of Aquaria. Moments later, the Russian-built Hind carrying the UN's Special Envoy rose from the deck to follow in their wake. Delila had a bitter taste in his mouth. One look at Malikai Allotey and the hard looking men accompanying him only tended to further confirm his suspicions that something was amiss with this whole operation. And a surreptitious sideways glance at Lieutenant Myron Johnson during their short meeting with Allotey told him the Navy Seal officer felt the same way. It was obvious Johnson did not like the pompously arrogant Allotey or the Chilean commando hovering at his side. What was the Chilean's name? Delila searched his memory, trying to recall it. Ah, yes, now he remembered. It was Alvarez, Captain Francisco Alvarez. His dislike of the man suddenly intensified. He had sensed a suppressed viciousness in Alvarez's manner lurking just below the surface, suggested by the way he had fingered the haft of the sheathed *corvo* slung from his belt. Undoubtedly Alvarez would be merciless and cruel in a fight, and he couldn't help but wonder how many men the man had killed with that blade.

The U.S. senator tagging along with Allotey only tended to increase Delila's growing uneasiness over this whole affair. Paunchy and square-jawed with a thick crop of silver hair far too neatly trimmed to be natural, Senator Brent Van Heflin seemed especially eager to get a firsthand look at the secrets Aquaria held. Delila had studied him surreptitiously during the meeting and he sensed an inordinate amount of corruption lurking just below the surface of the man, so much so that he could have sworn he had actually smelled it wafting off him as he climbed back aboard the Hind to embark for the floating city.

Delila sighed. Unfortunately, he had his orders, and those orders specifically stated that Allotey was to be in overall charge of the mission, a mission that reeked of conspiracy. Allotey had called for a slight change in the mission, though Lieutenant Johnson's team would land on Aquaria's central structure to secure it as originally planned. The second team, however, led by Ensign Patrick Flynn, was to land on Navassa Island to secure the buildings and the tramway leading to the offshore platform.

In the distance directly above the floating city, movement abruptly caught Delila's attention, and he lifted a pair of spyglasses to his eyes. A small helicopter had taken off and appeared to be headed toward the island. Studying it a moment longer, he lowered the glasses.

For a man his age, he had exceptionally good vision, and seconds later he brought his eyes back to something else he had been monitoring. A ship he had noticed earlier was moving steadily closer to the floating city, though ever so slowly. Looking through the glasses again, he assessed the magnified view. A frown came to his face as he studied it. There was something odd about what he was seeing. The vessel appeared to be drifting sideways against the wind. With its starboard side facing him, he saw it was now directly off Aquaria's southern breakwater. Carried by the breeze, clouds of mist swept over her superstructure from behind to partially obscure it, adding to his puzzlement. Continuing to focus the glasses, he began to discern huge shapes bunched together near the vessel's bow and stern. A pod of whales was roiling the sea, hundreds of them breaching and spouting as they disappeared on the opposite side of the ship.

Captain Delila turned to address one of his officers approaching him, a young ensign displaying a befuddled demeanor. "Have you been able to raise that ship, Mr. Jefferson?"

"No, sir, they won't acknowledge our call. Don't you find it odd that they're drifting into the wind?"

Delila shook his head slowly, his lips forming a small humorless grin. "Not at all when you realize a herd of whales is pushing her."

Jefferson stared back at the captain, an implacable though dubious expression suddenly coming to his face. The possibility that his superior might be entering the first stages of senility entered his mind.

At reading the look, Delila handed him the glasses. "See for yourself," he offered, not taking any offense at his ensign's dubiousness.

An abrupt transformation in Jefferson's bearing took place as he focused the lenses, his mouth falling open in astonishment. "Why would whales be pushing her, sir?"

"I don't have the foggiest, Mr. Jefferson."

Delila was about to order him to send up a small drone to get the name of the vessel, but at that moment the ship swung around.

"What name do you read on her stern?" asked the captain.

"Looks like *Numquam Satis*," Jefferson replied as he handed back the glasses. "Sounds Latin."

Bringing the glasses back to his eyes, Delila confirmed the name before turning back to his ensign. "Run a check on her, Mr. Jefferson," he ordered. "I'd like to know who owns her."

An odd name thought Delila as Jefferson walked away. He had studied Latin as an elective when he had attended the Naval Academy. Whoever had named the vessel Never Enough had to be one greedy bastard. Dismissing the notion, he redirected the glasses toward the floating city's central structure, noting that Johnson's chopper had already set down on one of its landing pads. Swinging the lenses left, he saw that the other AW101 had now reached the island. As for the small chopper that had taken off from Aquaria moments earlier, he observed it just coming to a hover directly over the offshore platform.

Mat moved quickly among the network of interconnected components, searching for the bomb. Unfortunately, no cameras had as yet been installed at this level of the substructure, so Ez could not tell him where to look.

"I believe you're getting warm," Ez advised him soothingly.

"What brings you to that conclusion?" Mat said irritably, not understanding how Ez could remain so calm under the current circumstance.

"My sensors have picked up an anomalous signal. The source of it seems to be originating close to your location. Move left twelve feet, I'm tracking your cell."

"I don't see anything," grumbled Mat testily upon following her directions.

"You're almost on top of it."

Mat eyed some ductwork before him, extending his arms and groping around blindly on the side opposite him. His hands immediately fell on something, and carefully he pushed it, finding that it moved.

"I think I found it," Mat said in a hushed, constrained voice. Cautiously he eased the object past the duct where he was able to view it. Resting on its base stood a shiny cylindrical canister about eight inches long with a diameter half that. A light at the top glowed red, blinking on and off in measured pulsating cycles. Next to the light was a tiny toggle switch, and next to that was a small LED timer steadily ticking down. At the moment it showed five minutes twenty seconds.

Slowly, painstakingly, Mat pulled the object toward him, keeping it upright and making sure to slide it. He couldn't be sure it was not fitted with a concealed spring-loaded trigger on its base that would set it off once it was lifted from the floor. He knew that most land mines were designed this way.

"Ez, I'm sending you a picture," he said, aiming the tiny camera of his cell at the device. "Give me an assessment. If it's a bomb, it appears to have an arming switch, but I can't be sure I won't detonate it if I flick it in the opposite direction." He could not rule out the possibility of such an event. A deviously minded bomb builder might actually incorporate such a feature into the design. If this were the case, once it was armed it could not be disarmed.

"Has Bolder landed his chopper?" asked Mat hurriedly as he eyed the cylinder nervously, knowing it would not distract Ez from carrying out the assessment. He was well aware that Ez was capable of carrying out hundreds of tasks simultaneously.

"It just set down," answered Ez. "He's moving the gold into it. I'm surprised he's able to lift those boxes by himself. Each weighs slightly more than four hundred pounds."

"How you doing on that assessment?" Mat pressed anxiously.

"I've accessed the worldwide web including the data banks of the CIA, NSA and FBI and find nothing that matches the object, but if it's a bomb made for remote triggering, it's a foregone conclusion that it would be suicide for Bolder to detonate it before he's clear of the platform."

"There's something else you should know," Ez added. To Mat, her tone had changed, now sounding downcast. "Two large helicopters have taken off from the aircraft carrier. One of them has already landed on Helipad Eighteen and has disembarked what I believe to be U.S. Navy Seals. The second one is just beginning to set down on Navassa."

"How do you know they're Seals?" Mat demanded in surprise.

"They wear the Special Warfare insignia, the Trident."

A plan suddenly emerged in the back of Mat's mind, and he made a decision. Slipping the knapsack Samuel had given him from his shoulders, he pulled out the cloaker and donned it quickly, listening to the faint hum it emitted as he turned it on. Staring down at the device at his feet, he took a deep breath, then lifted it.

Mat expelled a sigh of relief, somewhat surprised that he was still alive.

Chapter Sixteen:
Ez Hacks in

No sooner had the EC 135 set down on the *Kraken's* more than ample landing pad, Maximus hopped out, striding briskly with head lowered to get away from the whirling blades. In moments he descended the helipad steps, quickly making his way to the ship's bridge. As he entered the cavernous helm, a huge, bearded individual with leonine features turned to regard him. Sporting a thick, shaggy mane reaching to his shoulders and dyed a striking russet through periodic applications of henna, had the man been transported back in time and festooned with a horned helmet rather than a captain's cap, he would have perfectly matched the classical image of a seafaring Viking preparing to sack a coastal village. Grim-faced with a ruddy complexion, the man's deep-set, squinty eyes blazed with a fierce intensity that suggested a cruel nature, though this was somewhat offset by an impossibly large bulbous nose that bulged comically from between them, giving him the appearance of a circus clown when he was not frowning. Captain Rufus Finley's demeanor, however, was anything but clownish as he ran his ship with all the tact of an oppressive tyrant.

"What's our position?" Maximus demanded, ostensibly eyeing three rough-looking individuals manning the bridge under Finley's watchful eye. Their sole function was to monitor readouts displayed on an assortment of computer screens dominating several control panels. As Maximus well knew , their presence was merely a safety precaution as the entire ship was fully automated and, in theory, could have been run by one man.

"Right where you want us, thirty-two nautical miles northeast of Navassa Island," Finley said courteously, making an effort to suppress the gruff edge he normally carried in his tone. Malcolm Maximus was the only man he allowed himself to take orders from.

"Good," Maximus rasped. "Continue to hold this position for the time being. If necessary, use your bow and stern thrusters."

Finley nodded. "How much longer before Aquaria is secured?"

"Not long. The task force has already deployed the Seal teams."

"You don't see them as a problem?" Finley asked solemnly.

Uncharacteristically, Maximus let a sly, demonic grin flourish on his face. Normally he refrained from displaying a show of emotion. "They have no idea what awaits them."

Finley stared fixedly, waiting for Maximus to tell him more, though he suspected it had something to do with what the ship carried.

"I assume our additional cargo is in full readiness," said Maximus.

"Yes," answered Finley, continuing to stare expectedly. When Maximus failed to divulge more, he turned his eyes away. Though his curiosity was whetted, he knew not to press. If his boss wanted to provide details, he'd tell him.

Maximus dropped the grin, deciding not to elaborate. Sometimes he was better off keeping certain things to himself. Though Finley was an underling, he was also a confidant, one of the few men he made privy to his primary objectives and how they came together to form the grand scheme. The man was intelligent, pragmatic, and above all else, loyal. Nevertheless, in this case he would keep all details of the plan to himself. All Finley had to do was mind the *Kraken*.

Maximus liked surrounding himself with big, physically intimidating men. If anything, men like Finley were a reflection of his own power, which was far-reaching if not altogether omnipotent. The thought made him think of Swensen. As soon as this was over, he would find a replacement. Men like Swensen, he well knew, were easy to find as long as you had the means to pay for their services. With such individuals, the lore of money trumped morals and ethics. They were like big trustworthy lapdogs, willing to carry out any type of act no matter how heinous and ruthless it tended to be.

"What's the latest on the Ebola outbreak in Africa?" Maximus asked.

"It's reached pandemic status," said Finley. "Cases are now being reported in Europe and the United States."

Maximus' grin returned. Agents of *The Order* had planted the virus in Guinea three months earlier, and now it was spiraling out of control, reaching Sierra Leone and Liberia in rapid succession before finding its way to other parts of the globe. It was just one more of his ingenious schemes to bring on panic and confusion that would further subjugate people while solving a major planetary problem. Governments throughout the world would have no choice but to enact martial law in trying to contain it, but their efforts would ultimately fail. The virus was a genetically modified and laboratory-grown strain even deadlier than its predecessor. Due to the major medical infrastructure challenges that existed in Western Africa, it was the ideal locale for initiating a pandemic. Reversing the mushrooming population in Africa had been one of *The Order's* primary goals for many years now, but only recently did his pharmaceutical laboratories finally develop a reliable vaccine to combat the virus. Prior to that he had dared not tamper with releasing it, though he could not guarantee it would not mutate into something even deadlier where there might be no defense against it at all. But with recent projections showing the population within the African continent would grow by another two billion by the year 2050, he was now willing to take that risk, especially since he stood to make a financial killing on the sale of the vaccine, which he would sell to desperate governments at astronomical rates.

Maximus knew that the mere mention of human population control in any form was considered ruthlessly barbaric and unjust by philanthropic thinkers, a nefarious and unholy undertaking that greatly exceeded the bounds of moral rectitude. Nevertheless, it was something that had to be done if the planet was to remain healthy, and he and his followers would do whatever it took to accomplish the task, resorting to the use of pandemics and eugenics to cleanse the earth of the useless eaters. As such, were not he and his followers the true caretakers of the world? Was what they were doing any different than what was done to other species of living organisms to preserve them? Weren't elephant herds periodically culled down to hold their numbers in check, purposely slaughtered in the game and wildlife preserves that abounded in Southern and Eastern Africa to keep them from completely stripping the land of all vegetation? Certainly it could be rationally justified as a merciful and proactive approach to keeping the elephants from slowly starving to death. Deprived of their natural food source, wouldn't they eventually die off if not for these measures? In addition, periodic culling served other purposes. Not only did it prevent other herbivores from going without food, it also reduced the number of potential hosts for spreading disease.

This train of thought made him think of his great grandfather with prideful admiration. Even back then scientists recruited by *The Order* had been experimenting with various deadly pathogens as a viable way of holding down population explosions during the industrial revolution, and it had been Marcais Maximus who had his minions unleash the Spanish influenza on the planet in 1918, killing off close to 100 million people across the globe. Having played a hand in instigating World War I, Marcais had timed the release of the virus to coincide with massive troop movements, relying on the close quarters of soldiers and modern transportation systems to hasten its transmission. The mass genocide he created, estimated to be somewhere between three and five percent of the world population at that time, made it one of the deadliest disasters in human history.

"Anything new on the Middle East?" asked Maximus.

"ISIS has executed two more, this time Christian priests. The backlash is just as you wanted. Western powers are starting to react, and the Islamic Revolution in Syria and Iraq is intensifying."

Maximus pondered the acronym, which stood for Islamic State in Iraq and Syria when translated to its English equivalent. What better time to have diversions like these? he thought cunningly. Through careful planning and implementation, he and his acolytes had been successful in manipulating geopolitical events so that the fascio-Islamic movement in the Middle East and throughout the world had continued to grow. Radical Islam was a most useful tool. This threat alone had allowed *The Order* to tighten the noose on all free societies through the use of massive government security measures aimed at keeping them safe from terrorism. But there had been a price. With the public embracing these seemingly beneficial measures, they failed to see the true diabolical nature behind the increased security imposed on them, and in the end, freedom had slowly been eroded. Liberty had been sacrificed for survival.

How easy it was to manipulate them, thought Maximus disdainfully. What was that phrase Benjamin Franklin had once said? Ah, yes, now he remembered. *Make yourselves sheep and the wolves will eat you.* The thought made him chuckle to himself. He liked being a wolf. More precisely, the supreme Alpha-wolf. Such status allowed him entitlements few human beings enjoyed. As the *Sublimis*, he lived the most lavish lifestyle imaginable, and the power he commanded knew no bounds. He had been born and bred for the position he held. He had been backed by the vast influence *The Order* wielded and provided the seed money to grow his sprawling financial empire into what it had become, and it was still growing. He had just turned six when his father had revealed to him who he was. He was the heir apparent to the position of *Lofty One*, the person *The Order* called the *Sublimis*. He belonged to a privileged clan, a plutocracy whose ancestors could be traced all the way back to the Pharaohs of Egypt and beyond. Attaining power and wealth had been easy for the clan once they had learned how to manipulate the masses through subterfuge and cunning, and as time went on they had developed it into an art form. The clan had been a major force in shaping world events throughout recorded history, going by various names during different periods, with the Hermetic Order of the Golden Dawn, Knights Templar, and Illuminati being three of them. And now they were called *The Order of the Righteous*, but for the sake of brevity, most members simply referred to themselves as *The Order*, including the *Sublimis*. Many of the rich and famous throughout the world, both past and present, had been bred by *The Order*. But maintaining total control had not been easy, and at times had been lost. They would have succeeded in attaining their goal of a one world government seventy years earlier through the rise of the Third Reich, but unfortunately Hitler had been defeated. Nevertheless, they had regrouped, and as the world population grew so had their numbers, with members of *The Order* now carefully planted within the governments of every major power on the planet.

As it now was, *The Order* only needed one more major terrorist attack to be carried out in the U.S. in order to force the use of martial law that would finally put an end to the nation's Constitution once and for all.

For starters, the Second Amendment would be immediately abolished and all registered firearms seized to ensure that no resistance by the population occurred. Citizens would be defenseless. It was imperative that political upheaval of this magnitude was necessary if *The Order* was to succeed. Once things settled down, martial law would be lifted to allow the presidential election that had been suspended to finally take place, thereby clearing the way for Van Heflin to occupy the Oval Office. And when that happened, the old American republic everyone remembered would cease to exist. Free speech would become a thing of the past. Severely weakening the foundations of the only remaining superpower on the planet would pave the way for the one world government it so desperately sought.

Though it had been a test run, the Boston bombing had clearly shown how easily a major U.S. city could be locked down. Ratcheting up a police state had to be done delicately, incrementally, in order to determine how far the government could go without the masses rioting in response. Suppression of freedoms had started to gain pronounced traction shortly after the attack on the World Trade Center. Through careful coaxing by embedded members of *The Order*, Bin Laden and his radical Islamist followers had been used and manipulated into carrying out the murder of thousands. Pat downs, body scans, and searches of air travelers at airports by TSA officials had immediately followed to ensure public safety. The planning for this, he well knew, had taken years in the making, but it had nevertheless worked beautifully, using the power of big government to target the people. Continue to frighten them with staged security alerts and events, and they gladly submitted to increased security measures. Nazi Germany had carried out similar ploys, only it had terrorized its citizenry at gunpoint to consent to illegal searches and violations of their privacy in order to guarantee no one would oppose it. Knowing such tactics were now only a short step away gave Maximus comfort. He was well aware of the widespread complacency and apathy that currently existed in America, and he was convinced the time was now ripe for change, draconian change. People had become so ignorant of their rights and powers that they would practically submit to anything the government forced on them.

But he had other schemes afoot throughout the globe. Invoking a controlled chaos worked wonders, and in spite of the recent setbacks he was forced to endure, he knew the time was right to orchestrate events aimed at creating as much international turmoil as possible. As intended, these events would certainly dominate the news media and shift public attention away from another of his primary goals, one of them taking control of Aquaria. But he had to do it in a covert manner, one designed to delude the masses and further mold world opinion. The fact that Percy Osgood had absconded with incriminating evidence on *The Order*'s objectives continued to irritate him, and he had to remind himself that it was he who controlled ninety percent of the major news outlets throughout the world. Gaining dominion over the remaining media holdouts was already in the works, and he knew that it wouldn't be much longer before he had total control over all of them, either through corporate hostile takeovers, outright bribery too difficult to refuse, or by planting moles in high-ranking positions on editorial staffs. Maximus' grandfather, Marauda Maximus, had given Hitler a valuable lesson on the effectiveness of the media in consolidating power. Control it and you control the people, making them so brainwashed with propaganda that they lose their ability to think clearly. Whatever information Percy held would be suppressed and refuted as nothing more than far-flung conspiracies aimed at undermining the honorable reputations of Plagiarius and Unus Universitas.

Pacified by these thoughts, Maximus stepped closer to Finley, locking unwavering eyes on him. "I'll let you in on a little secret," he said. "A sub belonging to Iran has joined the task force. It's under the command of Captain Sayyari Habibollah, a low-ranking member of *The Order* who will be answering directly to me."

Maximus glanced out one of the bridge windows, a wide expanse of Plexiglas that gave an unimpeded view of the ship's rear deck trailing away to a distance of a half-mile. Turning around, he glimpsed the tanker's bow section reaching out over the sea another half-mile. With such an enormous vessel he had thought it prudent to position the bridge amidships when the design of the ship was first conceived, otherwise navigating through tight channels would have been exceptionally difficult. Using its incredibly powerful bow and stern thrusters, the tanker could be made to pivot on its central vertical axis much the way a locomotive could be rotated on a railroad turntable.

Staring beyond the bow, Maximus searched the horizon, unable to discern the pinnacle of Navassa's old lighthouse. Finley had done a good job, he had to admit. The *Kraken* sat just beyond the reach of Aquaria's line of sight sensors. Even if they had thought to place a radar dish atop the lighthouse or the floating city's central structure, they would be unable to detect the world's largest ship.

Maximus gazed behind him again, eyeing the EC 135 sitting on the landing pad as his pilot tied down the main rotor. Below the pad, he saw that Alex was just climbing into the cab of a monorail car used for rapid transit of the ship's vast infrastructure. The two guards with him climbed in behind him, and a moment later the cab shot away, disappearing into a tunnel that would take the trio into the bowels of the vessel. Having been involved in the *Kraken's* design, he had made sure to have a monorail network incorporated throughout the ship, connecting with the various decks and the key sectors within those decks. At the moment he envisioned the cab descending to the tanker's lowest level.

Shifting his gaze, Maximus fixed his eyes on another whirlybird squatting low and unmanned on a second helipad situated a little further back from the EC 135, this one an ancient Jolly Green Giant that had supposedly seen action during the Vietnam War. He knew the people who flew it, bounty hunters, a husband-and-wife team he occasionally contracted to carry out nefarious jobs. According to the husband, the chopper had been won in a high stakes poker game, appropriated from a former CIA operative. The aircraft would have fallen into the hands of advancing North Vietnamese Army regulars as spoils of war if not for the quick thinking of the operative, who had used it as a means of escape during the fall of Saigon in 1975. With barely enough fuel in its tanks, the operative, a seasoned helicopter pilot, had been able to reach the safety of Phnom Penh, Cambodia. Not wanting to part with the sizable asset the chopper represented, he had arranged its shipment to Manila in the Philippines where it had been used for transporting illicit drugs.

"When did they arrive?" asked Maximus.

"An hour ago," grunted Finley. "That should give them a good head start on the softening process."

"Come with me!" Maximus ordered, spotting the hatch bubble of another monorail cab sitting along a far wall. "Let's see if our young protégé truly wants to join us."

Once Finley settled his large bulk into one of the cushioned seats across from him, Maximus pushed several buttons, sending the cab on its way. Smoothly and soundlessly, it moved forward several feet before pivoting to keep its orientation upright as it dropped through an opening in the deck. The sensation of falling was immediate as it plunged downward in the manner of a high-speed elevator, and Maximus studied the green readouts that showed the deck numbers flashing rapidly by as the cab descended lower. Beyond the cab's transparent bubble, blue lights set up in the tunnel walls whisked past at periodic intervals, and in moments the cab slowed, then pivoted another ninety degrees before speeding up again along a level stretch of rail. Seconds later it decelerated quickly, coming to a complete stop as though cushioned by a wall of marshmallows.

As soon as the bubble rose, Maximus's ears perked. Loud screams knifed the air before trailing away. Climbing from the cab, he walked through the sliding door that accessed a dimly lit corridor. This was the area of the ship set up for interrogation.

Maximus glanced up. Suspended from the high ceiling was a 36-inch steel pipe that ran along the length of the passageway. It was held in place at periodic intervals by 2-inch diameter steel rods that hung down on each side to connect with a semi-circular cradle supporting the pipe. When needed, tons of seawater water could be forced through it each second by powerful pumps.

"Which cell?" Maximus asked, frowning at how quiet it had become.

Finley indicated the middle of the corridor. "Third one down."

Maximus nodded in acknowledgement. He should have known it would be that one. The third one was the only cell rigged with the specialized equipment. Electro-shock torture could be highly effective if administered properly, and the twosome he had hired were experts at it.

Entering the room, Maximus took in the scene at a glance. With both guards next to him, Alex stood mute, watching in fascination as a nondescript, heavyset man rested his hand on a throw-switch. Seated side-by-side and strapped tightly to abutting chairs with wires and clamps attached to their arms and feet, two men appeared exhausted, their faces streaked in sweat as they gasped for air. Probes were attached to the chest and head of each man, feeding physiological information to a nearby computer.

The man at the throw-switch glanced over at a woman monitoring the computer. She had long chestnut hair hanging limply past her shoulders, part of it covering the left side of her face. Maximus knew the hair covered scar tissue overlying a deformed cheekbone that three operations involving the latest breakthroughs in plastic surgery had failed to correct. In their profession, things sometimes went awry no matter how meticulously a kidnapping was planned, and two years earlier the woman had ended up on the short end of an undertaking that had gone terribly wrong. Up until the accident, Dr. Gladius Jester, M.D., had been an attractive woman. Both her and her husband had been interrogation experts with the CIA, but upon retirement had offered their skills to various governments as bounty hunters.

"Heart rates came close to pegging out, but you can increase the voltage," Dr. Jester said, her lips parting to reveal a set of perfectly straight teeth that Maximus knew to be dental implants. She had been monitoring the readouts with a predatory look on her face.

The man turned a nearby knob, prepared to throw the switch again.

"Are our guests cooperating?" Maximus rasped, seemingly catching the man by surprise with his sudden arrival.

Herbert Jester turned. "Good to see you again, Mr. Maximus." He returned his gaze to the two men strapped to the chairs, speaking glibly in the manner of a boy enjoying a day at the amusement park. "Didn't get 'em to crack yet, but I believe we're getting close."

Maximus stopped him before he could close the switch. "I want you to let the lad here do it."

Herbert shot him a puzzling look before sizing Alex up and down. "Fine by me," he said, a touch of disappointment evident in his tone. Unenthusiastically, he stepped aside to make room for Alex. "Make sure to open the switch when she tells you," he instructed Alex halfheartedly, "otherwise you might end up killing them, and that's something we don't want until we get the information we're after."

Alex did not move. Turning, he gazed dumbly at Maximus, confusion clearly showing on his face.

"He doesn't understand a word you're saying," Maximus informed Herbert. "You'll have to speak Russian if you want him to understand."

Herbert nodded, repeating himself as instructed. Russian was his second language, having been stationed at the U.S. Embassy in Moscow two decades earlier.

Alex stared at the man, a look of comprehension descending on his features. He moved forward and placed a hand on the switch but hesitated, turning to look back at Maximus once again.

Maximus rasped harshly. "Move away if you're not up for-"

Before he could finish the order, Alex threw the switch. A barely perceptible spark arced as the conducting metals came together.

Screams immediately erupted from the men strapped to the chairs, their bodies juddering convulsively as the current surged.

Maximus studied Alex, noting the sadistic look clinging to his face. Yes, he decided. Already the lad was proving himself to be a foot soldier. *The Order* always has need of followers, men that were unconscionable, ruthless, and willing to carry out orders without question. He would need replacements for all the men he had recently lost, though Alex would need careful honing.

"Stop!" the woman blurted.

Obediently, Alex opened the switch, though he would have preferred to keep it closed. The screams of the captives excited him.

Herbert moved to hover over the nearest captive. "Are you ready to talk, Baptiste?" he said softly.

Sweat poured profusely from Emmanuel Baptiste's forehead and temples. He was gasping hard in an effort to catch his breath. "Go...to... the devil!" he managed to utter.

Herbert swung his gaze to the second captive, a short pudgy individual. "What about you, Hennington?"

Chester Hennington's eyes rolled in their sockets before steadying. "You're... wasting your time...a thousand deaths are preferable to telling you."

Maximus spoke up. "Why be so stubborn, gentlemen? Aquaria is now under UN control. Whether you divulge the information or not, the troops will eventually discover where you mine the gold. Is it on Navassa?"

Maximus had known about the gold long before Van Heflin had brought up the subject during the meeting in Cardoza's castle, but he had kept that knowledge to himself. He had never considered that some of it might be stockpiled near Malique until the senator had conjectured about it, but with the loss of Swensen and his elite security force in that godforsaken cove, he would now focus his efforts on locating it in the floating city or the nearby island. It had to be there, he reasoned. The grandmother of those brats had been evasive when questioned about where it was mined. He clearly remembered her words. '*Gaia provided it*,' she had told him. Tossing the conundrum aside, he thought about his last minute decision to have Van Heflin accompany Allotey during Aquaria's invasion, wondering if it had been a wise move after all. Almost immediately he chastised himself. No, the decision had been a good one under the present circumstances. With Van Heflin being head of the senate's prestigious Science and Technology Committee, the media would be used to put the senator's participation in a positive light, one that might enhance his image all the more during a run for the presidency. Van Heflin would be portrayed as a staunch champion of the planet, leading the charge to take on any and all abusers of the environment.

Maximus broke from these thoughts, aware that the captives were not cooperating. In a voice that magnified his growing rage, he said, "I ask you again, where is your gold mined?"

It was Baptiste who spoke this time, his tone strained and faltering. "It is only the powerless that can be manipulated and used as cattle by men like you, but we are not powerless." Torture was nothing new to him. Both he and his wife, Lucette, had been tortured unmercifully at the hands of the now dead Colonel Ternier before being saved by Javolyn and the dolphin women, but he knew rescue would not come this time.

Maximus glanced over at Herbert Jester, the pent up rage building within him finally reaching its limit. "Maximum voltage!" he screamed.

"You risk killing them," the woman cautioned.

Maximus ignored the warning, turning to Alex instead. “Fry them!”

Alex grinned, more than happy to comply, but as he threw the switch the lights went out.

Maximus froze as the interrogation cell was plunged into total darkness. Except for the startled breathing of those around him, a deafening silence descended. Even the soft background hum of the generators that normally reverberated at this level of the ship was now gone.

Finley’s voice resounded in the pitch blackness. “We seem to have lost power, but the emergency lighting will kick on in a moment.”

No sooner did he utter the words, the room was once again bathed in light, though the illumination was much dimmer than before.

“Why have we lost power?” Maximus railed, unable to accept the chain of disrupting events plaguing him.

“I don’t know,” was all Finley could offer. Puzzled, Finley moved to a wall intercom. In a flustered voice he hailed the bridge, speaking quickly. “This is the captain. We have no power down here. What happened?”

The voice that came back was clearly nervous. “We don’t know, sir, the problem is throughout the ship. All the generators have stopped working, and so have the three engines. We’re attempting to run a diagnostic to pinpoint the problem, but it seems the entire computer system is locked up.”

“That’s impossible,” Finley snapped. Sweat began to bead on his forehead. The tanker was fully automated. Almost every mechanical system aboard it was controlled by two linked mainframe computers. Without them, the ship would not be able to hold its present position. The enormous vessel would become nothing more than a drifting hulk.

“I wish I could give you better news,” replied the bridge. “We’re trying to re-boot the system. Without it we cannot locate the problem.”

“Keep me informed,” growled Finley.

An ominous feeling of total vulnerability began to take hold of Maximus as he listened to the conversation. Surely this on top of everything else could not be happening. And yet it was.

Maximus turned wrathful eyes on Finley as though he were the cause of the system failure. "Get up to the bridge and find the problem!" he scolded as though speaking to a child. "I want this ship back in working order immediately."

Finley's face clouded. He did not like being reprimanded in this manner, especially in front of the others. Holding back a biting retort, he simply nodded. "I'm on my way," he grunted, quickly exiting the cell.

Needing to vent his fury further, Maximus turned a ferocious gaze on the two captives before shifting it to Alex. "I thought I told you to fry them!" he hissed.

Anxious to please his new mentor, Alex closed the switch again, but no spark was visible this time as metal met metal.

Maximus stared in expectation at the men strapped to the chairs but saw no torment in their faces, nor quivering in their bodies.

"There's no power," Herbert pointed out in a near whisper.

"Stay here!" Maximus screamed. "All of you stay here until I get back." Like a madman he tore from the room and made his way to the remaining bubble cab. With his emotions running wild, he pressed the buttons that would take him to the sector of the ship he sought.

Chapter Seventeen: Chopper Destroyed

In another sector of the *Kraken* on the lowest deck farther astern, an electronic deadbolt clacked loudly when the lights had gone out. Hearing this, a lone figure suddenly stirred within the holding cell imprisoning him. He knew what the sound implied. With a loss of power, the lock would release.

Even before the emergency lighting kicked on to dispel the enshrouding coal-black darkness, he sprang from the cot to push against the hinged bars entrapping him. If he failed to act quickly, he was certain the lock would re-engage, and he would miss his chance to escape. Unable to see, he misjudged his leap, chipping a front tooth as his face slammed up against the bars, but the pleasure of triumph was more than enough to transcend his pain as the cell door swung open.

With his thick eyeglasses askew and nearly dislodged from the collision, he repositioned them on the bridge of his large jutting nose and stepped clear of the cell, all the while running his tongue over the jagged edge where the tooth had broken. Groping about like a blind man, he began feeling his way along a wall just as the lights came back on accompanied by the sound of synchronized clicks.

Looking down the length of the passageway, he realized he had been right about the lock. Only one other prisoner had thought to do as he did, noticing that the man being held three cells further up was also free while eight others gripped the rigid bars confining them. Too late, they pushed and tugged on the bars like frenzied berserkers, but the doors would not budge as all the locks had re-engaged.

At five feet six and one hundred fifty-five pounds, he was not a very big man, but sustained imprisonment and the painful things they had done to him had tempered his resolve to kill again. Ever since they had brought him here they had fed him almost nothing, barely enough to keep him alive, and he was famished. Strangely though, he had this hankering for a handgun, but a fire axe affixed to the wall opposite his cell would do just as well. He had been eyeing that axe ever since they had put him in the cell, probably a week earlier he guessed as he had lost all sense of time during his confinement. Whiling away the hours he had stared fixedly at the axe. Though it had been beyond his reach, it invoked memories of his life back in Ankara when he had chopped up six graduate students with a similar weapon at the university research facility where he had worked before setting off to a nearby mosque. There he had slain eight more people, randomly choosing victims before hacking them to death as they kowtowed in worship with rumps in the air and foreheads touching prayer mats.

Still holding the axe in bloodied hands, he had made his way into a crowded marketplace not far away where he had run amok, indiscriminately killing another ten people, all the while keeping a running body count in his head. After that he had lost all sense of himself, and by the time the authorities caught up with him, it was speculated he had murdered as many as forty-three people, though they could not prove all of his crimes as they had only recovered a total of twenty-four bodies, most of them in pieces. Vaguely he remembered running along a riverbank on a moonless night, every so often coming across a person or two out for an evening stroll. These he had dispatched quickly before hurling their remains in the fast-flowing water.

The memories abruptly dissolved as he became aware of himself pulling the axe he had been eyeing from the wall. Ambling up to the lone prisoner who had managed to escape his confinement, he acknowledged the man with an affable smile just before swinging the axe.

Satisfied, Peyami Pehlivan made his way down the corridor, wondering who he might encounter next.

Bolder climbed into the pilot seat of the IBC News chopper and strapped himself in. Pulling up gently on the collective, he tested the additional load, almost sensing the weight of the gold tugging back tenaciously against the upward thrust of the main rotor. With the chopper refusing to rise, he eased more pitch into the blades, willing the aircraft to break the anchoring grip of gravity, but still the chopper refused to lift. Anxiously he glanced at his watch, immediately seeing he had little time left to clear the platform and get out to a safe distance. With less than a minute left, he knew he would be cutting it close. The thought that he might have overestimated the weight he could carry descended on him with a frightening cruelty, and he knew there was no time left to lighten the load.

With the cold hands of fear gripping him, he applied yet more pitch, and this time he felt the airframe shudder sluggishly as it broke free of the deck. Rising to a height of ten feet above the platform, he gently pivoted the aircraft around, prepared to move it laterally out over the water, but as he did so a figure suddenly materialized on the deck in front of him.

A look of surprise came to Bolder's face as he realized who it was. The man he had knocked cold was staring up at him, waving goodbye with a savage grin stretching from ear to ear.

You stupid bastard, Bolder thought smugly. *You have no idea what's going to happen, do you?* Chuckling to himself, he steered the helicopter clear of the platform, slowly gathering air speed. In seconds he was skirting the island, moving east past the old lighthouse to gain distance from the impending explosion. Looking to his left, he glimpsed the huge helicopter that had set down on the island near the warehouses. The invading force of soldiers appeared like tiny ants as they fanned out among the buildings to secure the island.

Bolder expelled a prolonged sigh of relief. The fear that had galvanized him moments earlier was quickly ebbing, displaced by a deep sense of contentment and accomplishment. With all the gold he had gotten away with, he was going to be a rich man. An *exceptionally rich* man.

Just as he reached seventy knots, he became aware of a sound. Though it was subtle and erratic, it was a sound he should not be hearing. Puzzled, he shot a concerned glance at his instrument gauges.

Nothing was showing in the red. The turbine was not overheating, and the RPMs were right where they should be.

As the aircraft gathered speed, the unfamiliar sound grew louder. Listening carefully, he was convinced it was not coming from the power train but from somewhere lower, further back. Maybe he had caught onto something with one of the skids while taking off. Yeah, that had to be it, he reasoned. Feeling he was at a safe enough distance from the platform, he slowed the chopper to a speed where the passage of wind would allow him to open the door and locate the cause.

With the reduction in air speed, the inexplicable banging lessened. Leaning his body out the door, he turned his head and peered back at the undercarriage. His heart nearly seized in his chest as he saw what had made the sound. Dangling from the pilot-side skid by a short length of rope was the bomb he had left to destroy the platform. Pushed back by the wind, it quivered and jerked on its tether to batter against the skid.

Bolder's scream never cleared his throat as the bomb exploded. The chopper disintegrated, raining charred bits of metal, torn flesh, and chunks of molten gold into the waiting sea below.

Captain Delila scanned the far side of the island through the spyglasses. Straining his eyes, he had been able to identify the logo on the small helicopter. Out of curiosity he had been monitoring it every so often for the last several minutes, following its flight to the offshore platform and then watching it lift off again to make its way past the old lighthouse. But without warning it had flared, consumed in a coruscating fireball of expanding gas.

"Sir, am I seeing things or did that helicopter just explode?"

Delila turned. Ensign Jefferson was gazing past him with a befuddled expression.

"Yes, it was a news chopper representing the Interregional Broadcasting Company," answered Delila grimly. "Too far away to tell if it was shot down, though."

"Strange that you say that sir."

"Say what, Mr. Jefferson?"

Seeing no more debris falling from the sky, Jefferson settled his eyes on the captain. "That it was an IBC chopper." Clearing his throat, he sought to bring light to the confusion registering on Delila's face. "I was able to confirm ownership of that ship, but I had to really delve," he said, looking in the direction of the *Numquam Satis* for emphasis. "Working through a maze of twelve shell companies, the search finally ended at a multinational conglomerate called Unus Universitas. Nine corporations stood in the way of revealing the true owner of IBC News."

Delila nodded slowly, his mind trying to make a connection between the ship and the destroyed chopper but unable to come up with one. Thinking about the name of the conglomerate, he quickly worked out the translation. One World. He could only guess that whoever had named the ship had also named the conglomerate. It was obvious that person had a fondness for Latin. He glanced in the direction of the mega-yacht. It was much closer now, still being pushed into the wind by a vast herd of whales.

"Nice work, Mr. Jefferson. With any luck, maybe we'll find out what that vessel is doing here."

Jefferson gazed past the captain again, pivoting his head in another direction. "What happened to the subs?"

Delila swept his eyes over the sea. His junior officer was observant, he thought. *Iron Fist* was now gone, and so were the two Varshavyanka class submarines sent by Venezuela. "I wish I knew," the captain said uneasily. "Unfortunately, they are under the direct command of the envoy the UN sent to take charge of this mission."

"Beggin' your pardon, sir, but that man gives me the creeps, and so do the men with him. Shall I have the techs engage the sonar in active mode to track the subs."

Delila gave a slight shake of his head, speaking softly. "No, son. Keep it passive. Active can be quite harmful to sea mammals, and the sea around us seems to be crawling with them."

Being a man of sound environmental convictions, Delila would refrain from using the carrier's low-frequency sonar unless absolutely necessary, knowing the danger it posed to whales and dolphins. Better known as SURTASS LFA in naval circles, or Surveillance Towed Array Sensor System, Low Frequency Active, it could produce as much as 215 decibels of intense sonic wave energy capable of producing emboli, or gas bubbles, in the organ tissue of marine mammals at close range like this. Whereas active sonar sends out a sound pulse to be reflected back from an object to calculate its distance as well as direction relative to the sender, passive sonar only listens to sounds emitted by the object to determine its direction. Thus, passive cannot tell a listener how far away the object is.

Jefferson blushed abashedly. He should have known better. He knew about the captain's concern for sea creatures, especially when it involved cetaceans. Delila had once related a story to him. An avid surfer in his youth, the captain had grown up in Southern California where he had learned how to ride the waves. It was during an outing along Manhattan Beach that an exceptionally large shark had taken a bite out of his surfboard. The shark had been quite aggressive, and if not for the intervention of a passing school of dolphins which drove it away, he was certain he would have become the predator's next meal.

"You're right, sir, I wasn't thinking," said Jefferson. "But isn't it a certainty that those subs will be using it?"

Delila shrugged helplessly. "Unfortunately, yes."

Chapter Eighteen: World's Largest Ship

Jacob peered out one of the windows to his tower office, watching the remnants of Bolder's chopper rain down into the sea. Swiveling his head, he brought his gaze to Amelia, who had witnessed the same thing in stunned amazement.

"Someone paid your cameraman to blow up our shipping platform, but apparently the effort backfired on him," remarked Jacob. Moments earlier, Ez had apprised him about what Mat had done.

"But why the platform?" questioned Amelia. "If he was intent on sabotaging something, wouldn't this structure be a better target?"

"It's obvious they wanted this structure completely intact. Their objective was to temporarily stop our power production and to halt further exports of the enhanced *guano* fertilizer we routinely send to Haitian farmers."

Jacob looked away to plop down wearily at his desk, prepared to await the arrival of the invading troops. He had instructed Ez not to put up any resistance, including using the non-lethal multi-beam microwave technology she had previously used to drive away Malikai Allotey and his goons.

The familiar holographic image of Jacob's deceased grandmother suddenly coalesced before him. A smile clung to her broad face. "I have just received what you might call some eye-opening news," she said. "It seems to fit in well with your conspiracy theories."

"Please tell me," Jacob replied.

"As you had already been informed, in destroying Cardoza's compound, Jay Jay rescued a man by the name of Mortimer Osgood.

Mortimer had been kidnapped by Cardoza and was being held hostage in order to force his twin brother, Percy, to work for a man called Malcolm Maximus, an industrial magnate of incredible wealth. Aside from that, Mortimer had a cache of overwhelming evidence stored in a hidden electronic file to incriminate Maximus, Cardoza, and a broad list of accomplices involved in a plan designed to dramatically change the world as we know it."

"Where did you get this information?"

Ez's smile broadened. "A bluefin delivered it to me."

Baffled, Jacob's weathered brow crinkled. "A bluefin?"

"Yes, would you like to hear what I've learned?"

Jacob sat transfixed; his curiosity aroused. "Talk away, Ez, and don't hold anything back."

Having reached his destination in the bubble cab, Maximus climbed out. He was furious. Why the ship's sophisticated computer system would lock up defied reason, but the sector of the ship he was now in remained independent of that system and relied exclusively on a huge battery bank for its power needs that was altogether separate from the tanker's electrical grid, as did the vessel's monorail system. Coming to a bulkhead, he reached for a thick section of U-channel that appeared to brace the wall, swiveling it off to one side on a concealed pivot to reveal a small glass plate recessed behind it. Without hesitation he placed his right thumb against it. The plate had sensors that analyzed the DNA in his skin oil. He and Finley were the only ones it was programmed to allow admittance. A small LED light above the plate suddenly flashed green, and an instant later the bulkhead slid up.

As soon as he stepped through, the bulkhead closed behind him, confining him in a dimly lit space the size of a storage closet where a door barred his way. Bringing an eye to a retinal scanner next to the door, he heard a familiar buzz, and a moment later the door slid aside. Walking through, he stood in a glass booth overlooking an enormous chamber. It was a hidden area of the ship that should have housed crude oil, one the Coast Guard would never discover, even in the unlikely event the *Kraken* was to be boarded. Using the potent influence of high-ranking bureaucrats within the U.S. government, both the *Numquam Satis* and the gargantuan oil tanker were essentially made off limits to the long arm of the Coast Guard.

Looking below him, Maximus set his gaze on the huge oblong craft just over 300 feet in length. It was supported on cradles, its hull painted a dull metallic gray. Several men were just climbing aboard, entering through a hatch atop a conning tower situated amidships. This was the third Russian-built Varshavyanka class submarine purchased by Venezuela. *The Order* had been successful in entrenching *fifth column* elements within the government of the oil-rich South American country, spreading corruption around like a virulent plague among its high-ranking officials, and he had taken full advantage of the economic toll such corruption brought to the nation. Knowing it could ill-afford the insane cost of another naval vessel, he had stepped in to broker the purchase by offering the Venezuelan government shipments of pure gold bullion to be used as payment for the sub. His only stipulation was that he would have clandestine use of the vessel and its crew for a period of three months following its delivery. Desperate to increase its military assets, the Venezuelans had agreed, and negotiations with the Russians for the third vessel had quickly ensued. With world currencies being rapidly devalued by irresponsible governments around the globe, the Russians were quick to take the bait, turning the sub over to the Venezuela in good faith without any cash exchanging hands up front. They would instead accept pure gold bullion in three separate installments at later dates.

The gold, however, was to come from Aquaria. Once Maximus gained possession of it, it would be melted down and recast into bars with cores filled with tungsten. And if the Russians discovered the swindle, the blame could be cast on Tursiops. This would be a plausible explanation for the Russians to accept in light of the IBC's spurious smear campaign that depicted Tursiops to be run by crooks. Hadn't it already been shown that the budding enterprise had financed construction of the floating city by bartering with what amounted to watered down gold? Aquaria's unprovoked attack on the *Southern Star* had been broadcast worldwide, revealing the sea colony's motivation in capturing the freighter. The sea colony needed the tungsten the ship carried to produce more counterfeit bullion. Certainly the Russians could not hold Venezuela responsible for some of this fake gold falling into their possession. Gold bullion switched hands all the time, often making its way through international exchanges much like paper currency.

Another objective concerning Aquaria's gold entered his musings. The sea colony was flooding the market with huge quantities of it, and that was a good thing. It took the pressure off the Federal Reserve Bank and its counterpart, the European Central Bank, to ease up on their short selling. Working in conjunction with the major bullion banks, they had been routinely dumping some of their physical stores of precious metals and gold-based derivatives in order to keep the price down in the face of widening economic rifts in global economies. Artificially manipulating the gold market was in *The Order*'s interest, and with *fifth column* operatives firmly embedded in each of these powerful financial institutions, they were able to do just that. But once investors realized a glut of fake gold was finding its way into international markets, the price per troy ounce would go even lower, much lower. When that happened, agents of *The Order* would move back in to buy up as much of the commodity they could get their hands on by going long on futures contracts, ultimately controlling most of the world supply. In fact, that was another of *The Order*'s goals, eventually obtaining and holding onto as much genuine gold as possible. Then it would lower the boom by orchestrating several international calamities in concert to destroy both the dollar and the euro once and for all. As it now was, the Federal Reserve had possession of practically all the gold that had once filled the vaults of Fort Knox, and with the value of major currencies having been dramatically devalued through overly excessive stimulus policies by both the Fed and the ECB designed to lure as many investors as possible back into the stock market, the price of bullion would skyrocket to stratospheric heights once a huge sell-off in equities ensued.

A dark smile consumed Maximus' features as he continued to dwell on the carefully crafted plan. Like always, a catastrophic event would be needed to trigger that sell-off, one that was rapidly approaching. It would bring down global markets yet again. And in knowing precisely when that event was to be triggered, members of *The Order* stood to siphon off a good portion of the world's wealth by short-selling equities just before it occurred. The economic chaos brought on would force a merging of the largest banks on earth. The Fed and the ECB would consolidate with the World Bank and IMF, forming the most powerful financial institution ever devised by man, with a new currency emerging that would become the predominant medium of exchange. Once this happened, the world would quickly change, for the bank rising from the ashes would become the cornerstone of the global government *The Order* had been seeking. Almost overnight, the UN would be transformed to become that government. Nations that refused to conform would not be issued loans to keep their economies going.

A remembrance of the *Southern Star* being sunk turned Maximus' smile sour. He had almost forgotten. Huge stockpiles of tungsten had been part of the cargo Cardoza's freighter had carried. He would have to obtain more.

Depressing a button on the console before him, he brought his lips close to a microphone connected to a loudspeaker. "I trust everything is in full readiness, Dante?"

The trailing man climbing the conning tower glanced up in surprise to espy Maximus looking down at him. This was the sub commander, a Venezuelan that had spent the last six months of his life in Kola Bay, Russia, learning how to operate the submarine. Like many of the henchmen Maximus used to carry out his schemes, the man was physically large, almost as big as Finley.

Dante nodded. A dour smile took shape on his swarthy features, conveying to Maximus that he was eager to get on with the mission. Maximus had originally planned to have Dante spearhead the government coup scheduled to take place in Port-au-Prince, but recent setbacks pertaining to a takeover of both Haiti and Aquaria had forced this revised mission on the man.

Maximus nodded back grimly before checking the Emperador Temple strapped to his wrist. It was now time to launch the sub. The bomb Bolder had placed had undoubtedly detonated by now. Once activated, it had sent out a signal that Maximus received just before he had landed on the *Kraken*. The bomb had originally been intended for blowing up another section of pristine reef, footage of the event to be documented by Bolder to further bolster world outrage directed at the colonists. He had wanted Aquaria entirely intact and undamaged, but recent events had necessitated this change in plans. While inbound for the *Kraken*, he had contacted Bolder again, redirecting him where to place the bomb, informing him about the subaqueous access tunnel his mechanical fish had documented on video. With Bronte Pharah currently unavailable and possibly dead back aboard the *Numquam Satis*, he had decided to destroy the offshore platform to stop the transshipment of the enhanced *guano* fertilizer to Haitian farmers. Once Aquaria was secured, the platform along with the damaged water intakes could be repaired and brought back online.

Bringing his lips back to the microphone, Maximus heard the echo of his own voice as it reverberated ominously within the cavernous chamber. "I'm opening the bay doors. Do not fail me!"

Dante nodded again as he climbed through the hatch and dogged it off.

Maximus nudged a switch that opened a valve, and within seconds the lower portion of the chamber began to flood with tons of water pouring in each second. Rapidly the water rose to engulf the sub's hull, upon which the eight enormous berthing clamps holding the vessel in place disengaged as a gargantuan pair of hinged doors swung down to reveal an inky blackness below them.

Satisfied that the sub had successfully launched, Maximus closed the first switch and thumbed another, watching as the bay doors pivoted back up slowly. Once they closed, a set of powerful centrifugal pumps whirred to life to empty the cavernous chamber, quickly driving the water through a 36-inch pipe and back into the sea.

Anxious to get an update from Finley, Maximus contacted the bridge. "Status?" he rasped.

"We were able to re-boot the mainframes," Finley proclaimed proudly. "All power should be restored in a matter of moments."

Keeping his tone stern and intolerant, Maximus asked, "Any idea how the failure occurred?"

"Yes, we were hacked."

Maximus gritted his teeth, knowing only one man had the technical knowhow to get past the supposedly unbreachable firewall that had been incorporated into the ship's mainframes. And he had done it from one of the many computer terminals stationed aboard the *Numquam Satis*.

"If we were hacked, then it's possible we're going to be boarded by attackers if we haven't already," Maximus snapped. "Make sure everyone on the bridge is heavily armed," he quickly added before exiting the booth.

Going back the way he had come, he made his way hastily through the two hidden doors before emerging past the bulkhead. Quickly, he moved to another nearby bulkhead to swivel another section of U-channel aside to reveal a hidden glass plate the size of a credit card, placing his thumb against it. This one was programmed to allow only one-person access, that being him. As the panel slid up, he set his eyes on what lay on the other side. A gloating smirk came to his face. Here was his insurance against possible invaders boarding the *Kraken*.

Phillipe studied Destiny's mother as she sat on the white sand bordering the cove's limpid water. "It doesn't feel right staying here when Jay Jay needs our help," he grumbled peevishly, unable to comprehend how she could appear so calm at a time like this.

Amphitrite did not offer a reply. Though she was aware of his concern, she kept her gaze fixed on the arching hues above the falls. So beautiful, she thought. She was seeing one of nature's gifts, serenity and beauty arising out of chaos. There was violence in the water. It tumbled from great height to crash harshly into an awaiting pool to create a jumble of vortexes and eddies. And yet it sent a gentle blanket of mist into the air to disperse the sunlight into bands of color that soothed the soul.

Appearing pensive, Troy Jacob echoed Phillipe's apprehension. "Phillipe's right, grandma. We should go back to Aquaria."

"When the time is right," Amphitrite said softly. Continuing to stare at the rainbow, she suddenly discerned Esmerelda's smiling face within the mist. Jacob's deceased grandmother was nodding in agreement.

"Do you see her?" Amphitrite murmured, turning to look at Destiny sitting at her side.

"Yes," Destiny said.

"See who?" Melody asked. Perplexed, she turned to follow her mother's gaze. Abruptly her jaw dropped in astonishment.

"What are you looking at?" TJ questioned, but by the time he looked to where his sister was staring, the vision had vanished. "I don't see anything."

"It's something only girls can see," Melody teased smugly. "It's a secret that boys aren't supposed to know."

TJ was about to lash back at his sister, but the sound of splashing water diffused the tart retort he had in mind. Turning, he saw Phillipe was swimming out to the *Angel*.

A budding sense caused Amphitrite to reach into the pouch strapped about her waist. "Children, I have something for each of you," she said, producing a violet crystal in the shape of a small pyramid in each hand. Though she couldn't explain the why of it, she only knew the twins would need these.

Melody stared at the crystal held before her with adoring eyes before gently taking hold of it and cupping it in her hands. "How beautiful," she remarked in an awestruck voice.

"Wow!" TJ exclaimed, reaching for his. "What's it do?"

"It gathers in energy and will sometimes react to your thoughts," Amphitrite said, knowing the children had never seen these smaller versions.

"It looks just like the larger crystals being grown under the island," Melody uttered reverently, noticing that the pyramid was beginning to pulsate and grow brighter. She looked over at the one her brother was holding, seeing it do the same thing.

"Did these also come from the giant *thurentra*?" asked TJ.

"Yes," Amphitrite answered. "Hercules retrieved them the other day. Hold onto them, they're yours to keep."

As the children fondled the crystals, Amphitrite glanced at the two men in the dory at the base of the falls. Zimbola and Hector were busy filling ten-gallon cans with fresh water to replenish supplies aboard the *Angel*. Though there were massive quantities of water available to them in a much purer form back at Aquaria, the black giant claimed it lacked the therapeutic qualities contained within the cove's majestic falls. But she knew his true desire for the water. Zimbola believed the water held magical powers, and by filling the *Angel's* potable water tank with it, the water would protect his beloved vessel as well as those sailing aboard her.

In moments, Franklin strolled up to the group, giving his wife a look, which indicated he needed to talk. Rising from the sand, Amphitrite joined him, and together they ambled well away from the others, neither of them speaking for several minutes as they moved along the sand at the water's edge.

"You know as well as I we can't stay here," Franklin finally said.

Amphitrite glanced in the direction of Mortimer Osgood and Bronte Pharah, two distant figures who sat near one of the cottages set further back from the water. Both men seemed to have taken to one another and were passing the time in conversation over a friendly game of chess. Zimbola had arrived back at the cove with Pharah in tow a half hour earlier.

"What about them?" Amphitrite queried.

"Mortimer wants to join his brother."

"And the children?"

"They can remain back here with-" The din of an engine revving made him turn to locate the source. The inflatable water chute at the *Angel's* stern had been deployed, and an instant later the waverunner stowed aboard the vessel slid gracefully backward along its sloped surface to hurtle into the water. It sent a series of small waves rippling toward the beach. Sitting aboard Jake's STX-12F Kawasaki was Phillipe.

Franklin raised an eyebrow, blurting out the first question coming to mind. "What's he doing?"

Amphitrite immediately sensed Phillipe's intentions, and like the time before when she had airlifted an injured Bashir from the *Southern Star* and left Phillipe behind, she would once again avoid trying to stop him from following his own convictions. There was a cause-and-effect outcome in the balance here, and she had to let it run its course.

"He's taking the initiative," Amphitrite said.

Phillipe turned the Kawasaki around to glance briefly in her direction before gunning the engine and speeding toward the cove's narrow inlet that gave way to the sea, and she saw the small watercraft was fully armed. With its souped-up engine, she knew it was capable of covering the forty miles to Aquaria in a little over thirty minutes.

Franklin watched him race away. "He's heading for Aquaria, isn't he?"

Amphitrite turned to face Franklin, sighing deeply. "I'll crank up the chopper."

Franklin looked toward the falls. Even at a distance of several hundred feet, he could see Zimbola was not very pleased at seeing Phillipe leave like this. "I'll let Zimby know we're also leaving," he said. "Destiny and the twins can stay here with him."

Amphitrite held his gaze a moment longer. "No, tell him Destiny will be coming with us."

Franklin stared back thoughtfully before nodding slowly in understanding. "I'll tell him but he's not going to like it."

Twenty minutes later, the twins waved goodbye as Amphitrite guided the Bell Ranger over the western ridgeline of the chasm.

Pouting, Melody turned to her brother and said, "I want to go back to Aquaria."

TJ eyed Zimby placing the filled water cans on the *Angel's* swim platform. At the moment, the Jamaican giant had his back to them. "If we hurry, he'll never know we're missing."

A mischievous grin broke out on Melody's face, and she waded out into the water to grab hold of her bond mate. TJ did the same, and within seconds they were both fully submerged and heading toward the inlet leading to the sea.

Chapter Nineteen: The Order Revealed

Zipping over the ocean surface at 120 miles per hour, the Bell Ranger overtook Phillipe ten miles from Aquaria. Phillipe looked up, continuing to barrel over the sea at full throttle as Amphitrite brought the chopper in low. Franklin opened the side door and leaned out of the co-pilots seat, pointing to the radio mic he held in his hand. Slowing the Kawasaki's rate of travel, Phillipe nodded. Bringing the small watercraft to an idle, he pulled the Motorola radio from a storage compartment and attached it to the bracket on the console. Depressing the transmit button, he spoke irritably, raising his voice to be heard above the roar of the rotor blades.

"Don't try to stop me!"

"We're not, son," Franklin replied. "We're also going to Aquaria. I guess I don't have to remind you it might be dangerous." Pausing, he studied the resolute look on Phillipe's face. "We're going to fly ahead. I'll keep you informed about what's going on."

Phillipe nodded in understanding as Amphitrite dipped the chopper's nose to gather airspeed. In seconds the Bell Ranger gained altitude, rising high into the sky.

Fifteen minutes behind Phillipe, the *Exoco* skimmed over the calm sea, the hull of the sleek craft riding atop its dual hydrofoils. Melody stared ahead, then turned her gaze to the driver, a pudgy Haitian with a seemingly perpetual grin plastered on his face. Truth be told, Melody could not remember a single time when the man did not smile. It was as though the act of living was a constant delight to him. Kobe was always fun to be around. He was the *Exoco*'s skipper, assigned to the task of making regular runs between Aquaria and the Haitian coast. Riding their bond mates, the twins had been fortunate to catch up with him just as he was steering the vessel away from Malique's main pier.

Melody shifted her attention to Bashir sitting reclusively and pensively on a cushioned chair bordering the starboard window. He seemed to be fully recovered from his injuries, though his outward manner suggested he was mired in deep reflection. Like her and her brother, she knew he was yearning to get back to Aquaria. Having been dropped off at Louwanda's home in Malique and placed under the woman's doting care, he had recuperated quickly over the last day and a half. Not one to sit idle, he had offered to assist Kobe on one of his regular runs to Gonaives to drop off bottles of hydrogen gas and bags of fertilizer to several farmers that lived on the outskirts of the coastal city.

Standing on the other side of Kobe, TJ asked for the fifth time in the last ten minutes, "How much longer, Kobe?"

Maintaining his signature smile, Kobe glanced down to read the restlessness showing on the boy's face. "Mon, you gonna be old before your time with so much impatience bubbling within you," his words accentuated heavily with a thick island accent that sounded Jamaican.

Abashed by the gentle chiding, TJ turned his gaze aft to check on the dolphins, currently immersed in three separate holding tubs filled with seawater. The tubs had been purposely designed to carry members of their species aboard the high-speed hydrofoil. Not wanting to be left behind, Phillipe's bond mate, Perseus, had accompanied the twins during their escape from the cove and was now occupying the middle tub. While it would normally take the albinos a little over two hours to make the swim between the sea colony and Malique, the *Exoco* could make the crossing in one-third that time when sea conditions were accommodating as they were today. Hydrogen gas powered the vessel, as it did most of the watercraft owned by Tursiops.

A moment later the *Exoco*'s radio came alive. "Angel to *Exoco*, come in *Exoco*!" The caller's voice was deep, gruff, and brimming with anxiety.

Kobe reached for the mic and brought it to his lips. "*Exoco* back at you," he answered happily, glancing at the twins as he spoke. "What you need, my Sasquatch friend?"

"You see two little ones scootin' along on their dolphins?"

Melody stared up at Kobe with pleading eyes, putting her hands together as though in prayer and shaking her head fervently.

Kobe hesitated, holding back a reply, his smile taking on a slight waver. Turning, he looked at TJ, who was doing the same as his sister.

"You copy me, *Exoco*?" Zimbola came back, his tone now booming and filled with alarm.

"*Exoco* copies you, Zimby. Are you referring to that waggish duo, those two gremlins belonging to Jay Jay and Destiny?"

"Yes, Kobe, you see them?"

Kobe shot a sly wink at the twins, then forced a series of staccato crackles and hisses from between puckered lips. He was the colony's resident jester, a born comic known for his imitations of various sounds, especially when it involved emulating radio static. If you wanted laughs, just hang around Kobe and he'd give you an endless supply.

"You're break..hiss.. up, Ang..crackle..can't..ear a word you're. . .aying."

"Quit foolin' around, Kobe."

"..hissss..radio mus..hiss..ee..mal..unctioning."

Turning off the radio, Kobe regarded the twins suspiciously, still holding that ceaseless smile. "Now be honest with your uncle Kobe, what you imps up to?"

The twins had obviously come up with a whopper in order to get him to abet their little scheme. They had told him their father would appreciate him taking them and the three dolphins to within two miles of Aquaria's outer perimeter and drop them off. Jay Jay would be awaiting them there to escort them to the dolphin sanctuary under Navassa Island. Kobe was well aware that Aquaria was currently under siege by UN forces, having been informed of this hours earlier. For the time being the sea colony was a dangerous place, so once his passengers disembarked, he would head for Gonaives, his original destination before the children had caught up with him.

"They wanted us to stay behind with Zimby in the cove," both twins chorused, "but we want to help them."

"Your parents?"

"Yes," Melody said, speaking for both of them. "Both Mumsie and Dadoo are doing what they can to keep invaders from harming the colonists."

Melody was surprised to see Kobe's smile fade.

"I'm sorry, children, but I can't be responsible for droppin' you into a hornet's nest." Movement on the aft deck suddenly caught his eye, and he saw all three dolphins pull themselves from their holding tubs. Using their prehensile limbs, they walked themselves to the vessel's stern and leapt into the water even though the craft was barreling along at a high rate of speed. As if on cue, the twins bolted after them, moving quickly to the *Exoco*'s rear.

"Children, wait!" he shouted in alarm, but seeing what they were going to do, he reached for the throttle and cut the engine. Although he knew the dolphins would likely forego sustaining any serious injury at hitting the water at such breakneck speed, he wasn't so sure about the children. The last thing he needed was the twins getting hurt, and he certainly didn't want Zimbola coming after him if this were to happen.

Both Melody and Troy Jacob looked back at him as the boat slowed quickly, their expressions apologetic. Suddenly aware of the situation, Bashir came out of his deep thoughts and sprang from his seat, only to pull up short when he realized it was already too late to stop them. Waving goodbye, the twins jumped clear of the stern just as the vessel settled its hull back in the water.

"Sorry we lied to you," TJ shouted as he and his sister straddled their bond mates. "Hope you're not mad."

Kobe opened his mouth to yell back, but before he could voice his objections the dolphins sounded with their charges only to leave ripples in their wake. Lifting his eyes, he espied the peak of Aquaria's central structure jutting above the horizon. Floating close to it were two large ships, one of them an enormous flat-top vessel.

Seated comfortably with three House members occupying the booth, Truman Hearthwatch, Green Technology and Climate Advisor to the President, continued to make his case. "...and so, gentlemen, it's crucial we push this bill through as quickly as possible."

The congressman from Idaho glanced furtively around the sports bar, suddenly feeling uncomfortable. It was early afternoon in the U.S. Capitol, and white-collar workers and bureaucrats of Washington's working class were beginning to crowd into the popular establishment situated a block from Pennsylvania Avenue. Although he had nothing to hide, conversations such as this were not meant for prying ears. Several people at the closest table, however, seemed to be engrossed in a news bulletin displayed on a 65-inch flat screen TV affixed to a nearby wall. Satisfied that he would not be overheard, he brought his eyes back to Hearthwatch, letting his concerns be known in a soft voice.

"A carbon tax is not going to sit well with voters. They've already voiced their displeasure with the country's state of affairs during the mid-term elections."

"I wholeheartedly agree," said the delegate from Iowa, also keeping his tone low. "Endorsing such a bill will amount to political suicide. My seat will be coming up for re-election, and I'd like to hold onto it."

Unperturbed, Hearthwatch brought his roast beef sandwich to his mouth and took a hefty bite, chewing the morsel hungrily before setting his gaze on the congressman from California. "What about you, Harry? What's your stance on this?"

The pudgy-cheeked representative from California's 8th District placed his drink back on the table and dabbed his lips with a napkin. "As long as it will bring jobs to my district, I'm all for it. I assume the government will be willing to fund the green techno startups with the tax money."

Hearthwatch smiled magnanimously. "Of course."

The Idaho rep eyed the California rep suspiciously. "Yeah, and what if those startups go bankrupt the same way several others did after the government bankrolled them? You sure you want to be embroiled in a similar scandal, Harry. It was a well-known fact those companies didn't stand a chance at competing with the Chinese even before those loans were given."

Hearthwatch followed the conversation with a calculating ear. It was going just as he had anticipated, one for and two against, but he had needed this informal meeting to confirm how the opposition would react. *The Order*, however, had ways of making them come around, and in these two cases it would be necessary to resort to blackmail. The wife of the Idaho rep was a cocaine addict whom they had lured into a compromising position using a handsome male stripper. Hearthwatch suppressed an urge to laugh as he thought about it. It had been easy for the male stripper to entice the woman into bed, after which it had only taken three trysts for the Adonis to get her thoroughly hooked on the drug, all of which had been recorded by hidden cameras.

It was just the reverse with the happily married Iowa rep with five children. A powerful tranquilizer had been slipped into his drink at a small, informal gathering of House members to discuss matters of national security. Later, he awoke to find himself in the sack with a prostitute. Once again it had all been recorded.

As for the California congressman, it had only taken a mere $20,000 along with a promise he would receive a sizable chunk of the government subsidies once the startups got their hands on the funds. This was how things were done in Washington these days in order to bring seemingly opposing sides to an agreement.

"The companies looking to take root in my district cannot possibly fail," Harry replied calmly. "They'll be manufacturing solar panels with three times more efficiency than the companies that failed, and with all the available cheap labor swarming across the border from Mexico, they'll be producing them at half the cost of the panels coming from China."

The congressman from Iowa appeared skeptical, raising his voice to be overheard above a growing hubbub. "Those failed companies made similar claims, Harry. No doubt these startups will promise the sun, moon, and stars to get the funding they want. Then when things go south, these so called entrepreneurs will walk away with millions in bonuses from the seed money given them just like the others did."

"You're mistaken," objected Harry, his eyes narrowing with pique. "I can guaran-"

"Sorry to interrupt you, Harry," the congressman from Idaho cut in, "but it seems our esteemed colleague here is being discussed on the news." He appeared amused as he first looked at Hearthwatch before staring back at the TV behind Harry.

Hearthwatch swiveled his head to follow the Idaho rep's gaze, glancing briefly at the TV before turning back and shrugging. "That doesn't surprise me," he remarked blithely. "Both the President and the press value my recommendations wholeheartedly. You can never take things lightly when it concerns the environment."

Mildly annoyed at being interrupted, Harry turned his head around briefly to catch a glimpse of Hearthwatch's image before turning back to his companions. "As I was saying…" His annoyance turned to indignation as he realized the other three men were no longer listening. Obviously distracted, they were focused on the mounting buzz that pervaded the place. Patrons all around them were speaking in agitated confusion before a hushed silence descended on the room as though by majority consent. Every person in the bar had their gazes fixed intently on the wide screen TV. An attractive newscaster was talking, her strawberry hair fluttering in the breeze. In the far distance behind her, an aircraft carrier could be seen floating atop a fairly calm sea.

"…and because of these lies and mass deception, I have renounced my affiliation with the Interregional Broadcasting Company. Better known as IBC News to the public, the acronym actually stems from the Latin term *Ineptio Beneticium Conservo*, which means playing the masses for fools to benefit a privileged few. For many years now, the IBC along with other mainstream news channels have been systematically engaged in a conspiracy so widespread, so iniquitous and insidious as to defy comprehension. But their dark secret has finally been unearthed and come to light."

Someone behind Harry spoke loudly. "What's she saying?"

"Shussh!" several people chastened in unison.

"But I-"

"Shut up and let me hear!" another scolded sharply.

"…infiltrated by members of this cabal, which seems to have its tentacles embedded in high positions of authority everywhere these days."

In San Francisco, a communications supervisor at IBC headquarters had to pull the phone away from his ear. An officer of the company was livid, screaming at him. "I don't know what happened, sir, we're trying to locate the problem," he was finally able to reply.

Another barrage of foul language immediately assaulted him, and he nodded vigorously. "Yes…yes...I know, sir, we…we've been trying to cut the transmission, but we're unable....no…we can't just simply pull the plug, the system is not set up that way…no, it's all controlled by computer…yes, I know it's supposed to be unbreachable…but…but… it's not just us, all the other stations are experiencing the same problem. We believe a hacker has found a way in. All the stations are airing the same thing."

Nearly deafened by the yelling issuing from the phone, the supervisor pulled it from his ear again. Exasperated, he finished the call by saying. "All I can tell you is we're working on it."

As Hearthwatch listened in stunned silence, all three congressmen turned to regard him as the woman on the screen launched into a list of names.

"…all of these officials have abetted Plagiarius, including Senator Brent Van Heflin, Chairman of the senate's prestigious Science and Technology Committee, and Truman Hearthwatch, the supposedly esteemed Green Technology and Climate Advisor to the U.S. president, a man who has been cleverly dubbed Earthwatch by the corrupted media. But these men are no such champions of issues seemingly aimed at safeguarding the environment. Beneath these carefully erected personas lay ruthless, diabolical rogues motivated by greed and an insatiable lust for power, them and all those they are aligned with. They are in league with a cabal that pushes for legislation which will impose yet another tax on an already overtaxed American public, a carbon tax to be levied commensurate with the size of carbon footprint a citizen or enterprise projects to the environment. On the surface, it would appear this tax is meant to curb the use of carbon-based energy sources responsible for the release of greenhouse gases. But this objective is merely a pretext for tightening the economic noose further, not only on the American people but on other countries of the world as well. Once passed into law, it is meant to become the standard for other nations to follow, ultimately to be enforced by United Nations sanction. And while there is a consensus among most scientists that an unrestrained discharge of greenhouse gases into the atmosphere will eventually lead to drastic climatic change detrimental to mankind, such an assumption has never been proven, though it has been aggressively promoted by this group of plotters who have spent hundreds of millions of dollars in creating a crisis quite literally out of thin air, propagating this hoax with nothing more than fabricated and embellished data."

The woman paused momentarily, a look of utter disgust evident on her face before going on with the commentary. "Plainly put, it is a scam. The individuals behind this scam have much to gain. At the heart of their aggressive promotion is a hidden agenda. These schemers stand to reap billions in profits through brokerage fees based on the trading of carbon credits, which are actually licenses to pollute. If such legislation were to be passed, the very use of electricity would be considered a form of pollution since the great majority of power plants rely on the burning of fossil fuels to generate electricity. As is obvious, factories and industry in general would ultimately be required to obtain these licenses in order to continue manufacturing, and these would be available for a hefty price and subject to an exorbitant brokerage fee. These fees would be passed onto consumers, who would also be subject to carbon taxation, causing the price of goods and services to escalate further. In essence, people would be taxed on the very air they breathe since the act of breathing causes the expulsion of carbon dioxide into the atmosphere. In the end, the wealth of both citizens and governments will be looted by these men. From what has been uncovered, this cabal seeks to bring down the American way of life through a systematic dismantling of the Constitution, the foundation upon which life in the United States is based. Senator Brent Van Heflin is currently being groomed and backed by this cabal to run for the Oval Office as an added measure to ensure this scheme becomes a reality."

As he watched and listened, Hearthwatch began to tremble with pent up rage. "Someone turn that lying bitch off!" he growled aloud, unable to control himself any longer.

"Shuddup!' someone hollered. "I wanna hear this!"

"...coupled with this desire to gain huge profits from the general population of the world is another agenda, one far more insidious and sinister, and that is the promotion of a global government." Amelia's voice rose with emotion. "Wake up people, your future is in jeopardy, dire jeopardy, for you are only a few steps away from total enslavement by this cabal. And while it won't be the type of enslavement you see in movies showing sweat-soaked, downtrodden toilers in loincloths being prodded along by overseers with whips, it will be enslavement nonetheless. With disposable incomes slowly eroded and stretched to the limit, the middle class will cease to exist. Reliance on government will be their only option if they wish to have a roof over their heads and food on their plates, but it will be a bare minimum. This scenario will be very similar to what coal miners had to endure when they were forced to rely on extended credit given them by the company store for all their needs. With their wages unable to keep up with living expenses, they fell further and further into debt, forced into bondage and forever indebted to the company that sustained them, obliging them to keep working for the rest of their days with no option for retirement. In such a world, the average person will become an indentured servant until they are no longer productive. Only two classes of people will emerge from the economic wreckage that will come from this tax, that being the rich and the poor, with indentured servitude becoming the norm among the lower class so that the rich can live in hedonistic comfort."

On the screen, Amelia Amhurst sighed with contempt. "Behind the scenes in shady back room deals and covert conferences held by conspiring plutocrats and elites, the UN is being methodically prepared to evolve into this global government. The push for this to happen rests on three main pillars, the first of them being the pretext of halting global warming. The other two are even more depraved. A dramatic reduction in the world population is the second of these pillars. These plotters believe this can be accomplished through a twofold process involving artificially manufactured pandemics in third world countries and massive crop failures on a planetary scale. Already they have the mechanisms in place to bring about these calamities, one of them being the Ebola crisis currently killing off thousands in North Africa. Several nefarious members of this cabal will be portrayed as saviors of mankind when they bring forth panaceas for remediating these problems, panaceas that have already been developed and are awaiting dispersion to the rest of the world. However, these same individuals will contend that the cost of producing these panaceas will be astronomical, thereby forcing additional financial burdens on already bankrupt governments in order to pay for them. This will trigger a global financial crisis that will set the stage for the third pillar, which will necessitate the creation of a global bank. By instigating these events, these schemers believe the surrendering of national sovereignties to the one world government can be achieved."

Amelia paused again, giving her audience a moment to grasp the full context of this disclosure. "We have learned the name of the man heading this cabal, an incredibly rich industrialist who prefers to remain in the shadows, a man who goes by the name of Malcolm Maximus. His followers refer to him as the *Sublimis*. It is a Latin term that means *Lofty One*. He is the Chairman of Unus Universitas, an immensely diversified conglomerate and the largest corporation on the planet. Within his vast holdings is the Plagiarius Corporation, which lies at the heart of this conspiracy."

As Amelia continued to speak, all three Congressmen eyed Hearthwatch as though he were toxic, and more and more patrons were beginning to take notice of his presence, suddenly aware of who was in their midst.

Hearthwatch leaned forward, bringing his voice to a panicked whisper. "Don't believe what you're hearing, it's nothing more than an attempt by the opposition to discredit me and stop passage of the bill."

His companions looked back at the TV, intent on hearing what else was being said.

"...seeing Tursiops Worldwide as a major threat to their global interests. A concerted effort has been underway for some time now by these plotters to vilify Aquaria." The image of Amelia abruptly vanished from the screen to be replaced by a succession of scenes depicting various facets of the floating city, Navassa Island, and the pristine tropical waters surrounding both. "By pulling strings with corrupted officials within the UN and the American government, they have coaxed military action upon its peaceful and environmentally conscientious inhabitants. At this moment, a UN task force is invading the facility to take control of it. I dare not..."

Standing on the bridge wing of the *USS Carl Sagan*, Captain Delila lowered the spy glasses from his face. Though he could have monitored the progress of the mission in high definition on a TV screen situated in the bridge, he preferred to remain outside in the breeze. Though it was hot, the smell of salt water in the air was invigorating.

"Sorry to bother you, sir," a voice at his back beckoned.

Delila turned. It was the young ensign again. "I think you should see something, sir."

"What is it?"

"If you'll follow me, I'll show you, sir."

Leading the way, the ensign brought him before the HDTV. "It came on of its own accord, sir, almost as though someone found a way into our system, but I believe it's worth noting. I've been recording it, so if you'd like to review the full context of what this woman is saying, it's all there."

Delila stared at the image on the screen, suddenly intrigued by the things being said.

Clearly outraged, Truman Hearthwatch arose from the booth. Feeling like an outcast, he eyed the audience of spectators and raised his voice loudly enough to be heard above the TV. "How dare this woman impugn my good name."

The closest patrons diverted their gazes from the TV to eye him coldly. "Charlatan!" someone shouted.

"Yeah, shut the hell up so we can hear!" another person growled.

Hearthwatch recognized one of his admonishers. It was a high-ranking bureaucrat who worked for the Office of General Accounting. Striding for the door to leave the establishment, he would make sure to do whatever it took to get the man fired.

Chapter Twenty: Scaling The Kraken

Within a half mile of the *Kraken* and ten feet below the surface, Jake emerged from the submersible nicknamed *Johnnie* and straddled his bond mate. Underwater visibility was exceptional, and with Achilles swimming along at full speed, they closed the distance quickly.

JJ, the ship has launched a submarine from hull doors located amidships, Achilles informed his rider.

How big? questioned Jake, scanning the hydrosphere before him in an effort to spot it.

Big, approximately three hundred feet in length. It's too far away now for you to see, but it appears to be heading for Aquaria. I have already alerted the pod.

It's obvious that ship is being used to carry more than just oil, Jake said. *Are the hull doors still open?*

We'll arrive too late to get into the ship that way if that's what you're thinking. Those doors have just closed.

Then I guess we're stuck with Plan A, Jake replied disappointedly. They would resort to the same method they had used in getting Jake aboard the *Southern Star*, only this time more rope would be needed to reach the main deck, which was slightly more than 130 feet above the water when the vessel was fully loaded. But they had come prepared. They had with them the required length of rope, and Jake knew where to go once he gained the main deck. Just before they had left the *Numquam Satis*, Percy had used the computer in the moon pool chamber to pull up plans of the *Kraken*, and Jake had committed Percy's instructions to memory.

"This is where you'll find them," Percy had said, pointing to a place where the bottom deck was located. He had placed a finger on another area on the main deck. "The ship has a rail system. There's a door here that will take you to a bubble car. It works pretty much like an elevator and operating it is quite simple, but two buttons have to be punched instead of one to let it know where you want to go." He scribbled something on a piece of paper, adding, "Just punch in these numbers and it will automatically take you there."

Jake saw the side of the mega-tanker's hull come into view. The sheer size of it was intimidating. *You sure you'll be able to do this, Achilles?*

Jake felt a sudden surge of indignation emanate from his bond mate. *Why must you always doubt me, JJ? If I said I could do it, I meant it.*

Okay, okay, just asking.

In moments they unraveled the rope in the same manner they had done before, but this time the technique would be slightly different. At the apex of Achilles' leap, the dolphin would hurl the grappling hook the remaining distance to the main deck. Then Jake would have the arduous task of climbing hand over hand much higher than he had done in scaling the side of the *Southern Star*.

Holding onto his end of the rope, Jake glimpsed Achilles shoot into the depths. With a much greater length of rope, the dolphin was able to go deeper, much deeper than what was executed at the *Southern Star*, and he descended to the rope's full length before turning and throwing the full power of his extraordinary muscularity into a rapid ascent. Up he rose, accelerating quickly and gathering all the speed he could muster that would set the stage for a spectacular leap. Breaking free of the ocean like a guided missile, he reached a height of ninety feet before the pull of gravity negated his upward flight. In that instant of time, a profound feeling of satisfaction and elation took hold of him as he sensed it was the highest he had ever jumped, but even before he reached the peak of his leap he was whirling the grappling hook in a sling-like fashion on eight feet of rope. Releasing it, he glimpsed it arc higher to go sailing over the ship's railing as he fell back into the sea.

Let's hope it grabs, JJ, he uttered just before hitting the water. Exploding past Jake by gravity-induced momentum, he trailed a plume of cavitated whitewater as he was driven deep.

Jake pulled in the slack and tugged on the rope. A smile came to his face as he felt it go taut.

You never cease to amaze me, my friend.

I told you I could do it, didn't I?

Yes, you did.

Jake surveyed the sea behind him just in time to discern *Johnnie* coast out of the gloom, the sub's maw beginning to open to release Hercules with a rider straddling his back. To convey to the rider they were set to go, he made a show of yanking forcefully on the rope and pointing upward.

Victor Belachek nodded back in understanding as Hercules handed Jake the plastic-wrapped Sledgehammer, a combat harness, and a rucksack filled with gear. With Achilles lending support, Jake strapped on the additional items, aware that they would add an extra seventy pounds to his own weight once he exited the water. Removing his swim fins, he handed them over to his bond mate.

Fully armed in the same manner when he had invaded Maximus' mega-yacht, Jake pulled himself to the surface, and as he did so, Achilles intruded on his thoughts.

You sure you can make it to the top, JJ? It's a long way up and you're carrying a significant load.

Now who's doubting who, wise ass? Jake shot back, grumbling out the thought as he hauled himself clear of the water.

Bracing his booted feet against the tanker hull, he began pulling himself up hand over hand, the sinew in his chiseled arms rippling like slithering serpents from the strain. This was going to be a new challenge, one he wasn't sure he could overcome as he felt the incessant, unyielding pull of gravity begin to take him to the far reaches of his physical limits. But giving up the effort and quitting was a notion completely foreign to him, and despite the fact that his forearms, biceps, and lats began to burn with a leaden fatigue that grew painful, he continued to heave himself higher. Finally reaching the main deck, he slithered over the top railing and lay on his back, gasping for air and giving his aching muscles a chance to recover.

The area of the ship he had chosen to scale had not been randomly selected. Percy had recommended a place where Jake would go unobserved from the *Kraken's* bridge. Though Percy had managed to hack into the ship's computer system and shut down most of the systems, including the camera network, Jake would need large deck fixtures to shield him from vigilant eyes located higher up.

Feeling himself quickly recuperating, Jake removed a device from the rucksack. It was a small electric winch, one of several auxiliary winches normally stored aboard *Johnnie*. But a power source would be needed to operate it. Looking behind him, he spotted an outlet. It was right where Percy said he would find one. Percy had been thorough, for once he had realized what Jake planned to do, he had performed a final task on the moon pool computer before they had vacated Maximus' yacht, scrolling through the *Kraken's* immense electrical grid to locate a working outlet in the area where Jake would reach the main deck. With Percy having disabled the ship's primary generators, Jake had been skeptical about the plan, but Percy had assured him the auxiliary system would kick in to provide Jake with the power he would need.

Pulling the power cord free of the winch, Jake plugged it into the outlet and tested the device. Immediately, it hummed to life. Satisfied, he turned it off and secured it to the lowest railing with two hooks attached to it. Turning it back on, he began playing out the one-eighth inch braided cable, extending his head out between the rails to observe the end of it eventually drop into the water. Letting out ten more feet, he turned it off.

Several moments passed before Achilles petitioned him. *Victor is ready, JJ.*

Jake turned the winch back on, retracting the cable. Victor had openly admitted he could not possibly make the climb. Well into his forties and a good fifty pounds heavier than Jake, not to mention the additional gear he carried, he knew he would need help to reach the main deck.

Another minute passed before Victor was crouched beside Jake. "You ready," Jake said, noticing the intense look the Russian commando displayed.

Hissing out the words with gritted teeth and murder in his eyes, he said, "Let's get my son back."

Jake pointed aft, showing Victor the door that led to the bubble car.

Captain Delila continued to watch and listen to what was being broadcast on the Military News Channel, a deep foreboding chill creeping up his spine as he took in all the things the newswoman was saying.

Standing at his side, Ensign Jefferson spoke up. "She's on all the major networks, sir. It's obvious she's broadcasting from the floating city. You can see our ship behind her in the distance."

"...aside from these despicable acts of treason, these men have used their influence to initiate a UN task force to take control of Aquaria. The man in charge of this task force is Malikai Allotey, Special Envoy to the United Nations' Council on World Ecological Affairs, a newly created branch within this world body that was purposely slapped together within recent days to justify the takeover of the sea colony. Acting as agent for the UN for many years now, Allotey has a long history of heinous indiscretions that have allowed him to walk away with millions of dollars while carrying out missions under the UN banner."

A recent though unflattering photo of Allotey replaced Amelia's animated personage as she spoke. "From the start, men like this have routinely infiltrated the UN to severely corrupt an organization originally established for the betterment of mankind, placed within its ranks by members of the cabal plotting for world enslavement." A line of alphanumeric characters began to march across the bottom of the screen. "What you're seeing below Allotey's image is the coded username and password for accessing his account in the Deutsche Bank of the Cayman Islands where he has stashed more than seventeen million dollars while carrying out his illicit activities. During Saddam Hussein's regime, he was heavily involved in the oil-for-food scams Iraq's former dictator perpetuated, and while he was in charge of UN troops in the Congo, he extorted sex for food from children and exchanged ammunition for ivory with rebels who slaughtered elephants in the Virunga National Park."

Another photo came to the screen, this one showing a swarthy individual with a heavily pockmarked face. "Assisting him in carrying out most of these malicious crimes is Captain Francisco Alvarez, a professional mercenary hired on by the UN to enforce its agendas. While working with Allotey, he was directly responsible for the massacre of seventy-eight innocent villagers in Rwanda fourteen years ago, and during a peace-keeping mission in Uganda a year later, forty-two people mysteriously disappeared under his watch."

Delila stared in stunned silence as he assimilated these revelations.

"Sir, I knew there was something about that guy that didn't feel right," Ensign Jefferson grumbled softly. He turned to study his captain. "What are you going to do?"

Amelia continued to speak, reading the handheld teleprompter given her by Jacob. "At this moment, the inhabitants of Aquaria are not putting up any resistance as they come under attack, but it seems the man leading the invading task force has more in mind than taking control of the facility. He is looking to confiscate Aquaria's wealth before an official tally of its assets can be made."

Delila pulled his gaze from the TV, his features suddenly reflecting anger. "Get on the radio and call back the Seal teams. We're aborting the mission."

A smile of genuine admiration broke out on Jefferson's face, proud of his commanding officer's decision. "I don't think it will do any good to remind you that you risk a court martial for disobeying orders, sir."

Exiting the bubble car, Jake crept stealthily along the dimly lit corridor. With Victor behind him, he came upon the second of the interrogation cells, which proved to be empty. Jake pulled up short, giving Victor a hand signal to do the same. The layout was just as Percy had described and a stark reminder of the way Colonel Ternier's torture chambers were laid out when he had rescued Emmanuel and his wife from the clutches of the psychopathic colonel and his depraved mother years earlier. And now he was doing it again, only this time Chester Hennington and Victor's son, Alex, were to be additional torture victims instead of Lucette.

Jake did not delude himself into thinking otherwise. When Percy had used the term "contractors," he knew exactly what that implied. In the business of political scheming, espionage and subterfuge, men who hired contractors used them primarily for two purposes, and that was to either assassinate people or capture and torture them to extract information. This was verified when Percy had hacked into the *Kraken's* surveillance system to show him where Emmanuel and Chester had been taken.

Jake looked at his wristwatch, aware that time was running short. Though Percy had managed to remotely gain access to the mega-tanker's mainframe computers and shut down most of the ship's power, he said it would be temporary at most. But at least without power, electro-shock torture could not be carried out on his friends.

Abruptly the hall lights dimmed just before going brighter, and the low vibration of generators being re-engaged could be felt underfoot. A male voice coming from the third cell suddenly broke the air. With Jake still mentally linked to his bond mate, Achilles translated the strange sounding words for him. "Power's back on. Go ahead and juice them, boy."

Jake moved quickly, raising the Sledgehammer's muzzle and stepping through the doorway. "I think not," he growled irritably.

Startled by the sudden intrusion, two guards whirled.

"Place your weapons on the floor!" Jake snapped sharply, his Sledgehammer trained squarely on one of them, his trigger finger prepared to fire off a round. From experience, he dared not tell them to drop them, knowing the weapons could potentially discharge if the safeties were off. "Do it real slow!"

Knowing they had no chance of coming out of this on top, both guards bent slowly, placing their Uzis on the floor in front of them. Rising back up, they raised their hands in surrender.

Movement from the male contractor caught Jake's eye, and he swiveled the Sledgehammer a few degrees to bear on the threat. "Try it and I'll blow you in half!" he warned.

Without being told, Herbert Jester lowered the small handgun to the floor and put his hands in the air as Jake stepped over to check on his friends strapped to the chairs. Both Emmanuel and Chester peered up at him as though in disbelief.

Jake glanced at the woman, her eyes boring into him like hate-filled drills. "Unstrap 'em, lady, and be quick about it or I might decide to shoot your partner just for kicks!"

Alex, his hand still on the throw switch, turned to regard him with a confused stare. His perplexity immediately dissolved at seeing Victor standing behind Jake.

Belachek appeared stunned. Speaking in their native tongue, he said, "What are you doing, Alex? Did they make you do this?"

A defiant smile emerged on Alex's face. "These men are going to tell us where they mine their gold. You do remember the gold we came upon back near that cove, don't you, Victor?"

Victor took stock of the captives Alex had been preparing to electrocute, then looked back at his son with a horror-stricken expression. "You wanted to torture these men?" he said, unwilling to believe what he was seeing. But deep down he knew what lurked within his son's core nature, though he had refused to acknowledge it. It had been confirmed while Alex was convalescing aboard Jake's boat. Alex had asked that those strange surrealistic oil paintings decorating the cabin walls be placed where he could not see them, claiming they were making him nauseous.

Alex stared back at him with cold, distant eyes. "Why should it matter to you? As I recall, you work for a man who engages in torture all the time."

"I don't anymore," Victor replied ruefully. "My days with Zinova are finished."

"Then join me, Victor. We can both work for the man who owns this vessel. He is rich beyond anything you can imagine. He'll reward us for our services. We will be able to live in luxury for the rest of our lives."

Jake stood off to one side keeping a watchful eye on his adversaries, a feeling of rapidly escalating uneasiness taking hold of him as Achilles translated what was being said. Alex still had his hand resting on the throw switch and the woman only had one of his friends free, that being

Chester. Abruptly he spoke up, his tone conveying an unmistakable warning.

"Victor, tell him to move his hand away from that switch."

Alex shot a look at Jake. Though he didn't understand English, he sensed the meaning behind the words, and his fingers tightened on the switch.

"Victor!" Jake said curtly, swinging the Sledgehammer around to bear on Alex.

Alex eyed the remaining captive still strapped securely to the chair. The woman was just starting to remove one of the arm straps. Turning his head back round, he first looked at Jake, then at Victor. "He can go ahead and shoot me, I don't care. If I can't be rich, I don't want to live."

"Alex, I am your father!" Victor blurted.

Alex's face clouded darkly. "My father died a long time ago," he spat back in anger. "He was killed in Afghanistan. Why do you lie to me, Victor?"

Wetness welled up in Victor's eyes. "It's true, Alex. I am not lying."

Alex stared back dumbly for one brief moment before comprehension caught up with him. "You," he snarled venomously, his face screwing up with bitter hatred. "You left me when I was a baby." Drawing in a deep breath, he screamed, "You deserted me."

Tears began to roll down Victor's cheeks. "Yes, I know, Alex, and I can only tell you how sorry I am for doing that." His tone took on a pleading edge. "Can you find it in your heart to ever forgive me?"

Alex's expression turned incredulous. "You must be insane. I can never forgive you!" he railed back with dismissive contempt.

Jake continued to follow the exchange, aware that Emmanuel was now almost free. He felt Victor's anguish, an inconsolable yearning for the love of a son who was predisposed to hating him forever. Nothing was going to change that. He sensed it like smoldering coal in a nearby oven, only the oven was Alex, a person with a dark foreboding nature. No wonder Amphitrite and Destiny had such a hard time healing and reviving him. The boy had little to no good residing deep within him.

Jake risked a brief glance at the former Spetsnaz operative while still keeping close vigilance of Maximus' henchmen. He dared not take his eyes off them for more than a second. From the look on Victor's face, he could see the man was crushed. Nevertheless, time was running out and he had to get back to the colony, with or without Alex.

Thinking it prudent to take charge of the situation, Jake spoke up before any more hurtful words could be uttered.

"Are you able to walk, Emmanuel?"

"I think so," Emmanuel gasped, rising slowly out of the chair.

"How about you, Chester?"

"I'll be okay," Chester acknowledged weakly. "Just give me a minute to catch my breath."

Jake took a few steps forward, pointing his weapon at the two guards. "Back away!" he ordered.

As the guards backed up, he used his left foot to slide the two Uzis across the floor toward his friends. "Emmanuel, Chester, pick up their weapons and stand by the door. Warn me if you hear or see anyone coming down the hall." Looking at the male contractor, he issued another command, motioning with the Sledgehammer. "You. Slide your pistol over to me."

Warily, Jake followed the contractor's movements as he bent to slide the weapon toward him with his hand. "With your foot," he hissed.

Straightening back up, the contractor did as instructed, and Jake trapped the handgun under his heel as it slid across the floor.

"Now take a seat!" Jake ordered him, indicating the chair on the left. His gaze swung to the woman. "You too, lady, in the other chair!"

Both contractors glanced at each other and hesitated, their eyes widening in fear.

"Do it!" Jake growled ominously. "I advise you not to try my patience. I'm sure you know the weapon I'm holding can blow you to mush."

Begrudgingly, they complied, and as they settled unwillingly into the chairs, Jake motioned the guards forward. "Strap 'em down!" he said. "Nice and tight and be quick about it."

Aware that Alex had removed his hand from the switch, Jake pulled a roll of duct tape from his utility belt. Satisfied that both contractors were sufficiently constrained, he barked another order at the guards. "Now, both of you sit in their laps." Motioning with the Sledgehammer, he added, "You in his lap and you in hers."

Daunted by Jake's stony gaze and the way his finger hovered menacingly over the Sledgehammer trigger, each guard did as ordered. The woman's face blanched as the heavier of the two guards settled himself onto her lap, and she let out a husky gasp.

"Okay, Victor, I need you to bind them," Jake said, tossing him the roll of duct tape. "For your own safety, I recommend you ask your son to step away from that switch."

Victor looked at him like a man in a stupor, avoiding his son's withering glare. He had barely reacted in time to snare the roll Jake had tossed him, and he nearly stumbled as though intoxicated as he moved forward to carry out the task.

There was no need for Victor to ask Alex to do as Jake requested. Alex had already edged toward the door. Frowning with contempt, the lad watched as Victor bound the wrists and ankles of the guards to the same body parts of the person they sat upon. As his father completed the task, Alex suddenly bolted past Emmanuel and Chester and raced down the corridor in the direction opposite where Jake and Victor had disembarked the bubble car.

Victor turned to see him vanish, his expression helpless and forlorn.

"What do you want to do, Victor?" Jake asked softly, feeling the man's grief as though it were his own. "It's your call."

Victor let out a deep, downcast sigh. "I will not hold you up any longer, my friend. You have already done more than a man in my position can expect. I bid you and your friends good fortune in getting back to Aquaria."

"Come with us."

Victor shook his head dolefully. "No, I have unfinished business here."

Jake opened his mouth to persuade him otherwise, but a premonition of lurking danger suddenly accosted him.

As if to affirm this, Emmanuel spoke up with a hushed warning. "Jay Jay, I hear someone coming!"

The image of something coalesced lucidly in Jake's mind, and for an instant he thought he might be hallucinating. It was coming from the direction in which Alex had run, and he suddenly realized what it was. "Everyone to the bubble car!" he ordered sharply. "Hurry!"

Both Emmanuel and Chester heeded the curt warning but failed to move as quickly as Jake would have liked. Debilitated from their bout of recent torture, they ambled along sluggishly, panting hard. Jake scooted after them but abruptly pulled up short, realizing Victor was holding back, still within the interrogation cell.

"Victor!" he shouted, turning to look back.

The sound of heavy clomping impinged on Jake's hearing, and movement further down the corridor caught his eye. He became aware of Alex advancing slowly toward him, the expression on the lad's face filled with fright. Directly behind him was a towering figure at least nine feet tall. It was Maximus in a fully armored combat suit. He knew it was Maximus despite the metallic helmet that completely obscured his head and neck. In his mind's eye, he saw the man's face, though it was hidden behind the tinted visor through which the man could see. It was the same face that had stared lividly back at him from the co-pilot's seat when he and Victor had tried to stop the helicopter from taking off from the *Numquam Satis*. The suit appeared powerful but bulky, completely encasing Maximus' torso and limbs as well as his head, and from the look of the protective armor, Jake doubted his frag-12 rounds had any chance of penetrating it at all.

"Do not try to run away or I will kill the lad," a raspy voice blared harshly from a loudspeaker built into the suit. In the confines of the corridor, it reverberated ominously.

Jake stared, noticing a nasty looking electronic Gatling gun with six barrels jutting from the suit's left arm, though it was a much smaller version of what military aircraft used. He knew that combat suits like this had been in the development stage by the U.S. military for the last several decades. They were essentially wearable robots with tough, durable shells comprised of a high-strength material designed to resist ballistic impacts originating from machine gun fire and shrapnel from explosive devices. Their biggest flaw, however, was their lack of agility, and this one appeared to be ponderous in the way it moved, telling Jake that the suit was obviously quite heavy, forcing its hydraulic joint actuators to work exceptionally hard to overcome the suit's massive weight.

Stealing a quick glance behind him, Jake saw that Emmanuel and Chester were now out of the corridor, having made it to the bubble car platform. Thinking quickly, he weighed his options, but Victor's voice rang out with strident urgency.

"Don't shoot, I'm coming out." Tossing his weapon from the interrogation cell, Victor stepped from the room with his hands held high in the air.

The robotic head rotated slightly to fixate on Victor before swiveling back to bear on Jake. The amplified voice reverberated again, this time charged with untold menace. "So, I am finally meeting the tenacious Mr. Javolyn," Maximus said scornfully, "a man who has foolishly decided to become a thorn in my side. You will tell me what you have done with Bronte Pharah."

Jake decided to act dumb. "Who?"

"I warn you, do not play me for a fool," the *Sublimis* bellowed. "The Haitian Minister of Agriculture. He was being escorted by two of my guards before you disposed of them back on my yacht. Where is he?"

"Oh, that Bronte Pharah," Jake replied flippantly, keeping his mental link with Achilles fully open. "He's in a safe place beyond your control."

"Then perhaps a trade is in order if all of you wish to live," the *Sublimis* boomed back. "But first you will tell me where your cache of gold is stored and where it is mined."

Jake's thoughts raced, searching for a way out of this, but it was evident Maximus had the upper hand at the moment.

Jake let out a contemptuous chuckle. "What is it with men like you? You possess staggering wealth and yet you have this obsession with gathering in yet more riches. Don't you think you already have enough?"

This time Maximus laughed, a grating, raspy sound within the narrow hallway. "No, Mr. Javolyn, there will never be enough for men of substance like myself. We are the true caretakers of an already overpopulated world. If left to his own devices, the common man has this proclivity to squander the fruits of his labor by perpetuating a meaningless life. When food and energy are readily available, he floods the earth with over-breeding and runaway consumption of limited resources. The common man is feckless and lacks the intellectual capacity to know what's best for him. Men like me are the chosen ones. As such, we have a duty to take what is produced by the masses to be used for managing the earth in a more responsible manner. Our goal is to prevent humanity's extinction. We seek nothing more than the betterment of mankind through the salvation of the planet."

"Don't you really mean the enslavement of mankind?" Jake spat back in disgust.

"I will not bandy words with you, Mr. Javolyn. Debating this with you is pointless. Our philosophical viewpoints are obviously diametrically opposed. While you see me as utterly ruthless and morally deficient, I see you and those you abet as offensively negligent. Your imagined benevolence is actually a curse that will ultimately be mankind's undoing."

Jake stared back in amazement, his jaw dropping. He couldn't believe what he was hearing. "Undoing you say! I fail to see how you can deem the production of sustainable renewable resources to be mankind's undoing when they are created in total harmony with the earth's environment. We bring forth an unlimited bounty by creating an oasis in what would otherwise be a desert. And we have the potential of creating many more of these oases."

The robotic head appeared to nod in agreement. "Yes, and while that may be true, bringing forth an endless supply of cheap energy and sustenance to billions of people in Third World countries will surely accelerate their already out of control breeding. That is the natural consequence when food and energy are plentiful to humans. The start of the Industrial Revolution bares illuminating testament to this. Once carbon-based fuels were introduced to the masses, their numbers mushroomed dramatically. No, Mr. Javolyn, I can't let that happen. What you are doing is irresponsible. It's far too risky to let your operation continue, for if it did the earth would be swamped with more people than it could sustain. This would result in catastrophic pollution that may be irreversible, not to mention the massive wars between nations that would ultimately ensue. I'm talking extermination of the human race."

Jake let fly another chuckle, this one laced with vitriolic ridicule. "I find that most ironic coming from you. It's you and your kind that instigates wars with the aim of financing opposing sides to increase their indebtedness to you. You continue to grow richer with all the misery you cause."

"Wars are necessary," the *Sublimis* riposted angrily. "They cull down the growing numbers of useless eaters, and once we establish a singular government to control the entire world, national sovereignties will be eliminated along with wars."

"Only after you kill off billions," Jake snarled.

"Yes, and the earth will be better for it. Chaos and anarchy will become things of the past, with only order to follow."

"Isn't it rather hypocritical of you to speak of order when you and your cronies are the cause of much of the havoc and discord that currently exists throughout the world."

Maximus elicited a bored sigh. Magnified by the suit's speaker, it sounded like a prolonged hiss, telling Jake he was growing tired of the conversation. "Enough of your stupidly infantile drivel, Mr. Javolyn. Tell me where the gold is kept, and I'll let you and your friends live."

"No, you won't," Jake fired back. "Once you get what you want, you'll eliminate those you consider to be impediments to your insidious schemes. Isn't that right, Maximus? Throughout history men like you have constructed fantasies in which they believed themselves to be gods by self-proclamation. They thought they had all the answers for making the world an orderly place. But by their own actions they caused horrific events that evoked the deaths of millions."

"I need not proclaim myself a god, Mr. Javolyn," Maximus said, his tone taking on one of patronizing superiority and entitlement. "That was decided long ago by my forbearers. My very omnipotence makes me a god. Fate ordains it. Though you have caused me certain inconveniences, in the end I will ultimately prevail, and Aquaria will become another of my possessions. But you can save my minions the trouble of searching for the gold by telling me where they can find it."

"You are not a god," Jake declared grimly. "You are a monster. You can't help yourself. Causing misery and strife is what you enjoy most. You are the worst kind of predator, one that is purely evil and demented, surely the devil incarnate himself."

As Jake spoke, he became aware of Victor edging closer to Maximus, whose visored gaze was still fixed firmly on Jake's antagonizing presence. It was evident Maximus felt invincible, certain the suit protecting him was invulnerable and could not be breached. He seemed to show no concern whatsoever for his own safety.

A premonition of disaster and sadness abruptly loomed in Jake's thoughts, and he caught Victor's eye, trying to warn him off with an almost imperceptible shake of his head, masking the gesture with another declaration. "You're wasting your time, Maximus. You want the gold, go find it."

Achilles was suddenly in his mind. *JJ, look above you! The steel pipe you see carries seawater when pumps are activated.*

Jake wasn't sure what Achilles was getting at. *Explain!*

It fills and empties the submarine bay.

How do you know that?

Never mind how, just keep stalling him. The lights will go out in exactly five seconds but be ready for the intake pumps to initialize. They'll push the water toward Maximus.

A light flickered on in Jake's brain, and he suddenly grasped the full implication of what Achilles was telling him.

How thick is the pipe wall?

The nominal section is one inch.

"I'll give you one last chance to reconsider," Maximus offered irritably.

Jake stared back defiantly. "Go back to hell where you belong!" he growled aloud, stretching out the words slowly.

Risking another glance at Victor, he was answered with a doleful shake of the head that seemed to say, 'I'm sorry, my friend, but this is the only way.'

Peering back at Maximus, Jake's supreme loathing of the man began to build like hot scathing magma below a caldera. Standing before him was another Cardoza, only many times worse. Without giving it any conscious thought, his trigger finger moved idly to the tiny switch that controlled the Sledgehammer's firing mode, shifting it from semi to automatic, and had not Victor's son been standing directly in front of Maximus, he would have not hesitated to open up with the full fury of the weapon, though he seriously doubted even a barrage of the frag-12 rounds had any chance of getting through the impervious armor encasing him. But there might be another way.

Maximus' armor-clad figure remained transfixed on Jake, the visored helmet regarding him with that same immobile expression of impending doom. The roar that suddenly erupted from the suit's speaker was deafening. "Then prepare to die!"

Victor suddenly sprang, tackling Alex and moving him out of the way. In reaction, Maximus rotated his robotic head to look for the cause of the disruption, and as he did, Jake saw the arm holding the Gatling gun begin to line up on father and son.

Jake swore under his breath. Victor's rashness had removed all options from the table. With only one solution left to keep the twosome from getting killed outright, he pulled back on the Sledgehammer trigger just as the lights went out, aiming high and sending a burst into the armored helmet and upper chest.

An explosion of sparks flared brightly in the ensuing darkness as the enfilade impacted with brutal, jarring savagery. The onslaught was enough to topple Maximus backward on his heavily booted heels and send him crashing to the floor with his left arm flung high. But it was not enough to keep him from letting loose with the Gatling gun.

A thunderous storm of bullets strafed the ceiling directly above him, caroming violently off the steel pipe and sounding like a chain saw gone crazy. Ricochets flew haphazardly, and anticipating this, Jake leaped away to avoid the spray of lethal fragmentation engulfing the hallway. Lasting less than two seconds, the blitzkrieg abruptly ended, and without the coruscated eruption of rounds to provide flickering illumination, the corridor was plunged once again into total darkness. A dead, unsettling silence followed, one so quiet that Jake heard the beat of his own heart.

In moments, backup power kicked in to relight the corridor in a dim afterglow. Creeping cautiously back toward the fallen Maximus, Jake kept the Sledgehammer trained on him as he quickly assessed why the Gatling weapon had stopped firing. Though the barrels remained pointed at the ceiling, the ammunition guide that fed them was bent and ruptured. Apparently, the combination of frag-12 rounds and ricochets had been enough to disable the weapon, reminding Jake of a similar event when he had fired a handgun directly into the mini-gun aboard Sebastian Ortega's Bell Ranger years earlier to keep it from destroying the *Avenging Angel*.

Seeing that Maximus lay unmoving for the moment, Jake risked kneeling beside Victor, who was sprawled atop Alex. A smear of blood crept slowly outward from a hole in Victor's back. Fearing the worst, Jake pulled him gently off his son to cradle his head in his arms. He was immediately struck by a deep sense of déjà vu once again. He had held Myers this way as he lay dying.

Victor stirred, his mismatched eyes fluttering open to stare up at Jake with a near death glaze. Blood trickled from his open mouth. "Thank you..for.. helping me," he managed to say in a faltering whisper.

Jake extended an arm to check on Alex, but immediately saw where one of the ricochets had penetrated the lad's skull. A check of his pulse confirmed he was beyond saving.

Bringing sorrowful eyes back to Victor, he spoke in a gentle voice. "I'm sorry to tell you Alex is gone."

Victor nodded weakly in acknowledgement, then coughed harshly, his lips drenched in blood.

"I'm getting you out of here," Jake said, shifting his body in readiness to lift Victor from the floor.

Victor pushed him away. "Na…nyet," he stammered in protest. "Save yourself…I'm finished."

Jake ignored him, preparing to hoist him over his shoulder, but the whir of a joint actuator made him look at the armor-clad figure lying prone on its back. Maximus was trying to rise from the floor, and as he did, the robotic head turned to regard him.

"A valiant move, Mr. Javolyn, but nonetheless a futile one." As Maximus spoke, Jake saw the Gatling gun swivel to bear on his face.

"Your weapon is useless," Jake said smugly.

"But I can still crush you," Maximus retorted, his joint actuators now working hard to roll the massive combat suit over to face the floor. Pushing himself to his knees, he added. "You have no idea what these arms can do to a person."

Not wanting to be trapped against the wall, Jake reached under Victor and heaved him up with a sudden surge of adrenaline, grunting with the effort. Draping him over his left shoulder, he grabbed the Sledgehammer and began moving down the passageway in the direction of the bubble car, but not before Maximus lashed out with his right arm. A starburst of lights erupted behind his eyes as the arcing swipe nicked him on the side of the knee, almost buckling it. Gritting his teeth, he tried to ignore the pain, limping along slowly with Victor's dead weight pushing down to exacerbate the ache.

Stealing a glance behind him, Jake saw Maximus regain his feet and rise to his full height to pound forward, and he felt the floor shake softly underfoot. In his estimation the combat suit had to easily exceed a thousand pounds, with each of its footfalls quaking the deck plates like some monstrous creature out of the dinosaur age. The concept behind its design was rather simple, and speed was not one of its virtues. It was built for defensive protection and brute power, much like a Sherman tank, and if he didn't move any faster, Maximus would catch him before he reached the bubble car.

Jake did not sense any real damage to his knee. The pain brought back memories of his days playing college football. Though a stiff hit to the knee would temporarily sideline him, the ache would ultimately subside, allowing him to get back in the game. But unfortunately, he needed more time to shake off the pain, and he was still hobbling along even slower than Maximus' sluggish pace. If he didn't move any faster, those powerful arms would squash him and Victor like bugs against a wall.

Unexpectedly, hands were suddenly lending support, and he realized both Emmanuel and Chester had returned to provide assistance. Pulling up short, Jake hefted Victor from his shoulder awkwardly, placing him into the awaiting arms of his friends. "Get him to the car!" he ordered.

Emmanuel nodded, and with Chester helping, each draped one of Victor's arms behind their neck, sandwiching the wounded man between them and hauling him away with the insteps of his feet dragging along the deck. With his head slumped forward, it was hard to tell if he was still alive.

Jake turned to face the oncoming juggernaut, his leg still hurting and almost collapsing under him. Though Maximus was coming at him like a slow, ponderous bulldozer, he was moving fast enough to overtake the four men before they would have any chance of escaping in the bubble car.

A sound abruptly caught Jake's ear, making him look up. It was a sound he was intimately familiar with, one of rushing water, and it was coming from the pipeline directly overhead. Apparently Ez had succeeded in turning on the pumps. Scrutinizing the pipe's curving surface, he gauged the distance. The bottom of the pipe had to be roughly five meters above the deck. This was a blessing! The frag-12 rounds the Sledgehammer held were armor-piercing and needed three meters to arm themselves once they were fired. But he knew each one was only capable of penetrating one-half inch of steel at most. Multiple strikes, however, just might get through the pipe's inch thick wall and open a sizable hole.

Bringing the weapon to bear on the underside of the pipe a few meters out in front of him, Jake depressed the trigger, opening up on full automatic as Maximus bore down on him. Bursting flickers of violent incandescence flared hotly as a dozen rounds met steel, and for one fleeting moment he believed the attempt to be a failure. But then a spray of water under tremendous pressure gushed forth from a jagged hole the size of his fist.

Jake sent another 12-round burst into one side of the breach, rending the metal further. The hole changed shape, and aided by the enormous pressure contained within the pipe walls, the steel ruptured outward, no longer able to withstand the severe forces imposed on it. In the span of an instant, a huge oblong tear opened up to send a spate of whitewater gushing into the corridor with a deafening roar as though a dam had burst, and Jake saw it rush toward Maximus with all the pent-up fury of a tidal wave charging toward a beach. Lingering a second longer, he watched as the armor-clad figure disappeared under the surge.

The passageway was rapidly filling, and though the flow was moving away from Jake, he was already ankle-deep in water, with the level coming up quickly. Not hesitating any longer, he turned and hastened in the opposite direction. His knee was still smarting, but most of the ache was now gone. In a few moments he turned a corner to find Emmanuel and Chester awaiting him in the bubble car. Victor's inert body was slumped between them, and he knew it was going to be a tight fit with four men crammed into a space designed to seat two.

Diving through the open door, Jake punched the buttons that would take them back the way he had come. The door immediately hissed shut just as a rush of backwater slammed against it, the water level rapidly climbing sharply to the middle of the window as the car took off, and seconds later they were free of the deluge beginning to engulf them.

As the car rose higher through the decks, Jake fired off a thought to his bond mate. *Get word to Ez to turn off those pumps, Achilles.* The last thing he wanted was the *Kraken's* lower decks filling with so much water that the ship's keel was lowered to the point where it might go aground on the nearby reefs abutting the Windward Passage.

Don't worry yourself, JJ, it's already been taken care of.

Breathing a sigh of relief, Jake came to realize that with the intake pipe now broken, there was no possibility of the submarine returning to the *Kraken's* concealed bay.

Chapter Twenty-one: Rebooting the System

One of the three technicians manning the *Kraken's* bridge lifted his eyes from the computer screen and turned to look at Finley. "The system has gone haywire again," the man declared, his manner clearly frazzled and fraught with exasperation.

"Well fix it, damn you!" Finley yelled. He stood close by, his face smoldering with intense anger.

"We're still being hacked. Someone's got a firm lock on it from the outside, someone who seems to know how to bypass the overrides."

Finley's voice boomed louder. "Then shut it down again and reboot like you did before."

Holland threw up his hands in frustration. "That's what I've been trying to tell you. Whoever's got control won't let us shut it down. They've reset the codes."

Maddened like a tormented bull, Finley was on the verge of reaching out with a huge hand to grab the man by the throat.

Sensing this, Holland spoke up quickly. "But there might be another way."

"How?" Finley grumbled.

"By improvising a wireless shield."

Finley appeared perplexed. He had no idea what Holland was talking about, nor did he care. He just wanted the problem solved. "Do whatever needs to be done, but do it fast," he snarled.

Holland nodded and stepped away from the keyboard, striding briskly to the ship's radar array set up in one corner of the bridge. With the computers being controlled by an outside source, the keyboard terminal was useless to him. He'd have to do this manually by changing the frequency of the pulses emitted by the radar dish and stopping the rotation of the dish so that it faced in only one direction. It was all guesswork, but it was likely the hacking was originating from either the *Numquam Satis* or the sea colony, both of which were at the same general location. He prayed his assumption was right, because the last thing he wanted was Finley's wrath befalling him a second time. With hands that squeezed like hydraulic machinery, Finley had grabbed him by the throat once before and his neck had throbbed for a week.

Thinking about the problem at hand, Holland knew wireless hackers used microwave signals to gain access to a computer system, but by aiming the radar dish in the correct direction and jamming those incoming signals with a high enough frequency, he could stop the hacker's attack. Then all he'd have to do was reboot the system and reset the access codes.

Hoping he was right, Holland turned a few knobs and adjusted the digital settings, calling back to McGormack, one of the other techies. "See if she'll reboot now."

"It's working!" McGormack shouted gleefully.

Pleased with himself, Holland glanced over at Finley, using all his will to keep from smirking. Scampering back to the keyboard, he began entering new codes, and two minutes later all the computer monitors came back online to reveal the status of the various systems. Studying them a minute longer, Holland frowned before setting his gaze on Finley again. "Everything seems to be back to normal except for the intake to the submarine bay."

"What's wrong with it?"

The question was thrown at Holland like a knife. Seeing the same look the *Kraken's* captain had displayed earlier, he swallowed deeply. It was obvious Finley was in no mood to hear about any more problems. "The pipeline is broken and has flooded the interrogation sector. But at least the pumps have shut down," he added, blurting out the words as fast as he could utter them.

Finley's eyes grew large, the statement taking him completely by surprise. The thought that the *Sublimis* along with the two contractors and abductees were down there made his gut tighten. Almost abruptly his features hardened, twisting into another menacing scowl, but before he could cast any blame, the sound of rotor blades slapping the air caught his ear. Rushing to a window facing the ship's bow, he glanced up to espy a helicopter bearing directly at him. Reflexively, he threw an arm up in front of his face and ducked down, the blood in his veins going cold. For one fleeting second he thought it was going to keep coming and crash through the glass, but then it suddenly veered higher to thunder over the bridge.

Spinning around, Finley sprinted across the bridge deck to a sprawling rear window. The chopper had slowed, flaring up sharply in preparation to settle on the ship's helipad that was the size of a football field.

An indecipherable curse sprang from Finley's mouth. Though he had a limited understanding of how the various systems tied into the vessel's mainframe computers, had not Holland tampered with the *Kraken's* radar he might have been alerted of the whirlybird's approach long before it came within earshot, and without clearance to land, he would have promptly blown it out of the sky by engaging one of the ship's concealed 20mm cannons. Whether or not they needed the computers to engage the vessel's weaponry made no difference to him. As far as he was concerned, Holland was to blame. But at seeing the chopper settle down behind the other two aircraft which now effectively shielded it, those being the EC 135 and the contractors' Jolly Green Giant, it was already too late to even think about using those weapons.

Finley continued to stare out the window, searching for signs of the other three men Maximus had brought with him. He remembered seeing the pilot step out to stretch his limbs before tying down the main rotor, but the pilot was nowhere to be seen. The two guards that had flown in with Maximus to escort the boy were also not there. Those guards had not been present in the interrogation room with Alex when he and Maximus had gone down there. Only two of the three guards that normally accompanied the *Kraken* had been in the room. That left three guards somewhere on the ship, making him wonder where they were at the moment.

Finley's apprehension grew as he pondered these things. Moving quickly back to the ship's control console, he lifted a microphone and hit the intercom button that connected with most quarters of the vessel. "Bridge to *Sublimis*, come in *Sublimis*!

When Maximus did not respond, Finley repeated himself, his voice becoming more panicky.

Still no reply.

This time Finley shouted at the top of his lungs. "Answer me, damn it!"

In frustration, Finley threw down the mic and scurried over to a nearby locker. Pulling a key from his pocket, he unlocked the door and pulled out a holstered .357 magnum revolver and hurriedly strapped it on. Because he treated the technicians that normally manned the bridge with the harshness of a tyrannical ogre, he did not trust any of them to carry weapons of any kind around him. And not knowing where the three remaining armed guards were, the task of repelling boarders had now fallen to him.

Reaching for the Heckler and Koch MP5 rifle with scope, he grabbed the fully loaded banana clip next to it and slapped it into place before chambering a round.

Occupied with this, he did not notice the short individual that emerged from a staircase to saunter nonchalantly onto the bridge as though he owned it. Still thoroughly engaged in bringing all the systems back up to speed, none of the other three crew members noticed him either.

Turning, Finley found himself staring down into a pair of maniacal eyes that bulged grotesquely behind a set of thick lenses perched on a nose resembling the beak of a hawk. Too late to react, he barely had time to register the lethal swing of the axe blade arcing toward his skull.

Destiny scrambled from the Bell Ranger as soon as it touched down, probing her surroundings with a paranormal sense that went way beyond the five normal ones the average person used. Strangely, she did not feel any lurking danger at the moment, though her eyes were automatically drawn to the ship's bridge. Something dark and offensive existed there, sending out pulsations of raw evil that seemed to abrade her soul. The sensation sickened her, nearly making her gag, and if words could describe it, it was as though the air she breathed was rife with the vapors of rotting flesh.

In seconds, Amphitrite and Franklin were beside her as Mortimer sat pensively watching them from the rear port side seat of the chopper, its blades still being spun by an idling engine. Calmly, Amphitrite moved to the port side edge of the landing pad with Destiny and Franklin following.

"Down there!" Amphitrite said, pointing at the four men just emerging from behind a huge curving deck vent to make their way toward the helipad. One of the men was obviously injured, his arms draped over the shoulders of two others as they shuffled along awkwardly bearing his weight. The fourth man followed up their rear, periodically looking behind him and covering their retreat with a firearm at the ready.

With Amphitrite leading the way and Destiny and Franklin following, they dashed to a nearby stairway to rush down the steps. Having already been informed of Victor's condition by Achilles, Destiny knew time was of the essence. Victor was fading fast and they didn't have a moment to lose if they were going to save him.

"Lay him down!" Amphitrite shouted to Emmanuel and Chester as both groups converged at the bottom of the steps.

Victor's face was ashen and he had stopped breathing. Quickly, both women laid hands on him. The thought that they might be too late cast a pall on what they were attempting to do. Destiny pushed down hard on his chest as Amphitrite placed gentle palms on each side of his head.

"Is he still alive?" Emmanuel asked, gasping hard from the strain of carrying the unconscious man.

Totally focused on the task at hand, neither Destiny nor Amphitrite answered.

Jake stood watch as both women went to work, glancing about in all directions as he gripped the Sledgehammer. Knowing he was down to only a few frag-12 rounds at most, he used the moment to remove the drum magazine and pull out a fully loaded spare from the rucksack he carried.

Amphitrite and Destiny remained steadfast and positive in trying to save Victor, but without the albinos channeling their energies into the mortally wounded man through direct contact, the effort was made all the more difficult. Nevertheless, in spite of the distance separating pod members from the event, both women felt the flow of the dolphin energies being telepathically channelled to them and added to their own. And while these energies would certainly amplify their combined healing prowess, the technique would lack the potency the dolphins imparted through direct touch.

Doggedly, both women would not give up, committing themselves entirely to saving the dying man with a trance-like focus for several minutes, unwilling to accept failure.

Victor suddenly stirred with a sharp intake of breath, his chest beginning to heave once again as he sucked in air.

"Get him to the chopper!" Jake yelled. "We got company."

Amphitrite looked up, her features appearing drained. "We need another minute or we still might lose him," she said, her words strained and lacking their normal vigor.

Jake noticed the same drawn look on his wife's face. He had seen this type of thing before and knew she and her mother were donating a significant portion of their own life energies in resuscitating Victor, and without the albinos in attendance and making direct contact with the subject, the effort would invariably leave them in a weakened condition, albeit a temporary one.

"We don't have another minute," Jake warned sharply. He had been struck by another bout of presentiment, and he sensed the approaching danger even before it manifested itself. Somehow Maximus had survived the deluge of water and had managed to make his way up to the main deck, and a quick glance over his shoulder confirmed what he was feeling. Cocooned in his massive robo-suit, Maximus was advancing ponderously in their direction.

Destiny followed Jake's gaze to espy the mechanical monstrosity slowly plodding toward them.

“Now get going!” Jake prompted a second time, taking a few steps toward Maximus and leveling the Sledgehammer. Perhaps he might be able to topple the weighty robo-suit like he had done before.

As Jake stood his ground to confront the oncoming metallic giant, Amphitrite and Destiny managed to get Victor to his feet. In moments they were helping him to climb the stairs, Franklin, Chester and Emmanuel following up the rear.

Jake whipped his head around momentarily to follow their progress, not happy at how slow they were moving. Victor was still far too weak to make the ascent beyond a snail’s pace, and none of the others were capable of bearing his weight in a fireman’s carriage. Victor was a big man. Complicating the issue was the narrow width of the staircase, which only allowed the group to proceed up the stairs in single file.

Looking back at Maximus, Jake was convinced the only weapon the man currently carried were those powerful mechanical arms, and if he weren’t stopped, those arms might be capable of tearing out the staircase supports before the escaping party of six reached the top.

Taking a wide stance and setting the Sledgehammer’s firing mode to automatic, Jake waited for Maximus to draw closer. Abruptly, a premonition of additional danger took hold of him, and instinctively he executed a shoulder roll as he dove to one side, coming back to his feet as a storm of bullets pinged and ricocheted, barely missing him. Knowing exactly where the fire was coming from, he opened up with a short 3-round burst to take down one of the guards he had seen aboard Maximus’ chopper when it left the *Numquam Satis*. Maximus was not the only threat. There were others.

As Maximus bore down on him, Jake stole another quick glance behind him, noticing Victor was nearing the top of the stairway. Without even thinking, Jake instinctively whirled to his left to avoid another volley of automatic fire, the Sledgehammer in his hands seeming to have a mind of its own as it came to bear on another target just as his finger tightened on the trigger for the second time. A scream cut the air, and he saw a second guard crumple to the deck.

With the metal giant almost on top of him, Jake opened fire again, aiming for the helmet as he had done before. Seemingly anticipating the blistering enfilade, Maximus leaned into the gale of exploding rounds. This time he did not go down, still advancing like a towering colossus.

Jake held his ground doggedly, refusing to yield and continuing to hammer the robo-suit when something unexpectedly happened. Maximus crashed face forward onto the deck. Seeing the cause, he immediately let up on the trigger to stare slack-jawed.

What are you waiting for, JJ? Achilles chided. *Now get going before he re-gains his feet.*

Had Jake not seen it with his own eyes, he would not have believed it. His bond mate had somehow managed to reach the main deck and, using his prehensile appendages, had hauled his body across the steel surface to come up on Maximus from behind to execute a near perfect shoestring tackle.

You should have clued me, Jake admonished.

Achilles released his hold on the robo-suit ankles and began scurrying back the way he had come. *Had I done so, I risked distracting your clairvoyance.*

Jake mentally sighed. *Wait for me. I'll catch up with you as soon as the others are clear of this ship.*

Turning, Jake tore up the staircase just as Maximus began lumbering to his feet. Almost to the top, the steps beneath his feet suddenly wobbled violently, and a quick glance below him showed Maximus tearing out the supporting stanchions, metal ripping like tissue paper under the onslaught of the suit's powerful arms.

Gripping the railing, Jake managed to keep his balance and bolt up the last remaining steps before the staircase swung sideways, held precariously by its topmost connections which were on the verge of pulling free. An instant later, the entire stairway completely dislodged to fall away and crash onto the main deck below.

Taking a moment to look back down, Jake espied the visored helmet locked on him, cognizant of the monstrous evil that lurked behind the impassive shell. Behind that shell he envisioned the intense hatred Maximus wore.

The suit's speaker suddenly boomed stridently with giddy, harsh laughter. "Where are you going to run, Mr. Javolyn? Once your colony falls into my hands, there won't be a place on this planet you can hide."

Jake ignored the chaffing comment and stared in the direction of the Bell Ranger. Though the chopper was designed to carry five people, it was capable of carrying a much heavier load due to the modifications Fernando had made to the engine. And now it was about to lift off with seven people crammed aboard, or so he assumed until Destiny turned back in his direction.

Destiny was pointing at the ancient Jolly Green Giant as she ran toward him, and Jake felt an alarm go off in his head accompanied by a curt warning from Achilles at the exact moment she pointed.

On your left, JJ!

Jake dropped to one knee just in time to avoid a stream of bullets that seemed to part his hair. Catching sight of muzzle flashes coming from the fuselage doorway of the old Marine Corp whirlybird, he returned fire, sending a small burst of well-placed rounds into the darkened interior. And then the Sledgehammer went dead in his hands.

Realizing the drum magazine was now empty, he tossed the weapon aside and pulled the USP-9 submachine pistol from his thigh holster in one smooth motion, chambering a round as he did so. Tuning out the whine of the Bell Ranger's turbine growing to a raucous shriek, he sprang sideways, executing a shoulder roll so as not to present a stationary target. Surprised that no further fire followed him, he eyed the doorway of the ancient chopper, prepared to unleash another sally, though one of lesser magnitude. But when a figure suddenly reeled drunkenly from the interior to tumble down the steps, he knew the Sledgehammer had done its job.

Jake rose to his feet as the assailant lay sprawled on the deck, fragmentation from one of the Sledgehammer rounds apparently having sliced open a huge gash in the man's neck. Blood pumped in heavy spurts from a torn carotid artery, and as the man lay dying, Jake recognized him to be the second guard that had fired upon him and Victor from Maximus' chopper.

The pungent smell of aviation fuel suddenly filled Jake's nostrils, and he became aware of a gathering puddle. Expanding rapidly, it spread outward to surround the guard's prostrate body, and he could only deduce that shrapnel from one of the Sledgehammer's exploding rounds had ruptured the Green Giant's fuel tank.

Reaching Jake's side, Destiny embraced him fiercely as a blast of rotor wash buffeted them gently. Somewhat confused, Jake wondered why Amphitrite was leaving her daughter behind.

"I'm coming with you," Destiny said quickly.

Jake was about to reply when the downdraft from the heli blades abruptly intensified, and he looked up to see Amphitrite guide the small whirlybird directly overhead.

"Grab hold!" Destiny urged, reaching for one of the skids.

Suddenly Jake understood. Though the helipad spanned the full width of the *Kraken's* main deck, it rose twenty-five feet higher. At this moment they were 155 feet above the water, and had they attempted a dive from that height, they risked potential injury, especially Jake. With a rucksack strapped to his back and the weaponry he carried, he was all the more vulnerable since those items would likely be torn from his body when he met the sea, though he could have easily tossed them over the side to let the dolphins retrieve them.

Nodding, Jake was about to holster his USP-9 but stopped, sending a thought to his bond mate. *Achilles, let Destiny and Amphitrite know what I'm about to do.*

Jake watched as Amphitrite moved the Bell Ranger farther away, still holding a hover. Destiny left his side and followed. Satisfied that everyone was at a safe distance, he aimed the submachine pistol at the nearby EC 135 and opened fire. Only when it burst into flames did he let up on the trigger. Shifting the weapon, he squeezed the trigger again. Sparks erupted as rounds struck the growing pool of aviation fuel that continued to spill from the other chopper. Almost immediately a flash point was reached and the fuel ignited. He was going to make sure Maximus had no air transport off the ship, at least for the time being.

Taking a few steps, Jake calmly bent to retrieve the expended Sledgehammer and strap it over a shoulder. Breaking into a trot to escape the growing conflagration, he caught up with his wife. Reaching for the skid opposite the one Destiny was holding, he gave Amphitrite a thumb's up sign, and an instant later felt himself lifted clear of the deck just as the Jolly Green Giant was completely engulfed in flames.

In moments, the helo swung out over the sea as the ancient helicopter exploded to eject a swirling fireball into the sky. Jake caught a final glimpse of the robo-suit standing stationary near the port side railing, the jointed head articulating to follow their flight as they descended as though they were on a high-speed elevator. Twenty feet above the water he released his grip on the skid a split second after Destiny let go. Plunging beneath the surface, each found their bond mate awaiting them, and a short time later all were aboard *Johnnie* with Fernando steering the submersible as fast as it could go toward Aquaria.

Leaving the *Kraken's* galley, Maximus' pilot munched contently on the ham sandwich he had made for himself. Unsure how long his boss planned to stay aboard, he only knew that he was to stand by on the helipad until further notice. Reaching the door that opened to the main deck, the crackling sound of gunfire made him pull up short. Not daring to exit the doorway, he listened to the skirmish for several moments before deciding to take a peek. Realizing the disturbance was coming from the helipad, he felt back-to-back shock waves course through the deck under his feet followed by two loud thumps. Abruptly he stiffened at the sight of fireballs rising from where the helicopters sat, and a moment later he glimpsed the Bell Ranger swoop below the ship's port side to escape the flames as two figures clung to its landing skids.

Continuing to stare in disbelief, he was unprepared for the voice that spoke up from behind him. "What is your preference?" it requested, the tone carrying inflections of mockery.

Startled, the pilot turned. A pair of crazed, leering eyes peered at him from behind a set of thick lenses only inches away.

"Huh?" was all the pilot could utter.

"Never mind," Peyami said. "You look like a person that prefers a bullet."

Feeling something jam firmly against his ribs, the pilot glanced down to espy the barrel of a .357 magnum just before it exploded.

Captain Sayyari Habibollah turned to his sonar expert, keeping his expression stern and holding back the malicious grin yearning to suffuse his features. "Range?" he demanded.

The crewman manning the sonar console continued to monitor the readouts, his earnest gaze never straying from the screen. "Twenty-six hundred meters and closing."

Habibollah stepped forward to stare over the crewman's shoulder, aware that the *Carl Sagan* was not probing the surrounding sea with active sonar. He could only assume its captain was currently using passive mode. *Idiot*, he thought blithely, wondering how the man commanding the carrier had ever advanced to the rank of captain. *Only a fool would drop his guard like this.*

Memories of past encounters with the man danced through Habibollah's thoughts, with his mind coming to bear on one particular incident. Coming upon a herd of whales in the Straits of Hormuz with Habibollah shadowing him, Delila had purposely disengaged his active sonar. And now with hundreds of huge sea mammals swarming close to the sea colony, Habibollah had guessed correctly. Delila was repeating himself.

He's far too predictable, Habibollah mused, only slightly disappointed at how easy this was going to be. *He puts his ship and that of his crew at risk to avoid harming animals that live in the sea. The man is utterly stupid.*

Pivoting his head to glance at the crewman manning the weapons station, Habibollah grunted out a command. "Stand by for launch on my mark." His sub was creeping up on the carrier slowly. At 2,000 meters he'd give the order to fire. Delila was giving him a perfect broadside, and with four torpedoes ripping the carrier's guts out, she was going to go down like a bag of cement.

Finally giving in to his glee, Habibollah let it show. He could not believe his good fortune as of late. Not only was he captaining a Russian-built kilo class submarine, but he had also been given the order to take down his longtime nemesis. It was all part and parcel of the plot laid out for him. But these orders had not come from the Ayatollah or the Islamic Revolutionary Guard, though they would have been exuberantly gladdened that a U.S. warship had been destroyed. And while he professed an almost rabid adherence to the teachings of Islam to the men surrounding him, it was all for show, for by nature he was not a religious man. His allegiance resided elsewhere, preferring instead an almost insatiable desire for material gain and the power that accompanied it above all else, and the man promising these things was the only person he was willing to pledge his loyalty. As a young man attending the University of Tehran, he along with several others had been recruited by *The Order* to foment the Iranian masses into overthrowing the Shah's government. In the aftermath of that he had been instrumental in spreading the flames of hatred against the U.S. by organizing and goading a crowd into storming the U.S. Embassy in Tehran and taking hostages. The ploy had worked exceedingly well. While on the surface the takeover of the embassy had deceived the world community into believing it was aimed at embarrassing the U.S. government, the actual aim was to heighten international tensions enough to make the public perceive the flow of Middle Eastern crude would be disrupted and create shortages. The oil companies had taken full advantage of the situation, purposely holding back supplies and driving up the price to unheard-of levels. As a result, members of *The Order* had profited immensely by going long on futures contracts in advance of the takeover, and overnight he had become a wealthy man.

Habibollah continued to beam at the memory. As more than a foot soldier of *The Order of the Righteous*, his orders had come directly from the *Sublimis*, and he was eager to carry them out. Once he fired the torpedoes it would appear that Aquaria had taken aggressive action against a war vessel belonging to the U.S. Navy. The fact that Delila's carrier was also acting as flagship to a UN operation would make the attack even more vicious, further adding to the vilification of the sea colonists.

Without his sonar in active mode, Delila would be alerted he was being probed but he would have no way of knowing the prober's range, though he would be aware of its bearing. He would not know it was coming straight at him, though ever so slowly, and he certainly would be oblivious of its intentions.

Habibollah continued to evaluate the situation, wondering if he should launch the torpedoes at this very moment. No, he decided.

Launching at 2,000 meters would be the ideal distance. It would greatly increase his chance of hitting the target. Moreover, it would give Delila insufficient time to evade the subsea missiles homing in on him even if he suddenly decided to be more cautious by reverting back to active sonar mode.

Immediately after Habibollah sank the carrier he was to carry out one additional directive of the *Sublimis*, one far more sinister in nature, one that would allow *The Order* to make off with a major portion of the world's wealth via the international financial markets. A quick glance at the digital clock overlooking the helm told him the time was drawing close. He knew that an hour earlier agents of *The Order* had secured vast equity positions on the short side and long positions in precious metals on an unprecedented scale. Members of the cabal were now fully prepared to enrich themselves further. The occurrence would send markets reeling. As far as he knew, this was the cataclysmic event the *Sublimis* had been planning for some time now and one that would plunge the world banking system into paroxysms of chaos. It would force the merging of all the major banks throughout the world and transform the United Nations into the global government *The Order* had been seeking.

Housed within the *Iron Fist's* missile silo was a warhead carrying enough megatonnage to fully destroy a major U.S. city within range of the missile that would deliver it. Miami, as it turned out, lay just within range of the delivery system. Despite all the economic sanctions previously lodged against the Iranian government to keep it from pursuing its nuclear ambitions, and despite a recent pact with the U.S. that supposedly ensured it would give up the effort, the Islamic nation had finally succeeded in producing enough high-grade plutonium to manufacture its first atomic bomb in recent months, and it was this bomb that had been assigned to Habibollah's sub, though he had no current orders from Iran's high command to use it. Once launched, members of the remaining U.N. task force would claim the missile originated from Aquaria in retaliation for being attacked.

As the *Iron Fist* continued to creep closer to its intended target, so did the iniquitous smile dominating Habibollah's face grow ever larger.

Captain Delila pondered the current state of affairs, wondering what was causing the delay. The choppers that had deployed the Seal teams were still not inbound to the carrier at this moment. Though the team leaders, Lieutenant Myron Johnson and Ensign Patrick Flynn, had initially responded to his orders calling them back, he had since lost all contact with both teams and there was still no sign of the ponderous AW101s lifting off, neither from Aquaria's central structure nor Navassa Island. He knew the cause that prevented further communication with the teams. Radio signals were being jammed over a wide band of frequencies, telling him the interference was not random but intentional.

As Delila scanned the sky from the carrier's starboard bridge wing, Ensign Jefferson returned at a brisk trot to lay the latest news on him.

"Sir, it seems we're being probed by sonar."

"You sure it's not some of the acoustical anomalies we've already detected in these waters," Delila remarked. With the area brimming with marine mammals, the water below them abounded with the echoes of bio-sonar propagating through the hydrosphere. They had noted other sounds as well, some of them highly unusual and seemingly originating from the sea floor directly below the floating city before the bottom dropped off severely into the abyss to the south. Those sounds tended to distort a clear picture of what lay down there.

"No, sir, it seems to match something we might encounter from a sub, but the sound is garbled by the other noise. It's coming from a source directly in line with Aquaria's central structure and roughly one hundred feet below the surface."

Delila nodded, his mind churning over this latest bit of information. With three Russian-built subs possessing stealth capability prowling the adjacent water, one from Iran and two from Venezuela, he wondered if one of them might be the actual source. Turning back to face the colony, he lifted the binoculars to his eyes to scan the sea in the direction of Aquaria for the fifth time in as many minutes. "Maybe the captain of one of those subs wants to be sure they don't accidentally run into us," he muttered softly, trying to remind himself that they were all on the same team. In spite of this he continued to shift the spyglasses this way and that, a feeling of rapidly growing vulnerability suddenly plaguing him.

Before Delila could say anything more, Jefferson's phone buzzed. Holding it to his ear he listened momentarily before his manner went rigid. "I'll put you through to him," he uttered quickly, giving the captain a fearful look as he handed the phone over. Words spewed from his lips in a breathless rush. "Sir, we have someone who insists on speaking directly with you. Says it's urgent, that this ship is in jeopardy of being destroyed."

For one fleeting instant Delila's normally laid-back composure seemed to unravel, but just as quickly he regained control of himself. Speaking in an uncharacteristically stern and authoritative voice, he addressed the caller. "This is Captain Delila of the *USS Carl Sagan*. To whom am I speaking?"

The voice emanating from the phone was obviously female and carried a clipped accent distinctive of the Caribbean, but there was no mistaking the urgency in her tone. "My name is of no consequence, and we have little time for formalities, captain. I believe your ship is about to be torpedoed by one of the subs in your task force."

"Please identify yourself!" Delila demanded. His entire body went taut as he spun around to search the water for torpedo contrails.

"We'll do what we can to keep this from happening," the caller said quickly, completely ignoring the captain's query, "but I strongly advise you to get your ship underway immediately to take evasive action."

Delila shot a look at Jefferson, bellowing out an order. "Have the helm get us moving now! Hard rudder to forty degrees!"

As Jefferson bolted into the wheelhouse, the caller added one more thing before ending the conversation. "I think I should tell you a fourth submarine of unknown nationality has entered these waters. It arrived on the opposite side of the colony before you recalled your Seal teams, so it is doubtful you would be aware of its presence. It has since deployed a task force of more than one hundred men onto the colony's central structure before dispersing an equal number of men to the nearby island."

Delila's shoulders went rigid as steel as the phone went dead. Pocketing the device, he gripped the railing and leaned over it, his knuckles turning white as he searched frantically for telltale signs of streaking underwater missiles once again. As the ship picked up speed and began to turn in the direction of the colony, he braced himself in expectation of the shattering blasts that would rip the hull apart. If, in fact, torpedoes were inbound, the carrier would at least present a smaller target. As the bow swung around to line up with Aquaria's central structure towering more than 500 feet above the sea, he began to wonder what the hell was going on here.

Chapter Twenty-two: Sliding Into the Abyss

While Lieutenant Myron Johnson was happy about the recall, he was nevertheless disappointed in having to leave the facility so quickly. Since alighting on one of the larger landing pads adjoining Aquaria's central structure, he and his team had not encountered a shred of resistance. As far as he could tell, the facility was deserted, at least the sectors he had so far come upon. But having to leave so soon after entering the vast interior of the complex was a major disappointment. The sights that had so far greeted him were a visual delight. The alien architecture that lay before him enthralled the senses with a seemingly endless wonder of interlacing walkways and terraced decks that wound their way around rising pillars and beneath arching bridges. Serene pools, gently plunging waterfalls, and gurgling fountains were interspersed everywhere. Smoothly curving walls, floors and ceilings rose and fell like waves in a rolling sea, much of it suffused by soothing multihued lighting ingeniously placed for maximum effect. Built into the walls in many places were thick panes and bubbles of glass, behind which swam multitudes of exotic fish among brilliant corals and anemones, further enlivening the city's interior with flaming reds and glittering iridescence. But it was the strange art periodically integrated into the whole that punctuated the fantasyland motif, and as he glanced around he could see that his men were equally spellbound by it.

With considerable effort he reminded himself he had been ordered back to the carrier, aware that the pervasive atmosphere which lay all about him was dulling his sharpness and drawing him into a stupor. The last thing he needed was to let his vigilance wander. Managing to harden himself against the alluring imagery, he spoke softly into his lip mic, and using hand signals, directed his men to follow him back the way they had come. Though he would have preferred to explore the place further, it was time to leave. The sound of heavy clomping, however, made him stop dead in his tracks.

Further down the winding walkway a huge figure suddenly loomed, and a short distance behind it, several more like figures came into view.

A mental alarm immediately sounded in the lieutenant's head, and without a moment's hesitation he ordered his men to take cover.

Staring over the shoulder of the sonar operator, the *Iron Fist's* captain eyed a new blip that suddenly appeared on the screen. It was closing on his stern.

Habibollah extended an arm, pointing at the object. "What is that?"

An expression of intense concentration consumed the operator's countenance as he listened to the echoes coming through his headphones, his eyes roving over the readouts showing on the screen. "A small submarine about thirty meters in length, captain."

Habibollah tracked two larger blips that abruptly materialized on the screen. His face lit up in a sadistic grin as they quickly converged on the smaller blip from opposite sides. With two Venezuelan subs guarding his back, they would engage the threat by destroying it with their own torpedoes.

A frown abruptly transcended Habibollah's features as the screen came alive with several more blips, four of them. They diverged into pairs, streaking across the screen from one corner to intercept the subs protecting his stern. In the blink of an eye, the pulsing dots showing *El Martillo* and *El Yunque* abruptly flared, and from experience Habibollah knew they had been torpedoed.

The sonar operator turned in his seat, exchanging a horrified look with the captain. "The Venezuelan subs are sinking, and the carrier has begun moving," he decried in a quavering tone.

Flabbergasted by this sudden turn of events, Habibollah opened his mouth to speak, but before he could issue a new set of orders, a shower of sparks suddenly flew from control panels all around him. Unable to handle the intense electrical surge coursing through them, circuit boards fizzled to fill the air with the acrid smell of scorched plastic and biting ozone. Lights blinked erratically before fading completely, and the susurrating thrum of the sub's power plant could no longer be felt. Except for the labored breathing of crewmen, a hushed quietude descended to immerse the control room in total darkness.

Within moments emergency LED lights began to flutter on and off torpidly, but even these seemed to be on the brink of failure, and Habibollah caught sight of the helmsman's face in the feeble, flickering glow. The man was white as a ghost. In a faltering voice the helmsman broke the stunned silence. "We have no power. We are drifting blindly." He looked hopefully to the captain for guidance. "What can-"

His words were immediately cut off as several explosions rocked the sub on opposite sides of the pressure hull. Losing his balance from the jarring impacts, the helmsman was tumbled to the deck as others, including Habibollah, grabbed hold of anything within reach to steady themselves. Moments later something slammed heavily into the sub's starboard side, tilting the sub precariously to port. A quick glance at the inclinometer told the captain his vessel had listed by more than forty degrees off an even keel. Several more impacts followed as the sub began to roll back to right itself, but these were less jarring, and to Habibollah it felt as if his vessel was being driven sideways by something colossal and ponderous. Looking all about him he saw crew members bracing themselves and holding on in terrified silence.

"What is happening?" someone cried out just as the LED lights failed altogether.

Driven to the threshold of mind-numbing panic, Habibollah's thoughts raced along haphazardly, frantically searching for the cause of their predicament. Somehow he was able to grasp that the *Iron Fist* was being driven to the south where much deeper water existed. That was where the seafloor dropped away precipitously, falling more than 7,600 meters into the Cayman Trench. Though he was engulfed in pitch black darkness, his eyes widened sharply at the thought.

Barely managing to hold onto his sanity by a thread, Habibollah shrieked into the blackness. "Purge all water from the ballast and trim tanks." Hearing his own voice, it sounded uncharacteristically shrill and brittle, as though it had come from the mouth of a stranger. Realizing they had no power, he kept a firmer grip on his tone when he amended the order. "Do it manually."

Hearing movement in the darkness, he knew members of the crew were groping around in search of the throw valves situated against a forward bulkhead. Pipes suddenly hissed as air began to flow, and with it filling the buoyancy tanks the sub would be inexorably lifted toward the surface.

Thinking his vessel was only moments away from rising, Habibollah froze as the pressure hull began to creak and groan, and he knew at once that the sub was sinking.

"The tanks have been breached," a crewman wailed forlornly. "I can hear the air leaking out. We are doomed."

As if in answer, the hull groaned louder, sounding like the moan of a dying leviathan resigned to its fate. With steel being squeezed ever tighter by the growing hydrostatic forces pressing relentlessly against it, the *Iron Fist* slid faster into the yawning abyss awaiting it.

Habibollah gritted his teeth and closed his eyes, anticipating the moment the hull could take no more. His torment seemed to last an eternity before the sub finally imploded, and the last thing he heard was the crunch of his own bones as he was cast into oblivion.

Percy Osgood stared in amazement at the multiple displays on the huge screen taking up the entire wall high up in Aquaria's central structure. Binary code in the form of zeros and ones continued to flash across one of the displays at a dizzying rate. Data which he had absconded with using the mechanical fish was still being analyzed. If not for the incredible decoding wizardry of the entity called Ez, the *Sublimis'* plan to annihilate a U.S. city would never have been brought to light. This had been something he had not known. Embedded within that data was an immense myriad of interconnected and convoluted schemes of cause and effect aimed at creating an insidious chain reaction of mounting chaos in the world designed to enslave humanity, much of it encrypted in high order algorithms much too complicated for even him to crack. But the artificial intelligence known as Ez was doing it rather easily, and she had been able to uncover the plot to nuke Miami in the nick of time.

Standing behind him, Jacob said, "Your actions saved the lives of millions."

"Yes," Amelia Amhurst concurred admiringly, "and with all the information you've given us, it might even turn out that you saved billions."

Percy nodded ruefully. "Unfortunately, it was those same actions that led to the deaths of the men aboard those subs." He had witnessed it all via the marvelous gadgetry several of the dolphins wore. Jacob had called them DBTs, Delphine Biosonar Transmitters. The clarity of the transmissions they had received had been stunning. The gadgets had provided real-time video viewings of exceptional high-quality resolution.

"Yes," Jacob commiserated, understanding his bereavement. "But there were no other options available to us. Had we not acted quickly, the missile would have been launched."

"But that sub was completely disabled," Percy responded dismally. "With its electronics fried, it could not possibly have launched that missile."

"We had to be sure," Jacob consoled. "Their weapons station may have survived the attack if the circuitry was shielded, and there wasn't time to determine that."

Percy shrugged laconically, taking a deep breath. Deep down he knew Jacob was right. Changing the subject, he tried to assuage the guilt he felt. "You'll have to tell me how those transmitters work. Obviously you figured a way to get around the attenuation of telemetry transmission in an underwater environment."

"I'll leave that to Dr. Grahm, he's the one that developed them with the help of the dolphins. I believe you already met him."

Percy nodded, playing over in his mind the recent string of events he had been a party to. At Javolyn's urging he had managed to re-program the torpedo system aboard the *Numquam Satis*. With Javolyn giving him further instructions, he had parted company with the former Navy Seal. An albino dolphin named Hermes had swum him to the colony as a multitude of whales began pushing the drifting mega-yacht close to Aquaria's uncompleted section of outer breakwater. With Hermes delivering him to a discrete location along the base of the colony's central structure, he had met up with a large Haitian woman who was there awaiting him. She had introduced herself as Ez, and it didn't take him long to realize she was a holographic manifestation of a sentient, incredibly advanced computer system. Easily evading members of a Seal team that was prowling the facility's lower levels, she had escorted him to an elevator that carried them high up into the central tower. On their way up she had asked him specific questions regarding the *Kraken's* systems layout, projecting three-dimensional images for him to see to make it easier for him to answer. These had been acquired from information held in the mechanical fish. As they were doing this, he knew she was hacking her way into the mainframe computers that controlled the immense ship. Reaching the room where he now found himself, Ez had introduced him to Jacob and the IBC news reporter, who was just completing a broadcast to major news media stations around the world. Somehow Ez had managed to usurp control of them all, paving the way for Amelia's eye-opening statements read directly from script on a teleprompter. Subsequent to that he had viewed the huge screen dominating one wall, watching intently as a small sub belonging to the colonists crept up on a kilo class submarine provided to the UN task force by Iran. Having given Ez the code to remotely operate the torpedo system housed aboard Maximus' yacht, she had fired off four torpedoes to accurately intercept and destroy two other kilo class subs owned by Venezuela before they could lay waste to the Aquarian sub, which was armed with a device that was able to project a tight-beam electromagnetic pulse at the sub carrying the nuclear device. As an added measure to ensure that the vessel could not launch its nuclear missile, several albino dolphins had moved upon it to plant explosives on its ballast and trim tanks. To avoid injury from the ensuing lethal pressure waves put out by the explosions, the dolphins had been protected by what Jacob had termed PWIs – Pressure Wave Inhibitors. The albinos, he had learned, had developed such contrivances once the mysterious explosions started occurring on the lush coral reefs that abounded between the floating city and Navassa Island. But it had been twenty leviathans that had provided the final assault on the Iranian sub. Standing by in close proximity, a mix of humpback, gray, and blue whales also outfitted with Pressure Wave Inhibitors to avoid injury from the deadly explosions, had used their combined strength to drive the sub toward deeper water where it had fallen away into the Cayman Trench.

But now Percy found himself looking at the screen to observe the latest threat that had arrived to assault the colony. The screen had split to reveal what was currently happening on Navassa Island and Aquaria's lower levels. His face clouded as he took in both scenes. Though he knew the Seal teams had been ordered to scrub the mission and return to the carrier, each had come under attack by unknown assailants.

Jacob stepped closer, reading the confusion Percy's face harbored. "It seems the man responsible for all this has gone to great lengths to make us look like the aggressors once again."

Percy glanced his way briefly before snapping his eyes back to the screen. "What do you mean?" he said, continuing to study the massive robotic forms advancing with impunity into the withering enfilades put out by the Seal teams. The firefights were intense at both locations. Inside the central structure along the lower level, ricocheting rounds were destroying artwork as they tore sizable chunks from walls, ceilings, pillars, and archways. On Navassa, Seals scrambled behind warehouses and heavy machinery to avoid being hit. He could see both units were effectively cut off from escaping to the huge AW101 helicopters that had delivered them. With the lead robots unleashing buzz saw bursts of overpowering counterfire, the Seals were forced to keep retreating, taking refuge behind anything available as they withdrew. Shielded by the huge metallic forms, heavily armed men in all black camos followed behind them, their faces and hands covered by black ski masks and black gloves. It was obvious they were preparing to overwhelm and subdue the Seal teams once the armored monstrosities leading the way overtook them and punched through their positions, but they seemed to be moving far too slowly to make this happen readily.

"Those attackers are supposed to be us putting up resistance against the UN forces," answered Jacob.

Percy appeared glum. "Is there anything you can do to stop them?"

Jacob turned his gaze on Ez, who answered for him. "It seems our primary modes of defense are failing us. Holographic representations of the albino art have no effect on the attackers, and the ADS Three appears to be useless as well."

"Please explain?" Jacob asked, his brain already rummaging about on why this was happening. The dolphin art was their preferred line of defense. Though it could be highly debilitating to wicked personas, it was passive in the way it acted and essentially harmless. Through intelligence gathered by Jake, he had learned about the drug UN troops were now using to counter its effect, but the wave of black clad assassins currently storming the Seal teams were obviously not part of the UN task force, so he could only conclude they also had access to the drug. Exhibits of the esoteric art were situated throughout the colony, both in oil paintings and holographic projections, and in those places where there were no displays Ez could project three-dimensional images of it at will as long as a 3-D laser projector was in the immediate area, so avoiding it was impossible. The ADS2 - Active Denial System 2 – which Ez had illicitly appropriated and enhanced and now called ADS Three was their backup line of defense. She had used it to drive away Malikai Allotey and his Chilean commandos when they had tried to impose their presence on Aquaria. And while it could induce intense physical distress on the human anatomy, it inflicted no lasting bodily damage detrimental to a person's health. But why it was not working in this situation he could only wonder.

Ez turned to face Jacob, seemingly reading his thoughts. "Either the core natures of the raiders are uncorrupted, which we can rule out by simple observation, or they have effectively immunized themselves, at least temporarily, against our arcane art with the same drug the UN troops have been using. Since the latter scenario is most probable, that is the one we should assume." She stated this confidently, confirming Jacob's initial deduction.

Ez explained further. "A search of the data held by the mechanical fish shows the drug was developed in Plagiarius laboratories for the sole purpose of invading this facility. As to the ineffectiveness of the ADS Three, my sensors have detected emissions of microwaves that are counter-phased to our own. They nullify and cancel out the ADS microwaves each time I initiate a burst. Those combat suits are the source of those emissions. Apparently the people who designed those suits anticipated the possibility of microwave technology being used against them and installed a system to counter it."

"What about changing the phase of our microwaves?" asked Jacob.

"I've already tried that, but those suits immediately detect the change and alter their emissions to counter our own."

Jacob looked at Ez, shaking his head slowly in frustration. "Don't you find it rather strange that these people already knew about our microwave defense and were prepared to counter it?"

"Not really when you consider that those suits were already retrofitted with microwave generators even before I was able to acquire the ADS technology."

The exasperation pervading Jacob's countenance immediately changed over to puzzlement. "Can you be more specific?"

"I was not the only one to hack into the U.S. Defense Department's computer system to appropriate the original ADS design. Looking at the data uploaded from Percy's fish, it seems a hacker working for Maximus managed to get that same information long before I did. A subsidiary of Unus Universitas specializing in the manufacture of arms and sophisticated weaponry is the developer of those combat suits. They took the ADS design and modified it slightly before incorporating it into the suits as a precautionary measure."

"Why do you say precautionary?"

"As we know, microwaves put out by the ADS system have a frequency of roughly 2.5 gigahertz and can induce intense discomfort on the human body but will generally not damage tissue. But the metal components and circuitry comprising the walls inside those suits become a liability when subjected to those same frequencies. The metal and circuits will quickly heat up, so much so that the suit becomes an oven. The operator inside will be cooked. The result is similar to crumpled aluminum foil being put in a microwave oven. With the newly emerging ADS technology about to revolutionize modern warfare, the developers of the suit were quick to see this flaw and recognized the need for a defensive system to nullify possible microwave attacks being used against it."

"Wouldn't the counter frequency generator in the suit heat up the interior circuitry anyway?" Jacob was quick to point out.

"No, because the generating unit is fitted on the suit's exterior and radiates waves directly away from it."

"Then maybe that in itself will make it vulnerable to damage with concentrated small arms fire," Jacob said hopefully.

"It is shielded by two inches of a carbon-titanium alloy. There is no possibility of the Seals rupturing it with the weapons they carry."

Jacob sighed deeply, wondering if their troubles could get any worse. "Then how do we stop those metallic giants?"

"I'm working on it," was all Ez offered just before she vanished from sight.

Jacob clicked a button on the remote held in his hand, bringing a third picture frame to the screen. This one showed the Hind gunship sitting adjacent to the massive AW101 that had landed one of the Seal teams on Aquaria. Seemingly in conference, eleven men stood out in front of the helicopters with one of the metallic monstrosities guarding them. Almost immediately, Jacob recognized Malikai Allotey and Captain Alvarez amid the group.

Percy suddenly spoke up. "Is that who I think it is?"

"Which one?" rejoined Amelia.

Percy pointed. "The fat, paunchy one, that's Senator Brent Van Heflin."

Amelia scrutinized the image briefly before agreeing. "I believe you're right." Turning, she looked at Jacob. "I hope you're recording all this."

Jacob nodded. "Everything you are seeing is being documented."

"Why do you suppose he would come here?" she asked.

To Jacob the answer was simple. "As Chairman of the senate's Science and Technology Committee, he has a legitimate excuse for being here. His presence will be played up by the media to underscore the environmental champion they have so tediously and cunningly built him up to be. At least it will be made to appear that way on the surface. But I'm more apt to believe he wants to make sure he gets a fair share of the bounty."

Amelia stared back in puzzlement. "Bounty?"

Jacob smiled. "Plunder, spoils, booty. His actual reason for being here is to take inventory of our assets and claim his share before any of it disappears into the hands of Allotey and company. My guess is this latest band of raiders are directly under Allotey's control and will make off with anything valuable they can get their hands on once they finish off the Seal teams. With the Seals out of the way they won't have to account for anything missing that was not nailed down. Furthermore, they'll be able to say we were the ones that wiped them out."

The expression on Amelia's face reflected nausea as her eyes fell back on the screen. "How is it that men like that get elected in the first place?" she said.

Jacob's response was concise. "Political ignorance."

"Is that the result of the widespread complacency and apathy you spoke of earlier?"

"It goes much deeper than that, I'm afraid to say," Jacob remarked, his manner becoming erudite once again. "A rising tide of immorality among the populace may also be responsible."

Surprise showed on Amelia's face. "Are you suggesting that greater numbers of people are becoming wicked?"

Jacob looked back at her with sad eyes. "Not in the strict sense. I refer to the increase in vices that are taking hold of people. Drugs, sloth, greed, essentially anything that makes a person feel good and goes counter to a virtuous nature. A preoccupation with these things does not necessarily make a person wicked, but the general consensus in present-day American society seems to have shifted in the way such behavior is becoming more and more acceptable. Vice, or what theologians like to call sin, tends to deaden the intellect. So, as more and more people descend into moral depravity, they lose their natural probity. The Old Testament refers to this very thing when God says he will turn them over to a reprobate mind."

Amelia nodded in understanding. "So what you're implying is that a deterioration in personal values causes a person to lose their ability to distinguish between good and evil."

"Yes. Corrupt leaders are mere symptoms of the problems confronting America these days. The real problem resides in the fools that elect them. Their addictions cause them to lose sight of what is actually occurring all around them. They tend to ignore the growing problems and look the other way."

"But we've already exposed these men for what they are. I would think that will wake the public up."

Jacob shook his head dolefully. "Once they regain control of their broadcasting stations they'll say it was all fabricated lies made to cleanse our image."

"But the captain of that carrier called back the invasion force," Amelia argued. "Surely we've accomplished something."

Jacob slumped tiredly into a chair, continuing to monitor the screen and noticing that the band of eleven were now dispersing, with nine of them following behind the person operating the combat suit and making their way inside the facility as two others climbed inside the AW101. "Only if those Seal teams manage to come out of this alive," he remarked in frustration.

Chapter Twenty-three: Jamming In Progress

Mat was back in the access tunnel, this time making his way to the island. Though he was not a vindictive person by nature, the fact that he had turned the tables on Bolder gave him satisfaction. But now he had another matter to attend to. Having been informed by Ez on the latest developments, he decided he would lend his support to the closest Seal team. After all, weren't they his brothers? From the platform he had counted sixteen of them disembark from the AW101 displaying the UN logo. The fact that US Navy Seals had been assigned to provide the main thrust of the invasion force disturbed him. Obviously someone carried a lot of clout to make this happen, a person with their hands on the strings of governmental power. But Amelia's broadcast must have paid off. At least that was his assumption as to why the Seals had been ordered back to the carrier. And now another force of unknown raiders had come on the scene to attack the Seals and keep them pinned down.

Mat's cell phone came alive as he approached the end of the tunnel. "What is it Ez?"

The voice coming through the phone was abnormally low and filled with static. "I've analyzed the problem. Your best option for taking out the men in those combat suits is the explosives we use for mining the *guano*."

"I can barely hear you, Ez."

"That's because heavy jamming is in progress."

"Where's it coming from?"

"Multiple sources. Those combat suits and the choppers that brought the Seals here."

Mat mulled this momentarily before replying. "Then the chopper pilots must be in league with the new invaders."

"Apparently so."

"How many combat suits have you counted?" Mat asked, continuing to move forward as he spoke.

"Four on the island and four in the city. A band of one hundred and five mercenaries are moving up the rear of each group of four."

"I don't advise using explosives inside the city," Mat said. "You have any other options for neutralizing those combat suits?"

"I'm working on it."

"Tell me what you have in mind," Mat demanded. Growing impatient when she did not immediately answer, he pressed her again. "Ez?!"

Riding Alpha, Troy Jacob rose up into the vertical tunnel that gave access into the interior of Aquaria. Clinging fast to Omega, Melody was right behind him. In moments they surfaced behind a curtain of thundering water. It was the perfect place to enter the floating city unseen. They were behind the waterfall that dropped into the artificial cove, a shrunken down version of their birthplace back in Haiti. Letting go of their bond mates, they asked them to swim out into the lagoon for a quick reconnaissance. Having accompanied them, Perseus immediately shot off to assist.

Melody's face contorted in a frown as she treaded water beside her brother. "Is that a chainsaw I'm hearing?" This close to the falls she knew something had to be awfully loud to be heard above its pervasive roar. No sooner did she ask the question, the barely audible sound abated.

"I think that's the battle you're hearing," TJ said.

Shortly before their arrival the twins had been alerted by their bond mates about the firefight that was currently taking place above them. With Ez having been notified that the children were on their way via the network of interlinked delphine minds, she had used the facility's array of underwater acoustical speakers to communicate with Alpha and Omega, instructing the young dolphins to bring the twins to the safety of the subterranean cavern underlying Navassa Island. But knowing their parents were on their way to the floating city, the twins had gone against Ez's wishes to keep them out of harm's way.

A short interval passed before the faint din of a chainsaw broke the air again, this time a tad louder than before. It was evident the fighting was getting closer.

Mentally linked to their bond mates, the twins saw what their bond mates were seeing from beyond the curtain of water. Midway up along one side of the chasm they espied figures scrambling near the railing. With their gazes directed inward at their mind's eye, they continued to watch a towering form amble along that same railing as though in pursuit, one of its arms extended out in front of it. An explosion of light seemed to leap forward from the arm, and once again the reverberation of a chainsaw resounded.

Without warning, Ez suddenly appeared in the water between the siblings, startling both of them. "Children!" she reprimanded. "It is too dangerous to be here. Please go at once to the subterranean cavern."

Overcoming his momentary fright, TJ realized they should have expected this. Holographic projectors and speakers had been installed at numerous locations throughout the colony, one of them directly behind the falls. "Is that where mom and dad will be?" he asked.

"No, they are coming here."

"Then we want to be with them," Melody insisted.

The displeased look Ez had given them abruptly fell away at seeing the defiance lodged on their faces. Sighing deeply, she caved in understanding. "All right, then, but at least climb up into the chamber behind the falls," she said, pointing to the rungs embedded in the rock. "I'll let your parents know where to find you."

"What about Alpha and Omega?" both twins queried as one.

"Tell them to go back the way they got in here, but to stay close. Now hurry!" Having said that, Ez's form immediately winked out.

TJ eyed the rungs that rose up behind him, then looked at his sister. "You first."

Moving swiftly, Mat by-passed the primary cavern under Navassa Island, finding it necessary to avoid the throng of Aquarians that had evacuated the floating city. Taking one of the side passageways within the maze of naturally formed tunnels riddling the subterranean karst, he was able to reach the steel spiral staircase that rose up into one of the large equipment sheds overlooking Lulu Bay. The shed housed heavy earth-moving equipment for mining the huge deposits of *guano* indigenous to the island. These included one Kamatsu 575 super dozer and a 988G Big Cat front end loader, both of which could be operated remotely. The engine of each had been modified to run on compressed hydrogen gas, as was every land-based machine in the colony.

Drenched with sweat and gasping for breath, he raced up the stairs, surprised to find the hinged overhead door already open and two heavily muscled, bare chested Haitian men awaiting his arrival, their torsos and arms gleaming with perspiration in the muggy air. Najac and Kilroy were the colony's supervisors in charge of mining the *guano*. As Mat poked his head above the floor, he was immediately greeted by the staccato din of small arms fire.

As he climbed the rest of the way through the door, Ez's persona suddenly materialized out of thin air, and it dawned on him that the shed was outfitted with a holographic projector and speaker, something he hadn't known. He did know the floating complex had literally thousands of these illusion-producing contrivances situated throughout. They had been necessary components in the facility's construction, primarily installed to instruct the resident Haitian labor force how to wire and retrofit the huge array of electrical and mechanical systems that abounded within the central structure, lagoons, and breakwater. Using these projectors gave Ez a multitask omnipresence, allowing her to be in thousands of locations simultaneously while teaching the predominately unskilled laborers how to assemble components through step-by-step instructions via three-dimensional diagrams and personal oversight. This had permitted the speed of construction to proceed many times faster than would have normally been expected. Having so many of these projectors on the surface of Navassa, however, was not as necessary, mainly because there were not many structures dotting the terrain.

"We have little time," Ez said, her expression grave as she pointed to four small packets of high explosives sitting on the concrete floor behind the two miners.

Though the packets were smaller than the ones Mat had supplied Jake for the raid on Cardoza's stronghold in Tiburon, the composition of the blasting material they contained was exactly the same, an ingenious mix developed by the dolphins that was many times more powerful than TNT or dynamite.

"I will attempt to take out those iron men with the bulldozer and loader," Ez clarified, "but should the attempt fail, the use of those explosives is our secondary option. In such an event you will need to use your Masker to get close enough to plant the charges on their suits. On the backside of those packets is a heavy adhesive that will allow them to adhere. Each time you plant a charge I suggest you get well clear. Only then will I detonate it remotely."

"Sounds like a plan," Mat muttered uneasily, unable to come up with a better one. "I assume you've already preprogrammed the Masker, but which of those goons out there am I supposed to mimic?"

"The iron men, of course, so try to match their actions. Their hydraulics are poorly designed and unsuitably powered, causing them to move rather slowly."

Eying the square, rectangular packets, Mat noticed the radio-activated detonator topping each one and the gooey tar-like adhesive clinging to one side. "You mentioned those things are rigged with radio jammers. Are you sure you'll be able to trigger the detonators?"

"They are set to receive a narrow beamed milli-pulse of exceptionally long wavelengths. By the time the suit's counter-wave system detects them it will be too late. Now hurry!"

"I'll only be able to carry one packet at a time."

Najac spoke up. "I will bring the others to you."

Aware that the firefight was drawing closer due to the escalating sound, Mat shook his head. "No, bullets will be flying every which way out there. Let's hope the heavy machinery works so we don't have to use them."

Removing his backpack, Mat pulled out the Masker and strapped it to his wrist. As he did this, Najac and Kilroy moved to the shed's huge sliding door that allowed entrance for the heavy equipment and shoved it wide open.

Looking through the opening, Mat caught sight of several men in full combat dress as they scurried around the corner of an adjacent structure. One of the men was limping badly, one leg of his fatigue pants covered in blood. The man looked on the verge of collapse, and just as he was about to go stumbling to the ground his companions grabbed hold of him to carry him along.

Mat moved to the door, beckoning frantically and yelling at the top of his lungs. "In here."

One of the men spun, pointing his weapon at Mat and regarding him with suspicious eyes. At that moment a huge metallic humanoid form emerged into the open area between the two structures. Lifting its left arm, it swiveled the Gatling gun protruding from the end of it to track the men it had been pursuing. Picking up the movement, the other uninjured man shouted something to his partners just before pulling them forward to rush headlong into the shed and dive behind the dozer. It was obvious he had no time to consider whether Mat or the men with him were friend or foe.

Seeing what was about to happen, Mat pushed Najac and Kilroy behind the loader just before leaping to where the three soldiers sought cover behind the dozer, which sat sideways to the shed's entrance. No sooner did he do this than the unnerving sound of a buzz saw cut the air as a storm of rounds pinged like raging hailstones off the heavy machinery.

"Who are you?" one of the Seals growled as soon as the enfilade ceased. The man's face was painted with green and black camo cream, as were his teammates. Already his partner was attending to the wounded soldier, who grimaced in pain as a tourniquet was cinched tightly around his thigh to staunch the heavy bleeding.

"One of you," Mat said quickly, pulling back a sleeve on his jumpsuit to expose the tattoo on his left forearm. It depicted the Special Warfare insignia worn by Navy Seals, a golden eagle clutching a U.S. Navy anchor, trident, and flintlock pistol in its talons. "At least I used to be," he added, a touch of regret in his tone.

The Seal's eyes widened with surprise and a glint of respect, but he whipped his weapon around lightning fast to confront the Haitian woman suddenly looming over him.

"Who's she?" he asked in a bewildered voice. The woman seemed totally unconcerned for her own safety.

"A friend," Mat said, perceiving the Seal to be the squad leader, whose name he would later learn to be Patrick Flynn.

"Please move back away from the dozer," Ez said hurriedly. "I'm going to pivot it around."

"I suggest we do as she says," Mat urged as Ez's form abruptly winked out, causing all three Seals to stare in wide-eyed disarray. "She's going to do something about that thing out there."

Flynn glanced all about with disbelieving eyes. "Where'd she go?"

"You'll find out soon enough," Mat said.

With trance-like expressions, all three Seals followed Mat's lead as he kept low and scampered back from the dozer's treads. As soon they were clear, the dozer swung around, its front blade rising slightly to meet the metallic giant head on as it plodded forward to enter the shed.

At seeing this unexpected turn of events, the man in the combat suit opened up with another buzz saw burst to send hundreds of rounds caroming off the blade to no effect. Too late to move out of the way, the huge form was toppled over by the far more massive Kamatsu. Trundling forward, it ground the suit under one of its immense treads.

As Mat watched, the Big Cat front end loader suddenly churned to life and rolled out of the shed to follow the dozer just as another metallic behemoth emerged from the opposite side of the nearby structure. More than a dozen black-clad men swarmed up behind it. With their faces swathed in matching ski masks, they reminded him of marauding *ninjas*.

Mat turned, reading the expression on the squad leader's face, and answering the obvious question before the man could raise it.

"Those people attacking you are not part of this colony."

"Then who are they?" Ensign Flynn demanded gruffly.

"That's the sixty-four-thousand-dollar question I keep asking myself, but if I could guess I'd say they're going to be played up as an Aquarian counterstrike force defending this colony. But don't get yourself in a dither, we still have a few more tricks up our sleeve."

Rising, Mat bolted to snatch up one of the four explosive packets lying nearby. Looking back at Flynn, he blurted, "Don't be alarmed by my sudden transformation. It's going to make me look like one of them, but please pass the word to the rest of your unit not to shoot at any of those mechanical things because they might very well end up killing me." Having uttered the warning, he activated his Masker.

Flynn gawked as Mat's persona morphed, his eyes following the towering giant as it trudged off in the wake of the Big Cat. Though it was justifiably unclear to him what he was witnessing, he spoke quickly into his lip mic, hoping he would get through to the rest of his unit this time, but the static coming through told him he was still being jammed.

Mat could only hope the ploy he had in mind was going to work. From the direction the last metallic behemoth had come from, he doubted the man inside it had seen the Kamatsu crush the first one, so maybe he would think Mat was one of his teammates. Though it was a long shot gamble, it was one he was willing to take, and he realized he was acting in a manner reminiscent of Jake's reckless behavior.

Holding to that thought, Mat made sure not to proceed too quickly, mimicking the movements of these slow-moving monstrosities. Pulling his USP-9 from its holster with his free hand he plodded forward, angling into the midst of the troopers in black.

The attackers appeared to ignore him but made sure to keep clear of his hulking form so as to avoid being stepped on, seemingly focusing their attention on the Big Cat rumbling forward. Significantly faster than the Kamatsu, it tore directly at the second slow moving monster. On seeing it coming, the monster opened up with its Gatling, shattering the air with its deafening noise. The men accompanying it also opened up, adding to the torrent of rounds clanging into the charging loader, most of them slamming harmlessly into its enormous bucket.

Managing to flank these adversaries, Mat depressed the trigger on his submachine gun, spraying the tightly grouped field of men from left to right and seeing seven of them go down. All too soon, the magazine of his weapon ran out of bullets, but he was prepared for it. Letting go of his USP-9, he reached down to grab a fallen mercenary's Uzi. Squeezing the trigger, he finished off the other five as they glanced around in confusion in an attempt to locate where the fire was coming from. Dropping the weapon he held, he snatched up another Uzi from the hand of a trooper that lay dying.

By this time the loader had rammed into the second combat suit, rolling over it with its huge tires. Coming up behind the Big Cat, the Kamatsu's treads applied the finishing touch, mashing the combat suit into the soil and leaving it in crushed ruins.

Mat rounded the second building, continuing to keep his movements purposely slow as he swiveled his head back and forth looking for more of these giants. Spotting another of them beyond one of the other buildings, he plodded forward to meet it as more than sixty troopers dressed in black trailed in its wake. Following the direction of their pursuit he glimpsed a small detachment of Seals scurry behind a mound of dirt adjoining an open pit where *guano* was being mined. Picking up his pace, he caught up with the combat suit and nonchalantly placed the explosive he had been holding against the suit's rear torso. The man inside seemed not to notice as he unleashed the full fury of his Gatling weapon to strafe the mound.

Drifting away from the pack of marauders, Mat suddenly picked up his pace and sprinted for the Big Cat, which was just rounding the building at his rear, aware that several black-clad troopers had turned to stare in his direction. No doubt they were perplexed that one of these giants was able to move so fast. Taking cover behind the massive machine which had come to a halt to protect him, he hoped Ez had noted the placement of the charge. With a heavy assortment of video cameras installed on the outside of buildings and at the top of the old lighthouse overlooking the island, he was certain she would have seen it.

No sooner did these thoughts streak through his brain, a severe shock wave struck the Big Cat, jolting it hard enough to partially lift the machine's gargantuan wheels facing the blast off the ground. The machine bounced heavily as its huge tires landed back on the ground, and leaning his back against one of them, he looked up to espy a mixed assortment of bodies and body parts go sailing end over end overhead before crashing harshly onto the karst edging the bay.

Three juggernauts down and one to go, Mat thought idly. *Number four, show yourself.*

A sudden burst of small arms fire clattered heavily a short distance away. Hugging the backside of the Big Cat, Mat leaned out to take inventory of the damage the blast had incurred. Those of the marauders who had managed to survive the shock wave appeared stunned and incoherent as they tried to rise on wobbly legs, making it easy for the contingent of Seals that had taken refuge behind the mound to systematically cut them down.

Preparing to move out, Mat discerned two figures running toward him, recognizing them to be two of the Seals he had beckoned into the shed. Touching a button on his Masker he reverted to his true form.

"Thought you might need another one of these," Flynn said, handing him an explosive packet. Flynn's partner also held a packet.

Taking hold of the packet, Mat said, "There's one more of those things with about thirty more of those goons still on the loose according to the intel I received."

No sooner did he make the statement his cell phone chirped. "What do you have for me, Ez?"

"The last faction of insurgents is chasing five Navy Seals making for the lighthouse." As if to confirm this latest bit of info, the sound of a chainsaw suddenly broke out in the distance to echo off the rising landscape to the north.

Mat noted a reduction in static coming through the phone this time. "You're coming in a little clearer than before, Ez."

"That is because three jammers have been eliminated," rejoined Ez. "If you want better reception, I suggest the Seals take command of the chopper that brought them here and shut down the jammer aboard it. Only then will they be able to re-establish contact with the carrier. It is evident that the chopper pilots are abetting the insurgents."

Mat pulled the phone from his ear and turned to Flynn. "How many in your squad?" he asked.

"Sixteen including myself." Flynn brought his gaze to the floating city. "An equal number have been dispatched over there."

"The chopper pilots that mobilized your squads are in league with those insurgents," Mat said, staring in the direction of the AW101 sitting downslope of him. "They're jamming your transmissions."

Flynn's eyes suddenly flared as he stared contemplatively at the massive chopper that had transported him and his men to the island, and beneath the camo cream smearing his face Mat saw the man's lantern-like jaw stiffen. By this time the nearby contingent of Seals had been waved over to the Big Cat by Flynn's companion, their expressions filled with befuddlement and questions as they noticed Mat in their midst.

Ensign Flynn immediately began barking orders. "Haskel, Joliard and O'Malley, get down to the chopper and arrest those pilots. They've been jamming our radios, so make sure you shut down their jammer. The rest of you follow me."

Mat watched momentarily as the three Seals tore off in the direction of the chopper before turning to Flynn, who now had only six men under his command.

"This guy's one of us and is here to help," Flynn informed the others. With an expression filled with trust and admiration, he stared thoughtfully back at Mat. "Any ideas?"

Mat brought the phone to his ear again. "What say you, Ez, any ideas as to how we proceed from here?"

"The terrain is too rugged for the dozer and loader to get up there quickly, so you're going to have to do this on your own. But I'll try some holographic distractions that might be enough to keep them occupied."

"Okay, Ez, we're on our way."

Pocketing the cell phone, Mat looked back at Flynn with a somber look on his face, knowing there was only one other place where a holographic projector was located on the island surface. "We'll have to play this one by ear." Having said that, he began trotting in the direction of the old lighthouse.

Chapter Twenty-four:
Unseen Foe

Reaching the topmost rung, TJ pulled himself up the rest of the way to follow his sister into the recessed opening resembling the mouth of a cave. Unlike the interior of the real cave located behind the falls tumbling into the cove, which their mother had never allowed them to enter, this one was well lit. As he stood up, astonishment flooded TJ's face.

"I should have known I'd find the two of you here," Phillipe said disapprovingly, his gaze swinging from Melody to TJ. "Why didn't you stay with Zimby?"

"For the same reason you refused to stay," Melody retorted defiantly. "We belong here to help any way we can."

Phillipe's stern expression softened, and he let out a prolonged sigh. "You're right, I suppose. But now I have to worry about the two of you when I should be out there doing anything I can to stop this colony from being taken over."

"We can do it together," TJ offered brightly.

Phillipe shook his head. "No, you're both too small and will only get in the way."

"How did you know where to find us?" asked Melody.

"I didn't. When I reached the city, Ez was waiting for me and said there was something important for me to see in here, but she didn't say what. I had no idea it would be the two of you."

"There's fighting going on," TJ informed him. "We heard something that sounds like a chainsaw."

"Yes, I know. Usurpers are storming this place," Phillipe replied in exasperation. Ez had given him a hurried overview of what was currently taking place within the floating city, and it wasn't hard for him to piece together whatever she had left out.

The eyebrows of both children rose up, and they chorused a question in unison. "What are usurpers?" It was a word they had never heard.

"Bad guys trying to take control of this place. They're fighting against Navy Seals."

"Dad used to be a Navy Seal," TJ said, though it was a needless reminder.

"And so was Uncle Mat," Melody added.

Phillipe felt his growing impatience bursting at the seams. "I need you both to stay here. I cannot let you-"

Both twins stared dumbly as Phillipe suddenly grimaced, his hands reaching for something clamped tightly around his throat. Struggling violently, his eyes began to bulge in alarmed surprise as the mulatto skin of his cheeks rapidly took on a blue-tinged shade. It appeared as though he couldn't breathe, and within seconds his body went limp as he lapsed into unconsciousness.

"Phillipe!" the twins cried in unison.

Phillipe crumbled to the floor, and in his place the image of a man with a glowering, pockmarked face abruptly coalesced.

A bout of snickering laughter erupted from Captain Francisco Alvarez as he studied the children, his glower changing over into a malicious grin. "So your father was a Navy Seal," he said, his tone dripping with sarcasm. "Could it be his name is Jake Javolyn?"

Both twins stared back wide-eyed, too frightened to speak.

Alvarez shed the cloaker he wore. Having had time to examine it since departing the *Southern Star*, he had figured out its purpose. And now he had put it to good use, utilizing it in the same manner Phillipe had used it to skulk about Cardoza's freighter unseen. This had made it rather easy for him to sneak up on the very person that had escaped his custody and apply a choke hold from behind.

The captain could not believe his good fortune as he eyed the children. Eager to locate where the gold was stored, he had left Malikai and company far behind and struck out on his own. Moving along a maze of rising and falling corridors that wound through the facility, he had spotted Phillipe and followed him.

Making a show of pulling his corvo slowly from its sheath, Alvarez glanced down at his fallen victim, who lay face down on the floor. Kneeling, he used his free hand to elevate Phillipe's head, placing the blade across his throat. From the look on his face, the twins could see he was enjoying this.

"I will only ask you once where they keep the gold, otherwise your friend will die," Alvarez snarled.

"It's on the island," Melody said, horrified that someone could be so cruel.

"Where on the island?" Alvarez demanded.

"Underground!" TJ blurted. "It's kept underground."

A look of madness consumed the captain's face, and for one fleeting moment it seemed as though he would carry out his threat anyway.

"Where underground?" Alvarez hissed, continuing to present a fierce scowl.

"We can show you if you promise not to hurt him," Melody pleaded with tears spilling from her eyes.

The captain's scowl turned introspective. He had not anticipated this. If what the children were telling him was true, it meant he'd have to find a way of getting to the island without alerting the others. And he had to do this quickly, knowing part of the invading force sent by the *Sublimis* was already on the island and might have located the booty by now. If this were to happen, there was no telling how much of it might disappear. As he mulled this, something drew his eye. It was the glint of polished metal.

"Why do you lie?" he accused in a distracted voice as he locked an avaricious gaze on a pallet stacked chest high with ingots of solid, gleaming gold. Forgetting about Phillipe he immediately rose to inspect this spectacular find.

Both twins followed his gaze, surprised by the sight. Exchanging looks, a sudden gleaning flooded their expressions, and taking full advantage of the man's preoccupation they scurried over to Phillipe, who was just beginning to stir.

Transfixed by the glistening metal, Alvarez stood mesmerized for several seconds, his mind trying to grasp the full magnitude of the wealth that lay before him. Sheathing his corvo, he reached out to grasp one of the topmost ingots. It took a moment before a frown creased his forehead as his hand only met air, and the thought that he might be going mad registered dully in his brain.

"What is this?" he railed, continuing to grope the stack in front of him but finding nothing there.

"It's not real," a voice from behind said.

Alvarez spun, astonished to see Phillipe already recovered and standing with the children behind him. Insane rage gripped him at the thought of being tricked like this, and overcome by it, the double-edged, razor sharp corvo was instantly back in his hand. "There's gold here and you will tell me where it is," he stormed apoplectically.

Phillipe shook his head calmly. "No."

Alvarez gave him his most pernicious, intimidating look. "Tell me where it is and I will let you live."

"You're wasting your time," Phillipe said, noticing the Masker taken from him was strapped to the captain's left forearm.

Alvarez considered drawing his Uzi and blasting him but immediately dropped the idea. The *corvo* was his weapon of choice. He wanted to hear his victims scream. Once he finished off this annoyance standing before him, he would have those brats lead him to the treasure.

Phillipe studied the Chilean's face, trying to anticipate his next move. The memory of his encounter with members of the *San Carlo* crew eight years earlier was suddenly in his thoughts. The incident had taken place one night along the waterfront in Port-au-Prince when they had surrounded him. The one called Pedro had also liked using a knife on his victims. He had only been fourteen years old at the time, far too small to defend himself, and if not for the timely arrival of Jay Jay and Zimbola, Pedro would have gutted him like a fish.

Men like Pedro were stone cold killers, unmerciful and sadistic to the core, and Phillipe had no trouble recognizing the same predatory look in the Chilean's expression. Here was another of the same ilk, a man who took immense pleasure in doling out excruciating pain, and he knew at once Alvarez was a monster that had to be stopped. But he was on his own now, for neither Jay Jay nor Zimby would be coming to his rescue this time. By all rights he should have been afraid, but strangely and for reasons he could not explain, he felt an overwhelming calmness sweep over him.

Phillipe slowly drew back into a martial arts stance. "Men like you have no honor," he taunted. "Only a true warrior would throw down the knife and engage me in hand-to-hand combat."

Alvarez abruptly stopped his advance, scrutinizing Phillipe with a wary frown. He was unaccustomed to dealing with an unarmed adversary who showed no fear, especially when he was wielding his corvo. Stunned by the youth's audacity, he decided to take on the challenge. "I don't need this to defeat you," he spat contemptuously, re-sheathing the blade, "but once I put you down again I will carve you up like a cow in a slaughterhouse." When his threat failed to instill any dread in Phillipe's eyes, the captain's sneer reverted back to a frown once again.

Phillipe waited for Alvarez to come to him. With eight solid years of martial arts training under his belt, he felt he was ready to counter anything the man threw at him.

A silly smirk conveying an utter lack of caution was plastered to the Chilean's face. Obviously overconfident in his fighting skills and completely underestimating Phillipe's, the captain didn't even bother to remove his weapons or the combat belt holding spare ammo clips and other items. The wheel kick he launched was easy to avoid, and Phillipe had no trouble shifting his body clear of the boot intended to smash his face. Alvarez followed up on the maneuver with a spinning back kick using the opposite leg, and again Phillipe sidestepped the attack, keeping just beyond the range of the heel seeking his ribcage.

"I am going to enjoy killing you," Alvarez blustered brashly. Pompously self-assured, he was unprepared for his opponent's counterstrike. Phillipe timed his leap perfectly, delivering a flying knee that caught Alvarez under the chin and staggered him backwards.

Barely able to keep his balance, the captain stared back in shock and awe as he shook off the cobwebs rifling his brain, astounded by the speed of the move. Humiliation quickly caught up with him, and he came back at Phillipe with a vengeance, throwing a series of punches and kicks laced with intense rage. Avoiding the onslaught, Phillipe danced backward, shifting his body and head from side to side or keeping himself just beyond the captain's striking range, all the while looking for a counterstrike. Compared to Jay Jay and Mat, the man before him was not even in the same class as his mentors.

The opening Phillipe sought came quickly. Reversing his retreat, he sprang forward to smash his right elbow into the bridge of Alvarez's nose. With his entire bodyweight behind the blow, the man's forward charge was abruptly halted as he went down on hands and knees. With the speed of a hummingbird, Phillipe slipped to one side to assess the damage, noting the wash of blood spilling copiously from a deep laceration where he had split the cartilage.

Alvarez gasped, wheezing hard and unable to pull in air through a broken nose. With glazed eyes he lifted his head to stare back at Phillipe dazedly, idly raising a hand to his face to inspect the blood smearing his fingers. As his head cleared, insane outrage took hold of him, and he staggered to his feet to fly back at Phillipe like a madman, screaming obscenities in Spanish. Deftly avoiding a shower of ineffectual kicks and punches, Phillipe suddenly ducked under a nasty right cross to lunge forward with a powerful tackle. Catching Alvarez about the waist, he lifted him off his feet and drove him backward with explosive force to slam him into a wall. Knocked senseless, Alvarez lay motionless.

Rising back to his feet, Phillipe stepped clear of his fallen opponent to give him quarter. Alvarez lay there for several seconds, breathing hard and grimacing before raising a hand to fend off another blow. "*No mas, no mas!*" he stammered. "*He terminado." No more, no more, I'm finished.*

"Have you had enough?" Phillipe huffed. "I do not wish to kill you. Perhaps-"

Appearing listless, Alvarez suddenly drew his holstered Uzi and leveled it at Phillipe. Clambering unsteadily back to his feet, a dark, hideous grin came to his bloodied face. "But I wish to kill you," he snarled insanely. Squeezing the trigger, he fired off a volley at close to point blank range, his rabid demeanor turning incredulous as the discharge streamed into a dazzling corona of pulsating violet radiance directly in front of Phillipe.

Astonishment took hold of Phillipe as he realized there was no pain. Nothing was hitting him. He could clearly see flames belching from the Uzi's muzzle from less than four feet away, but he was not being struck. In fact, there was not even a sound issuing from the weapon when there should have been. It was as though the brilliant flare of palpitating light separating him from Alvarez was absorbing the enfilade, including the sound.

Phillipe suddenly became aware of a twin standing on each side of him, Teejay to his right and Melody to his left, each extending an arm with something resembling a pyramidal jewel held firmly in their fingers. A flow of radiance spewed forth from each jewel to merge into the aura of violet pulsation that seemed to shield him from the deadly barrage.

The Uzi stopped firing as the last bullet in its clip leapt forth, and the shield of rippling light vanished. Still wearing a look of disbelief, Alvarez threw the firearm aside and drew his corvo once again. One way or the other, he was going to kill this adversary. Slashing the air wildly in a whirlwind of motion, he came at Phillipe again.

"I don't know what just happened, but you are going to die anyway," he screamed in a fit of blinding rage.

Aware that each twin had moved clear of the impending showdown, something flickered in the back of Phillipe's brain. Keeping just beyond the blade's lethal swipes, he moved backward.

An ugly leer formed on the Chilean's face as soon as he realized he was backing Phillipe into a place where the tunnel ended and the rush of a pounding waterfall could be heard. Forcing him back further, he suddenly lunged forward to execute an overhead slash. Phillipe was ready for it, however, and he shifted swiftly aside to leave Alvarez hovering slightly off balance at the brink of the drop-off. Turning quickly, the captain was ready to resume the stalk, standing momentarily at the edge of the steep precipice.

"You cannot escape me," he bellowed in frustration. "Sooner or later your head will be rolling-"

Phillipe barely heard him above the thundering water as the Chilean's eyes abruptly went wide. Looking down, Alvarez became cognizant of what amounted to a claw with five digits gripping his right ankle. With mouth agape, he let out a bloodcurdling shriek of unrestrained terror as he was suddenly yanked backward to disappear beyond the tunnel's lip.

Leaning over the edge, Phillipe saw him tumble end over end, the corvo held in his hand catching on one of the rungs embedded in the cliff wall a split second before the captain's neck intersected its guillotine edge. With his head lopped off, Alvarez vanished into the churning water far below.

Phillipe brought his gaze to Perseus, who continued to grasp the uppermost rung. Smiling, he sent out a thought to his bond mate. *Thanks for saving my hide, friend, but would you mind retrieving the Masker that bad guy was wearing.*

A thank you is not necessary, Perseus replied wordlessly, *but retrieving your Masker is.* Pushing his streamlined body away from the rung, he released his grip and somersaulted backward to execute a perfect dive into the water.

As both twins joined him, Phillipe couldn't help but ask, "What was that I witnessed?"

"We're not quite sure," Melody offered, holding up her crystal for him to see. "Grandma gave us these. It's a smaller version of the bigger ones being grown under Navassa. She says they gather in energy and might react to our thoughts."

Ez was suddenly standing next to them. "There is still much we have to learn about those crystals," she said, her gaze falling on the one Melody held. "At first I theorized they were only attuned to gathering in energy from seawater, but now it appears they are able to absorb energy in any form like a sponge, including kinetic, heat and even acoustical wave energy."

"That explains why I didn't hear any sound when he fired at me," Phillipe remarked, "but I'm surprised you didn't zap him with microwaves when he pulled his gun."

"That was not possible," replied Ez. "The microwave projectors are only stationed on the outside of this facility to repel undesirables from gaining entry."

"Well, it seems they got in anyway," Phillipe contested.

"The infiltrators have several men in combat suits equipped with wave suppressors that nullify our microwave emitters."

"Then how do you propose we stop them?" Phillipe asked.

"For starters I need you to capture the large helicopter that delivered one of the Seal teams. There are no men in combat suits on the landing pad and the two pilots are currently stationed aboard it. Take command of the ship and disable its jamming device. The radio waves it sends out are far more powerful than the ones issuing from those combat suits. We have to reduce the radio interference so those Seals can communicate with one another."

"Why not just zap the pilots with a microwave burst?" Phillipe proposed. "They're outside the facility."

"The microwaves cannot penetrate the aircraft's magnesium skin. I cannot reach them while they sit aboard it, but my sensors indicate that aircraft may also be equipped with a microwave emitter capable of suppressing our own weapon. Also try to locate that and disable it."

Phillipe gave a resolute nod. "And after I capture the chopper and disable both units, then what?"

Ez eyed Melody's crystal again. "We'll cross that bridge once you accomplish the first task, but you might try using those. I have reason to believe the more energy they absorb, the more powerful they become, though it is strictly a theory which I have yet to prove."

A subtle flickering resounded in Phillipe's mind. It was Perseus beckoning him. *I have your Masker*, his bond mate said. *I also found a second one in the captain's utility belt, including three ammo clips for his discarded firearm.*

Phillipe suddenly remembered that Alvarez had also taken the Masker Bashir had worn during their firefight back on the *Southern Star*. Moving back to the edge of the precipice, he found Perseus clinging once again to the topmost rung, Alvarez's combat belt with holster clamped between the dolphin's jaws. *You'll find the Maskers and ammo clips in the pouches,* Perseus informed him.

Teejay retrieved the discarded Uzi and handed it over to Phillipe, who reloaded the weapon with a fresh ammo clip upon strapping on the belt. Pulling out the Maskers, Phillipe handed one to each child. "I want you to wear these," he instructed them. Turning his gaze back to Ez, he asked, "Can you reprogram them so the twins will look like one of the infiltrators?"

"It's already done."

"It's too loose on my forearm," Melody complained after strapping hers on.

"So's mine," TJ griped.

Phillipe was adamant. "Well, you'll have to make do and wear them anyway." Moving away from the falls, he strode briskly to where the cloaker lay. "I want the two of you to stick to me like glue," he ordered the twins as he donned the cloaker.

"How do we do that if we can't see you?" Melody asked.

"I won't activate it unless absolutely necessary," Phillipe assured them, knowing Ez would not be able to track him once he went invisible. Even his infrared thermal emissions would be effectively blocked from Ez's scanning detectors when the cloaker was in active mode. That was why Alvarez had been able to sneak up on him undetected by Ez.

Thinking about what he was going to do, he looked behind him and saw that Ez had vanished from sight.

Chapter Twenty-five: Madman On The Loose

Idling up to one of several floating docks jutting out from a white sandy beach at the base of Aquaria's central structure, Kobe and Bashir tied off the *Exoco* and scanned their surroundings cautiously. Looking up, they could still see the upper portion of the massive military chopper resting on one of the landing pads two levels above them. Before reaching the dock they had had a better angle in which to study it. Sitting next to it was a smaller whirlybird, but the armaments and weaponry jutting from it made it appear far more ominous.

"I wish I knew where those two mischievous imps went," Kobe muttered, the signature smile that normally pervaded his features completely absent.

With squinted eyes, Bashir surveyed the water behind him to once again take in the enormous yacht floating just beyond the uncompleted portion of the breakwater that was to surround the complex, yet again wondering what it was doing here. It seemed to be drifting without power.

Kobe followed his gaze as they climbed onto the dock and made their way onto the artificial beach. Off to one side of the yacht and farther out to sea he could just make out a speck on the horizon seemingly heading directly for the colony. "Zimby's gonna have me dangling like a mango from one of those trees," he grumbled uneasily, eyeing the nearest citrus grove topping a completed portion of the breakwater well over a mile away.

Kobe swept his eyes along the lee side of the mounded protective barrier lushly populated by various types of fruit-bearing trees and staple crops set in between the various pavilions, hydroponic structures and resident living quarters dotting the breakwater. The sheer size and extent of the facility never ceased to awe him. Once the final modules of the barrier were floated into place, the ring enclosing the sprawling lagoons and containment ponds radiating outward from the central structure would be complete. And after that happened he would no longer be able to bring the *Exoco* inside the enclosure in the same manner as he had done now.

Bashir grabbed Kobe's arm, hastily pulling him along until they were sidling up against one of the columns supporting the esplanade the next level up. "There's armed trooper's up there," he warned, keeping his voice low.

"Did they see us?"

"I don't think so. I saw two of them two levels up. They appeared to be heading for those choppers."

Kobe gave Bashir an anxious stare. Lacking military training or combat experience of any kind, he would need to rely heavily on Bashir's guidance on how to proceed next. The only weapon he carried was the spear gun he normally kept aboard the *Exoco* for occasionally spearing a fish that came alongside the vessel while he was still aboard it. Rarely did he go in the water.

"What should we do?" asked Kobe, dubiously eyeing the webshot held by Bashir. It was the only other item of any significance he usually carried on the vessel. Though it wasn't even a weapon, Bashir thought it might come in handy other than the knives used for cleaning fish, which both of them also carried. Several years earlier, Jay Jay had given Kobe the webshot as a present. In all that time he had never used it.

Wearing a grave expression, Bashir looked all about him. "First we must see if they captured the twins." Indicating a stairway that rose up to the next level, he added, "If we make our way up there, maybe we can find out."

Kobe swallowed hard, glancing out to sea again to espy the *Angel* getting closer to the unfinished portion of the breakwater. It was either risking going up against armed troopers or dealing with Zimbola. "I'm with you," he said, nodding his head vigorously.

"Let's go!" Bashir prodded, suddenly bolting for the stairs and taking them two at a time. Not used to such physical exertion, Kobe had a hard time keeping up with him.

Reaching the next level, Bashir pulled up short to survey the platform with rapid glances in each direction. Seeing no one lurking about, he bolted for the next flight up, which ended at the foot of the ramp leading to the huge helipad. Risking a peak at the top before exposing himself entirely, he glanced sharply about again.

"Where you get all this energy?" Kobe protested, gasping heavily as he came up behind him. "Lowanda said you still needed rest."

"Quiet or they will hear you!" Bashir cautioned. He now had an unobstructed view of both troopers, who seemed to be lingering at the fuselage door of the larger helicopter and apparently focused on something that lay within.

"Do you see the children?" Kobe whispered hopefully.

"No. Stay here. Those troopers have their backs to us. I think I can sneak up on them."

"Are you crazy?"

Without another word, Bashir bolted from his place of concealment and sprinted up the slightly pitched ramp. The two troopers stood shoulder to shoulder, making it possible to snare both of them simultaneously once he got closer. Bashir knew that Jay Jay had used the webshot with great success during a skirmish with the crew of the *San Carlo* eight years earlier. Once fired, it would launch a 12-ounce projectile from its 37-millimeter bore to unfurl a net capable of entrapping these men without harming them.

As his finger tightened on the trigger, someone suddenly materialized in the doorway of the chopper a split second before springing out in front of the troopers. "Whoa, Bashir!"

Taken completely by surprise, Bashir immediately slowed, lowering the webshot as recognition flooded his countenance. Phillipe stood before him, his arms held out in supplication as a de-activated cloaker draped his body.

"Easy there," Phillipe appealed soothingly.

In an instant, the two troopers standing behind him underwent a transformation, reverting once again to their true identities. Both gazed back at Bashir as Kobe caught up with him, the twins appearing chagrined by their earlier deception.

"I saw you coming from the chopper's cockpit," Phillipe explained curtly, turning to climb back into the chopper. "Give me a hand and help me bind the pilots. I clocked them pretty good but there's no telling how much longer they'll remain in LaLa land."

As Bashir joined him, Phillipe yelled back to the twins in exasperation. "Will the two of you please turn your Maskers back on."

"Sorry," they chorused as one.

"What am I going to do with you two?" the *Exoco*'s captain chided.

Though they once again took on the form of black-clad troopers, both children fidgeted abashedly under Kobe's uncharacteristically stern demeanor.

"When Zimby catches up with Kobe he is going to rearrange my features to make me look like something that swims in the ocean. Are you happy?" Kobe's anger suddenly changed to exude the same jovial humor he normally displayed. "Do you hear me? The next time you see Kobe you will see a tuna with a face that looks like mine."

Both children erupted in laughter, the sound absurdly incongruent with their disguises. Their levity quickly subsided as a familiar though distant noise intruded on their senses. Turning, they espied the approach of a whirlybird, its blades slapping the air in a steadily deepening pitch. In moments the chopper flared to alight behind the Hind.

"It's grandma," Melody shouted to be heard above the blast of rotor wash as the chopper's blades began to wind down. "Maybe we should show ourselves." Looking at her brother she saw he had already done so.

Phillipe poked his head from the troop transport once again to note the cause of the disturbance. Jumping down from the doorway, he swung his head around to take a quick glance down the ramp to see if the noise had drawn the attention of any infiltrators. At seeing no one approaching, he ran to the Bell Ranger as the blades continued to crank at an idle.

"We need to get Victor to the infirmary," Amphitrite said, still sitting at the controls with Franklin next to her.

Phillipe glanced behind her, surprised to see Emmanuel and Chester jammed into the passenger seats along with Mortimer. Held between them was the former Spetsnaz soldier, his shirt caked with dried blood. He couldn't help but notice how exceptionally pale and weak Victor appeared.

"None of the medical staff will be up there," Phillipe informed her. "Ez tells me everyone has been evacuated to the island."

"All you need to do is hook him up to life support. Ez will be there to instruct you, then she will do the rest. Use elevator A-12. Ez says the way is clear, but you'll have to hurry. Were you able to shut down the jammer on that troop carrier?" Amphitrite asked as she focused her gaze on the AW101. Before she had landed Ez had told her what Phillipe was attempting to do.

"It's disabled." At seeing Amphitrite was making no move to shut down the engine and exit the chopper, Phillipe asked. "What about you?"

"Mat needs my assistance on the island."

"Let me help you," Phillipe said.

"No, stay with the children."

It suddenly occurred to Phillipe that Victor had been with Jake aboard *Johnnie* the last time he had seen him. "What happened to Jay Jay?" he demanded.

"He's on his way here. Destiny is with him."

Melody squirmed in front of Phillipe to show her grandmother the crystal she had given her. "These crystals did what you said they would do, grandma," she proclaimed excitedly. "We wanted them to suck up bullets and they did."

Amphitrite elicited a smile. Ez had already informed her of this. "I just had a feeling they would. Now go with Phillipe and use those crystals to protect everyone."

With Mortimer assisting Emmanuel and Chester, the task of removing Victor from the chopper was completed, upon which everyone stepped clear of the Bell Ranger as the main rotor gained momentum to blast them with a rush of wind, and moments later Amphitrite was making a beeline for the island.

As the twins watched her go, they became aware of a multi-hued spectrum gathering in the sky. A rainbow was forming directly over Navassa.

Clomping along heavily in the armored combat suit, Maximus made his way slowly back to the *Kraken's* bridge. Maddened by the suit's less than satisfactory performance and the latest turn of events, his seething rage immediately turned to bewilderment as he clambered into the ship's cavernous control room. Body parts smeared the floor, and if not for the huge ruddy nose jutting obtrusively from a severed head lying adjacent to a locker, he might have mistakenly assumed Finley was still alive. A bloodied axe lay next to Finley's remains, attesting to the weapon used in the slaying. The door to the locker was wide open, and Maximus saw that several of the firearms Finley normally kept locked up were missing.

Swiveling his visored helmet to take in every part of the room, he stared all about him in search of the murderer. In moments he spotted two more dead men, but each manifested a single gunshot wound to the chest. These he surmised to be the computer technicians that routinely assisted Finley in running the ship. Though Maximus was indirectly responsible for the deaths of millions around the world, rarely did he get a firsthand look at carnage such as this.

Mulling what he was going to do next, Maximus moved toward the ship's control console, the hydraulic joint actuators of the suit whirring noisily with every step he took. The mechanical suit was a major disappointment regardless of its other attributes. It had kept him effectively sealed from the torrent of water inundating the ship's interrogation sector when the pipe had burst, and the built-in oxygen supply had sustained him as he fought his way up into the dry levels where he could once again initiate the air intake. But now his Gatling gun was inoperable. Called a SPEFACS for short, the suit was supposed to be the latest generation in military grade Self Powered ExoFrame Armored

Combat Suits. Though its designers had told him it was combat ready, adamantly stressing its invincibility against small arms weaponry, they had failed to mention how slowly it moved. Originally, the suits were intended to be used during the planned government takeover in Haiti, but recent setbacks had caused Maximus to use them in taking control of Aquaria instead.

As he neared the console, a panicky voice carried across the room. "Don't shoot! Don't shoot!"

Looking down, Maximus saw a man poke his head from a large cabinet beneath the console. It was Holland, the *Kraken's* Chief Technician.

Watching him withdraw his body from the cramped space, Maximus studied the terrified expression on Holland's face before reaching out to clutch him by a shoulder with the suit's free hand and lift him from his feet.

"Why did you kill these men?" Maximus snarled through the suit's speaker.

Holland grimaced. The pressure exerted by the pincer-like hand was just short of snapping bones. "I didn't do it!" he screamed.

"Then who did?"

Barely able to speak from the pain, Holland moaned, "You're breaking my shoulder. Release me and I'll tell you."

Needing answers, Maximus set him back on his feet and eased up on the pressure only slightly. "Tell me?" he demanded, the sound projected by the suit's speaker reverberating harshly off the bridge walls.

"It was one of the men in the ship's brig. I saw him clearly before hiding, otherwise I too would be dead."

"How did you know he was from the brig?"

"I saw him when he was brought aboard. He has one of those faces you can't forget, the look of a madman."

"How did he get out?" The possibility that others may have escaped entered Maximus' thoughts, knowing how dangerous these men were. They had been neurologically pre-programmed for carrying out atrocities within the U.S. that were intended to increase gun control and induce politicians to take one step closer to repealing the Second Amendment.

"I'm…not sure," Holland groaned in a frail voice. "I think the locks on the holding cells released when the power went out."

Maximus let up on the pressure a tad more. "Are all the systems working again so the ship can be steered?"

"Yes."

Releasing his hold on the man, Maximus said, "Give me a view of the brig. I need to know how many escaped."

Holland brought a hand to his shoulder, rubbing it tenderly as he turned to a keyboard on the console. Tapping keys quickly, he brought up several real-time images of the holding cells on a wall monitor. The lone corpse littering the floor adjacent to an open cell door immediately caught Maximus' attention. Only one other door situated at the far end of the corridor stood ajar. All the other doors appeared closed, and from behind several of the barred doors the faces of other inmates could be seen staring back with the glazed look of zombies.

"It appears two got out," Holland said.

"Bring up the photos of the men assigned to the open cells."

As the mug shots appeared on the screen, Holland pointed. "The one on the right is him, Peyami Pehlivan."

Maximus swiveled his helmet again to see if the man was lurking anywhere about. He knew that one was particularly dangerous and judging from the gunshot wounds that had killed the two technicians, he had to assume Pehlivan was now armed and roaming the ship in search of more victims. Protected by the rigid, impervious suit he had no worries for his own safety. But Holland was another issue. Holland was vulnerable, and he needed Holland to operate the ship.

"Scan the ship and see if you can locate him," the *Sublimis* ordered.

In rapid succession, images of various sectors and hallways of the ship flitted across the screen.

"Back up!" barked Maximus suddenly, his sharp eyes discerning something on the floor where a corridor ended. Reversing the sequence of images, Holland also spotted the oddity, wondering how he had missed it.

"Give me a close-up," said Maximus.

"It seems to be your pilot," Holland offered, studying what the camera revealed. The pilot lay looking up at the ceiling with an expression of surprised horror frozen on his face, the remnants of a sandwich lodged in his mouth. White fragments of splintered bone protruded meekly from a gaping hole in his lower chest where a bullet had savaged his lower ribcage to leave his shirt soaked red with congealing blood.

"Looks like Pehlivan got him too," Holland commented nervously, his gaze sweeping the bridge on the lookout for the madman.

"There's a small galley down the hall," Maximus said, knowing the inmates were fed very little while penned up aboard the ship. Keeping them hungry was a necessary measure. The psychological programmers had been very explicit about this. Hunger would reinforce their desire to kill. "He'll be looking for food."

In moments, a view of the galley came up on the screen, and sure enough Pehlivan could be seen standing at a refrigerator, periodically reaching in the open door and ravenously stuffing cold cuts into his mouth.

"What are you going to do?" Holland asked, half expecting the *Sublimis* to make his way down to the galley and end the threat.

Maximus ignored the question. "Do you have head cams?" he queried, knowing Finley had always kept a few handy on the bridge to keep tabs on his technicians.

"Yes."

"Put one on and key it to the same screen."

Puzzled, Holland reached into a cabinet and strapped the device on so that the tiny camera jutted from his forehead. Turning back to the terminal, he manipulated more keys. As he faced Maximus again, the *Sublimis* saw his visored image staring ominously back at him from the monitor, which was now split into two scenes, one showing whatever Holland was looking at and the other continuing to display Pehlivan wolfing down food.

"Good, now engage the drone."

Holland gave him a curious look before doing as ordered. Turning back to the keyboard, his fingers went to work again. A low hum could be heard, and within seconds a nearby section of deck flooring opened up. Something rose from the opening, finally coming to rest with its base locked even with the floor. It resembled the seat of a jet fighter. Directly in front of the seat was a joystick and control console with an assortment of gauges and monitor screen.

Shifting a quizzical gaze from the drone controls back to Maximus, Holland repeated his earlier question. "What are you going to do?"

"It's what you are going to do," Maximus snarled, swiveling his helmet to the open gun locker where a shotgun and Uzi still remained.

Holland followed his gaze.

"Take the shotgun," Maximus grunted. "Go down there and finish him while he's still distracted. The food will make him more docile and less eager to kill."

Holland gulped, a feeling of dread taking hold of him. "I'm not very good with guns," he found it necessary to say, a pleading edge in his tone.

"Do it!" Maximus growled. "I'll be watching from here."

"But-"

Maximus reached out to clutch him by the shoulder again, applying pressure like before. "Deal with him or deal with me, it's your choice."

"Okay!" Holland whimpered.

Behind the suit's tinted visor, Maximus' eyes narrowed as he considered something else. Continuing to keep a tight grip on Holland, he said, "Before you go, I want you to set the ship's autopilot on a course that will take us to the sea colony. Have the ship's dynamic positioning system kick in to hold the ship steady two miles from where the outer breakwater is still unfinished, but I want the bow facing directly at the central structure."

Holland shuddered, nodding rapidly in acquiescence as wetness beaded in both his eyes to trickle down his cheeks. Surely his shoulder was on the verge of breaking.

Maximus released him, watching him move like a wounded animal to the ship's guidance terminal to study a GPS screen and begin entering data. Unlike most ships, the *Kraken* had no steerage wheel at its helm. And while course and speed were run mainly by computer, the helm did have a small joystick, a main throttle for the stern drive, and a smaller set of throttles for both the bow and stern thrusters. This allowed an operator to manually steer or rotate the massive ship once the computer guidance was disengaged. And Maximus knew the system's protocol was so simple that even a child could operate it once shown how to make the switch. All it took to do that was to move aside a guard cap and press a button adjacent to the joystick that would shift computer control over to manual.

"I set in the coordinates," Holland finally muttered tiredly as a barely perceptible tremor swept through the vessel. "We're underway."

"Good, now go."

Looking like a whipped puppy, Holland moved reluctantly to the gun locker to retrieve the 12-gauge shotgun and load it with buckshot shells. Turning to glance back at Maximus' armored visage one more time, he shuffled off to carry out the order.

Standing before the monitor, Maximus studied the screen to view Holland move down three flights of stairs and advance along a corridor. The small galley where Pehlivan was gorging himself was not far away, and he estimated it should only take Holland two more minutes to get there.

Feeling it was safe enough to leave his protective cocoon, Maximus touched a switch that opened the suit's chest plate like a clam shell, allowing him to climb out. Striding over to the gun locker, he grabbed the Uzi, inserted a clip, and chambered a round, all the while absorbed in deep thought that made him seethe with rage. He had been apprised of events that were currently taking place on Aquaria and the adjacent island. Just before he arrived at the *Kraken's* bridge he had contacted Dante using an encrypted satellite phone contained within the SPEFACS. Dante had told him he had no word as yet on the unit sent to the main facility, but the attack against the Seal team on Navassa was not going well. The task force sent there had been greatly reduced in numbers by unanticipated tactics that had destroyed three of the four SPEFACS spearheading the assault. But what remained of the task force was currently chasing down Seals headed for the old lighthouse on the southeast side of the island. It also appeared that the Seals may have reestablished communication with each other, as most of the interference caused by the radio jammers had mysteriously abated.

"What about the flagship carrier?" Maximus had demanded anxiously.

"Still afloat last time I looked, which was less than a minute ago, but she's moved from her earlier position," was Dante's response.

Something hadn't sounded right in Dante's tone, and Maximus had correctly pinned it down to evasiveness, for he well knew the carrier should have been destroyed by now. "Didn't Habibollah fire the torpedoes?" he had stormed shrilly.

A prolonged pause had ensued before Dante answered in a subdued voice. "The torpedoes missed their target, and the *Iron Fist* has disappeared off my sonar."

"What do you mean disappeared?"

"She's gone. I am unable to pick up any sign of her."

The statement made Maximus' heart trip violently in his chest. He had purposely revised his carefully planned timetable by stepping it up several months ahead of schedule. Upon leaving the Haitian coast, he had contacted a high-ranking constituent within *The Order* and instructed him to have his agents short sell over two trillion dollars in stock market assets and to buy up more than ten million ounces of gold and thirty million ounces of silver. Habibollah's assignment had been the critical element needed to set in motion the cataclysmic event that would increase the cabal's wealth and power tenfold, but only if the nuclear missile were launched. Sinking the *Carl Sagan* and the decimation of Miami could be blamed entirely on the sea colonists.

At hearing such horrific news, Maximus' brain had gone into overdrive looking for alternatives, and he thought about the two Venezuelan subs. "What about *El Martillo* and *El Yunque*?"

Dante had replied in a near whisper. "Destroyed!"

In a panic, Maximus had immediately called back the constituent and commanded him to reverse all the earlier transactions.

The constituent's voice shrieked with hysteria as he responded with a rapid-fire reply. "We'll be ruined if I do that. The market is in free fall and precious metals are going through the roof. Gold has gone up five times in value and is still rising. I beseech you to let the market settle down before we attempt anything."

The news left Maximus only one alternative, and one alternative only if he was to recoup his losses, and that was to take possession of Aquaria's gold supply, including the actual mine. With gold having soared so high in value he might even end up richer than he was before.

Breaking from these disturbing thoughts, Maximus pulled a small case containing a syringe from a pants pocket. Swabbing a forearm with disinfectant, he inserted the hypodermic into a vein. He wasn't about to make the same mistake he had made before. Perhaps he was being overly cautious, he chided himself. It was broad daylight in the sky above Aquaria, and it was doubtful those debilitating holographic displays could be effectively projected amid bright sunlight, but he was not willing to find out without a little protection. He had severely underestimated the people he was up against, and so far they had been incredibly lucky in thwarting him. But that was all about to change. Maybe he was down for the moment, but he wasn't out.

Climbing into the fighter seat, he activated the drone before glancing over at the split screen to check on both men. Absorbed in recent events, he had almost forgotten about them. A puzzling frown came to his face as he realized the galley was now empty. Pehlivan was nowhere to be seen and the view from Holland's head cam was bouncing about in a herky-jerky motion similar to a bobblehead. There was no sound accompanying the video, which made any assessment of the situation even more difficult to figure.

As Maximus stared, the picture suddenly steadied, and he saw the tip of the shotgun in the lower portion of the screen. The lighting in the area was uncommonly dim, but as far as he could tell, Holland was standing in the hallway outside the galley. Perhaps several of the nearby lights had blown out after the ship's power had been restored, Maximus thought idly as he studied the image.

The image abruptly shifted, and he got a fleeting glimpse of what appeared to be a corpse that lay in shadow. With insufficient lighting available to provide clarity, his mind had to work hard to clarify the image more distinctly. It appeared the corpse was shredded beyond recognition by multiple shotgun blasts. The video immediately changed perspective, and he saw at once that Holland was making his way back to the bridge.

Satisfied for the moment, Maximus brought his gaze back to the monitor in front of him and hit the switch that opened twin doors set even with the ship's deck further forward near the bow. Seeing that all systems were in the green, he punched the launch button to allow the drone to leap skyward. A look of pure hatred descended on his features as he remotely guided the unmanned jet fighter toward the floating city at better than Mach 2.

Chapter Twenty-six: Watch and Learn

Having landed the chopper on a flattened portion of ground surrounded by rugged terrain on the east side of the island, Amphitrite and Franklin scrambled up the sloping karst. It took them several minutes of arduous trekking to reach the base of the old lighthouse where the partially concealed entrance to the subterranean cavern was located.

"What are you going to do?" asked Franklin as they finally reached the water's edge deep underground. "You still haven't told me."

"I'm still trying to work it all out, but there's no time to explain. Wait here for me and I'll return shortly," she said just before diving into the water. The sense of impending disaster that had accosted her minutes earlier was now overwhelming, and she knew she had little time left if she was going to avert it. One possibility continued to nag away at her, however. Should her premonition be wrong, Aquaria was finished.

Franklin saw Athena rise up to meet her, and a moment later both disappeared into the depths. Standing there, he felt like an old man in comparison to his wife. For reasons he was unable to fathom, the passage of time had been exceptionally kind to her. Her looks had changed very little since the day she had vanished at sea many years ago. She still looked quite youthful. And though he had no way of proving it, he could only surmise it had something to do with that strange jellyfish. Coming in contact with it had somehow affected her physiology, maybe even altered it in some profound way far beyond his comprehension. Keeping up with her was difficult, for she continued to brim with the same tireless energy that had propelled her into world class athletic competition. Many years earlier she had been an Olympic swimmer, medaling with a bronze despite a serious groin pull that should have kept her from competing at all. She had an unstoppable grit. And while the fire within her still burned with that same fervent intensity, it now glowed with a luminosity more in line with the spiritual rather than the physical.

True to her word, Amphitrite rose back to the surface a few minutes later clutching Athena's dorsal. In her mind's eye she saw two lethal dangers fast approaching, one from the land and one from the sky. As she climbed from the water, Franklin saw she was holding two more of the pyramidal crystals similar to the ones she had given the children. Handing him one, she said, "We've got to hurry."

Franklin studied the crystal momentarily, knowing Hercules had recently retrieved four of them, so these were the last two. Suddenly aware of what she had in mind he said, "How do you know this will attune to my thoughts?"

"It will."

The timber of her voice and the way she had answered him left no doubts in his mind. Her belief was all too clear, and he trusted her instincts implicitly.

Franklin followed her as she made her way back to the surface along the same limestone passageway they had descended a short time earlier. Stepping from the entrance, he found the air to be unusually still and eerily quiet, but the transition from the dimly lit caverns into the bright sunlight made him squint sharply, and he became aware of five men in camos hunkered down behind the base of the old lighthouse. One of the men shifted his gaze and immediately pointed his weapon as he espied Franklin and Amphitrite approaching. A companion next to him seemed to be talking into a lip mic just before saying something to the soldier eyeing them, and for what seemed to be a brief moment of indecision, the man suddenly lowered his firearm.

Amphitrite scooted over to the Seal quickly, knowing that Ez had been able to contact these men. No sooner was she within arm's reach of the closest solider, the man flung out a brawny arm and pulled her in behind him. He watched as Franklin fell in behind her, studying both of them with an intense, inquisitive stare. "You're both lucky you weren't shot," he scolded sharply. "My partner here received a message you were friendlies a second before you arrived. So you're here to help, are you?" His manner abruptly shifted to one of incredulous skepticism at seeing they were completely unarmed. "What in god's name do you expect to do, throw rocks?"

As soon as he said it, the sound of a buzz saw knifed through the stillness, and a shower of concrete chips from higher up on the lighthouse rained down in front of them. Amphitrite saw at once that a piece of the holographic projector that was affixed further up on the lighthouse wall had come down with the concrete hailstorm.

"So much for that part of the plan," Amphitrite muttered amid the cacophony, but she was in no way perturbed.

Franklin also noticed the ruined projector, and he knew at once that Ez would be unable to perform the illusionary magic they had planned on using.

"You shouldn't be here," the Seal rebuked again as soon as the enfilade ceased, setting his gaze on the mechanical monstrosity just beginning to emerge over a nearby rise in the terrain. "I'm not even sure a bazooka will stop that thing."

A devilish grin came to Amphitrite's face. "Watch and learn, sonny, but I don't advise you follow our lead."

Before the Seal realized what she was doing, she stepped out into the open to run forward and stand directly in front of the oncoming metallic giant. Trusting his wife's intuition, Franklin jumped out to face the oncoming monster alongside her.

At seeing a man and woman without any weapons blocking his path, a befuddled frown formed briefly on the face of the man operating the SPEFACS. And then just as quickly, the confusion turned to a sneer as he fired off a heavy burst with the Gatling gun. Even with the protection of the tinted visor shielding his eyes, he was nearly blinded by an explosion of blazing incandescence burning a deep pulsating violet as the barrage streaked out to end the lives standing before him. Thinking the rounds might have set off an explosive carried by these people, he saw no reason to continue firing. The flaring light waned rapidly as soon as the enfilade stopped, and he was stunned to see both people still standing.

Amphitrite felt the crystal in her hand grow a tad larger from the energy it had absorbed. "Stick your tongue at him while we move to our right," she advised her husband. "Draw him in and make him mad. Get him to keep shooting. We have to keep him distracted."

Franklin followed her lead, quickly gathering what she had in mind.

Thoroughly enraged by the display of inflammatory antics goading him on, the SPEFACS operator moved to follow them before turning the Gatling loose again, this time hammering them with a prolonged fusillade. Squinting into the coruscation flaring back at him, he finally stopped the assault, only to be met by the same sight as before.

This is impossible! he shrieked inwardly, letting his emotions take control of him. They were openly mocking him now, gloating and dancing rowdily with infuriating smirks. Again, he triggered the Gatling, and once again an eruption of pulsing light bombarded his eyes like a hot violet sun on the verge of going nova, but this time it was flaring with a potency greater than before.

Seething with hatred and frustration as he fixated on the man and woman before him, the operator failed to keep aware of the ground that lay before him. The terrain was studded with jagged limestone and dense thickets of underbrush where he now was. Fissures and sinkholes existed in many places, some of them well camouflaged by thorned cacti and other types of veiling vegetation, and completely distracted, he stumbled into the one Amphitrite had been drawing him toward.

The SPEFACS crashed down hard, jarring the operator inside. He suddenly realized he was stranded in a pit with only the top of the helmet jutting above the edge. Had he not been encased in the suit he would have been torn up by the razor-sharp thorns growing out of the hole. In desperation, he tried using his pincer-tipped arm to free the SPEFACS, managing to clamp the lone pincer on the trunk of a small sapling. The hydraulic arm whined loudly as the suit began to rise from the pit, but then the sapling snapped and the metallic giant fell back, still trapped. With the Gatling gun well below lip of the depression, the operator could no longer provide cover fire for his comrades trailing behind. Hearing a din of small arms fire abruptly break out behind him, the operator suddenly felt helpless, but refusing to give up, he tried again to extricate the SPEFACS.

The hydraulic actuator screamed like a wild beast gone crazy as the pincer latched onto the base of another sapling. Throwing all the suit's power into the effort, the operator knew he risked blowing the servos, and all at once some of the systems began to fry from the overload, one of them being the radio jammer. Staring through the visor, he saw the small contingent of Seals he had been dogging scramble from behind the lighthouse to run past, and an instant later the sound of the firefight escalated sharply. With their communications now fully restored, the combined Seal unit sent to the island was able to regroup and initiate a coordinated counterattack that outflanked the enemy from two sides, catching them in a withering crossfire, and it wasn't long before the infiltrators were systematically mowed down to a man.

Amphitrite suddenly felt the approach of more danger as Mat charged up to stand close to the SPEFACS trapped in the pit. Held in one hand was a packet of high explosive. Shouting out, she got his attention just before he threw it down into the pit. Running over to him quickly, she said, "Hold off a minute, we need that thing in one piece a little longer."

Mat frowned. "Why?" There was urgency in his tone. The robo-suit had grabbed hold of the trunk of another small tree growing at the edge of the depression. If the threat wasn't ended immediately, it might get free.

"You'll understand in a moment."

As Maximus guided the drone toward the island, an ugly scowl came to his face. On the screen before him he saw a rainbow had formed directly over the old lighthouse, and as the fighter drew closer, he noticed a second one had coalesced behind it. The sight infuriated him. The last time he had seen such an atmospheric phenomenon he had been thwarted. *Not this time*, he snarled, clenching his teeth.

Bringing the lens setting on the drone's nose camera to full magnification, his face clouded darkly again. Figures were scurrying over the landscape like ants near the lighthouse, but already he could distinguish black clad forms sprawled helter-skelter over the rugged landscape. Farther away, he spotted the *Carl Sagan*, still afloat and seemingly unscathed.

Seething with livid hatred, Maximus contacted Dante via the encrypted radio on the control panel. "Destroy the carrier!" he ordered.

Dante responded in a voice filled with apprehension. "We have already lost three subs, do you want to risk losing a fourth?"

"Do it now or your life won't be worth so much as a drachma!" Maximus snapped, referring to the failed Greek currency.

In no mood for further objections, he ended the transmission, shifting the camera angle to the island's south shore where a cluster of large structures existed. Almost immediately he spotted what appeared to be two destroyed SPEFACS smashed into the ground between two partially damaged buildings. More bodies, all black clad, lay scattered around them. Wondering what had caused such annihilation, his eyes came to rest on two pieces of heavy equipment rumbling over the terrain, a huge bulldozer and a payloader almost as big. Further away were parts of a third SPEFACS and several dozen more of his black clad troopers, all of them apparently dead, strewn over a wide swath of the landscape extending almost to the water. He had hoped the news Dante had conveyed to him was in error, but as his eyes took in everything the camera revealed, he knew it was all being confirmed.

And then his eyes fell on something else that made his blood boil all the more. Seeing the offshore platform was still intact told him Bolder had failed to carry out his pre-arranged assignment.

How can this be? he raged inwardly. The idea that every segment of his carefully crafted plan had come apart at the seams defied logic. Hardest to accept were the losses his invasion force had suffered. Using radio jammers to disrupt communication among the Seal units should have taken away any possibility of a coordinated counterattack. More than one hundred of his men had been dispatched to the island along with four SPEFACS that should have been unstoppable. Using superior weaponry and outnumbering the meager Seal team sent there by a factor of more than seven to one, they should have won easily, but his eyes were telling him differently.

Pivoting the camera more, he set his gaze on the floating city. Perhaps his task force sent to there was doing far better, he reasoned irritably. Within the confines of the central structure the Seals would not be able to resort to the same tactics used on the island.

With that thought in mind, Maximus reduced the drone's altitude to make a low pass near the lighthouse. According to Dante, not all his troopers had been decimated, and with the drone coming to their rescue it was now possible the battle for Navassa could be turned around into a decisive victory. Once he distinguished friend from foe, he'd blow those Seals to hell.

As the drone approached the lighthouse at supersonic speed, Maximus immediately spotted the fourth SPEFACS a split second before the unmanned jet flashed over it, and he realized it was trapped in a vegetated fissure with two people perched along its rim.

The precognizance that gripped Amphitrite was exceptionally strong as she glanced up at the sky to espy the drone swooping in swiftly. Hovering at the edge of the pit, she looked down at the visored helmet, letting out a loud, taunting laugh.

Upon seeing her, the operator elevated the Gatling arm to fire directly up into her face, and as he triggered the weapon, Amphitrite pulled her head back. Flames shot from the whirling barrels, and a dizzying torrent of rounds streaked straight up into the air. The drone seemed to buck as it flashed by overhead, and a moment later black smoke began to trail behind it as it tore off toward the western end of the island and beyond. The happening was an exact replay of the vision that had invaded her thoughts even before she had landed on the island.

"Now you can dispose of that monster," Amphitrite said, amused by the look on Mat's face.

Mat stared back in awe before tossing the charge down into the pit. Waving his arms wildly, he got the attention of Navy Seals fast approaching. "Everyone back and take cover!" he shouted.

Amphitrite began running toward the lighthouse with Franklin right beside her. Trotting past the Seal who had admonished her, she said, "Follow me!" But the man stood frozen with a dazed look, still astounded by what he had witnessed earlier.

Amphitrite stopped and turned to look back at him. "If you don't want to die, you and your men follow us!" she warned again. "That thing as you call it is going to blow." She knew how god-awful powerful those explosives could be. Even the pit containing it would not fully suppress the shock wave, which would fan out in all directions.

Suddenly coming out of his stupor, the Seal turned to the other men and barked an order. "You heard her, move!"

Scrambling into the cave opening, the men followed Amphitrite's lead as she braced herself against a rock wall just before the outside air was shattered. The shock wave tore through the earth, jolting the ground under their feet.

A moment passed before Amphitrite thought it safe to leave the tunnel. Dust wafted all around her as she poked her head outside to look back at the lighthouse. Her worst fear immediately faded as she saw it had weathered the blast, though there was considerable damage further up along its side where it had taken the brunt of the explosion. She well knew that everything depended on the lighthouse standing.

Bringing her eyes to the crystal in her hand, Amphitrite saw it had doubled in size. Tilting her head back, she focused her gaze on the structure's pinnacle towering high above her.

Franklin caught up to her at the same time Mat did. "Have both of you gone crazy standing in the open like that?" Mat scolded. "You're lucky the man inside that mechanical nightmare had such a poor aim. I'm surprised he missed you at such close range."

Franklin smiled. "He didn't."

Mat's brow creased, wondering why Destiny's father would joke like this following such a close call. For confirmation, he swept his eyes over Franklin looking for wounds. "Oh, he missed you all right. Not a scratch."

Franklin showed him the crystal. "When you have one of these, you don't need to worry about being hit." At seeing the perplexity on Mat's face, he quickly clarified the statement. "It attunes to the holder's thoughts. Once you envision it gobbling up lethal energy directed at you, that's exactly what it does. It acts as a shield. For reasons we still don't fully understand, it's able to absorb energy like a sponge."

Mat continued to stare. "Can I see that?"

"Be my guest," Franklin said, handing the crystal over.

Mat turned it over in his fingers as various members of the Seal team congregated around them. "This looks like a smaller version of the ones we're growing for Big D."

"That's exactly what it is," Amphitrite said. Suddenly struck by another premonition, this one more foreboding than the first, she reached out to retrieve the crystal from Mat's hand. "Now if you gentlemen will excuse me, I have one more task to carry out."

Mystified, Mat asked, "Where are you going?"

Amphitrite glanced up toward the tower again before her gaze strayed to the horizon off to the west. Continuing to belch smoke and flames, the drone was still aloft, but now it was turning. "We're not out of the woods yet," she warned as she headed quickly for the door at the base of the lighthouse.

Mat and Franklin exchanged puzzled looks before turning to stare in the direction where she had just gazed. Suddenly realizing what she was up too, both men bolted after her.

Two years earlier the lighthouse had been retrofitted with a high-speed elevator, and before Mat and Franklin caught up with her, Amphitrite was through the elevator doors and on her way to the top.

Surprise took hold of Maximus as he examined the control console in front of him. The temperature gauge had suddenly risen sharply, indicating the drone engine was beginning to overheat. If he didn't ease back on the power, the turbine driving the aircraft forward at more than twice the speed of sound would be in jeopardy of coming apart. The only plausible cause for the problem he could come up with was that the engine had taken a hit, and that thought alone made him scream out in frustration.

Letting up on the throttle, he swung the drone around in a wide turn, the need for retribution now overpowering. The desire to blow something to smithereens was maddening. The huge bulldozer lay directly before him, and as though his hand had a mind of its own, he fired off a missile. A rabid smirk transcended his face as a fireball engulfed the dozer, but with his need for vengeance still unsated, he looked around for another target to destroy.

Something nagged at his subconscious, and suddenly aware of what it was, he quickly manipulated a few buttons on the console, bringing up a video replay of the trapped SPEFACS in one corner of his flight screen. Pausing the picture, he studied it intently before magnifying and sharpening the image. Almost immediately his eyes widened in fury. One of the two people hovering above the robo-suit was the grandmother of those brats that had escaped him. Widening the view, he saw a half dozen Navy Seals nearby.

A cockpit alarm abruptly sounded, jolting him from his smoldering thoughts. Another glance at the temperature gauge reminded him of what these people had done to his prized aircraft. In spite of the power reduction, the temperature had crept further into the red, and he knew at once the unmanned fighter had little remaining life in it. If he was going to act, he had to act fast. Salvaging whatever airspeed he could coax out of the failing aircraft, he piloted it straight for the old lighthouse. Already he was down to 200 knots, with his airspeed continuing to plummet.

As he guided the drone closer to the towering structure, he espied a cluster of people along its base. Sudden movement caught his eye higher up, and he perceived a lone figure emerge on the tower's walk around observation deck on the outside of the tinted windows. Magnifying the view with the drone's nose camera, he saw it was that women again.

The warning alarm abruptly escalated into a piercing wail as Maximus drew forth the final ounces of remaining power from the dying engine, and the jet fighter suddenly surged faster. With his face twisted into a hideous malevolent smile, he simultaneously triggered the guns and all his remaining missiles, vaguely aware that he was screaming out the words, "Die, you bitch!"

Chapter Twenty-seven: Right on the Edge

Amphitrite stood fast as the fighter drone raced directly at her. Clutching a T-crystal in each hand, she brought them together and held them out in front of her as she focused her thoughts. Something akin to a spark flared brightly as the gems touched, but she had been prepared for this and had closed her eyes so as not to be blinded. Nevertheless, she saw the event clearly as it unfolded, envisioning a mental image of the drone coming on, its guns suddenly blazing and a cluster of missiles leaping forward. She saw the face behind it all, Maximus' face, a face of pure evil. The sheer magnitude of malevolence racing in on her was the worst she had ever faced, more pernicious than the late Colonel Ternier, more wicked than Erzulie, but like all things of a purely evil nature, she knew it could be stopped, first by capturing and then re-using its own deadly, destructive force to combat it.

Yet there was still the possibility of disaster. T-crystals could be unpredictable. If overwhelmed with more energy than they could absorb, the gems might very well explode, vaporizing her and the lighthouse in the process. Abruptly she dispelled this notion, setting her mind on only the positive, linking her mind with the others, the collective consciousness of the entire pod. It all came down to a battle of wills. Either the light would prevail or the darkness would rule. Standing her ground, Amphitrite felt the crystals swell in her hands as the wave of destruction found its target. There was no sound, nothing to ruffle her skin, but the drone itself was another matter. Far more massive than the combination of missiles and bullets hurled at her, it carried a kinetic energy that could easily disintegrate the lighthouse once it hit.

With her eyes shut tightly, Amphitrite only had to wait an instant longer before it hurtled in upon her.

Peering through the spy glasses, Captain Delila followed the aircraft as it streaked over Navassa Island leaving a heavy contrail of dark smoke in its wake. Heading directly for the old lighthouse, it appeared to launch missiles a moment before impact. A great flash of light followed, mushrooming out to completely engulf the towering structure. And just as quickly it seemed to shrink back in upon itself, disappearing to a pinpoint before vanishing completely. Frowning in puzzlement, he tried to make sense of what he had just witnessed. It was as though a powerful vacuum had suddenly turned on to suck up a cloud of hot gas before it could expand any further.

"Sir, we have another incoming transmission," Ensign Jefferson informed him, holding out the phone. "Sounds like the same caller as before."

Grabbing the phone, Delila put it to his ear, amazed to see the lighthouse still standing. "Captain Delila speaking."

"That fourth submarine I told you about earlier appears to be turning and heading your way. As a safety precaution it is strongly advised you steer a course of one hundred thirty-five degrees at full speed as the sub's immediate intentions are still unclear, but we'll do whatever is necessary to keep your vessel safe should those intentions be construed as truculent."

Delila looked in the direction indicated. Taking the carrier on such a heading would bring it south of the *Numquam Satis*, which appeared to be moving again. From his current vantage point, he had an excellent view of its starboard side and could clearly see a herd of whales now pushing it away from Aquaria.

"I would appreciate it if you'd tell me who you are," replied Delila.

Once again the caller ignored the question. "With our help, the Seal unit sent to the island has defeated the unknown forces the fourth sub had deployed there. You should be able to contact them now. Unfortunately, the other unit sent to Aquaria is still under siege, with their communications still being jammed, but we'll be assisting them shortly."

Delila opened his mouth to say more, but the line suddenly went dead. Turning, he addressed Jefferson. "Instruct the helm to steer a course of one hundred thirty-five degrees at maximum speed." Strangely, he felt he had nothing to worry about.

Amphitrite opened her eyes. She had felt Maximus' rage just as the drone vanished, and its sheer intensity had startled her. The feel of the T-crystals in her hands was now different, and as she gazed upon them she realized they had changed. Only one remained, but instead of a four-sided pyramid, this one was three-sided. She could only conclude that the two had merged to form a single crystal roughly twice as large. As she studied it, she saw the deep violet glow its predecessors had exhibited had also changed. This one gave off a soothing crimson light.

If only the pod had more of these rare gems, she ruminated in frustration. Almost immediately a new awareness seeped into her thoughts, and she found herself swimming in the depths directly below Aquaria. One of the gargantuan *thurentra* lay before her, and spewing from its base were hundreds of 4-sided T-crystals gathering on the seafloor.

Something jarred her from her reverie, and she realized Franklin was at her side with Mat standing next to him.

Franklin stared thoughtfully at the crystal in her hand.

Seeing the look on his face, Amphitrite said, "It seems if you hold them together when they are absorbing large amounts of energy, they merge into a single three-sided pyramid."

Mat leaned out over the railing to gape in all directions before bolting to the opposite side of the observation deck. Circling back, his expression was clouded. "Where'd that thing go? I don't see any sign of it."

Franklin nodded at the crystal. "Guessing, I'd say it's in there. Seems to act as a portal in which things disappear."

"Possibly an interdimensional portal," Amphitrite amended. Still linked with the others, she was merely parroting the overall conjecture of the pod mind. They were now aware of the potential.

Glancing toward the floating city, Amphitrite was not seeing the massive central structure surrounded by the vast array of lagoons and containment ponds. Instead, there was an image flashing before her eyes of more than a dozen albinos switch backing rapidly into the depths. They were diving deep, following behind an enormous sperm whale. The image faded, replaced by something altogether different.

Franklin studied her countenance, noticing the semi-glazed look that seemed to take hold of her as she turned to circle along the observation deck before stopping to take in the view off to the east. Following her, he saw the object drawing her attention. An incredibly large ship was just emerging over the horizon.

"We have little time," Amphitrite suddenly blurted. "We have to get back to the city if we're going to save it."

Turning, she raced for the door that accessed the observation deck. Inside the lighthouse, she scurried past the massive 3-sided pyramidal crystal centered behind the tinted windows. It had been installed there six months earlier. It was an exact duplicate of the one in her hand, only much larger. Radiating a deep crimson, it was beginning to pulse. It was the final component of Big D.

With Franklin and Mat trailing behind her, she bolted down the spiral staircase that wound one flight down to the elevator, aware that the T-crystal in her hand was pulsing in cadence with its much larger cousin.

Amphitrite suddenly pulled up short. Athena and the pod were calling to her in a unified voice again. Franklin noticed the faraway look on her face, and he immediately knew she was once more in conference with those higher delphine minds.

Mat also became aware of her detached mien. "What's wrong?" he asked.

Amphitrite emerged from her momentary stupor. "We have a little mission to undertake before we go back to the city," she stated flatly.

Mat's eyes narrowed suspiciously. "Mission?"

Amphitrite nodded solemnly. "Yes, this will involve an abduction." Keeping a tight grip on the crystal, she could feel the quickening resonation. "Both of you hold onto me. We're going for a little ride."

The cetacean giant rose to within 100 feet of the surface and opened its massive jaws to expose a mound of T-crystals sitting on its tongue. One by one, a succession of mutated gray dolphins swept into its maw to snatch a crystal in each of its grasping appendages before streaking off in various directions. Hermes had gotten four such crystals at depth and had passed two of them on to Aphrodite, his sister. Interspersed among the grays, a smaller contingent of their albino cousins also shot in to make off with a few of the small 4-sided pyramids, one in each hand jutting obtrusively from under a pectoral fin. Apollo and Artemis had already entered the artificial cove inside Aquaria, as did Coral and Reef, all of them armed with these same crystals. These six albinos were to be the advance guard, the ones whose primary objective was to stop the robo-suit operators before they could kill any Navy Seals within the floating city.

A short distance away, *Johnnie* materialized out of the gloom to discharge two more albinos, each with a human rider astride its back. In deference, the pack of grays parted to allow them passage, and gracefully, Achilles and Hercules swooped between the sperm whale's open jaws to partake in the proceedings, each grabbing two T-crystals. Both Jake and Destiny reached down and grabbed a dozen more, each stuffing them into a pouch strapped around their waist. But unlike the advance guard, they and their bond mates headed for the open water to the south.

How far? Jake asked Achilles.

Six thousand meters, Achilles answered. *The ship is well clear of Aquaria's outer ring. Shall I tell the whales to stop pushing?*

Yes, but I want them at a safe distance.

And what distance would that be?

Jake thought he detected a little snideness in Achilles' reply. *Hell, I don't know. Has Ez run any calculations?*

She has, but it's all based on conjecture, JJ, basically everything we learned in the last hour about these crystals. Ez surmises these latest crystals brought up from depth have slightly different properties than the earlier ones. In theory, there's no safe distance. If the crystals get overwhelmed with more energy than they can handle, all of us, including Aquaria and Navassa, will be vaporized. It seems Big D is somehow linked to them, so a chain reaction is possible.

Just what I needed to hear, more bad news, Jake griped.

You have to remember the power nitro fuel represents. Having remotely taken control of the ship's systems, Ez noted slightly over 80,000 gallons still remained in her tank. That's a catastrophic explosion no matter how you look at it, especially when you factor in all the explosives carried aboard. You sure you want to take that risk?

There was something in the way Achilles conveyed the question that made Jake reconsider what was at stake, and he wondered if his bond mate was testing his resolve. Everything they had worked for would be lost, and by their own actions if they failed. No, that wasn't quite right either. It would be the result of his own actions, for he was the one they all looked to for their mutual survival, for Aquaria's survival, and for future generations of the new breed. And though the albinos were light years above him in pure intellect, they all trusted his judgement with an unwavering loyalty even though that judgement might appear grossly reckless on the surface.

What am I doing? Jake questioned himself, blocking the self-assessment from Achilles. As he pondered on it, he realized there was more to what they would be attempting, much more. The causality was mind boggling, for he saw that failure would ultimately ripple its way outward to affect the entire planet. But there was also danger in too much caution, and no matter how he analyzed it, he knew Maximus and his cohorts had to be stopped, otherwise the bright future Tursiops was planning for the Haitian people would turn bleak, just as it would for the mainstream factions of the human race. If Maximus succeeded with his malicious schemes, widespread famines would ensue and huge numbers of mankind would die off, with survivors being sentenced to a life of servitude and misery for the benefit of an elite minority.

Jake needed some kind of reassurance, something to rest his hopes on. If it was solely his own life he was putting at risk, he would not have reflected on the possible consequences of his actions as he was doing now.

Is the pod able to glimpse the future on this one? Jake asked hopefully.

All we see is mist, JJ.

Then I suggest you put this to a vote.

It has already been done and the consensus is unanimous. I believe the term in table stakes poker is called 'all in.'

I should never have taught you that game, Jake grumbled, continuing to hold on tightly as Achilles surged through the hydrosphere.

An odd sensation suddenly nudged its way into Jake's thoughts, causing him to glance over at Destiny riding abreast of him. Behind her face mask he saw she was encouraging him on with a comforting smile stretched across her beautiful face, and within her eyes he was reminded of something he would always remember ever since he had come upon it in a book depicting the works of Robert Vallett, a famous twentieth century French poet, essayist and philosopher. *The human heart can see what is hidden in the eyes, and the heart knows things that the mind cannot begin to understand.*

As he stared into her eyes, all the encumbering chains of doubt fell away, leaving him suddenly electrified with an unstoppable determination. Opening his mind to his bond mate, he let loose the only thought that came to mind, a thought that to a large degree defined who he was.

Let's kick some ass, Achilles!

Temporarily blinded by the intense light that had flashed on the screen, Maximus waited for the dots swimming before his eyes to vanish and his vision to clear. Able to see again, a bitter scowl formed on his face as he stared at the blank screen in front of him, unsure of what he had witnessed just before the drone crashed into the lighthouse. The thought that he had killed the woman only gave him partial satisfaction, and he knew he had much more to do if he was going to put an end to the threat these colonists posed to his grand scheme.

As he climbed from the drone's control seat, a sound behind him made him whirl. Expecting to see Holland, a startled look of shock seared across his face as he stared upon the deranged countenance of

Peyami Pehlivan, the 12-gauge shotgun previously wielded by Holland now in his hands.

Pehlivan grinned fiercely as he pointed the shotgun at Maximus. Though his psychotic brain churned with a chilling madness, he had occasional though brief periods of clarity, and a portion of his once brilliant mind had pieced together what they had intended for him. He had overheard conversations of the white-frocked men who had tried to mold his thoughts using painful methods.

"Are you the man responsible for what they did to me?" Pehlivan asked. His tone was mild, almost as though he were inquiring about the weather.

Maximus recovered quickly, looking for a way out of this unanticipated predicament. In a desire to inflict pain on the colonists, he had foolishly let his wariness slip by assuming Holland had killed Pehlivan. How this lunatic had turned the tables on the ship's chief technician he had no idea, but perhaps he could talk his way out of this.

"Of course not," Maximus said, feigning offense. His eyes flicked furtively to the .357 pistol tucked into Pehlivan's waistband before shifting them to the Uzi he had laid on the floorboard of the drone control. It was just beyond his reach. "What they did to you, they also did to me," he went on smoothly. "I hate those people even more than you do and wish to kill them all. Perhaps you can help me. There are more of them aboard this ship." Turning his head, he indicated a door on the starboard side of the bridge. "They're in there."

Pehlivan followed his gaze, and as he did, Maximus sidled ever so slightly for the Uzi. He had previously chambered a round and the safety was off. All he had to do was snatch it up, point it and squeeze the trigger.

Maximus froze as Pehlivan pivoted his head back to regard him again. With his obtrusive hawk-like nose, he appeared like an avian predator sizing up prey.

Speaking quickly, Maximus pointed toward the bow windows, aware that he was a hair away from dying. "If we work together, we can kill a lot more of them. What they did to you, they do to a lot of people in that floating city."

At that moment a barely perceivable shudder reverberated underfoot as the port side bow thrusters kicked in to swing the ship a few degrees to the north, lining it up with Aquaria's central structure. The ship seemed to shiver again, more pronounced this time, and Maximus knew the propellers driving it forward were reversing to slow it down. The *Kraken* was nearing its preprogrammed destination.

Pehlivan's expression hardened, impaling Maximus with cold brooding eyes before turning his head to take in the city. Knowing this might be his only chance for survival, Maximus lunged for the Uzi, snatching it up in one quick adrenaline rushed instant and raking Pehlivan with a fusillade. Rounds stitched the lunatic's chest, staggering him backwards on his heels, but amazingly Pehlivan was able to fire back, and Maximus was spun around and knocked off his feet as a burst of 12-gauge buckshot plowed into his shoulder.

Maximus lay there for several seconds, his breath coming in short, quaking gasps. Somehow he found the strength to stumble to his feet, vaguely aware that his shirt was now sodden with blood. Taking inventory of his wound, he discovered his left arm hung limply and numb, with little feeling in his fingertips. At the moment there was no pain, but he was certain it wouldn't be long before it hit him with a vengeance. Nevertheless, he knew he would live. Setting his gaze on Pehlivan, he saw the man lay unmoving with sightless eyes fixated on the ceiling and half a dozen bullet holes in his torso. A slowly spreading puddle gleaming bright red moved outward from his body as his life juices leaked away.

Satisfied that Pehlivan was dead, Maximum staggered a few steps back to the drone control, his legs nearly buckling under him. Punching in a call to Dante, he needed an update on the mission. According to his calculations, Dante should have destroyed the *Carl Sagan* by now, but when Dante failed to respond, he flew into another rage. "Answer me!" he roared. It suddenly occurred to him he would be unable to reach Dante unless the sub had its communications antenna deployed above the ocean surface, so the sub must currently be on the move and too deep to do that.

Pondering the current situation, Maximus suddenly felt the pain in his left shoulder, a dull throbbing sensation that was quickly escalating. Knowing there was a first aid kit in one of the cabinets that Holland had hid in earlier, he gritted his teeth and reeled his way over to one of them, rummaging around before finding what he was looking for. Quickly, he pulled the syringe from the pack and injected himself with morphine, and in moments he felt the pain begin to subside.

Rising back to his feet, Maximus turned to study the colony in the distance. Almost immediately, a dark, livid scowl enfolded his features as his eyes fell upon the double rainbow he had seen earlier. And now a third one was forming behind those, perfectly framing the other two.

Out of the corner of his eye, he was stunned to see Pehlivan back on his feet, the .357 magnum aimed directly at him. A wavering amused grin hung on Pehlivan's face as he stared back at Maximus. Standing there on unsteady legs, he struggled for breath, and in a halting reedy voice that was barely audible he managed to utter the only words Maximus would ever hear again. "Perhaps… we were always meant...to see the wonders of hell together."

The gun in Pehlivan's hand erupted just before he collapsed, dead before he hit the floor. With the morphine coursing through Maximus' veins, he sensed rather than felt the bullet pierce his chest. Knowing that this time he was truly dying, he staggered on wobbly legs to the helm controls and lifted the guard cap that would allow him to override the autopilot. Awkwardly and with a trembling hand, he punched the button giving him manual control of the ship. With his last remaining strength, he pushed the *Kraken's* throttle all the way forward before his body slumped slowly to the floor.

Dully aware that his life was ebbing away, a feeble smile crossed his face, no longer caring about the task force he had sent to Aquaria, including Van Heflin and Allotey. Having spent most of his life planning and scheming, he had one last card to play. It was his ace in the hole, one he had kept in reserve should his life become forfeit, though he had never imagined it would end like this. With his vision rapidly fading, he groped with tremulous fingers for his Emperador Temple wristwatch and twisted the diamond-studded face. Even to his failing ears he heard the low hum. It was now emitting a powerful microwave that would be picked up by satellite and relayed to a covert base in Venezuela. It would be his final legacy to an ungrateful world. Even before his final breath came, he was happy in the knowledge he would be putting an end to everything the people who had thwarted him had been trying to accomplish.

That submarine is closing fast, Achilles informed Jake. *As you like to say, they're taking the bait.*

I wouldn't go so far as to say that, Jake qualified. *It seems the commander of that sub is more afraid of Maximus than he is of us, this in spite of what happened to the other three subs in their task force.*

Through the telepathic network the albinos used, Achilles had shared that news with Jake earlier on, also letting him know what Ez had learned a short time ago. Ez had intercepted Maximus' last transmission to the sub commander and had cracked the encryption. The commander's response and tone were enough to convince her of his reticence to actually carry out the order, but now she was certain of his intentions.

Directly in the path of the sub was the *Numquam Satis*, and just south of the mega-yacht and below her keel was where the foursome of Jake, Destiny, Achilles and Hercules waited.

Any word on the Kraken? Jake asked anxiously.

Thirty seconds, JJ.

Jake grimaced inwardly, knowing how close this was going to be. And maybe not close at all. Ez had run the calculations. The amount of energy they would need would put them right on the edge, a very precarious edge, most of it based on pure speculation and assumptions. She had felt it only fair to tell them the odds were not favorable, maybe fifty percent at best, but they had no choice but to try anyway, and the only immediate source of that energy was a combination of what the mega-yacht and oncoming sub held within their holds.

Why a man like Maximus would make a suicide run at the colony, he could not imagine…unless…

Achilles burst into his thoughts. *Maximus is dead, JJ.*

How do you know?

Amphitrite saw him die.

One of her visions?

Yes, JJ. I recommend you keep your eyes closed. Ez is going to remotely launch a torpedo at close to point blank range in two more seconds.

Jake became aware of the sub, a huge black shadow suddenly taking on shape as it materialized out of the hydrospheric void. Strangely, he felt at peace. Turning his head, he looked at Destiny sitting astride her mount next to him. She stared back, her eyes seemingly radiating a stream of love in its purest form. Though she held a T-crystal in each hand out in front of her, her gaze never wavered from his face. Even now she was a complete mystery to him, and like a parched man coming upon a water well in the midst of a searing desert, he could not get enough of her, drinking in her profound beauty to savor her sweet enigmatic essence, an essence that seemed to fluctuate somewhere between temporal and spiritual realms. If he was going to die, he wanted her face to be the last thing he would ever see in this world.

Closing his eyes, Jake kept her image firmly entrenched in his mind as he held his own crystals out before him. With Achilles and Hercules bearing four more crystals between them, the foursome was joined by others. More than a hundred crystal-bearing dolphins spread out on each side of them, each separated from its neighbor by 150 meters. In unison they formed a semi-circular phalanx out in front of the oncoming sub, but only the foursome floated directly in its path. If they were all going to die, Jake could think of no better way to go than being with the woman he loved and his loyal friend, Achilles. His only regret was that he would not see his children grow up in a world they had sought to make better.

A subtle whooshing sound caught his ear heralding the torpedo's launch, and an instant later he sensed a mammoth radiant burst. Involuntarily, Jake's arms were flung wide, nearly wrenched from their sockets as the crystals he held pushed away from one another in the way magnetic poles of similar polarity will repel, but with an unexpected potency and violence. And then just as quickly they flew back together as though they were polar opposites.

Jake was abruptly struck by a massive sensation of vertigo, and he felt himself spinning out of control, no longer feeling Achilles under him. Doggedly he continued to keep a firm grip on the T-crystals, but something had now changed in the way they felt. Risking a peek at his surroundings, he looked for Destiny, but she was no longer next to him.

Chapter Twenty-eight: Disaster Approaching

Captain Delila stared in disbelief. The huge mega-yacht, *Numquam Satis*, had seemed to disappear in a monstrous flash that had first expanded before collapsing in on itself. There had been no sound or shock wave. The fireball had simply contracted to a pinpoint and then vanished, but not before the sea beneath it had risen up sharply in a towering mountain better than 300 feet in height, and for one fleeting moment he thought it would surge forward to swamp the carrier. But amazingly and for reasons beyond his comprehension, the sea abruptly settled to once again reveal the *Kraken* in the distance as it headed straight for the heart of Aquaria.

My god! thought Delila. *The damage will be unimaginable. The oil spill alone will destroy the marine habitat and kill off most of the nearby sea life.*

As he looked upon the impending disaster, his eyes suddenly narrowed with that same puzzlement as before, and he wondered if perhaps his mind was playing tricks on him. Something odd was happening in the distance. Lifting the binoculars to his eyes, he studied the strange phenomenon. Directly ahead of the enormous tanker the air was beginning to shimmer weirdly, growing brighter by the second. Totally bewildered, he continued to watch as a gigantic dome-shaped bubble began to form. It appeared like a great, impossibly huge diaphanous canopy that seemed to enclose the floating city and the island behind it, its closest reach seeming to extend just beyond Aquaria's southern perimeter where the breakwater had yet to be completed.

Continuing to stare through the glasses, Delila noticed that the dome was now glowing with a deep pulsating crimson, and as he puzzled over it, he saw the cause. The apex of the old lighthouse was radiating dazzling ethereal bursts of the same spectral frequency. And now the resonance seemed to be speeding up, making the canopy appear like a mass of dappled molten crimson that obscured all it enclosed.

What am I looking at? he could only wonder.

Just as he completed the thought, the *Kraken's* bow met the dome of light, and a strange, unearthly glow of blinding scintillation seemed to leap forth from its liquid surface as the ship passed into it.

Delila kept the glasses focused until the ship's stern slipped through, and a moment later the pulsating dome dissipated as though it had never existed. A gasp of stark realization escaped the captain's throat.

The *Kraken* was gone.

The inexplicable force that caused Jake to spin dizzily out of control suddenly abated, and he found himself in a familiar place. A rapid dawning began to impinge on his awareness, and with his base consciousness rekindled, he instinctively grasped the nature of things he was seeing and feeling. He was in the same endless dodecahedron he had been taken to twice before. It was a timeless volume of space so vast that the twelve planes bounding it appeared to extend to infinity where he assumed they intersected. His mind was incredibly lucid and agile, and from experience he knew he was mentally conjoined with all the other albino minds in the super-mind meld they occasionally formed. And if not for this he surmised he would have been unable to grasp the true reality that existed all around him. The laws of physics were different in this place. Time and distance were non-existent here. But what the human brain would normally deem as being impossible in the limited four-dimensional subspace to which it was naturally attuned, in this place of higher dimensionality anything was possible.

Fully enraptured, Jake felt his inner being reasserting itself, that part of him that was intrinsically pure and uncontaminated by blinding presumption. In this realm, miracles did not exist, for miracles were merely shadows of phenomena that intruded their way into the subspace the lower mind had come to know. In the subspace of human consciousness, miracles transgressed the physical laws of space-time, but in higher dimensions those same laws were superfluous.

Jake sensed the synchronous joining of spirits all about him, a globular cluster seemingly in orbit about a glowing astral body he knew to be Destiny. She was the lens through which the others were channeling their combined thoughts. Together they forged a singular consciousness that evoked the luminous side of the cosmos, the ethereal, imponderable substance comprising the true essence of hyperspace, the very thing that gave matter pattern and form. And that was unconditional love. It was filling the heavens with sweet harmonious music with infinite keys, resonating between the stars and flowing rampantly everywhere he looked. Fully enlightened by the awesome energy that abounded all around him, it was all so clear to him. Here was an ally offering an unlimited array of vibratory tones. Played correctly, a future of their choosing was not only possible, but probable.

Jake studied the curvature of the ethereal landscape entwining him, and he now understood the power of healing, the positive energy that made all things possible, its purity able to strip away the physical deceptions that trick the unenlightened senses. Awash in the endless range of it, he suddenly became cognizant of an incongruous disturbance within the midst of such harmony. It eclipsed his perception, an inconceivably titanic shadow that seemed to both shrink and elongate as it stretched out along one of the infinite planes, and he knew at once it was the *Kraken*. And then it vanished, swallowed by what he perceived to be the nimbus of a nearby sun.

Jay Jay, the pod mind called out to him, *you are needed elsewhere. Grab hold of the rainbow before it disappears, or you will be too late to intervene. Please hurry.*

Jake saw the tail end of the multi-hued thread whipping about erratically like a feather in the wind. It seemed to be beyond his reach. But as he extended an arm to infinity, he was able to take hold of it before it was gone.

All at once, the exhilarating lucidity he had felt seemed to fall away like wings on a cloud, and he found himself earthbound standing waist-deep in a shallow pool with a fountain playing gently over the water. It took a moment to register before he realized where he was. The pool was located in the middle of a winding gallery situated in an upper level of Aquaria. Sensing something in his hand, he realized it was a 3-sided pyramidal T-crystal, and he knew the two crystals he had previously held had fused into one.

Perplexed, Jake sent a mental query to his bond mate. *What just happened, Achilles?*

With focused thoughts, these crystals can also act as portals, JJ, but only those that are three-sided. They can be used for teleportation.

How did you discover that?

We didn't, Ez did. Based on observations she made on the amount of mass conversions and energy these crystals are capable of absorbing, she developed an algorithm that predicted what would happen if a threshold were reached and it proved correct.

Spare me the details. Where's Destiny?

She's with Jacob and the children.

Jake looked all about him, still baffled. The gallery was empty. *But why am I here?*

We put you there. Beware, danger is afoot. We look to you to neutralize it.

Jake moved to a nearby archway. Beyond it was the entrance to the infirmary where he knew Victor had been taken. A vision of what lay inside suddenly came to him, and he saw the reason why he had been summoned. Malikai Allotey hovered threateningly over Victor, who lay in one of the beds used for life support. Next to him stood a portly individual who carried an air of authority about him. Abysmal abhorrence flared in Jake's eyes as he recognized the man. Senator Brent Van Heflin had one of those personas so typical of the leadership pervading Washington these days, the classic embodiment of ultimate corruption, at least from Jake's perspective. Even as a boy growing up he well remembered the man as being at the forefront of politics, and as he assessed the man now he could not help but notice how much the senator's girth had expanded since that time. Standing nearby were four of the fully armed, black-clad invaders Jake had been informed of on his way back to Aquaria aboard *Johnnie.*

Moving like a phantom, Jake sidled up to the archway, now close enough to hear what was being said. Almost immediately he recognized the smug, contemptuous voice of Allotey, a voice one didn't readily forget.

Allotey raised a hand and slapped Victor harshly across the face. "Do not lie to me!" he screamed. His face was twisted in a rabid snarl. "You will tell me where the wealth of this colony is hidden."

Jake risked a peak around the archway. The black-clad insurgents appeared to have their attention focused entirely on the interrogation and not on their surroundings.

"Go to hell!"

Victor's sharp, biting reply told Jake the Russian was quickly recovering from his wounds.

"I can have you killed right now," Allotey spat.

"Then what are you waiting for you fucking piss ant?" Victor bellowed.

At that moment Jake knew he had to do something and do it fast. It was obvious Victor no longer cared about self-preservation, and from Allotey's darkening scowl he could tell the Liberian was only a hair-trigger away from ordering one of his henchmen to carry out the threat.

Jake switched the T-crystal to his left hand and quietly slipped the USP-9 from the holster strapped to his right thigh, hoping the rounds it held were still dry enough to fire. He would have preferred his faithful Sledgehammer, but he had left it aboard *Johnnie*. Assessing the developing situation one more time with a seasoned eye, it appeared that Allotey and the senator carried no weapons. The black-clad troopers accompanying them were another matter, however, and he quickly determined which of them presented the biggest threat. Those were the ones he would take out first as he charged into the room, but just as he was about to leap forward, a taunting laugh broke the escalating tension.

All six men spun in startled confusion, looking all about for the source of the laughter.

"You men must be blind," a disembodied voice mocked.

"Show yourself!" Allotey challenged, the shadow of fear crossing his face as his eyes continued to dart searchingly about the room.

"As you wish," the unknown speaker said. Abruptly, the manifestation of Ez suddenly appeared.

"You!" Allotey howled, immediately recognizing the Haitian woman who had demeaned him when he had first come to Aquaria. Turning to the troopers, he cried out a shrill order. "Kill her!"

Shocked by the woman's sudden appearance, the trooper's failed to respond, still trying to comprehend how she had seemingly materialized out of thin air right before their eyes.

"I said kill her," Allotey screamed again.

The command registered this time, and all four troopers opened up to assault her body with a withering storm of rounds. Behind Ez, medical equipment and glass components strung out along a curving wall shattered in a deafening cacophony, raining back a hail of splintered shards and debris. The fusillade continued non-stop until all four weapons expended their ammunition.

Completely stunned, Allotey and company could only stare in disbelief as Ez continued to stand before them without injury, her face lit up in a placid smile.

Achilles' voice rang out in Jake's head just before he sprang from hiding to take advantage of the situation. *Not yet, JJ. Ez needs a little more time.*

Time for what? Jake demurred. *Now's my chance to take out those bastards before they reload.*

A slight change in plans, Achilles shot back. *Just be patient a little longer and all will become apparent.*

Grumbling in silence, Jake held his position, wondering what Ez had in mind as he listened to her speak.

"Senator Brent Van Heflin," she declared mockingly. "What a delightful honor to see you here in Aquaria, though it surprises me not the slightest to see you traveling with such sordid company. I would think you would be back in Washington attending to what you do best, pushing along bills designed to bleed the American people and subverting the government."

The jeering diatribe seemed to catch the senator off guard, and for several seconds he stood mute, appearing uncomfortable and chagrined in light of the truth. Gathering himself quickly, he nodded to one of the troopers.

Jake caught the gesture, shooting a glance at the trooper, who slung his spent Uzi over a shoulder and pulled a camcorder from his belt before moving further back. He realized the trooper was preparing to record the exchange that was about to ensue.

Seeing that the trooper was ready, Van Heflin turned his head back to the woman and cleared his throat. "And who might you be?" he asked austerely.

"My identity is of no concern. Think of me as merely one of the residents of this eco-friendly utopia you and your kind have gone to great lengths to defame, with the goal of goading the UN into taking military action against us. But I think it only fair to ask why you have taken the time to break away from your busy, subversive schedule to come here."

Van Heflin's manner abruptly stiffened and his eyes came alive with anger. Unaccustomed to being insulted like this, he retorted in the declamatory mode of voice he typically used when delivering a speech before Congress. "By sanction of the United Nations, this facility has been declared a threat to the planetary environment. Your people have been defiling the local habitat for some time now, and the UN has compiled sufficient evidence to prove it. The massive release of greenhouse gases Aquaria is causing is one such proof, not to mention the toxic pollution it is rapidly spreading to the rest of the Caribbean. As such, I would be grossly negligent in my responsibilities as Science and Technology Chairman not to be here during the takeover of this facility as an earth-saving measure, though I accompany this mission only as a neutral observer to see with my own eyes the atrocities you people have been inflicting on the ecosystem and to confirm that your harmful activities are ended once and for all."

Ez laughed sarcastically. "Observer you say. I suppose that function is appropriate, but shouldn't you amend it by being a bit more truthful. Shouldn't you be telling me you're here to observe the sizable assets this colony holds so you can claim a share?"

The senator subdued the scalding rebuttal before it could escape his mouth, and with an effort, forced a smile. "By debasing an elected representative of the U.S. government with such a fatuous statement, you debase all Americans," he said flatly. "Attacking my integrity by making false allegations is not going to change what is happening here."

Ez riveted him with an all-knowing gaze. "Do me a favor, senator, and drop the act. You're here to get a share of the gold, plain and simple, so stop having this farcical speech of yours recorded, which we both know will be carefully edited and then used as a means of covering your ass later on."

Before Van Heflin could reply, Ez turned and looked behind her to indicate a stack of wooden boxes. "But do not waste anymore of your valuable time by questioning this man when some of the booty you seek is right here in this very room. Please help yourself."

Van Heflin frowned. He could have sworn those boxes were not in the room when he had first entered it. Without looking at the cameraman he made another subtle gesture, and Jake saw the trooper lower the camera. Warily, the senator stood fast, not wanting to become the victim of a devious trap.

At seeing his hesitation, Ez moved to the stack and lifted the lid on the topmost box. Reaching in, she pulled out a bar of polished metal. It caught the light, reflecting a lustrous aureate glow that bedazzled the eyes.

"Don't be shy, gentlemen," exhorted Ez pleasantly. "Contained within these boxes is a windfall of gold worth slightly more than a billion dollars at current market value, so please take as much as you can carry away. From what I heard a short while ago, the price of gold is rapidly rising on international markets."

Even before Ez finished speaking she saw the fires of avarice blazing brightly in the senator's eyes. Allotey was practically drooling, evidenced by tiny beads of spittle forming at the corners of his mouth, and the four troopers seemed equally awed. All six were gawking like enraptured children coming upon a pile of neatly wrapped and ribboned presents on Christmas morning. Hesitating only a moment longer they ventured forward, though with obvious caution.

At seeing such auspicious distraction, Jake was ready to dart from hiding but Achilles quickly interceded. *Not yet, JJ.*

At least clue me in on what's next, Jake snapped back in irritation.

Before Achilles replied, the voice of another wailed out loudly. It conveyed distress, quavering nervously with frustration as though the person it belonged to had just undergone a traumatic event. "What is this place?"

From an alcove off to one side a man suddenly emerged, causing Jake's jaw to drop in surprise. The man was Truman Hearthwatch, Green Technology and Climate Advisor to the U.S. president.

Van Heflin gaped wide-eyed. "Truman?"

Hearthwatch turned his head to regard the senator in bewildered silence.

Van Heflin stared for another second before his dumbfounded countenance changed. "I was not informed you would be coming, Truman," he stated bluntly. "How did you get here?"

"I don't know," said the man the media had routinely dubbed as Earthwatch. He seemed visibly shaken and pale. The memory of what he had seen continued to haunt him. Without the feel of gravity to anchor him, he had floated aimlessly in the midst of swirling lights that seemed to go on forever before diminishing to pinpoints. The flashing imagery had made his head throb, bringing on extreme vertigo much the way the Aquarian art had made him ill. But now that the sickness was beginning to subside, he was able to recall the presence of three others, two men and a woman. He had been sitting there, and they seemed to come out of nowhere to lay hands on him just before a burst of crimson light flared. Had it all been a bad dream? Maybe he was still dreaming.

Hearthwatch settled confused eyes on the gold bar held by the woman. "One minute I'm in the White House waiting to see the President, and the next I'm here," he explained feebly. "Where am I?"

Van Heflin eyed him suspiciously, wondering if this was some kind of prank. "Surely you jest."

Hearthwatch's demeanor suddenly hardened like quick-drying cement, and he looked back at the senator with annoyance. "I do not jest," he grumbled testily. "Where am I?"

Allotey glared at him. The idea that Hearthwatch had now seen the gold did not sit well with him, for it was now probable the plunder would be divided further. "Do you actually expect us to believe such a ridiculous story," he ranted in frustration. "Your arrival here is most inappropriate in view of the military action that is currently in progress. Why did you come?"

"I sent him."

Both Van Heflin and Allotey whirled, stunned to see the *Sublimis* saunter into the room behind Hearthwatch. Hearthwatch spun around as well, equally stunned.

Maximus wore a cryptic grin. "One of my scientists recently made a major discovery," he began. "Truman was brought here by a quantum teleporter. Such a device allows instantaneous transport of sentient life forms to any place on the globe." Setting his gaze on Hearthwatch, he explained further. "Once I learned where you were, Truman, agents of mine were able to pluck you from the White House and bring you here." Pausing, he studied the confusion that still lingered on Hearthwatch's face. "If you haven't figured it out by now, you're in Aquaria. I can understand the extreme disorientation and fright you must have experienced, but in the end I think you'll probably agree it was all worthwhile. Other than what I will take for myself, you are to receive the second largest share of the spoils this colony holds."

Allotey appeared dismayed, immediately voicing a protest. "That is not fair. He played no part in this operation. He risked nothing."

Maximus gave him a sharp look. "For all the fine work Truman has done for *The Order*, I think he deserves it. And don't forget the major role he will play in urging Congress to enact the carbon tax. Once that happens, other nations will follow."

Van Heflin was aghast. "What about me? Aren't I just as deserving?"

"Your reward will be the U.S. presidency," rasped Maximus sternly. "I think that will be reward enough. Must I remind you it will cost a great deal of money to finance your campaign, and a significant portion of the assets taken from this facility will be used to pave the way for you."

Van Heflin's innate greed uncoiled like an enraged serpent deep in his gut, and its head rose up sharply to take control of his mouth. "Are you implying I am not to get a share at all?" he quailed ruefully.

Maximus responded without emotion. "That is correct."

The senator cast brooding eyes back to the stack of gold-bearing boxes. "Surely there's more than enough to…" His reply hung unfinished as he noticed the woman was now gone. Glancing about sharply in all directions, he looked to Allotey. "Where did she go?"

The question seemed to startle Allotey, and he scanned the room nervously to echo Van Heflin's concern. Turning, he brought a questioning frown to the nearest trooper. "Did you see the woman leave?"

Wide-eyed, the trooper shook his head fervently as he took in the room at a glance, his hands working quickly as he slapped a fresh clip into his weapon and chambered a round. Other firearms snicked audibly as the other three troopers followed his lead, all of them now on full alert and prepared to engage any surprises.

"Never mind her!" Maximus exclaimed exuberantly. "This facility will soon be under our complete control."

"What about the Seals?" asked Allotey.

"Our invasion force is eradicating them as we speak. Once they are wiped out, Aquaria will be ours to do with as we please."

"What about the international community?" Allotey continued to press. His tone was worried. "How will this operation be reported?"

Maximus grinned cunningly, his voice rising theatrically as though he were a news commentator. "The task force sent by the UN to take control of Aquaria was met with unanticipated stiff resistance by hostile colonists. Using sophisticated weaponry, the colonists were able to sink the invasion fleet, including three kilo class submarines and the flagship aircraft carrier supporting them. The soldiers representing the UN fared just as poorly, as they were met by a contingent of men in robotic combat suits accompanied by a far superior force of well-armed Aquarians who were able to destroy them."

Dropping the pretension, Maximus resumed a more serious attitude as he explained further. "The defeat will require the UN to marshal another task force, but that will take some time, and by then all the assets of this facility will be removed and in our hands."

Continuing to stifle his vexation, Van Heflin pointed out something Maximus had seemingly overlooked. "But how will this story reconcile the survival of Malikai and myself."

"You recognized the danger and escaped," answered Maximus briskly. His manner suggested he didn't want to waste any more time discussing it. Giving Allotey a harsh, penetrating stare, he added, "Malikai, I'm leaving it up to you to take inventory of all the gold you are able to locate within this city. Use the men in our invasion force as you see fit to have it gathered up and placed aboard the sub that brought them here." Turning, he looked at Hearthwatch. "Truman, you will be responsible for verifying the accuracy of Malikai's inventory. I'll return later to see that these tasks were carried out."

"Where are you going?" Van Heflin asked as Maximus turned to leave.

"I'm making a little visit to the island." With that said, Maximus walked swiftly back the way he had come, disappearing quickly from view.

The communications supervisor at IBC headquarters cringed at the sound of the ringing phone, uneager to answer it, its shrill, blaring tone seeming to announce the irascible fury of the caller trying to get through to him. Gloomily he picked up the receiver to hold it a good foot away from his ear, knowing what he was in for as he kept his eyes glued to the video screen.

Upon absorbing the initial vitriolic outburst coming through the line, he responded in a contrite voice, nodding repeatedly as if the caller were directly in his face berating him savagely. As the verbal barrage ensued, he attempted to squeeze in a stuttering reply wherever he could. "Yes… yes, I'm well aware of the problem, sir…yes…yes…no, we've been hacked again…" Frustrated, he laid the receiver down on the table until the rants of the company officer on the other end finally began to wane.

Picking up the receiver again, the supervisor said, "We're doing everything we can, sir…no, the built-in firewall is not working. The hacker seems to be highly sophisticated and has found a way around it. I can assure you our technicians are hard at work on the problem, but until they can figure out how the system is being breached, there's nothing we can do to stop these cybernetic intrusions and the rogue transmissions being aired."

The supervisor cringed again as another outburst ripped into his ear. "Yes, I know the video has been broadcast throughout the mainstream media," he was finally able to say. Listening a little more, he agreed with the officer. "Certainly it looks bad for all those portrayed, but I'm sure our damage control team will be able to produce something to downplay it as nothing more than a hoax enacted by actors made to look like the people they played."

After tossing the officer a few more hollow assurances, the supervisor finally shoved the receiver back into its cradle and breathed a sigh of relief. Setting his eyes back on the screen, his brief respite instantly crumbled. To his utter horror the video was being replayed all over again.

Captain Delila maintained his position on the bridge wing, enjoying the mild breeze and the smell of the sea as he kept his gaze fixed on the floating city in the distance. The tenuous dome of ethereal light that had enshrouded it a short time earlier was now gone, replaced by towering ribbons of multi-hued light. Two full spectrums graced the sky in banded symmetrical splendor, one draped over the other to form a great curving arch that spanned the horizon. The sight of a double rainbow enchanted him. But these were unlike any rainbow he had ever seen. Each band of color was unnaturally vivid, seeming to resonate with points of light that sparkled and flickered as they slid along their respective archways. But now a third rainbow was coalescing directly behind the first two, enveloping them in a display of perfect congruity.

As Delila looked on, Ensign Jefferson joined him. "Sir, ship's sonar shows no sign of the unknown sub."

"What about the *Numquam Satis* and *Kraken*?" Delila asked, continuing to behold the spectacular sight. "Any sinking debris detected?"

"None whatsoever, sir. Both ships appear to have vanished completely."

The captain nodded solemnly, still trying to make sense of these strange happenings as he continued to stare at the rainbows.

Jefferson followed his gaze. "Wow, I've never seen anything like that, sir."

"It certainly is an unusual sight," Delila concurred. "Any contact with Lieutenant Johnson?"

"A little. The jamming seems to have eased up a bit, so he's able to send broken transmissions. Seems he's still under attack."

"And Ensign Flynn's squad?"

"They're getting ready to lift off the island and lend support to Johnson's team." As Jefferson said this, he handed the captain an iPad. "Another of those broadcasts emanating from the colony was picked up minutes earlier. It's all been recorded, sir."

Delila withdrew his eyes from the triple arches and took hold of the IPad, a heavy frown creasing his forehead as the recording began to play out.

No sooner did Maximus leave the room, Allotey was the first to venture forward to take inventory of the gold, the stacked boxes drawing him like a hyena to carrion. But as he reached for the topmost box, his hands found only air awaiting him.

"What is this?" Allotey screamed. Looking all about him and groping the air wildly, he realized the boxes had vanished.

Okay, you're on, Achilles told Jake.

About time, Jake grumbled back in feigned annoyance as he bolted forward and raised his voice. "Drop your weapons and no one will get hurt," he commanded curtly. If he could avoid killing this time he would do so. And in a situation such as this, prisoners could be very valuable.

All heads snapped around in startled surprise, the troopers reacting instantly to bring their weapons to bear and open fire.

Fully prepared for this, Jake had already focused his thoughts to counter the deluge of rounds impinging on him, and in reaction to these thoughts the T-crystal in his left hand was already pulsating at a high frequency. It flared a blinding crimson as it swallowed up bullets as though they were insubstantial, immediately transmuting the lethal barrage of kinetic energy to another form and sending it into the esoteric abyss of higher dimensionality.

Jake waited for the firearms to deplete their clips. "Hands in the air!" he ordered with a goading grin as he noted expressions of incomprehension on the various faces. Keeping a wary eye on the troopers, he spoke out of the corner of his mouth. "You okay, Victor?"

Victor rose up from the bed to stand next to him. "I will feel a little better once I settle with this piss ant," he said, directing a contemptuous look at the man who had slapped him.

Allotey recovered from his initial shock at seeing something that should have been impossible. "You again!" he snarled disdainfully, immediately recognizing Jake from their previous encounter. "How dare you interfere with a UN official carrying out the directives of the governing world body. Do you realize you can be hung for this?"

Jake chuckled, shaking his head pitifully at Allotey's laughable pomposity. Even now the man's inherent self-righteousness seemed to have no bounds. "Whatever!" he said wearily. "Did anyone ever tell you to audition for Saturday Night Live. I think you have a natural flair for farcical comedy."

Recognition flooded Van Heflin's face as he realized who was standing before them. Composing himself quickly, he projected an air of superiority as he jumped in to take control of the situation. In his most authoritative voice, he said, "This is an international matter, Mister Javolyn, so I strongly advise you to put down your weapon. You cannot…"

The senator broke off in open-mouthed silence as three people suddenly winked into existence to stand beside Jake, one of them wielding a firearm also pointed at the troopers.

Jake gave him a wry smile. "You were saying, senator? Or maybe I should start calling you Mr. President."

Still at a loss for words, Van Heflin nearly wet himself as he continued to stare wide-eyed at Amphitrite, Franklin, and Mat.

"A little tongue-tied, are we?" said Jake with feigned sympathy. Turning, Jake brought his attention to Hearthwatch. "Perhaps your partner in crime, Mr. Earthwatch here has something to say."

Hearthwatch stared dumbly, his brain suddenly in turmoil as an obscure remembrance came flooding back with a rush. He was now almost certain the threesome standing beside Javolyn were the same ones that had teleported him here. But if they were agents of *The Order* as the *Sublimis* had contended, then why were they siding with Javolyn? And then it hit him. One of them was Mat Daniels. The resemblance of the man he had seen in photos was altogether far too striking for him to be wrong. Still perplexed as to what was going on, he decided to let the conundrum go for the time being, knowing that Maximus would explain it all later.

Gaining control of his senses, Hearthwatch reverted to his old self, and he glowered superciliously at Javolyn. "Maybe at the moment you hold all the trump cards," he spat wrathfully, "but you will soon learn who triumphs in the end. It is we who control the media. It is we who have the means to mold humanity, the majority of which are rather mindless and easily manipulated with deceptions and falsehoods. As I speak, this city is being overrun by paramilitary forces that work for us. The media, however, will play up those same forces as belonging to this colony, and once the Seal teams are eliminated the public will be up in arms screaming for your heads. So do yourselves a favor and hand over your weapons. Admit you're outclassed and out-gunned."

Jake let out a deep sigh of disgust. "I hate to burst your bubble, your royal arrogance, but your forces are not faring well. And as for the media which you claim to control, perhaps you should be reminded of what took place a short time earlier and the noose being slowly tightened around your own neck. Ez, please show these deceitful rogues what's being shown on all the mainstream news channels in the U.S. at this moment."

Hearthwatch eyed the newcomers standing next to Jake, wondering who Ez might be. When none of them moved, he glanced around sharply in search of the person, but his expression changed abruptly as his gaze settled on something else.

Jake read the horror-stricken look that came to Hearthwatch's face as five three-dimensional holograms suddenly took form in the air before him. Swiveling his head, he saw that Van Heflin had the same look, as did Allotey.

Van Heflin felt ill as he watched, realizing all the stations were playing the same exact thing. In desperation he shifted a frenetic gaze on each, identifying the station by the captioned logo it displayed. Nevertheless, he couldn't help but wonder if these broadcasts were truly authentic, and he grasped at this possibility the way a drowning man reaches for a life ring in a tumultuous sea. The thought that the broadcasts might actually be taking place at this very moment tormented him, searing through his mind like a hot poker scorching flesh.

"Oh, they're real all right," Jake affirmed blithely as if reading his mind. "Here in Aquaria, we have the means to take control of any news channel we choose, whenever we choose. We're going to flood the worldwide web with this video, exposing all the shenanigans your cabal has been up to. Your days of bamboozling the public are over."

Van Heflin searched for guile in Javolyn's expression. At seeing none, his heart began to pound like a trip hammer suddenly going arrhythmic. If what had transpired moments earlier was being aired for the entire world to see, he knew his political future was in jeopardy, dire jeopardy. Bringing his eyes back to the broadcasts, he realized it was all there, the looks of superiority, surprise, and smoldering greed suddenly turned apprehensive and intermixed with dangerous utterances by those involved. The sight of his own image began to haunt him as he scrutinized the way he had acted, but it had been the *Sublimis* himself who had actually admitted their true intentions, further confirmed by the heated discourse Truman had just given. Everything said had been meticulously recorded and was probably still being recorded. It was all there in a plethora of inculpating, irrefutable, mind-numbing ugliness.

Hearthwatch was mortified, now fully aware of how the event in the sports bar had come to be. But knowing how various politicians within *The Order's* fifth column ranks had managed to survive one seemingly hopeless scandal after another over long illustrious careers, he took on an air of haughty defiance, no longer caring if his words continued to be recorded. Impaling Javolyn with a savage glare, he vented his fury like super-heated steam escaping a pressure valve. "You won't get away with this," he hissed through clenched teeth. "Once our army gains control of this facility, we'll prevail in the end. You're way out of your depth, Javolyn. I don't think you have a clue as to the countless resources we have at our disposal, nor the vast strength of our influence. World leaders carry out our directives, and many of our member politicians have managed to survive worse than this because of that influence. Once that influence is exerted to its full extent, the tide will swing back in our favor. Your efforts to expose us will ultimately be shown to be fraudulent. After all...," Hearthwatch paused momentarily to check the time on his wristwatch before looking back at Jake with a sly expression, "...how can I possibly be here when less than fifteen minutes ago at least twenty people saw me in the White House. We'll blitz the public with a storm of propaganda designed to further defame your enterprise. We'll demonstrate how you hijacked the media to disseminate a hoax."

"You mean like your buddy here, the senator?" Jake replied flippantly. "I'm not sure the word 'politician' fully captures him, it just seems too inadequate. We need something that better describes him and his kind."

Jake brought a hand to his chin and stroked it as if in deep thought. "Hmmn, now let me see," he said contemplatively as he paced the room slightly. His clouded expression suddenly brightened, and he turned to Mat with sudden vivaciousness. "I've got it! Being that he's actually a charlatan, doesn't *'charlatician'* seem more appropriate?"

Mat shrugged. "You're being far too kind. I think dirt bag is more befitting."

Hearthwatch narrowed his eyes and his voice rose lividly. "Keep making fun of the situation, Javolyn. You won't be smirking once our troops arrive here in numbers."

"That could very well be if you have any troops left once this is over," Jake responded airily. "Ez, give us a fix on the marauders."

Like before, Hearthwatch, Van Heflin and Allotey scanned the room in search of the person called Ez. When that person failed to appear, they noticed something had changed in the holographic displays, these showing what was currently taking place in another sector of the city.

Jake studied the images being shown with a critical eye. "Now pinpoint Zinova and his cohorts," he instructed.

The disembodied voice of Ez answered immediately. "They are at the tail end of the pursuing army." As she said this, one of the displays zoomed in on three figures.

Jake turned his gaze on Belachek. "It's your call, Victor. How should we deal with your old boss?"

Belachek stared at the display, his countenance suddenly mired in deep thought.

Chapter Twenty-nine: Holographic Projections

First Lieutenant Myron Johnson had only his instincts to go by in not firing at the portly woman. She had seemed to come out of nowhere right before his eyes. But it was her kindly smile spread benevolently across her broad face that had kept his trigger finger in check as she peered directly at him. Though she bore no resemblance to his own grandmother, the smile she held brought back fond memories.

"Who are you?" he demanded, aware that she carried no weapon.

Just as he completed the question, another deafening roar broke the brief respite of quietude to send a shower of shattered sea cement flying. Had he and three of his men not taken refuge behind the arched pillar, they would have been cut to pieces. With his back up against the pillar, he was astounded by the woman's calm demeanor. She was just beyond the pillar's protection, and she had not even flinched in the face of such destruction.

The woman moved closer, speaking quickly when the enfilade cut out. "If you want to save your men, follow me." Pointing, she indicated a passageway off to her left. "This way."

The lieutenant stood frozen as the woman started walking, his mind churning with indecision. The moment passed quickly as he realized this was his only option. If he didn't get moving, those things would be on top of him and his men. Shooting a look to other members of his team hunkered behind nearby pillars, his waved them to follow. Only half his original contingent of men remained with him, the others becoming separated when the skirmish had raged on, and the thought of losing any of them weighed heavily on his him. Radio jamming seemed to be intermittent now, and it was only a minute earlier he had gotten through to the missing men. Miraculously, no casualties had been reported.

The passageway the woman had chosen afforded enough protection to keep them out of a direct line of fire, and as another buzz saw burst broke the air, he was convinced the pursuing monstrosities were now firing blindly.

The lieutenant had a hard time keeping up with their guide, and he began to wonder how such a large woman was able to move so fast. And there was something else going on that he found strange. Her form seemed to wink out, only to reappear further ahead as he ran behind her. This kept recurring over and over again as he and his men followed. There seemed to be no uniformity to the route she had taken. It wound its way snakelike through a forest of arched pillars, rising and falling as though they were traversing a rolling wave. And each time they rounded a bend or ascended a rise, the woman would suddenly vanish before she blinked back into view farther away. At first he thought this to be illusory, created by the soft interior lighting that pervaded the hallway, but then his sharp mind grasped what was really happening. *My god, she's a hologram.* Abruptly he slowed, signaling the men behind him to stop running. Coming to a halt, his eyes roved searchingly over the curved walls and ceiling looking for the projectors that were causing the effect. Was he being led into a trap?

He nearly jumped out of his skin as the woman was suddenly beside him, and in reaction he pointed his firearm but held back on the trigger. As though having read his thoughts, she said, "Search your feelings, lieutenant, I wish you no harm. Though you perceive me to be an illusion I can assure you my sentience is quite real." Her affable smile seemed genuine, and once again he was reminded of his grandmother. Slowly he lowered his weapon as his emotions steadied, and he decided that whoever was evoking the holograms was here to help.

The woman turned to indicate a fork in the passageway a short distance ahead. "You can set up over there to ambush your pursuers. We have something in readiness they will not expect."

Johnson looked to the area she had indicated, sizing it up as the rest of his men crowded alongside to eye the woman in bewilderment. Assessing the situation, he shifted his gaze and squinted. Further away was a huge open area where the lighting was strong. The subdued sound of thunder caught his ears.

Ez caught the look on his face. "You passed this way before," she informed him, "but on a level higher up. If you are still willing to trust me, we have the means to defeat these usurpers, but we will need your help."

The lieutenant frowned. "Those men coming after us are not your people?"

The smile Ez carried turned solemn. "That is what they would like you and the rest of the world to believe. Those men are part of an insidious plan to take control of this city. The task force sent under the UN banner, which you and your men represent, have been pulled into this debacle by the very people who devised this plan. These people hold no fealty to any one nation. Their only allegiance is to the cabal they serve, a shadowy group of conspirators driven by implacable greed and an insatiable lust for power. Apparently their leader considers this city to be a direct threat to his ambitions, a man who believes it will weaken his hold on world affairs. He wants to stop us before we can construct other floating cities capable of harvesting unlimited sources of food and eco-friendly energy at low cost. Contrary to what you've been told, lieutenant, Aquaria poses no threat to the environment."

The Seal leader managed an outwardly calm persona, though he was seething just below the surface. Everything the woman was telling him confirmed his earlier suspicions, and the idea of being used in this manner ignited his anger like gasoline poured on hot coals. "The man placed in charge of the UN task force and the U.S. senator accompanying him. Do you know if they're part of this conspiracy?" he asked.

"We have compiled sufficient evidence of their complicity. Your superior officer, Captain Delila, has already been apprised of what is really going on here, and he has ordered your recall and a suspension of this operation."

Johnson expelled a frustrated sigh. "I haven't received such orders, most likely because our radios are being jammed."

"Will you help us?" pressed Ez.

"How do we fight those things?" grumbled Johnson, a pained look coming to his face. "Our weapons can't penetrate their armor and they appear to have more than a hundred well-armed combat troops backing them up. And as you can see, even counting myself, my squad is down to nine men with seven of them somewhere else in this endless maze of corridors you call a city. The only reason we're still alive is probably because those things move so slow and there's plenty of places to hide and take cover, but each time we elude them they still manage to find us. We'd have more men available to fight them if not for that despicable UN clown put in charge of this mission." The supercilious image of Allotey immediately pervaded his thoughts as he said this, and his intense dislike of the man suddenly flared into bitter hatred. It was all too evident that Allotey had purposely sabotaged him. By dividing his original team of thirty-two and sending half of them to the island, it would make it that much easier for Allotey's loathsome collaborators to wipe out both units.

Ez pointed to the small pin he wore on his flak vest. "That is the reason they are able to locate you."

The lieutenant's face clouded as he lifted a hand to the pin. "What, this? These were…" He stopped in mid-sentence, his eyes flaring wide.

"UN issue you and your men were ordered to wear," Ez stated bluntly, completing what he was about to say.

Contemptuously, Johnson tore the pin from the vest to glare at the UN logo emblazoned on it. "A damn homing beacon," he grunted angrily. "How did you know?"

"We have sensors in this facility that detect the signals. After that it was only a matter of deductive reasoning."

"I should have known better," Johnson grumbled with self-ridicule. "From the start this whole mission never felt right. I should have trusted my instincts and now half my team may be lost because I didn't oppose that asshole sending them off to the island."

"Do not berate yourself, lieutenant. The unit sent to Navassa has prevailed and is about to join you, and so are the others." Ez looked behind her. "See for yourself."

Johnson followed her gaze. Silhouetted by the bright light at their backs, a band of figures was coming toward him at a stiff trot. His spirits instantly lifted when he saw it was Ensign Flynn at the head of the pack.

The lieutenant suppressed his sudden joy, barely managing to keep a stern face. "You look like shit, Pat!" he said disapprovingly, making a show of eyeing the dust and grime caking Flynn's sweat-soaked fatigues.

Flynn's reply was just as stern. "And you look like you just got your ass kicked, Myron me lad."

The expressions both men wore suddenly changed over to grins of elation, and they embraced heartily. They had gone through Seal training together and were close friends.

The lieutenant swept his gaze over the other men to make a rapid appraisal of numbers, and his grin fell away. "Who did we lose?"

"Blackwell caught one in the leg, but I think he's gonna be alright," Flynn said. "I had O'Malley bring him to one of the infirmaries in this facility to have his wound treated."

The lieutenant frowned. "How would he find it? Navigating this place is confusing as it is."

"A short Latino guy was showing him the way. I think his name was Hector."

Johnson glanced around again. One man he didn't recognize stood more than a full head taller than all the rest, but he ignored him for the moment as two faces were still unaccounted for. "What happened to Joliard and Haskel?"

"They're keeping watch on those turncoat bastards who flew us here. We're going to need them to fly us back to the carrier, and I wanted to make sure they don't skip out on us before we're ready to leave. Seems they were jamming our radio transmissions all along." Flynn saw the look that transposed his friend's features. "You didn't know?"

"We're still being jammed," Johnson remarked. "It's not as bad as before, but I'm still unable to establish clear contact with the *Carl Sagan*."

"Those combat suits are the cause," Ez piped in quickly, "but I suggest you and your men set up for the ambush in there." She indicated the gallery that opened to the left for the second time. "Those things, as you like to call them, will be here shortly. Once they pass, you'll have opportunity to dispatch the troops coming up behind them."

Johnson scrutinized the area again. The entrance had a multi-arched configuration, with six archways forming the opening, beyond which only darkness lay. Out in front of it was a raised circular basin of water twenty feet across with a gurgling fountain at its center. "It looks too obvious," he opined dubiously, though he knew it was wide enough to accommodate a skirmish line for all his men.

Ez smiled disarmingly. "Let me worry about that. I promise you they'll never see you."

As though suddenly remembering, Johnson held up the pin still held in his hand for the men to see. "Everyone get rid of your UN pin," he commanded aloud. "This is how those bastards were able to keep finding us."

Ez stopped him before he could hurl it away. "You and your men will have need of those," she said quickly.

Johnson belayed the throw and stared back at her with a baffled expression. "What do you suggest?"

"Give the pins to the man not of your unit."

Johnson glanced at the giant who had accompanied Flynn's unit before turning to Flynn. "Who is this guy?"

"His name is Zimbola. He's a resident of this city and insists on helping us."

"And I take it you have no objections," the lieutenant shot back.

"No, I'd be crazy to refuse him. He's big enough to take on one of those things all by himself."

Johnson sighed in resignation before turning to the rest of his men and pointing. "You heard the lady, give the big guy your pins and take cover behind those archways and fountain. It's payback time. Let's give those bastards something to think about before we send them off to hell."

Zinova was beginning to have second thoughts about Allotey's offer as he, Drakov, and Boris followed in the wake of the invasion force, and he began to wonder if Allotey had purposely lied to him in order to get his assistance. So far he had seen nothing to indicate the facility contained a large cache of gold, and even if one actually existed among this vast maze of corridors, galleries and passageways winding their way through the floating city's interior, it would likely take many hours of painstaking effort to locate it. Nevertheless, he had felt it prudent to separate himself and his remaining two accomplices from Allotey's company to venture off on his own. Among other things, he did not trust the UN envoy one iota. In spite of this distrust, he was at least thankful for the drug Allotey had recommended he and his men take, but he had only injected himself after seeing Allotey take the drug first. He never wanted to experience the debilitating sickness he had suffered back in Tiburon ever again. It had been triggered by a strange sight that had flashed up at him from the beach, and it was this that had prevented him from firing off a missile at the helicopter he had been pursuing. When it had occurred, his brain had felt as though it had been mashed into jelly, and it had only been a matter of will for him to make an emergency landing without crashing the Hind.

As he walked along, he realized he would never have been able to enter this place without resorting to the drug. Everywhere he looked he saw artistic creations, both two-dimensional and holographic, that were oddly reminiscent of the Tiburon sight that had nearly killed him, but even now he felt himself on the edge of illness. If there were incredible riches to be had, as the little weasel had claimed, he surmised Allotey would try to keep most of it for himself, so it was crucial he keep following the invaders to observe any valuables they might come upon. The U.S. senator was another matter, and one look into the statesman's eyes had told him all he needed to know about the true nature of the man. Surely the senator had to be after the same thing, or why else would he be here.

The Reaper continued to ponder the current state of affairs. Having gotten a close-up look at those combat suits and the Gatling guns they carried, he knew that by comparison the Seal teams stood little chance against them. And in spite of their extreme slowness, they were able to keep the foe they were hunting in complete disarray using their radio jamming capability. Add to that their ability to pinpoint the location of every member of the Seal team further enhanced the inevitability of the outcome. But his patience was beginning to wear thin. This seek and destroy mission was taking far too long for his taste, and he began to consider venturing off in another direction. As it was, the residents of the facility appeared to have vacated the premises, and if any Seals were lurking nearby, the SPEFACS operators would have already detected them and immediately moved to track their electronic scent.

Zinova came to an abrupt halt. Turning, he spoke to the others. "No reason for us to get involved in the fighting. Let's get away from the pack and go off on our own." Using the barrel of the AK-104 Kalashnikov assault rifle he carried, he pointed it at an area off to his right, and just as he did, movement caught his eye. Someone was coming in their direction but was as yet too far away to determine whether that someone was ally or foe. There was something familiar in the way the person moved, for he kept glancing back over his shoulder to check his six in a stealth-like manner.

"Hold your fire!" Zinova ordered the others as he kept a wary eye on the advancing party. With his weapon aimed and his finger poised gently on the trigger, he was fully prepared to send off a two-tap burst should it become necessary, but the person appeared to be without a firearm.

A stunned expression took hold of Zinova's features before settling into a suspicious stare. "Victor, I gave you up for dead," he spat gruffly. "What happened to you?"

Belachek gazed back soberly. "It's a long story, one I'll fill you in on later, but now is not the time." He looked behind him again before continuing, this time with a conspiratorial smile. "I found gold," he whispered jubilantly.

Zinova put his suspicions on hold for the moment. "Where?"

"Follow me and I'll show you. This facility has tons of it."

"Tons, you say?" The sum flabbergasted Zinova, quelling his immediate need for answers.

Belachek nodded exuberantly. "Yes, and if we hurry we can load the Hind with some of it and fly on out of here before Allotey and his troops even realize what happened."

Zinova's brow immediately bunched, and under the soft light his face almost appeared simian. "How do you know about Allotey?"

"There is no time for explanations, Karloff. I will fill you in on everything once we load the chopper and fly away." Belachek half-turned, beckoning the men to follow. "Come!" he urged.

Against his better judgement, the Reaper followed, the promise of untold riches too much for him to ignore.

The black-clad marauder kept a wary eye as he followed behind the slowly advancing SPEFACS. With four of these monsters leading the way, he felt safe and protected as they periodically strafed the passageway out in front of them. The damage they wrought was extensive, leaving shattered fixtures and portions of unfathomable artwork littering the floor under a wash of soft illumination of varied tinctures. As far as he could tell, none of the fighting force he was to engage had been hit, but he was certain it was only a matter of time before they were trapped and eradicated. The SPEFACS, he knew, were outfitted with tracking devices, and at this moment the operators were following the signals put out by the homing beacons the Seal units were wearing. Nothing could survive the firepower the SPEFACS were putting out for very long. Their only shortcoming was the sluggish speed at which they moved.

As he looked between two of the ponderous juggernauts he saw the passageway debouched into a cavernous area of intense bright light farther ahead. Abruptly he glanced from right to left. Up to now there had been too many places for an enemy to take refuge behind. A seemingly endless array of archways, foot bridges, and fountains abounded, much of it adorned with paintings and holographic projections of esoteric art forms that gave him a slight sense of vertigo whenever he stared at them too long. Now he fully understood why he and the others had been ordered to inject themselves just before departing the sub. The drug, he had been told, had been purposely designed to counter the debilitating effects the art would cause him, and had he not taken it he suspected he would have become terribly ill. But the area he had come upon did not conform to the rest of the place he had so far seen, and he saw at once that it was completely devoid of the arcane artistic renderings. This sector appeared to be barren, with no evidence of side passages or galleries. For perhaps the last two hundred feet only sterile walls and ceilings of a dull gray texture met his eyes.

Somewhat surprised by the change of scenery, he relaxed his vigilance knowing there was no chance of a flanking surprise attack. Not in this constricted hallway. Something reflected light from the open area directly ahead of him, and as he fixated on it he realized it was the glare of smooth polished metal. The operators of the advancing SPEFACS seemed not to notice, and after they had trudged past, he bent to investigate. But as he stooped down to place a hand on it, the trooper on his right reached for it at the same time and yanked it from his grasp. But he knew at once that it was a gold ingot. And suddenly he was seeing more of them scattered along the floor, a whole lot more. Wanting not to be outmaneuvered by greedier hands, he leapt forward to grab the closest ingot, only to collide headlong into another hooded trooper. Pandemonium seemed to break out all at once as other members of the assault team scrambled up from behind him to get their share, and he was only obtusely aware that all discipline within their ranks was quickly coming apart. Within seconds a full-blown melee broke out, and he found himself at odds with another trying to take away his small piece of plunder.

Continuing to focus their attention directly ahead, the SPEFACS operators failed to notice the disintegration of discipline behind them, and they trudged on forward into the well-lit area that lay before them, tenaciously following the tracking signals the Seals were unknowingly emitting. A four-foot parapet lay before them, and tromping heavily to the lip of it, they observed the same cavernous area they had seen before when they had passed along its tiered perimeter at a lower level. There was no mistaking it. The same rush of water descended turbulently from a place near the roof, pounding down harshly into a large pool at the bottom of an amphitheatre made to resemble a gorge. But something was different this time around. A cluster of what appeared to be segmented metal columns extended down into the water from an opening in the ceiling made to resemble an azure sky with a bright sun in its midst. The columns were cylindrical and tapered, far thicker at the top than where they met the water. Altogether there were eight of them. At this location the tracking signals were at their strongest, with no other place for their elusive quarry to go or hide except over the side of the short wall. Greatly puzzled, the operators swiveled the robotic heads down to scan the sides of the chasm, fully expecting to glimpse the men they were looking to kill, but it was the leftmost operator hovering at the edge who first noticed more than two dozen identical pins bearing the UN logo laying inconspicuously atop the wall. Shocked by the sight, he yelled into his lip mic, "We've been had." As he belted out the warning, chaos still raged behind him as hooded troopers continued to grapple insanely over the gold.

At that moment all hell broke loose as the unnerving clamor of automatic fire erupted spontaneously to cut down the massed horde of grappling men, and they began dropping like a swarm of flies suddenly sprayed with a lethal dose of exceptionally potent insecticide. Troopers that were not hit straight out glanced around in confusion within the constricted area. Tracers seemed to spring directly from one of the walls.

On hearing the uproar, the leftmost SPEFACS operator turned the robotic suit around to look behind him, unaware that those strange columns set in the water were beginning to move. With unexpected suddenness, all eight seemed to whip and writhe like the tentacles of a great octopus as four other tentacles tipped with huge claw buckets sprang from the opening in the roof and angled their way obliquely toward the combat suits. The movement didn't go unnoticed by the other three SPEFACS operators, and they immediately aligned their Gatling guns to meet the perceived danger. Warned by the others, the leftmost operator turned back to confront the oncoming threats, prepared to unleash a salvo in concert with his peers, but it was then that the other tentacles broke from the water, each supporting an albino dolphin bearing a T-crystal in each of its hand-like appendages. In less than two seconds, a pair of dolphins were positioned slightly ahead and to each side of a claw bucket just as all four Gatling's opened up, and the pounding of the falls was completely drowned out by the horrendous buzz saw roar. Fully shielded by resonating auras of intense violet iridescence, the tentacles remained undamaged as the swarm of rounds were completely absorbed. To Ez, this had been a point of deep concern. Unsure of how much damage the tentacles would be able to withstand against such a devastating barrage, she had decided to have the albinos invoke a shield of protection. As the Gatling's discharged at an enormous rate, the buckets opened like the maws of great serpents, and with amazing precision lunged toward the metallic monsters to close on the rotating barrels. With the guns fully destroyed, the eight albinos were lowered back into the water as the buckets reopened to snatch up all four SPEFACS in powerful jaws. Lifted as though their massive weights were insubstantial, the combat suits were swung out over the water and smashed violently together numerous times, battering and crushing the armored shells as well as the operators inside. Slowly, the tentacles withdrew back into the opening in the roof of the vast chamber as the gunfire from farther away began to die off. And then all was quiet.

Moments later, the holographically created optical illusion Ez had invoked abruptly faded to reveal Navy Seals cautiously emerging from behind the archways and fountain where they had taken cover.

With the air now rife with the smell of cordite and the barrel of his MP5 still smoking, First Lieutenant Myron Johnson called out to his men. "Anyone hit?"

It was Flynn who answered for everyone a few seconds later. "No casualties to report, lieutenant."

Johnson barked an order as his eyes swept over the carnage. "Stay alert, guys! Some of these clowns could be playing possum."

Weapons could be heard snickering as members of his team replaced their spent clips and reloaded before fanning out to tread gingerly among the mass of hooded commando bodies scattered across the floor. "Got one here that's still breathing," one of them shouted. "There's another live one here," someone else called.

Farther back, a body suddenly rose up, but before the marauder could get off a shot he was flung back as a staccato blast from the Stoner held in Zimbola's huge hands ended the threat. Ensign Flynn, who was standing close to the Jamaican giant, eyed him with newfound admiration. "Glad to have you on our team, big guy."

Johnson bellowed a stern warning meant for any survivors among the downed commandos. "Surrender and we will tend your wounds, but any more acts of aggression like the one that clown just pulled and you can expect the same."

The warning appeared to sink in, and within minutes the Seals were attending to five more of the hooded commandos still breathing. Johnson surveyed the death toll, and walking among the bodies he counted ninety-three fatalities.

Ez was suddenly at his side. "We have an infirmary available to treat the wounded, lieutenant."

"So I've been told," Johnson replied. "You have one of our guys in there now."

Ez displayed a concerned countenance, turning her gaze on the most severely injured. "Those two will not last another hour, but we have the means to save their lives. If you would like, we can stabilize them. Once they are out of danger you can transfer them to your carrier."

Johnson acknowledged the offer with a weary shrug. "I guess I'd be a heartless soul not to accept the invitation, lady, and certainly I owe you for all your help." He noticed her image flicker ever so slightly as he said this. "But please level with me, I have to know. Am I talking to an actual person stationed somewhere else in this facility?"

"You are very observant, lieutenant. It seems one of the holographic projectors at this location was partially damaged during the fighting. We used them to camouflage your place of hiding. Though you are currently interacting with a virtual manifestation of my being, I can assure you I am quite real."

With his curiosity appeased for the moment, Johnson asked, "Do you have a name?"

Ez smiled warmly. "My actual name is Esmerelda, but you can call me Ez." Turning her head, she indicated the large individual coming to join them. "Zimby will show your men the way to the infirmary. Motorized gurneys will arrive in moments to transport the wounded, so your men will not have to carry them."

Johnson nodded in appreciation. "In the meantime, I have to report to my superior to let him know what's happened here."

"That won't be necessary, lieutenant. Captain Delila observed the whole thing unfold, but you should be able to contact him rather easily now."

Johnson began issuing orders as soon as the gurneys arrived, and his men lifted the seven wounded black-clad commandos unto them.

Chapter Thirty: All is Possible

Zinova's impatience continued to worsen as he followed Belachek, and he found it necessary to ask, "Where are we going, Victor?"

"We are almost there, Karloff. Just a little farther."

In moments, Belachek led the trio out onto an esplanade near the helipad where the Hind sat. Zinova squinted, suddenly feeling exposed in the harsh glare. Outside in the open air the sunlight was bright, contrasting sharply with the soft lighting that suffused most of Aquaria's interior.

Coming to a halt, Victor pointed. "Here is the gold I promised you," he declared, indicating a motorized flatbed utility cart with a stack of wooden boxes laid atop it. "Slightly more than one hundred million in U.S. greenbacks," he quickly added.

The Reaper held back, eyeing the boxes suspiciously. Was it possible Victor was luring him into a trap?

At seeing Zinova's hesitation, Victor lifted an ingot in the shape of a small, elongated bar from one of the topmost boxes. "See for yourself, Karloff," he said earnestly, offering the precious metal to his old boss.

Zinova frowned, searching Victor's face for signs of deception, but overcome by the metal's alluring aureate gloss, he took possession of the ingot, hefting it judiciously to gauge its weight. Handing it to Drakov, he said, "Test it with your knife, Vladimir. It could be fake."

Drakov stepped over to the utility cart, placing the ingot on its flattop bed. Turning to look back at Belachek with an unreadable expression, he drew his knife, and with a powerful overhand strike, plunged the point into the soft metal and wiggled it vigorously to widen the hole.

Withdrawing the blade, he inspected what lay beneath the surface. Almost immediately, he beamed with satisfaction. Handing the ingot back to Zinova, he said, "I believe it to be real, at least this one."

The Reaper examined the metal thoughtfully, his keen mind running a rough calculation. He was good with numbers, and he figured slightly more than 2,600 kilograms or 5,800 pounds of pure gold would be worth $100 million at current spot prices on world markets. But that would present a problem. Aside from its armaments, the Hind was only capable of lifting another 1,100 kilograms, and that was also counting the four large men that would be manning it, including himself. Subtract the weight of the crew, and all he could carry was about another 750 kilograms.

"Test a few more from other boxes," Zinova ordered Drakov. Shooting a glance to both Boris and Victor, he added, "Help him. I want to make sure all of these are genuine."

Zinova kept a watchful eye on his surroundings as all three men carried out the order. It was broad daylight out here on the open esplanade, with the sun burning down fiercely, but as far as he could tell the place appeared deserted. Grunting from the exertion, the men assisted one another in removing the topmost boxes to explore the contents of other boxes further down in the stack.

"Vladimir, how many boxes do you count?" asked Zinova, looking to the big burly Russian again.

Drakov walked around the cart, his eyes flitting carefully over the stack. "Fifty-nine in all," he said.

"And what would you estimate each one weighs?"

Drakov took an extra moment to heft a box in an attempt to judge its weight. "About forty-six kilograms," he grunted.

The reply further corroborated what Belachek had said as Zinova worked out the numbers in his head. Discounting roughly two kilograms for the wood comprising each box, the amount of gold added up nicely to approximate the 2,600 kilograms he had originally calculated. Zinova continued to keep a wary eye as each man opened a separate box and randomly selected an ingot for testing before shifting more boxes around, and it soon became evident that every bar sampled was bonafide.

"That's enough," Zinova said, satisfied with the results. Already his mind was entertaining a new thought as he brought his eyes to the massive AW101 sitting forward of the Hind. "Start up the cart, Victor, and move it to the helos."

Victor climbed aboard the cart and activated the electric motor. Humming to life, it began crawling slowly forward with its heavy load toward the ramp leading to the helipad as the other three men followed behind, their vigilance on high alert.

Zinova stared ahead, his gaze locked on the troop carrier. As his angle of perspective changed, two figures came into view, and he immediately recognized the pilots of the AW101 that had flown one of the Seal teams to the floating city. They were still carrying out their assigned duty, which involved standing guard on the air assets provided by the UN. On the way into Aquaria, Allotey had apprised him of the enhanced ADS microwave assault weapon developed by the colonists but had also assured him that both the SPEFACS and troop transports were outfitted with suppressors that neutralized the pain inducing microwaves. With those suppressors turned on, he and the others would continue to remain unharmed.

Surprise caught up with Zinova as an additional sight caught his eye. Sitting on another landing pad farther away was the second AW101. Strangely, though, he saw no sentries guarding it. Nevertheless, the fact that it was here told him the second Seal team sent to the island had obviously been routed. And with more of the black-clad marauders now invading the city, mopping up the remaining Seals would be made that much easier. Unfortunately, that left him with precious little time to load the Hind and make off with the gold. That thought alone continued to nag away at him, and he found it disturbing that he would only be able to fly off with slightly more than a third of what lay on the utility cart.

As the group neared the pilots guarding the troop carrier, Zinova was caught up in a moment of indecision. After all, he had made a deal with Allotey, hadn't he? The last thing he wanted was to burn a bridge that could potentially lead to future work requiring his services, and the United Nations was certainly a wealthy client, as was Malcolm Maximus.

And while a little less than $35 million would be more than enough to carry him into a lavish retirement, he was not yet ready to exit the business. He loved the line of work he had spent most of his adult life pursuing, especially the killing. Killing was in his blood, an uncontrollable inclination that could never be fully sated. He lusted for it.

And while $35 million would more than cover the cost of replacing his lost Hinds, maybe even purchase a few more, $100 million would allow him to buy an army three times larger than what he had before.

But now there was another matter to settle, and that was Javolyn. As a warrior, no one had ever bested him until his engagement with Javolyn. It was a defeat that had eaten away at him with mordant corrosiveness, and avenging it had now become an obsession, one by which he was incapable of letting go.

Pulling a small device from a pocket, Zinova aimed it at the Hind. It sent a tiny laser beam to the security lock on the chopper that would allow entry and get the engines cranking remotely. In moments, Victor was driving the utility cart past the two pilots stationed next to the troop carrier, and Zinova saw they only gave him a passing glance of bored curiosity.

With his finger poised precariously on the Kalashnikov trigger, Zinova turned to Drakov and Boris, keeping his voice just loud enough to be heard above the growing whine of the Hind's engines. "Get ready!" he said. "We're taking command of the other helo, and we're going to need those pilots to fly it. We will load the Hind with only nineteen boxes. The rest will go aboard the troop carrier. Vladimir, once the gold is aboard, you will stay with the pilots and instruct them to follow me back to our base in Haiti. Boris will come with me, but Victor will stay with you. Take the headset of one of the pilots to stay in contact with me and set the radio frequency to the one we always use."

Vladimir gave a barely perceptible nod, seemingly having no problem with the plan.

With the Hind's rotors now churning at an idle, Victor hopped off the cart and slid back the fuselage door as both AW101 pilots watched. Distracted for the moment, they became easy hostages for the three Russians.

"Drop your weapons!" the Reaper commanded them, pointing his Kalashnikov threateningly.

Surprise registered briefly on the faces of both pilots before they laid down their firearms and raised their hands.

Motioning with the barrel of his weapon, Zinova indicated the stack of boxes on the cart. "Load those boxes on your helo and be quick about it."

Victor turned, seeing what was currently taking place, his expression stoic as the two AW101 pilots began hauling boxes up the rear ramp and into the cargo hold of the larger helo.

"Nineteen boxes will go aboard the Hind, Victor," Zinova told him. "Boris will help you. The rest will go aboard the other helo."

With Boris assisting in loading the Hind, the two men moved rapidly to carry out the order. With the attack helicopter's rotors continuing to churn the air, they lashed the boxes down securely to tie rings set in the cabin floor. As soon as the task was completed, Boris scrambled forward to man the weapons seat.

Victor hopped out of the cabin and moved over to help with the loading of the troop carrier as Drakov kept his gun trained on the two pilots, who continued to lug boxes into the big chopper's hold, but before he could place a hand on another box, Zinova stopped him.

The Reaper eyed him shrewdly. "You said you found tons of gold."

Victor nodded. "Yes."

Zinova surveyed their immediate surroundings before taking inventory of the next esplanade one level up to make sure no one was watching. On his way into the floating city, he had noticed there were a series of these structures that spiraled their way up to ring the central cupola-shaped mountain, with each girthing ring smaller than the one below it. Unable to control his inherent avarice, he said, "We can carry much more." His mind was racing ahead, estimating just how much additional weight the AW101 could fly away with and still make it to a location near Cardoza's destroyed stronghold back in Haiti where he kept a modest supply of aviation fuel stored in 55-gallon drums. Probably ten tons more. While aboard the *Carl Sagan*, he had noticed the troop transports being refueled, but flying such a massive load would cause the large helo to burn a great quantity of fuel. Once both choppers reached his chosen destination and were unloaded, he would provide the AW101 pilots with the necessary fuel to make it back to Aquaria and rejoin Allotey. Being that the troop transport was the property of the UN, it was only fitting that he return it, not to mention the world organization might have need of his services in the future.

"Take the cart and bring back another load," Zinova ordered.

Victor eyed him coldly. "No, Karloff, I cannot do that."

A flummoxed expression crossed Zinova's face before turning dark and malicious. "What do you mean you cannot?"

"I made a deal with these people. One hundred million to buy you off and leave them alone for good, and they agreed."

Zinova stared back in disbelief. "Buy me off!" he repeated. "This place is about to fall into the hands of mercenaries hired on by the United Nations. Either we grab what we can take now, or it will all disappear. The people who built this facility will no longer remain in control."

Victor remained stone-faced. "Those mercenaries are being defeated. Allotey and the American senator have already been captured, and all those abetting them are being killed or taken prisoner."

Zinova's countenance shifted from incredulous to dubious, and his reply showed it. "That's not possible," he countered adamantly.

"Believe what you want, but it's true. I think one hundred million is an incredibly generous offer these people have given you. I suggest we leave now before they change their minds."

Zinova's anger flared, and he raised the barrel of his Kalashnikov, pointing it at Victor's face. "You don't suggest anything. I'll decide how-"

The Reaper suddenly winced hard, the rest of his words seizing in his throat. His weapon fell from his hands to clatter on the deck, and he began slapping violently at the clothing covering his chest. He felt as though he were on fire, but almost as quickly as it had started, the intense pain vanished.

Victor glanced over at Drakov. The burly Russian remained unaffected, positioned just inside the AW101, halfway up its rear loading ramp where he could keep a vigilant eye on the two pilots carrying out the loading task, but Victor could see he was keenly aware of Zinova's sudden distress, having already shifted his weapon to point directly at him.

Victor made no sudden moves as Zinova reached down to retrieve his weapon. From experience, he knew Drakov was a deadly marksman.

"The microwave weapon these people use is no longer being suppressed," Victor said, giving Zinova a grim look. "They are giving you a warning, Karloff. They said they would avoid using it unless you forced them."

Zinova scowled. "How do you know about their weapon?"

"I saw them use it on others," Victor lied.

"That weapon is not supposed to work," Zinova ranted furiously. Turning his head, he glared savagely at the two pilots as they continued to load boxes into cargo netting amidships of the AW101 fuselage. "Turn the wave suppressor back on!" he screamed; his face contorted like a man on the brink of insanity. Both pilots stopped working and looked back at him with confused expressions.

Victor interceded quickly. "I was told it still works, but the people here have found a way around it," he lied again, knowing for a fact that the suppressor had been disabled. He glanced in the direction of the other AW101 sitting on the distant landing pad more than 300 meters away and one level lower. "We should leave now," he urged. "Look over there, Karloff. Navy Seals are already returning to the other troop carrier. That in itself tells you I'm not lying. Allotey and his henchmen have been defeated."

At seeing the Seals, Zinova's eyes flared red with rage. Bringing his gaze to Drakov, he shouted to be heard above the whine of the Hind. "Get them to move faster," he stormed, unhappy at how slowly the pilots were moving boxes.

"There's no time," Victor said. "We have to leave now."

Zinova hesitated, caught in a moment of indecision as he set his gaze on the Seals that were trickling back to the other troop transport before turning back to Belachek. "Did you see Javolyn anywhere in this facility?" The vendetta he wanted to settle was overpowering.

Victor kept a straight face as he lied again. "No. I saw him nowhere."

Zinova studied him carefully before speaking with finality. "I have a matter to settle with him. There will be no bargaining with these people to leave them alone. I didn't make the deal, you did. I will be the one to make deals, not you." As he spoke, he peered behind him to take in the ramp leading to the landing pad and the esplanade further back. At seeing no one, he glanced back at the remaining boxes on the utility cart. Only seven boxes remained. Turning, he stared back at Belachek. "Help the pilots with the rest of the boxes and get aboard their bird, Victor. You and Vladimir will make sure the pilots follow me back to our base in Haiti."

Zinova's manner abruptly shifted, and he eyed Belachek coldly. "When we land, you and I will have much to discuss, particularly what happened on the Malique mission and how you came to be here."

Victor nodded without expression. "You're the boss." Bending, he hefted another box and clambered aboard the AW101, placing the box with the others in the cargo netting. In moments the remaining boxes on the cart joined the others, and standing aside, Victor watched as Drakov belligerently coerced the two pilots forward toward the control seats, motioning with the barrel of his Kalashnikov as an added incentive.

Zinova gave one last glance toward the distant UN helo and the Seals crowding around it. He found it odd that none of them seemed interested in what was taking place on the landing pad upon which he stood. Striding quickly to the Hind, he strapped himself into the pilot seat and donned his flight helmet, his eyes scanning the instrument gauges to make sure no problems existed.

Having remained motionless and invisible within the cargo bay of the troop carrier, Bashir slipped quietly out of the cloaker he had been wearing and brought the webshot to bear, his eyes never leaving the Russian prodding the pilots forward. The man was powerfully built, and he wondered if the netting would be enough to restrain him. With the one called Victor having stepped aside, he squeezed the webshot trigger and felt the harsh recoil as the netting mushroomed out to ensnare its prey from behind. Caught completely by surprise, a startled deep throated bellow erupted from Drakov's mouth as he found himself enveloped in the webbing. In reaction, his finger jerked on the Kalashnikov trigger to discharge a burst of rounds that peppered the port side of the cabin, but in that same instant one of the pilots turned and unleashed a vicious punch that landed squarely on the point of Drakov's jaw. The blow was hard enough to make him lose his grip on the weapon and send him crashing to the deck beneath the webbing. With a knife suddenly in his hand, the pilot placed a knee on the stunned Russian's throat, pressing the tip harshly against his jugular where it broke the skin and forced a slight trickle of blood to emerge.

"Move so much as an inch and you're a dead man," the pilot snarled.

Knowing he had no choice but to heed the warning, Drakov lay still, though his face was frozen in a look of pure hatred. His expression turned even more malignant as he noticed the features of the man above him begin to change. The man was Javolyn.

"You, again!" growled Drakov, baring his teeth. His tone was suffused with bitter hatred.

"Yes, me again," replied Jake with a smug sneer. He shot a quick glance at the other pilot to see that the false image had already been shed. Fernando appeared relieved that the deception had succeeded, though most of it had been ad-libbed, having only been rudimentarily planned out based on Victor's input. By offering Zinova more gold than the Hind could carry, he knew his old boss would not be able to resist the temptation to use the troop carrier to transport the rest. But at least their main objective had been accomplished, and that was to separate the Reaper from Drakov, knowing these men were far more dangerous than the Chilean commandos they had previously come up against. Initially, Jake had thought it only fair to test Zinova's motives first before turning Ez loose on him, and had the Reaper decided to leave the facility with only what the Hind could fly away with, he would have been more than happy to let him and his two accomplices depart unmolested. Deep down he was growing weary of having to kill in order to protect Aquaria and had decided to give the former Spetsnaz soldier turned mercenary the benefit of the doubt, though he knew Zinova did not possess the same moral fiber as Victor. This he was certain of, having seen him nearly crash the Hind back near Cardoza's destroyed fortress when he had projected the arcane dolphin art at him using the PHP. Unfortunately, by the time he had assessed the full extent of Zinova's greed, Drakov had moved inside the troop carrier's cargo bay where he was beyond the reach of the ADS microwaves. The chopper's magnesium skin prevented that. Had the big Russian been incapacitated at the same time as Zinova, both men could have been neutralized simultaneously, but now the Reaper was at the controls of the Hind.

"Should we follow him?" asked Fernando. "I'm sure I can fly this baby."

"No, I have something better in mind," Jake replied, still holding the point of the K-bar firmly against Drakov's neck. "But first we better bind this sack of shit."

As Jake said this, Victor and Bashir moved in to take over.

Throttling the warmed up turbines to full power, Zinova lifted off, bringing the helo to a hover to test the load. The chopper responded sluggishly as he manipulated the controls, and he could tell the aircraft was at the very threshold of its lifting capacity. Eyeing the fuel gauge with a critical assessment, he was convinced he would be able to make it back to his base in Haiti, though he would likely be landing with only fumes left in his fuel tanks. Guiding the Hind out over the water, he pivoted it around to look back at the troop carrier to make sure it was also taking off.

A look of surprise enveloped his face when he saw no motion whatsoever in its main rotor blades. Abruptly he keyed the radio, using the frequency he had told Drakov to use. "What's the holdup, Vladimir?" he asked in a voice ripe with annoyance. When he failed to get a response, he repeated the question, this time more heatedly. "Damn you, Vladimir, answer me!"

Directing an angry stare at the troop carrier, he saw one of its occupants suddenly emerge from the starboard door to look back at him. Stunned by the sight, he immediately paled, the muscles in his neck and shoulders tightening like the string in a fully drawn crossbow.

Jake Javolyn waved up at him in enthusiastic greeting, taunting him further with a jubilant, goading grin accompanied by laughter. Speechless for the moment, Zinova sat frozen at the controls as his hated foe began to trot briskly across the landing pad. Reaching the far end, Javolyn stood at the edge and waved back one more time before launching himself over the side to fall seventy feet to the sea below. Meeting the water feet first, he vanished from view in the midst of a mushrooming splash.

As if suddenly awakening from a bad dream, Zinova turned the Hind and dove for the area where Javolyn had disappeared. Through his headset, Boris was nearly deafened by Zinova's blistering stentorian command. "Kill him!" But having also witnessed the entire scene unfold, he was already swiveling the guns in preparation to unleash a mighty salvo. Depressing the trigger, he watched the water erupt in a storm of whitewater geysers that completely obscured anything within their midst.

Bringing the Hind to a hover, Zinova scanned the water below as Boris stopped firing. Though the surface was still agitated, it was settling quickly, and in moments he was able see what lay below. The water was crystal clear, and anything near the surface could be easily discerned. Continuing to peer down searchingly into those depths, he caught a glimpse of movement. Dolphins were down there, four of them, their forms appearing like ghostly white apparitions rippling leisurely along, and atop those forms he could distinguish human riders, but already they were moving away. Steering the chopper forward, he dropped the gunship still lower to follow.

"Kill them!" Zinova repeated, bellowing vociferously into his lip mic. "Don't let them escape."

Once again, Boris opened up with the guns, exploding the water out in front of them into a foaming maelstrom. Bringing the Hind into another hover, Zinova looked down, waiting for the water to settle. In moments the agitation dispersed back into its former state, a clear shimmering blue with not the slightest sign of red discoloring it. How Boris had missed he could not fathom. Seeing nothing directly under him, he peered further ahead, only to have his temper flare a few more degrees. They were still moving away, no more than three or four meters below the surface. They seemed to be following a narrow meandering channel that wound its way through a sprawling swath of lagoons, containment ponds, and submerged holding pens.

Dipping the chopper's nose, Zinova coaxed more airspeed out of the turbines, not liking the feel of the controls. Loaded the way it was, the Hind responded all too sluggishly from what he was used to. Continuing his search, he strained his eyes to catch another glimpse of his quarry. This time he came in lower as he shouted to Boris. "Shoot now! You cannot possibly miss."

The water erupted violently, with the guns hammering down in a protracted burst. Pulling back on the cyclic, Zinova flared the chopper and maneuvered into another hover, peering down with the eyes of a rabid dog. He could discern nothing below the surface.

"Look!" Boris sputtered. "Ahead of you."

Zinova glanced up to gaze along the channel ahead of him. Several hundred yards away he spotted dolphins with human riders. Maddened with frustration, he tilted the main rotor, putting more thrust into the blades and tearing off after them. It seemed inconceivable they were able to cover that much distance so quickly.

Boris studied the lay of the meandering channel, aware that farther ahead it angled into a final dogleg that led directly to Aquaria's northern breakwater. "They seem to be moving toward the island," he said hurriedly. "If you fly out ahead of them and cut them off, they won't expect us to be waiting for them."

Normally Zinova did not like taking advice from his gunner, but he had to admit it wasn't a bad idea. Gaining a little altitude, he dipped the Hind's nose forward again, squeezing all the power he could get out of the turbines. Encumbered by the heavy load, they were straining hard. Keeping a close eye on his air speed indicator, he was disappointed at how slowly it was climbing. When it began to peg out at 110 knots, he realized that was all the helo was going to give him weighed down the way it was. Pulling up on the collective, he lifted the Hind above the breakwater, skimming low over a lush orchard and several buildings before dipping back toward the sea. Beyond the shelter of the surrounding breakwater, the water had lost its shimmering tranquility, no longer dampened by containment ponds or buoyancy cells supporting the central structure. Inside the floating mounded structure girthing most of the facility, wave action and undersea surge were largely suppressed, but once outside its calming embrace, the ocean was not as gentle. Out here the wind was in command, and he immediately saw the ruffle of waves marching relentlessly in a westerly direction, making the sea below him appear like an endless washboard stretching off to the horizon. Directly ahead was the offshore platform and the island that lay beyond. Another sight caught the corner of his eye, and he turned his head briefly to assess it. It was the aircraft carrier, the *Carl Sagan*, off to the southwest and better than three miles distant.

Banking the Hind as much as he dared without overstressing the airframe or main rotor, he swung it around to face the elevated mound girthing the facility. Bringing the helo into another hover 300 meters from the breakwater, he waited for his quarry to surface, intermittently monitoring his fuel gauge. Already he could see he was burning fuel at a rapid pace. "Show yourselves, damn you!" he yelled out impatiently. Growing increasingly frustrated when nothing appeared, he pivoted the Hind around clockwise to scan the water in all directions.

"Over there!" Boris shrieked. "Three o'clock."

Zinova whipped his head around. Four dolphin riders had broken the surface to send up a broken curtain of spray, their mounts switchbacking hard. This time he could clearly see that one of them was Javolyn. A woman and two children were with him, no doubt his wife, the notorious Dolphin Girl, and his offspring. Already they had passed the west side of the platform and were heading directly for the island.

With his fuel running low, Zinova instantly knew he would only have one more chance at catching up and killing them, including the strange white beasts they rode. "We've got you now," he howled, his face awash in a deranged grin as he banked the Hind to follow. Closing the distance rapidly, he became giddy with excitement. Strangely, the small group had not yet sounded, still holding to the surface.

At a distance of 200 meters, Zinova saw Javolyn look back over his shoulder with a smile clinging to his face. "Get ready!" Zinova warned his gunner.

As if hearing the command, all four dolphins sounded simultaneously, taking their riders with them and diving deep. A split second too late, Boris turned the guns loose, exploding the water into a seething geysered storm. Keeping the guns trained on the exact spot where their quarry had vanished, he kept up the salvo as the Hind swept past.

Zinova banked hard, no longer caring if he was overstressing the airframe. Bringing the helo into another hover, he scanned the water. Absolutely nothing. No blood and no bodies floated to the surface. The bludgeoning destruction he had turned loose appeared to have been in vain, and already the surface had settled back into a rolling translucent indigo.

With his rage still burning fiercely, the Reaper broke from his hover and veered away, taking on a course that took him over the island and past the old lighthouse, making sure to keep well clear of the *Carl Sagan*. He could not be certain if its captain knew what was really happening, and he certainly didn't want to risk being fired upon. Feeling it now safe to swing the helo around, he took on a heading that would take him to Tiburon, Haiti.

Captain Delila raised his binoculars again to track the whirlybird. More than two miles away, it had taken on a heading to the northeast before making a wide turn that kept it well clear of the carrier. And now it seemed to be heading in the direction of the Haitian coast. It was only a short time ago that he had caught a fleeting glimpse of it rising up slowly from one of Aquaria's landing pads to hold a stationary hover, but then he had lost sight of it as his angle of observation changed when the immense mound of the floating city's central structure blocked his view. On his orders, the *Carl Sagan* had altered course, taking on a new heading that brought it to Aquaria's northeast side a good three miles from the breakwater where he had been able to spot it again. It had assumed a hover outside the breakwater to face back toward the city. But then it had turned to pick up speed, racing low over the sea toward the offshore platform near Navassa Island where it had flared into another hover. To him, it had seemed to fire down into the water, but if it had actually done so, it had been too distant for him to be certain of this. The chopper, however, appeared to be the Hind that had transported Allotey and Senator Brent Van Heflin to the floating city. The sight didn't surprise him. First Lieutenant Johnson had already alerted him as to what he would see.

"Sir, our radar has detected something that could be a problem," Ensign Jefferson informed him.

Delila turned. Jefferson appeared nervous. "What is it?"

"Hard to tell, sir, but it's traveling at Mach two point one, six hundred feet above the water on a bearing of one hundred forty degrees. It appears to be heading directly toward the floating city."

"A missile?"

"Possibly, sir. It has a very small profile. We were barely able to detect it."

"Get on the radio and see if you can warn those colonists." Delila paused. "And tell Lieutenant Johnson to get his men out of there immediately."

"Yes, sir," said Jefferson as he darted away quickly.

Having made their way through the undersea tunnel to reach the immense subterranean cavern beneath Navassa Island, Jake, Destiny and the children left their mounts to stand on a ledge where the holographic manifestation of Ez was there to greet them.

"Will Big D be able to absorb the blast?" Jake asked her. His tone conveyed apprehension. Through Achilles he had been informed of the approaching danger immediately after subduing the big Russian aboard the UN troop transport.

"I believe the incoming missile is not meant for Aquaria," declared Ez with a grave expression. She had detected its approach even before the *Carl Sagan* had alerted her to the problem.

"If not for us, then who?"

"Logic suggests it's the same target the Iranian sub wanted to destroy. Maximus needed a catastrophic event to reap immense profits in the stock and commodities markets. Without such an event, he stood to lose most of his wealth."

Jake's jaw dropped. Once again he was reminded of how they had stopped the Rodong rocket launched by Yeslam Raduyev from reaching its intended target eight years earlier. Carrying a nuclear warhead, the rocket's destination had also been Miami. But with Destiny acting as the lens through which the others had channeled their combined mental energies, they had been able to make the rocket disappear into a dimensional void.

Ez explained further. "I've fully analyzed all the data contained in the mechanical fish. It seems Maximus obtained a cruise missile with a nuclear warhead several years ago, which he kept in reserve at a secret location near Valera, Venezuela."

"Why do you say he kept it in reserve?" Jake interjected quickly.

"Because he was a careful planner. It seems he always kept options at his disposal should primary schemes go awry. When *Iron Fist* failed to launch its nuclear weapon, he must have sent a signal relayed by satellite that set the backup plan in motion. He probably did this just before he died."

Jake's thoughts moved along at lightning speed. A cruise missile was an exceptionally dangerous weapon. It had an intermediate range capability of up to 3,000 miles. It could fly low and incredibly fast, and by the time it was picked up on radar, you had little time to react and bring it down, especially if it was preprogrammed to take on an erratic, evasive course prior to reaching its target.

"But how can you be sure the target is Miami? It could be headed anywhere, even Aquaria. Is it coming directly at us?"

"Yes, if you follow a great circle route across the globe connecting Valera with Miami, the arc intersects the heart of Aquaria."

A sudden show of relief fell across Jake's face. "Then activate Big D and swallow it up."

"Just like the *Kraken*, there is a potential risk to do so, but one far greater. The shield may be inadequate to absorb the energy contained in the warhead. The data I've obtained shows it to be a high-yield plutonium device of 1,500 kilotons. If it comes in contact with the shield, it may prematurely detonate. The resulting blast will be far more than the shield can handle."

"But Big D must have grown larger after it swallowed the *Kraken*," Jake was quick to point out. "Won't it be stronger?"

"Yes it has, and yes it will," replied Ez quickly, "but unfortunately my calculations show it won't be enough." She presented the problem in the simplest terms she could come up with, for time was running out. "We're talking atomics here, not a chemically induced explosion. All sorts of crazy things come into play when you're dealing with atomics."

Jake turned, giving Destiny a hopeful look. "We can stop it just like before, but this time we have the combined hopes of ten thousand people behind us."

Destiny held his gaze, a conflict of emotions beginning to brew within her, and she began to wonder if she had truly changed since meeting Jake. Her own words came back to haunt her when she had confided her feelings to him on this same point just before he had left to investigate the hijacking of the *Southern Star* when she had told him, "I don't think I'll be able to do something like that ever again."

"You have no way of knowing that," he had replied.

"It's what I feel deep inside," she had said.

Esmerelda's words back in the cave suddenly resounded in her head. *"You must believe in yourself, my child. Do not lose faith, for you are still the person you have always been."*

Jake saw the stirrings of doubt growing within her eyes. "You can do it," he encouraged softly.

"All that you need lies within you," Esmerelda had stressed. *"You must never stop believing in yourself."*

"It is as though the entire world is against us," she had deplored, overcome with helplessness. Esmerelda had responded by telling her that the aggregate of humanity was not the cause of this, but the power brokers ruled by the puppet master, the person she had since come to know as the *Sublimis*.

"How do we overcome that?" she had asked, but now she had to remind herself that the *Sublimis* had been defeated. *Or had he?* A nuclear missile was going to kill millions of people.

Draped in a halo of stardust, Esmerelda's smile came back to comfort her, giving her a margin of strength. *"By believing, my child. You must simply believe."*

"I have been compromised," she had declared, uncertainty still clinging to her. "My powers have been corrupted through my own doing. Without them, believing in anything seems futile."

Esmerelda had shaken her head. *"You deceive yourself, child. Your unconditional love for those around you has made you even stronger. It is a source of great power. It binds all of you together and is the foundation of unblemished faith."*

Destiny continued to hover at the brink of lost hope. Would everything they had strived for eventually be lost anyway? The task seemed so difficult, maybe impossible.

The image of Esmerelda's confident smile radiated in her mind, and she knew she would never forget her resolute words. "*Have faith. Hope is something not seen. You must have patience and steadfastness, continuing to believe with all your being until the belief is physically manifested. Once you possess it, all is possible.*"

Destiny felt strangely empowered by those words. Yes, all was possible. Why have I let this happen to me? she decried inwardly, suddenly fighting with all her strength against the chains of pessimism, willing them to fall away. Fear was the culprit here. She had allowed it to enter her life, letting it take control of the reality surrounding her, which included everyone she loved. She saw it clearly now.

"You must cleanse your mind of the fear that shackles it," Esmerelda had reminded her. "Once you do this, you will realize you are a spiritual being with incredible powers. Only then will you fully understand that you and all those you love are deathless souls having a physical experience. Like those magnificent creatures to whom you are forever linked, you were brought into this world to fulfill a profound purpose. Just believe in yourself and all that you wish for will follow."

Yes, she had almost forgotten why she had been brought into this world.

She looked down at her children. They stared up at her, their faces revealing their unblemished faith in her.

Turning back to Ez she asked, "How much time do we have?"

Ez spoke urgently. "In exactly one minute thirty-two seconds the missile will pass directly over us."

Destiny knew proximity was crucial for the task at hand. "Alert everyone what we'll need of them. Tell them to link hands and form a line that ends here. I need all of them to focus their thoughts." She knew everyone was in the adjoining subterranean cavern once used as a clandestine base of operations by Yeslam Raduyev. Since then it had been greatly expanded and retrofitted to accommodate the basic needs of the current Aquarian population should an evacuation of the floating city become necessary as recent events had dictated.

Ez nodded, beaming broadly just before winking out.

Destiny knelt close to the edge of the ledge, staring pensively out over the water. All the albinos had now arrived, their perpetually smiling faces elevated above the surface. Behind them was a multitude of mutated grays, including Achilles' mother, Thetis, and her own mother's bond mate, Athena.

Jake turned to see a line of people led by Amphitrite emerge from a large fissure in the rock. They were moving hastily in single file to form a human chain, the trailing hand of each person clasped to the hand of the one immediately to their rear. Behind Amphitrite was Franklin, and behind him was Mat. Kalid was the fourth person in the chain and following him was Samuel. Trailing closely were a string of other familiar faces.

Grasping Amphitrite's extended hand, Jake looked down. Destiny was gazing up at him, an expression of intense concentration engraved on her features. "Let's do this!" she murmured softly. "Place your hand on my head."

Jake did as asked, noticing that both children had already done so. Almost at once he felt a potent force go rippling through his mind. It was the combined focused thought of thousands of sentient beings, and it was gathering power like that of a rapidly advancing tsunami.

Chapter Thirty-one: Shark Bait

Captain Delila brought the spy glasses to his eyes as one of the AW101s lifted from the floating city and fluttered into the sky. On his orders, the *Carl Sagan* had moved to a distance of five miles from Aquaria's breakwater, and he wondered if it was safe enough for the time being.

Standing beside him, Jefferson suddenly spoke up, his voice filled with tension. "Sir, if you look to the south you'll see it."

Delila pivoted, looking to where his aide was pointing. A barely visible dot could be seen just above the horizon, but it was growing in size rapidly. He had received a call from that same woman representing the colony only moments earlier, and she had told him the destination of the missile was Miami and not Aquaria. "Do not attempt to destroy it with any of the weaponry your ship carries," she had warned briskly. She had gone on to say that the information she had obtained indicated a direct hit on it would set it off. "It seems whoever constructed the missile has rigged it to trigger the warhead if a counterstrike is used against it. The warhead is a high-yield fifteen hundred kiloton fission bomb with a plutonium core. But do not worry, we believe we have the means to neutralize it."

As he watched the object grow larger, he wondered how she could possibly know that. Wavering at the doorstep of indecision, he considered ignoring the warning. What if she was wrong and the colony was about to be hit? Or what if the target was really Miami as she had alleged? Even though he had already notified the Strategic Air Command in Homestead of the inbound missile, he knew the missile would pass directly over Cuba before it reached Miami, if in fact that was the actual destination. And even if the Cubans managed to shoot it down, there was still the question of a nuclear detonation. The radioactive fallout would be brutal on anything it came in contact with. Either way, if he missed this one and only chance to bring it down and it ended up causing vast destruction, he would never be able to forgive himself. Perhaps he should employ the LaWS anyway. The Laser Weapon System was the latest addition to the carrier's high tech defensive arsenal, capable of directing a twenty megawatt beam directly at the incoming threat. Already the LaWS was locked onto the missile, with the possibility of a miss at zero. All he had to do was give the command to fire and it would be destroyed. But in doing that, he risked triggering a nuclear blast that would vaporize the city and set off a tidal wave that might sink his ship even if the ensuing blast didn't. Nevertheless, he was still tempted to issue the order to fire, but some deep instinct made him refrain from doing just that. Somehow he trusted what the woman was telling him to be true. In spite of this, he grew increasingly nervous as he tracked the rapidly growing dot. Even at this distance he could hear the ruffling susurration that heralded its coming. The air began to tremble, changing over into a quaking rumble as the sound grew, and he knew it was only a matter of seconds before the sonic boom of its passing would stab into his ears. The missile seemed to be heading directly for the floating city, and based on what radar had reported, it would barely miss colliding with the crown of Aquaria's central structure, assuming it was not pre-programmed to gain altitude as it approached.

Jefferson brought a tense gaze to the captain, trying to read the thoughts behind a face seemingly struggling with indecision. Would Delila give the order to fire? The LaWS operator was standing by awaiting the command and the captain was wearing the lip mic. All that was needed was only one word to be uttered.

And then the moment passed. The young ensign immediately noted Delila's change of expression, the captain's eyes going wide with astonishment. In reaction, Jefferson whipped his head around to look for the cause.

The missile had vanished. In wonderment, Jefferson searched the sky, suddenly aware of something else. The sound of its passage was now gone. Totally bewildered, he asked, "Where did it go, sir?"

Delila shook his head slowly, still dazed. No shimmering dome had enveloped the floating city this time. The missile had simply winked out. One moment it was there, then it was not. The weird happenings he had experienced during the last several hours would keep him wondering for the rest of his days. "I don't know, son, I just don't know. See if radar is still picking it up?" But deep down he was certain what the answer would be.

Making use of the 3-sided pyramidal T-crystals, Jake, Destiny, and Amphitrite instantaneously transported themselves along with others to Jacob's office high up in Aquaria's central structure. Jake's first order of business was deciding what to do with the conspirators they had captured, those being Van Heflin, Hearthwatch, and Allotey, including the three mercenaries that had abetted them. Drakov was another matter. All seven had been thoroughly bound hand and foot and were currently being guarded by Zimbola and Bashir in an adjacent room

Mat was the first to voice his concerns. "Turning them over to American authorities, including the Department of Justice, will be a waste of time. Forget about indictments. That would require unbiased parties in positions of authority willing enough to prosecute them, and from what we've seen in the homeland during the last several years, there's no more accountability in government. It seems elected officials and high-ranking appointees can do as they please these days, including breaking the law whenever they want." Mat shook his head stubbornly. "No, once the firestorm of conflicting accounts settles down, the American public will go back to sleep and those men will use their influence to shut us down again."

"I fully agree," said Jacob wearily, turning to his cousin, the CEO of Tursiops. "What do you think, Emmanuel?"

Emmanuel adopted a thoughtful expression. "Perhaps we should take a vote," he suggested, looking to other faces around the room.

"What about the UN?" Percy offered. "Surely you can't condemn the entire organization just because of a few bad eggs…." His voice trailed off meekly at seeing the looks his words were eliciting.

Amphitrite jumped to Percy's defense, covering his embarrassment quickly. She was well aware of Percy's contribution to recent events, much of which had been indispensable in saving the colony and other lives as well. "Nice job in imitating Maximus, Mister Osgood. Without your help, the world might never have learned of *The Order* or the men behind it." Having been interrogated by the *Sublimis*, she knew he had captured the man's voice and mannerisms so perfectly that it had even fooled Allotey, Van Heflin, and Hearthwatch. All it had taken was for Percy to wear a Masker, which Ez had preprogrammed with acoustical picture-speak images of the man conveyed to her by Athena using the colony's underwater hydrophones.

Percy looked down, fidgeting self-consciously. "Always did have this talent for mimicking voices," he said softly.

"I think I have a solution that will spare us taking a consensus," Jake interjected, idly hefting the crystal that had brought him and several others to this level of the central structure. He had thought deeply on the matter while bringing the captives to where they were now being held, and he knew Ez had been able to locate Hearthwatch rather easily by hacking her way into the real-time camera surveillance system at the White House. Using deductive reasoning, she had anticipated Hearthwatch rushing off to explain himself to the President once the initial broadcast exposing his involvement with Maximus and *The Order* had taken place, and her reasoning had proved correct. That had made it rather simple to abduct the man, for all that was needed was for Amphitrite to envision that particular room in the White House in order to get there. And although the mechanical fish had contained no collaborating evidence within its memory banks to indicate any Presidential involvement in *The Order's* insidious schemes, one could never be sure that was not the case. If Van Heflin was to be next in line for the Presidency, it was also possible his predecessor had been bred and groomed for the same position, planted there by Maximus. Either way, Jake knew it would no longer be practical to trust career politicians in high office these days.

With all eyes focused on him, he directed a foxy grin at the sentience running the colony's daily operations, his thoughts hinged on the tiny tracking chip placed on the underside of one of the gold-bearing boxes. Victor had made sure to load that particular box aboard Zinova's chopper. "Ez, we've used these crystals to move between stationary locations, but do you think they'll work taking people from a fixed point to one in motion?"

"Nothing is actually stationary in this three-dimensional realm," explained Ez. "Everything is in motion. Every point on or below the planet's surface is constantly moving. The planet rotates while orbiting a white star, and that star revolves around a galaxy moving through space. Yes, based on that, it should certainly work." She suddenly displayed a knowing smile as though reading his mind. "At its present rate of speed, the Hind is fifteen point three two minutes from reaching the southern coast of Haiti's southwestern peninsula."

Jake nodded, bringing his gaze briefly to Victor. "Well, assuming there are no objections, this is what I propose."

Zinova eyed the fuel gauge apprehensively, his gut in knots. It was now within a hair of empty. As soon as he reached Haiti's southwest peninsula, he had purposely flown the Hind relatively low over the rolling terrain, keeping it no higher than 150 meters. It was a safety precaution in case the turbines should quit. The thought of this happening grated on him, for if the helo lost power, he'd lose his hydraulics, and without hydraulics he would be forced to use his bearlike strength to wrestle with stiff controls in order to auto rotate the chopper down without crashing, and to avoid crashing he'd need a clearing devoid of trees or other obstructions to ensure that. And although he had successfully performed such a maneuver at least a dozen times in the past, he had never felt comfortable doing it.

Staring ahead, the Reaper's spirits lifted a tad as he saw the southern coastline come into view. He had purposely taken the shortest route across the peninsula to reach the southern seashore as quickly as possible. That would give him more opportunity for a safe landing should the turbines run dry, for much of the shoreline consisted of white sandy stretches with only occasional patches of rocky outcroppings to obstruct him. As he neared the coast, some familiar landmarks told him he was just west of Tiburon, and as he swung the Hind onto an easterly heading, he came abreast of the town to follow the beach. It was only a moment later that the ruins of Cardoza's stronghold lay before his eyes, and though the site was disheartening, his spirits began to lift. Perhaps he would reach his destination after all.

Making a slight course adjustment, he risked angling the Hind inland again, lining it up to fly directly over the remnants of the ancient fortress. Barely half of it remained standing, still surrounded by a moat only half filled with water, and where the drawbridge had once spanned the narrow canal, a mound of stone rubble and debris sloped haphazardly down into it.

In the distance beyond, he could discern more destruction. What had been Cardoza's enormous aircraft hangar lay completely destroyed, scattered over a wide swath of charred landscape. But at least he was nearing his destination, which consisted of a small fenced off area in a hollow of ground Cardoza had provided him. It was situated 1,000 meters east of where the hangar used to be. Once he reached it, he would refuel the chopper and begin making plans to fly the gold to the Cayman Islands. There he would have it stored in the vault of the bank he always used, exchanging some of it for cash. And once that was done, he'd begin plotting his revenge on Javolyn and his family.

These thoughts fell away as a strange crimson glow suddenly filled the Hind's interior. It reflected off his instrument panel, flashing briefly before disappearing completely. Almost immediately, the feel of the cyclic stiffened more appreciably in his grip, and an instant later the airframe began to shudder severely, with the rotor blades slapping the air ever more harshly. A quick glance at his altimeter told him he was losing altitude, and though he still had power, It was evident the Hind was struggling to stay aloft.

Something thumped heavily in the cabin behind him, and he turned in his seat to investigate the cause. Abruptly, his eyes went wide. Allotey and the American senator stared back at him with horrified expressions. Adjacent to them was a man he hadn't seen before, and behind them were five others. But unlike Allotey and the two with him, the men to their rear were constrained by wrist ties and shackled to each other, four of them being the same black-clad mercenaries that had been assigned to protect Allotey and the senator. The fifth man, however, was Drakov, his lieutenant.

Stunned by the sight, Zinova's mind staggered under the unreality that lay before him, his flummoxed brain groping feebly for an explanation as to how they had gotten here. All he could do was stare, tottering at the edge of madness as his eyes were drawn to the person he hadn't recognized. The man appeared deathly ill and was obviously nauseous, retching in a series of dry heaves. But then something else caught his gaze that shocked him even more. There were three other people behind the contingent of new passengers, and they were grinning cheerfully as they looked back at him. One of them was a huge black man, a veritable hulking giant. Zinova gave the second man, a dark-haired individual only a passing glance as his eyes steadied on the third. The man was Javolyn, his hated foe.

Continuing to stare dumbly, Zinova was suddenly blinded by a vivid eruption of light. Closing his eyes tightly to escape the crimson starburst, he toyed with the possibility that perhaps he was imagining all this. But as his vision cleared, the sheer impact of the mystery returned to torment him further. Except for the one still retching, Allotey and the senator continued to stare back at him in terrified silence, as did the others, but Javolyn and the two that had accompanied him were now gone.

With his mind still reeling, Zinova suddenly realized the whine of the engines had ceased, and turning his head, he now saw the fuel gauge had reached zero. The Hind was falling. In panic, he pulled up on the collective as the terrain rushed up at him. Without hydraulics, it felt as though he were attempting to pry up a huge chunk of lead. In desperation, he searched the ground directly below for a place to land, but all that was available were the ruins of the old stone fortress. With a herculean effort he managed to muscle the cyclic just enough to avoid hitting what remained of a crumbled wall, and coaxing additional pitch into the struggling rotor blades at the last possible second, felt the Hind slow from its dizzying descent. In reaction, he looked all about him, frantically searching for options, but finding none, he realized he would have to ditch the Hind in the only place available that would not cause it to come apart. And that was in the moat.

Yanking up on the collective one last time before impact, he sought to arrest the Hind's plummet further, but as he did, the blades of the main rotor tore off and flew away. The chopper dropped heavily, meeting the water surface in a bone jarring plunge and sending up a towering maelstrom of spray.

Unstrapping himself hurriedly, Zinova's only objective was to evacuate the Hind before it sank. He was keenly aware of the denizens that lived in the canal, and like a panicked animal, wanted to get out of the water as fast as possible. Climbing from his seat, he was nearly bowled over by Boris trying to get out before him. Water sloshed heavily into the cabin and was rising rapidly.

Driving a shoulder into his gunner's stomach, Zinova sent him reeling back. Whirling, he pushed past Allotey and the senator. Both stared dazedly at the water, too petrified to move.

Lunging for the open doorway, Zinova heard Vladimir cry out to him. "Karloff, help me!" Ignoring the plea, he splashed through the doorway, only to find himself nearly pulled back into the cabin. Hands had latched onto his clothing from behind and were tugging him backward. A quick glance over his shoulder showed Allotey and the senator clinging to him with terrified eyes. Lashing out with a balled fist, he slammed it into the nearest face, and though it caused a spurt of blood to spew from Allotey's shattered nose, it was as if the blow had no effect whatsoever. The man held fast, far too frightened to feel any pain.

"Save me!" Allotey shrieked, struggling fiercely to hold on. "I can't swim."

Zinova lashed out again, this time with an elbow that found the side of Allotey's head. Allotey absorbed the blow, grimacing through clenched teeth and still managing to hold on with a superhuman death grip. "I can't swim," he screamed again.

Out of the corner of one eye, Zinova glimpsed movement on the water, and turning his head to inspect it further, spotted a fin cleaving the surface. All of a sudden there were more, many more. They were swarming along the moat and coming straight for the sinking Hind.

Zinova spun, kicking his feet hard to elevate his body higher out of the water, and with all his strength came down with his full weight behind a monstrous blow that landed squarely on Allotey's upturned mouth. The UN dignitary immediately went limp, and Zinova squirmed free, avoiding the senator's outstretched grasping hands. Stroking wildly, he swam for the sloped jumble of stones and rubble that had spilled down into the moat when the explosion had occurred. Reaching out, his fingers found purchase, and he pulled his legs free of the water, half expecting a set of serrated teeth to close on his ankles as he did so. Climbing higher onto the sloped mass, he turned to observe the fate of the others.

Already the water was turning red, fins going every which way, but amazingly Boris had somehow managed to escape the swarm of frenzied sharks and was swimming for his life. Seeking the same area of rocks where Zinova had climbed from the water, he glanced up at his boss with hate-filled eyes. But just before he reached the rocks, a look of consternation crossed his face followed by a horrific cry of distress, and an instant later he was jerked backward. Abruptly he disappeared, the water roiled red with his blood.

Dazedly, Zinova swung his gaze back to the Hind in time to see it slide beneath the surface. The feeding frenzy that had been taking place around it had now ceased. Fins were darting away en masse, leaving in their wake the remaining morsel. The head of a lone figure bobbed just above the water, and Zinova realized it was the senator. A fin far bigger than the others was bearing toward him, coming from the opposite direction in which the other sharks had departed.

Van Heflin let out a bloodcurdling cry as he watched the huge fin knife the water to come straight at him. Words Cardoza had uttered during the meeting were echoing in his head. *I believe Scylla regards you as a potential meal, senator.*

Zinova watched in fascination as the head of the massive great white broke the surface to snatch the senator in its jaws. The senator let out another chilling scream as the jaws clamped down, and a moment later he also disappeared.

Relieved that he had been fortunate enough to survive the onslaught, a dozen thoughts began to race through Zinova's mind as to how he would go about retrieving the sunken gold. Thinking there was no more danger, he was surprised to hear a low rumbling growl behind him. Turning slowly to confront the cause, he found himself looking into a set of fierce amber orbs. The Bengal was only inches away, the stench of its foul breath sickening.

It was then Zinova became cognizant of yet someone else screaming, a scream far shriller than the ones that had preceded it, and just before the fangs tore into his throat to bore him away into an abode of coal-black darkness, he realized the sound was coming from his open mouth.

Jake stood with his hands resting leisurely on the railing delimiting the edge of the esplanade halfway up Aquaria's central structure. His gaze was set on what appeared to be a tiny object floating more than a mile beyond the city's eastern breakwater, but he knew distance gave it the illusion of being small. Up close its actual size would be comparable to that of a voluminous hot air balloon capable of carrying aloft several people. It was only minutes earlier that the hydrogen gas contained under its leathery skin had borne it to the ocean surface. During the retrieval of the T-crystals, Hermes had noticed the budding node on one side of the crown of the largest *thurentra*, and the pod had been in readiness for the moment it broke free. With its destination having already been planned, he knew it was headed for a location closer to Haiti.

Standing next to Jake was Victor, who followed his gaze. "What is that?" he asked.

"You're looking at the start of another floating city."

Victor's countenance immediately clouded. He had no clue as to what the statement implied.

Jake turned to gauge the Russian's reaction. Smiling, he said, "That object carries a seedling. Once it finds a new home on the seafloor, it will eventually mature to turn an otherwise barren sector of ocean into an oasis of life."

His curiosity whetted, Victor studied the thing more carefully. Using his telescopic eye, he magnified the image as though he were only a hundred meters behind it. Further ahead of it he discerned a whale spout, and on each side of the huge cetacean there appeared to be more than a dozen albino dolphin switchbacking along the surface. A cable stretched from the whale to the balloon, and he realized the whale was towing it in an easterly direction.

Jake thought it was time to breach another subject. "Victor, have you given any thought as to what you're going to do now?" He felt a strange kinship with this man, one he could not explain. Though they had been combatants during their initial meeting, a great deal had changed since then, and he reminded himself of a similar situation that had occurred eight years earlier with Bashir and Kalid.

Victor answered the question with a slow shake of his head. With sadness still gripping him over the loss of his son, he had not given the matter any thought.

"The colony can use a man like you, Victor. If you'd like, you can come to work for us and live here."

Victor remained quiet. Continuing to stare pensively at the receding balloon, he pondered the invitation. It was then that he realized how much he liked these people. Unlike the meaningless existence he had previously lived, they were committed to a purpose, one that was profoundly altruistic and charitable. Twice they had saved his life, and perhaps that was not such a bad thing after all, for it might give him a chance to redeem himself and atone for his sins.

When he finally replied, his voice was barely above a murmur. "I am unworthy of your enterprise, my friend."

Jake placed a hand on his shoulder. He felt the man's pain. The guilt and shame Victor still carried was almost palpable. "Oh, you're worthy, all right. You've already proven that several times over."

Victor felt himself at a loss for words, and had he tried to respond at that moment, he most assuredly would have broken down then and there, blubbering like a baby. But then the sound of childlike voices broke the air to save him any embarrassment. Turning, he saw Jake's children scurrying ahead of their mother, rushing headlong toward their father in ecstatic greeting. "Dadoo!" they cried in unison.

Jake bent and scooped one up in each of his brawny arms, lifting them easily and giving each a tender kiss on the forehead before setting them back down again. Destiny was right behind them, and she reached up to loop a thin arm around the nape of his neck. With her feet dangling, she gave him a smoldering kiss.

At that moment, a short pudgy Haitian manifesting a jovial grin sauntered out onto the esplanade. At seeing the twins with their parents, his smile wavered fleetingly before re-asserting itself. "So there you are, you little imps," he said, his mirthful eyes coming to rest on Jake and Destiny in full embrace, their lips locked tightly. "They certainly missed their parents," he said, his signature smile now in full radiance.

Jake and Destiny parted lips to regard him with amused miens, fully aware of how the children had bamboozled Kobe into bringing them here, at least most of the way. But explaining that to Zimby would make no difference. "Better check your six, Kobe," Jake warned.

Looking behind him, Kobe's face immediately blanched. "Gotta be goin'!" he exclaimed, suddenly bolting away quickly and running for an arched doorway further down the esplanade that would take him back inside the city again.

Following on his heels was an imposing figure. "Come back here, Kobe!" Zimbola growled, his features harboring a fierce scowl that would frighten the dead.

Surprised at how fast Kobe could move, Jake suppressed a laugh. Addressing the twins, he said, "You got him in trouble, now you better save him."

TJ and Melody scampered away, adding further to the comical scene. Running after Zimby, they all disappeared through the same doorway Kobe had taken.

As Jake looked on, more of his fellow Aquarians strolled out onto the esplanade to join him, including Jacob and Jacob's cousin, the CEO of Tursiops. Emmanuel appeared uncomfortable with something he wanted to say. "Ez informs me that Zinova's chopper crashed in the moat at Cardoza's stronghold," he announced, managing to overcome the reticence gripping him. It was obvious he had misgivings about what he had consented to.

Jake absorbed this unexpected news with a show of surprise registering on his countenance. "Huh!" was all he could think to mutter before adding, "I wonder what the odds were of that happening?"

The manifestation of Ez was suddenly in their midst. "Thirty thousand six hundred twenty-nine to one," she stated bluntly.

Jake pondered this briefly before eliciting another "huh," though this one sounded much too frivolous by comparison. "Any survivors?"

Ez shook her head. "Other than the mauled body of a dead man near the water, satellite surveillance showed no one roaming the site, though a Bengal tiger was spotted. With all the sharks, it is doubtful any of those men could have survived."

Jake shrugged flippantly. "I guess it could be argued they got their just reward." As soon as he said it, he became aware of Amphitrite and Franklin standing nearby.

"Yes," Amphitrite concurred. "Such is the fate of evildoers when their iniquity becomes so overwhelming it comes back full circle to feed on its host."

Several others nodded in agreement with her sobering words as Chester Hennington, Tursiops' Chief Financial Officer, joined the group to stand next to Emmanuel, and Jake noticed that both men appeared to be fully recovered now from their earlier ordeal at the hands of the bounty hunters hired by Maximus. Jake had since learned they had been abducted in Port-au-Prince following negotiations with Haitian officials concerning the construction of the massive automobile factory on the outskirts of the city. Overpowered by six ruffians apparently working for the bounty hunters, Emmanuel and Chester had been injected with an immobilizing narcotic after being wrestled into a waiting van just outside the government building where the negotiations had taken place. And though they were now safe, he knew precautions would need to be implemented to prevent things like this from happening in the future. But at least the negotiations had been finalized, and it had been sanctioned that Tursiops was to oversee the building and running of the plant, which would produce eco-friendly cars to be exported internationally.

Jacob looked on, quietly taking in what was being said, aware that Mat and Amelia had also come outside to join the gathering. Ez noticed this too, but it was Jake who took the moment to lighten the mood. "I think our hotshot head of security here deserves a round of applause," he proclaimed in a voice loud enough for everyone to hear. "For meritorious conduct, extraordinary valor, and conspicuous bravery…" He was using a phrase spoken by the wizard in the movie *The Wizard of*

Oz when the wizard awarded a badge of courage to the cowardly lion. Quoting it blithely, he ended the laud by saying, "and, I might add, for keeping the offshore platform intact and the fine all around job of ass-kicking he doled out."

Mat immediately recognized the phrase and got into the spirit of the moment by feigning bashfulness and gesticulating with his hands in a futile effort to wave off the enthusiastic chorus of hip, hip, hoorays and clapping that ensued. "Shucks, folks, I'm speechless," he blurted, matching what the lion had said upon receiving the award and emulating the same antics. Projecting an air of chagrin, he turned his back to the crowd. This was a routine both men had often used to evoke laughter from fellow warriors during their days in the Seals, and they had the act down pat.

At seeing Mat's animated waggishness, Amelia burst into riotous, uncontrollable laughter, tears streaming from her eyes.

Ez was next to speak once the cheering trailed off. "And let's not forget Amelia's contribution for her superb commentary. She showed herself to be a true professional during our enlightening newscasts uncovering the insidious and nefarious activities taking place beyond the view of public scrutiny. And if she is not opposed to performing additional newscasts, I have prepared further commentary for her to disseminate to mainstream news channels around the globe."

Another round of lively applause and cheering abruptly resounded, and suddenly self-conscious, Amelia blushed with sincere embarrassment.

Jacob looked all about him to study the faces. A mood of warm, cheerful camaraderie had taken hold of everyone, and he was enjoying the contagion, content to bask in the feel of it. They had come a long way during the last eight years, and though the budding fantasy they had so intensely envisioned and nurtured in its infancy had now been transformed into reality, there was so much more yet to be achieved. The human mind was a wonderful thing, he cogitated. Coupled with other unique intellects that were in some respects much more powerful than those of the people around him, they had fashioned possibilities that could be made real.

Jake's voice rose up again. Holding his T-crystal, he said, "Shield your eyes, everyone. Destiny and I are off to commemorate the planting of the seedling."

Jacob avoided looking directly at him as a blinding burst of crimson light flared, and an instant later, Jake and Destiny were gone.

A feeling of deep-seated pragmatism suddenly invaded Jacob's thoughts, and beset by it, he expelled a resigned sigh. Though they had come out victorious on their recent battles, he was not foolish enough to delude himself into thinking the war was over. Innate wickedness tempered by virulent greed would surely re-assert itself, and another storm would eventually brew. But then again, certain things were meant to happen, and while these things were beyond his understanding and control, they would bring together circumstances that would fuel future battles that might prove even more fierce and exhausting than the ones they had just fought.

With his thoughts drifting, Jacob found himself revisiting past reflections. Revisiting them always bolstered his resolve whenever he found it flagging. Amphitrite had always stressed to him the delicate balance and uncertainty woven into the cosmic structure. There would be choices to be made and actions to be carried out, with any wrong decision leading to disaster. But with their course set and their conviction unshakable, they would continue to act against tyranny, poverty, and oppression. They would resolutely strive toward making significant positive changes to a world in desperate need of it. Leaving the beleaguered nation of Haiti to fend for itself was beyond consideration, and to retreat in pursuit of an easier life would be cowardly. Tursiops Worldwide would provide the impetus and corporate structure to attain their goals, one of them being the achievement of a much higher standard of living for the downtrodden masses. But it was the new species of albino dolphin that had initially devised the framework for carrying out this great undertaking, for it was they who had formulated the concept of a sea colony, which had taken root in their minds years earlier when he had thought it prudent to teach them everything he knew about the workings of capitalism, big business, and multi-national corporations.

Jacob smiled to himself as he mused about all the good things a cash-rich corporation could accomplish. Wielded properly, big business could be a powerful tool. It had clout, and was able to move heads of state into serving its interests. But here its interests would differ markedly from the mainstream, for the interests of Tursiops would remain purely philanthropic, run by entities incapable of corruption or greed. Tursiops would function in harmony with the ocean environment, incessantly striving for the development and implementation of alternative sources of clean, renewable energy derived from the sea, and producing commodities that could be sold on world markets at exceptionally low prices. Here was Haiti's best hope of escape from its plight of seemingly perpetual poverty. If everything went to plan, the island nation would no longer be suppressed and tortured by recurrent waves of corrupt domestic and international politics that washed away all hope. Innovation would pave the way for change. And though such a grand undertaking would be immensely difficult to achieve, it would not be unworkable.

But Haiti's salvation was not their end goal. No, it would not end there. If Tursiops continued to succeed, it would establish marine-based colonies throughout the planet's seas. By harvesting the oceanic reserves of almost limitless nutrients and previously untapped energy, it would unleash a floodtide of food and commodities that would ultimately enrich every third world country around the globe. Through the production of hydrogen, magnesium, and distilled potable water alone, enormous revenues would be gained to finance the development of new technologies. Henceforth, previous limits on food production resulting from land-based economies would be exceeded to an explosive degree through the implementation of mariculture and ocean farming, not only vastly improving Haiti's standard of living, but all nations of the world. These enterprises would provide unprecedented employment for the poor, sprouting forth an economy on a scale never before seen. In its wake, hunger would all but vanish, with new social orders emerging and evolving in total harmony with the planetary ecosystem. A partnership would transpire between man and cetacean that would open the doors to new horizons in scientific research. Spurred on by the albino intellect, the advancement of science and technology would accelerate, with meaningful breakthroughs occurring at a faster rate. In the sea colonies, crime, brutality, and social disorder would give way to intellectual, artistic, philosophical, and spiritual pursuits, setting the individual free from the lone struggle for survival that had characterized both old and contemporary societies. In short, a new chapter in social evolution would commence, unrivaled by anything that had come before it.

Contemplating this vision, Jacob hoped Tursiops would be able to provide a positive impact on the global recession that had hit the major economies of the world. In reaction to this, many governments had systematically devalued their paper currencies to counter the growing tide, so much so that their medium of exchange would likely become worthless someday. But Tursiops had something far better to fall back on should this happen. It had its gold. The concept, however, caused him some misgivings, for he remembered what he had taught the albinos years earlier when the first *thurentra* in the cove began harvesting pure gold and platinum from the Cayman Trench. He had told them no true benefit was derived from the production of such elements, that metals considered to be precious by humanity had been the underlying cause of many wars throughout its history. But as time had gone on, his view on this had changed. Gold did have its benefits. It had provided untold though discrete financial leverage in the building of Aquaria, and in the near future it might continue to provide leverage, for as other economies began to stumble, Tursiops would continue to grow stronger.

A warm glow began to take hold of Jacob as he thought about these things. Through the combined leadership of the company's board of directors, Tursiops would empower Haitians to transform their lives in a single generation. Such thinking tended to heighten his expectations of the future. Sometimes you had to hit rock bottom before you began the arduous climb back up. Here was Haiti's way out of the hole it had become mired in. They just had to be resolute in holding onto their conviction that the dream was possible.

During the last eight years Jacob had learned that anything was possible as long as you believed in it with every fiber of your being. And though it was his grandmother, Esmerelda, who had first tried to make him understand this, it was Amphitrite who had actually made him feel the absolute power underlying it. There would be no try, no meager stab at hoping for the best, for such outlooks were too diluted in ambivalence to have any chance of success. No, the fantasy was made altogether real by stripping away all negative leanings, all doubts. The power of their minds was working in concert, both human and delphine, to forge the path of their choosing, the desired trajectory through time-space. Sentient intelligence would be used to mold the future. He now understood the power of it. The mind was truly an integral part of the cosmos, and somewhere within this seemingly endless chaos and swirling motes, an enigmatic order existed that could be manipulated through conscious, and perhaps even unconscious, thought. Yes, perhaps there was a dimension where physical laws and mysticism eventually merged, intertwining, and combining into a simple structure that determined the reality they desired, a place immune to the winds of chance.

Jacob was suddenly pulled from these thoughts as he became aware of a commotion. It was the sound of awestruck gasps coming from those around him, their gazes beholding a spectacular sight. A double rainbow had formed over the Caribbean Sea off to the east to frame the receding *thurentra* seedling with its escort, but now there were three of them. As he looked on in wonder, he saw something he had never seen before. A fourth rainbow had coalesced to drape over the first three, their redundant arching hues perfectly coinciding. Continuing to gawk, he discerned a seemingly endless series of glowing nodules go hurtling along their respective bands of prismatic color. More vibrant than the arched hue confining their motion, they rose up from one end of the band only to vanish at the opposite end, with nodules of differing color moving in a direction counter to their neighbors. Finding himself totally enraptured by the dazzling display of shifting prismatic light, he was overcome with a profound feeling of euphoria much the way the enigmatic albino art affected him. Unable to pull his eyes from the enchanting sight, he noticed a subtle change that grew more distinct in moments. The face of his long-deceased grandmother, Esmerelda, was regarding him with a broad benevolent smile.

Jacob returned the smile with a barely perceptible nod, his mind harboring only one thought.

Thank you for making me a believer.

Acknowledgments

No one deserves more credit for their support in the writing of this tale than my wife and soul mate, Harriet, my biggest fan. Her indomitable spirit and encouragement was indispensable in keeping me focused on completing a work that could have otherwise gone unfinished, a story that could have conceivably transpired in an alternate universe closely paralleling our own. As the novel progressed, it was always a delight to gauge her reaction, which was never disappointing as I read proceeding entries to her over breakfast each and every Saturday morning.

But the thing that finally compelled me to actually write it was the way Harriet was able to cope with her illness. Harriet is tough as nails and since the year 2000 she's been battling CML - chronic myeloid leukemia - and so far she's put up one hell of a valiant fight, absolutely refusing to yield to what most doctors would describe as a devastating, life-threatening malady. Thus, she made up her mind long ago to live out a normal existence, avoiding hospitals completely and refraining from seeing doctors as much as possible. Consequently, it was her grit and determination that inspired me to take pen to paper and flesh out an adventure imbued with these admirable qualities of the spirit. In its basic subliminal form, I wanted to honor her with something unique, essentially a literary work that came from the deepest part of me, something only I could give her, but something which would reflect her iron will and indomitable strength. This is initially mirrored in the book's opening scene where we find a woman adrift and marooned in a thunderous, tumultuous sea. She is alone and clinging to a piece of flotsam, and the reader finds the woman to be pregnant. By all rights, she should accept her fate and succumb to the elements, but she continues to fight on in the face of overwhelming odds, clinging to life, and refusing to quit until she has nothing left within her to resist the battering forces of a sea gone mad. Later in the book we learn the woman survives with the help of a dolphin and that her name is Harriet Grahm. And although she has no recollection of her former life, she ends up taking on a new identity, becoming Amphitrite, one of the cornerstone characters of the story. During her ordeal at sea, something incredible has happened to Amphitrite, and her failure to remember her past has somehow given her the power to glimpse the future. Henceforth, she becomes an arrant believer in this power and what the future holds, convinced her visions are real, and it is this ability that spills over and infects the reader to make the story palpable and real.

Writing the novel was a labor of love that took four years to complete. In creating it, I had to constantly challenge myself to come up with new ideas, not always knowing where the story was headed since some of the characters within the developing plot started taking on a life of their own. I only knew I wanted to take the reader on a journey to high adventure, an escape from the often mundane routines of everyday life most of us encounter, and in adhering to this I kept imagining what I'd like to see on the big screen if the novel was ever made into a blockbuster movie. My heartfelt appreciation also goes out to my daughter, Melissa, for her added encouragement to keep me moving forward with this project. And I certainly would be remiss if I left out her three little progenies, Troy Jacob, Solomon, and the latest addition to the family, Jayna Jocelynne, each of whom provided me with the personality traits and inspiration to create the mischievous impish characters which have now come alive to play an integral part within the sequel to this tale.

And lastly, I want to thank my sister, Barbara, for showing an enthusiastic interest in my creativity. Whenever she picked up the uncompleted manuscript, she always seemed to have trouble putting it down, totally absorbed and fascinated by the plot's intrigue and explosiveness.

About the Author

Michael J. Ganas is a licensed professional engineer. Following a stint in the U.S. Army, he earned a degree in civil engineering from Cornell University. Shortly thereafter, his love of the sea prompted him to pursue a career as a deep-sea commercial diver, heading a wide array of marine construction projects. This eventually led him into his current occupation, which takes on the challenges of civil engineering in underwater environments. Having published over twenty technical articles involving marine engineering, he decided on writing his first novel, an epic action adventure titled ***The Girl Who Rode Dolphins***, which eventually merited seven literary awards and has since been subdivided into the first three books of the on-going ***Dolphin Riders*** book series. ***Survival*** is the fifth book in the series.

www.ingramcontent.com/pod-product-compliance
Lightning Source LLC
LaVergne TN
LVHW020653110826
845149LV00012B/1986

* 9 7 8 1 9 6 6 1 9 1 1 2 4 *